P9-DFN-423

THE SINGER FROM MEMPHIS

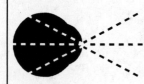

This Large Print Book carries the
Seal of Approval of N.A.V.H.

AN ATHENIAN MYSTERY

THE SINGER FROM MEMPHIS

GARY CORBY

THORNDIKE PRESS
A part of Gale, Cengage Learning

GALE
CENGAGE Learning

Farmington Hills, Mich • San Francisco • New York • Waterville, Maine
Meriden, Conn • Mason, Ohio • Chicago

GALE
CENGAGE Learning®

LIBRARY OF CONGRESS CATALOGING-IN-PUBLICATION DATA

Names: Corby, Gary, author.
Title: The singer from Memphis / by Gary Corby.
Description: Large print edition. | Waterville, Maine : Thorndike Press, 2016. |
  Series: An Athenian mystery | Series: Thorndike Press large print historical
  fiction
Identifiers: LCCN 2016021341| ISBN 9781410492623 (hardcover) | ISBN 1410492621
  (hardcover)
Subjects: LCSH: Private investigators—Greece—Athens—Fiction. | Nicolaos
  (Fictitious character : Corby)—Fiction. | Diotima (Legendary character)—Fiction. |
  Herodotus—Fiction. | Egypt—History—To 332 B.C.—Fiction. |
  Greece—History—Athenian supremacy, 479-431 B.C.—Fiction. | Large type
  books. | GSAFD: Mystery fiction. | Historical fiction.
Classification: LCC PR9619.4.C665 S56 2016b | DDC 823/.92—dc23
LC record available at https://lccn.loc.gov/2016021341

Published in 2016 by arrangement with Soho Press, Inc.

Printed in Mexico
1 2 3 4 5 6 7 20 19 18 17 16

For Helen

*. . . because you can never dedicate
too many books to your wife.*

THE ACTORS

Every name in this book is a genuine one from the classical world. Some are still in use. To this day there are people named Nicolaos. It's also the origin of our Nicholas.

Other names you might already know because they belong to famous people, such as Herodotus and Pericles.

But some names from thousands of years ago are unusual to our modern eyes. I hope you'll say each name however sounds happiest to you, and have fun reading the story.

For those who'd like a little more guidance, I've suggested a way to say each name in the character list. My suggestions do not match ancient pronunciation. They're how I think the names will sound best in an English sentence.

That's all you need to read the book!

Characters with an asterisk by their name were real historical people.

Nicolaos, NEE-CO-LAY-OS (Nicholas), Our protagonist	"How do you get off a rotating crocodile?"
Herodotus★, HE-ROD-O-TUS, A would-be author	"My plan is to set down in writing the history of the wars between the Hellenes and the Persians, so that the deeds of men will not be forgotten in time."
Diotima★, DIO-TEEMA, Wife of Nico	"Dear Gods, what is it with you men?"
Inaros★, IN-A-ROSS, Prince of Libya	"Send me an agent, a man of cunning and resource."
Pericles★, PERRY-CLEEZ, A politician	"It was too good an opportunity to pass up."
Charitimides★, CARRY-TIM-EED-EEZ, Admiral of the Fleet	"I'm aware of this scheme of Inaros's. I think his idea is crazy. You'll probably get yourself killed."
Kordax, CORD-AX, Captain of Dolphin	"We had a minor problem."

Markos,
   MARK-OS,
   An assassin

"Don't go looking for any moral high ground, Nico. You won't find it."

Djanet,
   JANET, A singer

"You have to hate the camel more than he hates you."

The Tjaty,
   JATTY, Head of the Public Service of Egypt

"This is the Public Service. We never take competence into consideration."

The Blind General,
   King of the beggars

"Of course I was a General, you dolt! If I had been a Lieutenant then I would be the Blind Lieutenant."

Maxyates,
   MAX-E-ATE-EEZ (Max), A Libyan with unusual fashion sense

"My tribe are the descendants of Troy. I am proud to call myself a child of Hector."

Tutu,
   TOO-TOO,
   An embalmer

"Now please relax while I demonstrate how we'll remove your organs."

| Alekto, AL-EK-TOW, A mercenary captain | "I seen a lot of men die in a lot of ways, and you know what? Not a single one of 'em looked happy." |
| The High Priest of Amun, Chief priest of the Oracle at Siwa | "The God says these things. We generally find that they turn out to be true." |

THE CHORUS

Assorted Egyptians, sailors, pirates, beggars, soldiers, crocodiles and some angry camels.

TIMELINE

This timeline lists the battles and intrigue that lead up to The Singer from Memphis.

You don't need any of this to enjoy the book, but if you'd like to know how the Egyptians, Persians and Athenians ended up in a three-cornered war, here is sixty-nine years of treachery, invasion, rebellion and murder.

526 BC Amasis, the second-last native Pharaoh of Egypt, dies after a long and successful reign. His son Psamtik III takes over. Unfortunately, Psamtik proves a terrible leader.

A Greek military advisor to the new Pharaoh defects to Persia. His name is Phanes. Phanes advises Cambyses, the Great King of Persia, how best to invade Egypt.

11

525 BC A Persian army arrives in Egypt, with Cambyses and Phanes at its head.

The ensuing battle is very close, but eventually the Egyptians break and run. They retreat to Memphis, the capital of Egypt.

Cambyses sends an ambassador to Memphis, down the Nile by boat, to ask Psamtik to surrender on terms. Psamtik has the ambassador torn limb from limb, then orders the entire crew of the boat murdered.

Taking that response as a no, Cambyses orders the attack. The Persians thrash the Egyptians.

Psamtik's aggressive approach to diplomacy has not endeared him to his conquerors. His daughter, and the daughters of the Egyptian noblemen, are led away to spend the rest of their lives as slaves. Psamtik's son and two thousand young noblemen are led away to be executed. Psamtik himself is spared for a few months, then executed when he agitates against the new rulers.

Egypt is now a province of the Empire, with a Persian as governor.

490 BC Persia turns its attention to Greece. The Athenians, outnumbered almost ten to one, face a Persian invasion on the plain of Marathon.

The Athenians thrash the Persians.

480 BC The Persians try again. They invade Greece with the largest army the world has ever known.

The Greeks unite and beat the Persians. This is the war that included the last stand of the 300 at Thermopylae, and ended with the famous sea battle at Salamis.

For the next twenty years, the Athenians and Persians are locked in the ancient version of a cold war.

458 BC The Egyptians rebel against their Persian overlords. They are led by a prince of Libya, a charismatic and highly competent man named Inaros. Inaros claims to be a descendant of the last true Pharaohs.

457 BC The Athenians send a force of two

hundred triremes to assist Inaros and the rebels. The Athenians are only too happy to help, because a Persian army pinned down in Egypt is an army that can't be invading Greece.

The Egyptian/Athenian allies win an enormous victory, during which the uncle of the Persian Great King Artaxerxes is killed.

The survivors of the Persian territorial army hole up within the White Fort in the capital, Memphis. It's the same place where Psamtik held his last stand, sixty-nine years before. The Persians send home for reinforcements.

The rebels now hold all of Lower Egypt, except for the capital.

Everyone knows that when the Persian response comes, it will be vicious. Not only do the Persians need to recover Egypt, a very rich province, but they must avenge the death of a senior member of the royal family.

Inaros must reduce the White Fort, take the capital, and consolidate his grasp on

Egypt before the Persian relieving force arrives.

456 BC A man named Herodotus chooses this moment to visit the war zone that is Egypt. He needs to do some research for a book he's writing.

Thus begin the strange events of *The Singer from Memphis.*

An Unexpected Visitor

"Master, there's a man at the door who wants to see you. He says his name is Herodotus."

I looked up from my cup of wine. The house slave stood over me, awaiting my instructions on what to do with the visitor.

I relaxed on a dining couch, under the stars in our courtyard, on a fine evening, in the quiet company of my family. I had no wish to be disturbed. I especially didn't want to be disturbed by a stranger.

"I've never heard of him," I said. I turned to my wife and asked, "Honey, do we know a Herodotus?"

My wife, Diotima, lay on the dining couch beside mine. She looked up from the wax tablet on which she scribbled notes, because she had taken it into her head to write a book of philosophy. Diotima chewed on the end of her stylus while she thought about it.

"Never heard of him," she said.

I turned to my younger brother. "How about you, Socrates?"

He was reading a scroll. He tore his attention away long enough to say, "No." Then he returned to his scroll.

The slave spoke up again. "Master, the man says he's from Halicarnassus."

Ah, that explained it. Halicarnassus is a city far away, on the other side of the Aegean Sea.

"He's a tourist to Athens then," I said. "Give him directions to the *agora* and tell him to go away."

"But Master, he says he has work for you!" the house slave said.

That made me sit up.

"Then why in Hades couldn't you say so at once? Show him in."

The visitor sat opposite me, in our *andron*, the room at the front of the house reserved for male guests, which I also used for business. He had a glass of wine in his hand and a bowl of olives by his side. He sipped the wine but ignored the olives. I studied him closely, because it is always wise to know a client, or a potential client.

Herodotus was a man not much older than myself. He could not have been more than twenty-six. He wore a beard of a

18

conservative cut, which oddly he had ring-leted in the Persian manner. His clothes were of fine linen. He wore the ankle-length chiton of a gentleman who had no need of manual labor to earn his living. Yet his sandals were of the heaviest workman leather, and his feet showed the sort of cal-luses that you would expect to see on a veteran soldier.

The overall effect was a man who was both young and old, Greek and Persian, rich and poor. This man, I decided, cultivated contradictions.

I asked our visitor what I could do to help him.

He said, "I require an escort for my safety. You were recommended to me."

I am the only private agent in Athens. I was used to hearing requests like this. I had once gained some notoriety when I pro-tected a woman who sought a divorce. Her violent husband had proven a genuine threat. Yet it seemed odd to me that a healthy man like Herodotus should admit he couldn't defend himself. Nor did he look like a coward. I asked the obvious question.

"Do you have any enemies?"

"None," Herodotus said. "But where I am going, I will require protection nonetheless."

"And where is that?" I asked.

Herodotus set down his cup. He leaned forward, and said, "I want you to be my personal escort when I travel to Egypt."

I was startled. What Herodotus proposed was a very long journey. I knew right away that I would have trouble avoiding this commission, even if I wanted to. Diotima loved to travel. Besides which, my wife was a philosopher, and Egypt was the land of ancient wisdom.

There was only one problem. I voiced it.

"But there's a war on there."

Everyone knew about the war. The people of Egypt had risen up against their Persian overlords. When the rebels had called for help, Athens had instantly dispatched a fleet of two hundred *triremes* to assist our new friends, because anyone who kills Persians can't be all bad. We'd done enough of it ourselves, when the Persians had attacked Hellas thirty-five years before. Now there were three armies roaming across the land of the Pharaohs.

"Yes, precisely. That's why I need the escort," Herodotus said.

"Sir, I'm a private agent, not a small army."

"But it's you I need," Herodotus said earnestly. "If you are with me, then I'll have a safe passage through any territory controlled by the Athenians. The Egyptians are your allies and I am a Hellene; they will not trouble us."

"What about the Persians?" I asked.

"My native city might be Hellene, but Halicarnassus is a client state of the Persian Empire," Herodotus said. "I am technically one of their citizens. Thus with you to escort me, I will have safe passage everywhere."

I thought about it for a moment.

"Where do you want to go in Egypt?" I asked.

"Everywhere," he said simply.

"The place is bigger than all of Hellas!"

"Everywhere that I reasonably can," Herodotus corrected himself. "You need to understand that I am embarking on a noble course, for I am writing a book."

I wasn't impressed. "Isn't everyone?" I said, thinking of Diotima in the courtyard, scribbling away.

Herodotus looked at me strangely. "This is a book of . . . *histories,* I suppose you would say."

"A book of inquiries?" I repeated.

"Just so." Herodotus nodded.

"You're a playwright then," I said.

"No," Herodotus said. "The stories I'll be telling are all true." Herodotus spoke more quickly, with excitement. "My plan is to set down in writing the history of the wars between the Hellenes and the Persians!"

He spoke as if I should instantly recognize the genius of this idea.

After a short pause I asked, "Why bother?"

"So that the deeds of men will not be forgotten in time," he said. "This conflict between us and the Persians is the greatest war since the Trojan. It deserves to be remembered."

I had my doubts. Why would anyone care about our war more than any other? But that wasn't my problem. "Let me see if I understand. You want to go to a war zone, not to fight, but so you can write about it?"

"You understand," Herodotus said, unaware that with those words he brought his sanity into question.

"How did you hear of me?" I asked. I wanted to know what person thought I was crazy enough to do this.

"You were recommended, as I said before," Herodotus told me. "I was speaking to your head man here in Athens —"

"Pericles?" I said, surprised. Pericles had never in his life done a man a favor that didn't have something in it for himself. The mention of Pericles made me instantly suspicious.

"Yes," Herodotus said. "I met Pericles the

other night, at a symposium. I told him of my plans and asked his advice. Pericles said you would be just the man to lead me around Egypt. He was most helpful."

"I'm sure he was." I rubbed my chin. "Well, Herodotus, I thank you for your proposal. To travel to Egypt is a long under-taking. I'm sure you understand that I must think on this. Does it suit if I give you my answer tomorrow?"

"That would be wise." Herodotus nodded gravely. He indicated my cup of wine. "I recommend that you get drunk tonight."

"Oh? Why do you say that?" I asked, for though I thought his advice sound, it did seem a little unusual.

Herodotus said, "I merely suggest to you the custom of another land. In Persia, when a weighty matter is to be decided, the men consider it first when they're drunk, and then again when they are sober the next morning. If their plan seems good when both drunk and sober, then they proceed with it."

I had lived among the Persians. Not once had I ever seen them do such a thing.

"Thank you for your advice, Herodotus," I said, showing him to the door. "I will give this assignment every consideration."

What I didn't say was that first thing in

THE MISSION

I was at the door of Pericles's home before Apollo's rays had touched the city.

Pericles was already awake. The most powerful man in Athens had more work to do than any other three men combined. His first words when I walked into his office were, "*Kalimera,* Nicolaos. I've been expecting you."

"*Kalimera,* Pericles." I asked Pericles what he had intended when he sent Herodotus to see me. I finished with, "Do you want me out of Athens for some reason?"

"Not out of Athens, but in Egypt, yes," Pericles said. "I will explain. The thing is, Nicolaos, we have a situation, and this fellow Herodotus has given us the perfect opportunity to deal with it. We've received a request from our allies in Egypt." He handed me a scroll. "Here, read this. It came by boat not ten days ago."

I took the scroll and sat down on the

25

couch opposite Pericles's desk. It was the comfortable old dining couch that had been placed to catch the sun that streamed through the window overlooking the court- yard. I sat without being invited, as I always did when I visited, and Pericles took no notice. I was struck by the easy familiarity of it all. How many years had I sat in this room, from time to time? Five now, I re- alized, counting back. Five years since my first commission.

The first time I sat in this room, I had been half-terrified. Now familiarity — and Pericles's habit of landing me in the raw end of every crisis — had reduced me to this assumption that I was free to take my comfort among the rich and powerful, though I myself was neither.

The scroll had been written in a firm hand, in good Greek. The message said:

Inaros son of Psamtik greets the Athenians and says this: the war against the Persian proceeds well. Together the Egyptians and the Athenians have won a great victory. Most of Lower Egypt lies in our hands.

The enemy has retreated to their strong- hold within Memphis. It is their final chance.

There was more, but I looked up at Pericles. I said, "This is a status report. Who is Inaros?"

"The leader of the rebels," Pericles said. "Inaros inspired the uprising. He raised the native army. If it weren't for him, there would be no rebellion. Oh, and he's a Prince of Libya."

"Libya?" I said. "I thought the rebels were Egyptian."

"They are. Inaros is a Libyan prince who claims to be a descendant of the last Pharaoh."

"That sounds doubtful," I said. "Is it true?"

"Does it matter?" Pericles countered pragmatically. "The man is causing trouble for the Persians, and that's good enough for me. Read the next part. It concerns you."

Inaros says this: the battle for Memphis will be a formidable task. In the south of the city lies the White Fort. It is almost impregnable. The Persian holds this fort with all the strength that remains to him.

The fort can be reduced by starvation. But that takes months or years, and the Great King of the Persians will certainly send another army before then. The fort can be taken by assault, in a glorious battle. Such enterprises are risky, as all men know.

There is a way to reduce the Persian's hold without a great battle. Send me an agent, a man of cunning and resource, someone I can trust, as I could trust no Egyptian in this matter. Do this, and Memphis shall fall, and the Persian shall be driven from Egypt.

Thus speaks Inaros to the Athenians.

That was the end of the message. I put it down and said, "So Inaros wants an agent. What does he want the agent to do?"

"He doesn't say," Pericles said.

"I noticed that," I said unhappily. I had little doubt who Pericles would nominate to be this agent of cunning and resource.

"Obviously the Prince of Libya wants you to represent him in some delicate matter," Pericles said.

Inaros had used the same word we would for a commercial agent, or someone delegated to act on another's behalf. It could mean anything from negotiating to buy a house, to arranging to have someone killed. There was no way to know. I also didn't like that part about Inaros not being able to trust an Egyptian. I asked Pericles what it meant.

28

"I don't know," he admitted. "However there's something else you need to hear. We've had word that another agent has been sent to Egypt. The word is that this man is a Hellene, but a Hellene who works for the Persians."

This job was getting worse every time Pericles opened his mouth. I said, "So just as Inaros has asked for an agent from us, the Persians are sending their own man."

Pericles nodded. "Whatever's happening down there, it's important."

"How did you hear of this?" I asked.

"A source from within the Persian Court," Pericles said, somewhat evasively. "We have friends there — visitors to Susa and the Great Court — sometimes they hear things. One of them wrote to us with this news."

"There's a traitor among the Hellenes then," I said.

"Not necessarily." Pericles shook his head. "Many Hellenes are legitimately members of the Empire. Those who live in cities on the far coast of the Aegean, for example."

"Do we know who the agent is?" I asked. "His name? His city?"

"No."

I suddenly caught the drift of Pericles's argument.

"You think this Herodotus is the Persian

agent!" I exclaimed.

"He might be," Pericles said. "Think about it, Nicolaos. Herodotus comes from Halicarnassus. It's a city on the other side of the Aegean Sea. It's under Persian sway; he could hold Persian sympathies. Consider that at the moment he arrives in Athens, on his way to Egypt, we hear of an enemy agent dispatched to that very same destination."

"It could be a coincidence," I said. "Many traders travel to Egypt."

"Yes, that's why I deliberately sought out this man Herodotus, to judge for myself, when I heard he was in Athens and enquiring about Egypt."

"Then the coincidence of you two meeting —"

"Was no coincidence," Pericles agreed. "I arranged for a friend to invite Herodotus to a symposium that I would be attending. I made a point of speaking to him. The moment he said he needed an escort, I suggested you. Thus if Herodotus is an agent of the Persians, I've planted on him an agent of the Hellenes." Pericles smiled a sneaky smile. "As I said before, it was too good an opportunity to pass up."

This was typical Periclean convoluted thinking. Pericles thought he was smarter than everyone else. The fact that he was right did nothing to make his devious schemes any less worrying for the people who had to execute them. If Herodotus was an agent of the Persians, then Diotima and I would be in mortal danger every moment we were with him.

"This is important, Nicolaos," Pericles said. "All eyes are turning to Egypt. All armies, all strategies are concentrating there. There's certain to be a major decision in that country. I don't know what it will be — there are too many factors, too many chancy options — but whatever happens will change the future of every city and every nation of civilization."

Pericles's words strangely echoed Herodotus himself when he had said he wanted to go to Egypt to record the great deeds of men.

"Your mission, Nicolaos, is to go to Egypt, talk to this Inaros, do whatever he wants, within reason, and report back to me on what is happening down there."

"What of Herodotus?" I asked. "What if he proves to be the Persian spy?"

"Then kill him," Pericles said.

ALL AT SEA

I accepted the commission from Herodotus. As the fee for my services, I asked for ten *drachmae* a day, plus expenses. It was twice what I thought I could get. After all, the average workman only earns one drachma a day.

I expected Herodotus to haggle with me. Instead, he agreed instantly to my outrageous demand and told me to find passage to Egypt at once. He said he was worried that something exciting might happen before we got there.

I was more worried that something exciting might happen after we arrived, but I had little choice in the matter since I had Pericles's secret commission to enact.

As I walked down to the docks at Piraeus, I thought about Herodotus. Money was no object for him. Either Herodotus was a wealthy man, or he was backed by someone with a great deal of coin; such as the Persian

Empire. It was something to think about. In either case, for the sort of money my new client was paying, he had every reason to expect perfect service. I went to find us a boat.

Cargo ships leave for Egypt every third or fourth day. It's one of the most profitable trade routes for luxury items. The Egyptians send us papyrus and jewelry. We send them ceramics and *amphorae* of wine. The big, fat traders were prepared to take a passenger or three. The problem was, they would all be far too slow. Every trader followed the coastal route. They would spend interminable days haggling at every port of call.

Luckily I had an answer. I arranged our passage to Egypt with my friend Captain Kordax. Kordax was a retired navy captain who had reluctantly given up command of a warship, and then instantly created his own shipping line. Four of his five boats were slow tubs designed to carry grain to the islands. There was always money to be made in that. The fifth was the pride of his small fleet. It was a courier boat that he commanded personally. Kordax hired it to wealthy businessmen, state emissaries, or other important men who needed to be somewhere else, fast.

Friendship didn't prevent the good Captain from charging me a fortune. I didn't mind, because Herodotus was paying, and because we'd chartered the entire boat for our own use. What Kordax asked seemed a fair price for a sleek private ship.

Next morning at dawn, Herodotus, Diotima and I stepped onto the deck of *Dolphin,* so named, Kordax explained, because his ship was as fast and clever as that remarkable creature. As the boat gently glided away from the Piraeus docks, we left behind a loudly protesting Socrates. I wasn't willing to take my little brother into a war, and in any case our father absolutely forbade it. Nor was Father thrilled that I was taking my wife with me, but there is a long-standing tradition of businessmen taking their wives with them on long journeys, and as far as the world was concerned business was all this trip was about.

We weren't the only departure. Dawn is the usual time for boats to make way. The moment the sun rose, every boat in the harbor took off almost simultaneously. Around us were small merchantmen, large cargo carriers, a handful of navy triremes, and more fishing boats than I could count. *Dolphin* was more nimble than the triremes and faster than every other boat. She soon surged ahead to lead the oddly assorted flotilla out of the harbor and into the Aegean Sea.

As the crew rowed, Herodotus, Diotima and I stood at the back of the boat — out of the way of the steersman — to watch Athens fall away. The Acropolis stood like a mighty champion above the city.

Kordax came to the back of the boat to talk to his client about the voyage. This was the first time Kordax and Herodotus had met. Our captain was courteous. Herodotus in his turn made Kordax a friend for life by saying he would love to hear every detail of how *Dolphin* was constructed.

Dolphin would need five days to reach Egypt, Kordax said to us. The first three would be spent island hopping from Piraeus to Crete. It was a simple, easy run from one island to the next. As Kordax explained it, this was the perfect combination for a sailor who wanted to travel fast but safely. The water was smooth on this leg and we would never be far from a coastline.

Then he warned us there would be a very long day from Crete to the coastline of Africa. We would leave Crete before dawn and arrive at night. Kordax said that he would delay in Crete until the wind favored us, so that he could raise the sail for speed, and so that if there was an emergency the crew would not be too exhausted to handle it.

Dolphin was a light ship compared to the wide, spacious, but slow cargo ships beloved by traders. In shape she was more like the sleek triremes of the navy. Kordax had copied her design from the ships he used to command. Yet *Dolphin* was barely a third the length of a trireme, and she carried no battering ram at the front, as a warship would.

Navy triremes are crewed by two hundred men, a hundred and seventy of them rowers. *Dolphin* was served by forty men and three officers. All forty looked to be experienced, hand-picked men. Certainly their skins had been weathered by the sea in that unmistakable way. These men could row through the day without flagging, or judge the wind and set a sail, or repair anything on board that was broken. Kordax paid high wages and he got the best.

We sheltered the first night at Siphnos. It was a small, pleasant island with a bay and a sandy beach. There was no dockyard. The local fisher folk had hauled their craft onto the sands for the night. After only a day of running there was no need to beach our boat for supplies — we were only stopped because to carry on through the night was too dangerous — so Kordax anchored *Dolphin* a safe distance from shore.

The night was warm. I suggested to Diotima that we go for a swim.

"But Nico, I don't know how to swim," Diotima said, matter-of-fact.

"You can't swim?" I said to my wife, astounded. We'd been married almost two years, and I'd never realized.

Yet now that I thought about it, it was obvious. Athenian girls run races on land, and they paddle in the nearby river. But I'd never, ever seen any father take his daughter to the beach, to teach her to swim. Of course Diotima couldn't swim. No one had ever taught her.

I resolved to teach my wife to swim at the earliest possible instant. But falling dusk in a foreign bay that neither of us knew didn't seem the time or place. We spent the evening eating the ship's rations and watching people move about in the distant town. Then we slept on the deck — the only place possible on a boat — upon soft pallets under the stars, among the snoring sailors.

Throughout the first day and the next I kept a close eye on Herodotus. I wanted to see if he acted like a secret agent. The only problem was, I wasn't sure how a secret agent acted on a boat. When I mentioned this difficulty to Diotima, she pointed out that I was a secret agent and I was on a boat. Therefore if Herodotus acted like me then he must be guilty.

Herodotus did act like me, but only because we were both bored. I thought about offering to help row, but the men at the oars were professionals and they wouldn't welcome an amateur, no matter how well-meaning. Herodotus dealt with the tedium by quizzing the sailors about any stories they might have heard from distant lands. He sat beside the rowers with a brush in his hand, a jar of ink by his side, and a scroll in his lap on which he kept his notes. That scroll was like a sponge. No man could say a word that would not end up on its paper, if Herodotus was there to hear it. The sailors soon became sick of this — it's hard to talk and row in time to a steady beat. They began to ignore him.

Herodotus moved his inquisitive attention to Diotima and me. I still didn't know if he was a secret agent, but he would have made a fine detective: he never stopped asking questions.

Somehow Herodotus knew that Diotima

and I had been to Ionia, a province of Asia Minor. What was more disconcerting was that he knew we had been in Magnesia, to the court of Themistocles, at the time when that great man died. I didn't recall ever mentioning that to Herodotus, and I was sure Diotima had said nothing. Our presence had been public knowledge, so perhaps that explained it, but it seemed odd to me that he knew such a detail.

Herodotus proceeded to ask us questions about Themistocles. We were able to fend off almost every sensitive issue, since we had only met Themistocles at the end of his life.

"How did he die?" Herodotus asked. He held the brush poised over his scroll and looked up at us expectantly.

The answer to that question was a state secret. I turned to Diotima. Diotima turned to me. We had both sworn never to reveal the truth of those terrible days. But Herodotus was waiting. We had to say something.

I said, "He died of an illness. It was natural causes."

The explanation might have held, except that at the very same instant Diotima said, "It was suicide. He drank bull's blood."

Herodotus looked from one to the other of us in surprise. "Surely it must be one or the other."

"It was both," I answered, thinking quickly. "When Themistocles learned he was dying of natural causes, he drank bull's blood to end it all."

"I see." Herodotus said doubtfully. "I didn't realize bull's blood was poisonous."

"Oh, it is," Diotima said with a straight face. "I thought everyone knew that."

"Thank you," Herodotus said. He scribbled notes.

After that we resolved to avoid Herodotus whenever he had his scroll open.

It was mid-afternoon of the second day when we arrived at Thera, an oddly shaped island that was incredibly beautiful. The bay was surprisingly deep. Kordax told me that no one had ever succeeded in swimming to the bottom. Yet the water was a warm translucent blue, and because the high land curved around on all sides, almost in a perfect circle, it seemed more like a giant pond than a part of the sea.

Diotima was entranced. She said to me, "Nico, when this mission is over, we're coming back here for a holiday."

"Sure," I agreed at once.

Herodotus begged Kordax to let us off. Herodotus was particularly keen to talk to the locals. "Did you know that Thera was once a colony of Sparta?" he said.

I didn't. Nor did I care.

Since Herodotus was paying for the trip, his request amounted to an order. Kordax took *Dolphin* in close enough to the sands that we could all spend the afternoon off the boat.

The deck hands warned me not to expect much in the way of excitement in town. Nothing ever happened on Thera. But that didn't prevent them from wanting to hit the local tavern.

Kordax made a stern speech to the men. He promised to leave behind any man who was too drunk to row next morning, then gave all but a rump crew permission to go ashore. The sailors leapt overboard and waded to land.

Diotima jumped into my arms while I stood in chest-deep water. All day I had watched her anxiously, knowing now that if she fell off the boat she would sink. Every time she went near the side, my heart had leapt to my mouth and I had grabbed her arm. My solicitous attention had finally exasperated her, and the men laughed at me, but I didn't care. I wasn't going to lose my wife to Poseidon's depths.

Herodotus invited us to go with him to

interview the locals for his book. We declined. Herodotus was safe enough here, and I could imagine better ways to spend our short time off ship than to irritate farmers and fishermen with endless questions.

So Herodotus went his way with scroll in hand, and Diotima and I found a secluded spot at the end of the beach, where we proceeded with one of those better things to do. Married life is hard to maintain on an open boat with fifty sailors. Afterwards we splashed in the water, and I showed Diotima the basics of staying afloat. She was a natural. I put it down to the outstanding buoyancy of her breasts. She doubted this.

We dried off by lying on the beach, then walked into town in search of dinner.

The main road was parallel with the shore. A few dusty streets hung off it, all of which led away from the water. We passed a temple to Zeus (wooden), a warehouse, a baker, a blacksmith, a temple to Athena (wooden, with wood rot), a few non-descript buildings. Thera was a typical Hellene settlement.

Diotima was offended that such a tawdry town should have been built in the midst of such spectacular scenery. "How could they do it?" she complained.

"Did you hear Herodotus say this place was colonized by Spartans?" I asked her.

"Oh, right. Good point."

Spartans are not known for their architecture.

An idler told us there was a bigger city up the mountain, but we weren't tempted to visit. Instead we asked for the local inn.

The inn was down one of the side streets, on the opposite side of a small agora that smelled of stale fish. It was the largest building we'd yet seen in this dingy town, and the only one that looked alive. Thera was one of those places where everyone went to the inn to meet, rather than visit each other's homes.

We pushed our way in, past the drinkers standing at the door.

The inn was the usual provincial affair: rough wooden tables whose tops had been smoothed to a sheen by years of supporting elbows and spilled wine; benches worn by the behinds of countless drinkers; a dirt floor covered with rushes to hide where the drinkers hadn't made it outside before they pissed, or worse.

Herodotus sat at one of the benches, looking boyish and animated in that way he did when he had a victim to interrogate. His papyrus scroll was open before him and his inked brush was in his hand. He was talking to a man who sat with his back to us.

The room paid brief attention when we entered, as locals always do when a stranger walks in. This caused Herodotus to notice us. He waved and called, "Nicolaos, Diotima, there's room over here. Come meet this man. He has many stories!"

We walked over and around the table to meet Herodotus's friend. A thin man, almost gaunt, his face pale — he looked unwell — but the eyes were alive.

I stopped in shock when he looked up at us.

"Hello, Nico," said Markos. "I thought you might be coming this way."

I took a step back and moved my right arm to cover Diotima. Diotima's hands fell instinctively to the pouch she always wore on a strap over her shoulder. In the pouch she carried her priestess knife. The blade was short, but sharp as a sword.

Herodotus looked from one to the other of us in confusion. "You know each other?" he asked.

"At the last Olympics," I said, without taking my eyes off Markos. "It was a brief acquaintance."

"Brief but intense," Markos added. "And memorable. I really should have killed you then. It's good of you to drop by, Nico. I did hear the Athenians were sending an agent to Egypt. I guessed it would be you."

How in Hades did he know that? Was there a spy inside Athens? The answer to that was probably yes. I made a mental note to tell Pericles.

The pressing question was, what was Markos doing here? Was he too on his way to Egypt? Could Markos be the agent working for Persia? But that didn't make sense. Markos was *Spartan,* not Persian.

Markos was the finest assassin Sparta had ever produced. I had been present three years ago when Markos had gone too far during an assignment. The king of the Spartans, a good man named Pleistarchus, had ordered his soldiers to arrest Markos. Markos had been carried off to Sparta to be executed. For these last years I had assumed that Markos occupied an unmarked grave.

"Why aren't you dead?" I asked.

"King Pleistarchus tried," Markos said. "He had me thrown into prison and bound in chains. Every day he ordered my execution. Every day the Council of Ephors vetoed him. Every day for three years they argued over whether I should live or die. Every morning I waited to hear if I would live another day."

Markos held up his wrists for us to see. Ugly white, calloused scars ran all the way round. They looked like bracelets. Markos flexed his wrists. The skin around the scars moved in an unnatural way. From numerous thin red lines at the edges, I guessed the skin and scars parted frequently and bled.

"My ankles too," Markos said in response to our visible distaste. "You've probably already noticed I lost a lot of weight. They fed me pig slops. I spent three years in agony — because of you, Nico."

"I can't say I'm sorry."

"I wouldn't expect you to be," Markos said honestly. "I hope you'll still feel the same when I exact my revenge."

Forthcoming revenge had been uppermost in my mind since the moment I recognized Markos. I had scanned the room as we talked, calculating the likeliest route to get us out.

Our exit would have to be the door we'd come in. There was probably a back route, but I didn't have time to find it, and didn't know what we'd run into if we tried.

I had to remind myself that we weren't actually being threatened. We stood, while a weak and unwell Markos sat, yet such was the strength of the rivalry between us that it never occurred to me that Markos would not attack if he had a chance.

I assumed that in any fight, Herodotus would be a bystander, which made it two against one. A healthy Markos would be more than a match for me and Diotima, but weakened as he was, I wondered if even Sparta's assassin might consider the odds too great.

Then the words of Herodotus came back to me. Did I know that Thera had once been a Spartan colony? I hadn't cared when the historian told me at lunchtime, now I cared a great deal. If it came to a fight every man in this room would support Markos against me.

Herodotus had listened to our exchange with increasing perplexity. He had no idea of the history between us and Markos, but he could hear the frigid tone. So could everyone else. It had gone quiet around the room.

As we spoke, Markos had gestured with his hands quite a lot. They had rested below the table when he spoke to Herodotus; he had held them up to show us his scars, and afterwards he had gesticulated with one hand as he spoke. Markos hadn't been the gesticulating sort three years ago. He shifted in his seat, but he wasn't the seat-shifter type either.

There was only one possible explanation:

Markos was deliberately drawing our attention upwards. That made me look down. There was a strange contraption on the bench beside him, something that pointed beneath the table. Markos was slowly edging this machine, whatever it was, not towards me or Diotima, but towards our employer Herodotus.

I saw a glint of something shining amongst the gears and knew instantly that it was an arrowhead. An arrowhead that was slowly but surely moving to point to the other side of the table.

Markos wasn't planning to attack *me*. At any moment he was going to kill Herodotus, and Herodotus had no idea what was happening.

I yanked Herodotus out of the way at the same instant Markos shot the arrow. My sudden movement made Markos flinch. The arrow hit the bench where Herodotus had been sitting with such force that it sent it over backwards. Every man sitting on that side fell over.

Markos rose to attack. I slugged him, hard, before he could get to his feet. He fell back across the drinkers behind us and spilled their drinks. Cheap wine went into the laps of local farmers. As one they swore mightily and got to their feet in search of whoever had attacked them.

Markos pointed at me and shouted. "The Athenian hit me. He's insane!" He even managed to sound aggrieved.

Herodotus was sprawled across the dirty floor, where he'd fallen after I saved his life. He hadn't seen a thing. If we had arrived a moment later, Herodotus might already be dead.

Diotima hauled our employer to his feet.

"Why did you hit him?" Herodotus demanded.

Diotima and I grabbed Herodotus by an arm each and dragged him into a run.

We didn't have a hope of making it to the door. Not when there were at least twenty angry drinkers after our blood, and at least forty more interested in joining in.

Ten men stepped in our way. We had to stop. They raised their fists.

I had only a moment to think this was going to hurt before they were bowled over sideways by the sailors from *Dolphin*. Kordax had given his men the night off to go drinking, and that's what they'd done. They must have been sitting in a corner, I'd never noticed them.

The *Dolphin*s and the men of Thera brawled in the crowded room. The Therans had the numbers, but it's a rare sailor who doesn't know how to fight dirty. It seemed they were evenly matched.

Now Diotima, Herodotus and I had a chance. Diotima placed a well-aimed kick into the nether regions of a man who came at her. I backhanded a drunk. Together we dragged Herodotus out of the inn and into the rancid agora.

Behind us, Markos was ignoring the riot and pushing his way after us. He had his arrow-shooting weapon in hand.

"Get Herodotus to the boat," I said to my wife. Herodotus was a fit young man, he should have been able to run fast, but I knew Markos could outpace Diotima. "I'll hold him up at the door, then join you."

Diotima was too smart to argue in the middle of a crisis. She said, "Be careful," and then she took off with Herodotus in tow.

Markos burst through the knot of brawlers and stood in the doorway. He saw me outside waiting for him. For the first time I got a good look at his weapon. The machine he held was in the shape of a T, with an arrow resting upon it and a taut cord behind the arrow. It was a like a small bow, but held sideways, with a long wooden stock. I'd never seen anything like it.

Markos raised the weapon to his stomach.

I didn't know what the machine was, but I knew that arrow was pointing at me and I knew it was going to hurt.

I'd pulled my knife, but there were ten paces between us and I couldn't cross that distance before he could shoot me.

I dodged from side to side, to spoil his aim. Markos moved the arrow shooter to cover me. He grinned and said, "This is going to be fun."

A man flew through the doorway and hit Markos square in the back. Markos stumbled forward and as he did, jerked a lever. The machine fired.

The arrow whisked past my head and hit the wall behind me. But the heavy arrow didn't stop there, oh no. The arrow went *straight through a wooden wall,* leaving behind an arrow-sized hole and a few splinters.

Dear Gods, if that thing had hit me in the chest it would have passed right through. If Diotima and Herodotus had been standing behind it could have killed all three of us with a single shot.

Markos cursed. He reached behind his back and brought out another arrow.

I didn't stay to find out how long it would take him to nock and shoot.

I ran, zigzagging hard, like my drill sergeant had taught us to do against archers when I was in the army. My back felt hideously exposed. Another shot whizzed by as I turned the corner, but it was nowhere close.

By the time I arrived at the beach, Diotima and Herodotus had already waded out to *Dolphin*. Kordax was hauling them up the side as I hit the water.

Either Markos was more crippled than I thought by his years of imprisonment, or he had decided to take his time. Either way, he wasn't on my heels.

I was relieved to see all the sailors return to the boat, as I sat on the deck panting with exhaustion. It seemed they'd retreated in good order after the three of us had made our escape. Sailors are generally very good at getting out of town when there's trouble behind them.

The hands reported that along the way they'd knocked unconscious a man who was following me. I could only wish they'd killed him, but as far as the sailors were concerned, this had been an everyday, run-of-the-mill barroom brawl. Nothing worth getting killed over.

"Row," I said to Kordax, when our men were all aboard.

He looked at me as if I were insane. "Are

you crazy? It's the middle of the night."

I thought about Markos on the shore with his new toy, using us for target practice all night long.

"If you hope to see the dawn then you'll row," I told him. "Now."

Herodotus spent all of the next day berating me.

"I hired you to keep me safe, not land me in the middle of a riot!" he shouted.

This from a man who was hurrying to a war zone. I forbore from pointing out that there wouldn't have been any trouble if Herodotus had stayed on the boat.

Instead I said, "It's hardly my fault if an enemy was lying in wait for us."

"Us? He was waiting for you. He's not my enemy."

"Herodotus, he was aiming that thing at *you.*"

Diotima nodded at my words, but Herodotus didn't believe me. He hadn't seen what I'd seen.

"I don't even know the man," Herodotus said. "Who is he, anyway?"

I explained that the man who had tried to kill us the night before belonged to a special, clandestine unit of the Spartans, men who were trained to act independently as expert scouts and silent killers. Markos was the best of them.

"You sound like you admire him," Herodotus said.

"I do," I admitted. "Who wouldn't want to be the best of the best? If it's possible to fear and hate and admire a man at the same time, then I admire Markos."

In this explanation I included Kordax, who had a right to know. Kordax had transported me on missions twice before, back when he was a naval commander. He wasn't surprised to hear that something was afoot. He looked from Herodotus to me and back again. I was sure Kordax realized there was more to this than I had said.

I finished with, "It's a bit of a coincidence, don't you think, running into Markos?"

"Not so much as you might think," Kordax said. "Crete via Thera is the fastest route to Egypt for both us and the Spartans, and as Herodotus has pointed out, Thera was once a Spartan colony. What more natural place for your enemy to stop?"

Kordax's words sounded reasonable, but I wasn't satisfied. The more I thought about it, the more I realized that luck was playing a strange hand here. That Herodotus had randomly chosen someone to interview for his book, and ended up selecting a Spartan assassin, was too much of a coincidence to be credible.

So I asked, "Herodotus, what made you approach Markos?"

Herodotus shook his head. "I didn't. He approached me. I was walking about the town, talking to people, gathering stories for my book, you understand —"

I could imagine Herodotus accosting people in the streets. Any busy man would have told him to go away.

"Your Spartan friend said he was a stranger in town, and we got to talking."

I nodded. That made much more sense.

"Herodotus, you were targeted."

Herodotus scoffed. "It's impossible. How would he recognize me? How would he know I was going to be here?"

That was the part that worried me. I didn't know *why* Markos had tried to kill Herodotus. It might be that when I found out, I would want to kill Herodotus too. I wondered if Markos had been assigned to eliminate the Persian agent who, on that theory, might still be my client.

"Herodotus, that Spartan is an incredibly dangerous man," I warned him.

"Then you shouldn't have provoked him,"

Herodotus said.

I didn't recall provoking Markos. I recalled running away from him.

Herodotus was still angry with me. We barely spoke for the rest of the voyage. The men blamed me too, for having to row all last night and today without sleep. Diotima was exhausted. She curled up under the shade cloth that the men had stretched across the center of the boat, and she went to sleep.

That left me plenty of time to think.

Markos had said he knew the Athenians were sending an agent. Pericles had said he knew Persia had an agent from among the Hellenes. It was like someone was issuing news reports on what the world's secret agents were doing. Everyone was getting updates but me.

The very early start meant we made landfall in Crete in excellent time, though I'd never seen Kordax so nervous as when we sailed through the dark, with no way to see what was in front of his boat.

The men hadn't slept. As *Dolphin* glided into Itanos Port they collapsed in exhaustion over their oars.

Kordax insisted the men take a day to rest. Herodotus, who was generous to a fault whatever his dubious status might be, paid for the men's meals, drink and accommodation in a good inn, on the strict condition that I stayed away to avoid starting another riot. Once again I wondered about the source of my client's wealth.

Kordax meanwhile proved true to his word. He refused to move on until the wind came from the north. Every night he stood on the deck of *Dolphin* and inspected the skies and frowned. Every morning he rose at dawn, held a feather in the air, and frowned again. Until the fifth day, when dawn saw Kordax smile. He sent a runner for the deckhands, another for Diotima, Herodotus and me, and we were on our way for the final leg of our journey. There was nothing between us and Egypt but open water. Nothing could go wrong now.

"Pirates! Pirates on the port bow!" Our *proreus,* the officer at the front of the boat, pointed to the southeast and called out in a worried voice.

Diotima and I had been dozing under the awning, but that announcement was enough to wake us up. Kordax came forward and hooked his arm around the mast, where I joined him. Sitting directly between us and our destination was a tiny blob that floated on the water.

I could barely discern even a shape, but Kordax stared at this blob for long moments before he said, "That's a pirate, all right."

"How do you know?" I asked. It was mid-morning, and the glare of the sun in our eyes made it impossible to see any detail of the other boat.

"Because he isn't moving," Kordax said. "See how he becomes slowly larger as we approach? He's just waiting on the standard shipping route between Crete and Egypt. That bastard's probably from Gortyn, or maybe Chania. Or pretty much any other town in Crete. The whole accursed island is full of pirates."

"It's a big sea. We can go around him," I said. "Can't we?"

Kordax smiled. "He's expecting that. He has a shorter distance to go to cut us off than we have to travel to bypass. He could easily get his grappling hooks onto us. Also, if we spend too long looping, his friend behind will catch up."

"What friend?"

Kordax jerked his thumb backwards. There, coming up behind us, was another boat. It wasn't a cargo carrier. It was long, thin, low and fast, like us, with many rowers. From the movement of the oars I could see they were pulling hard.

"I thought he was just another traveler, like us," Kordax said. "Now that I see this fellow in front, I realize the boat behind is his friend." He shook his head ruefully. "It's the good old-fashioned squeeze, with us in the middle."

"What do we do?" I asked. I was worried now.

"We hold course and we wait."

At that moment our pursuer put on a turn of speed.

By this time the whole crew and Diotima and Herodotus had worked out what was happening. Everyone who wasn't rowing stood on the deck at the rear, by the steersman, to watch our fate approach.

The pirate behind us edged closer, until our two boats were running at speed in parallel, the sea splashing up salt spray between us. Now I saw who their commander was. There, on the starboard side, stood Markos.

Markos waved to us cheerily and called out, "Hello, dear friends! *Kalimera,* Nicolaos! Hello, Diotima, you're looking lovely this morning!"

Diotima made a rude gesture.

Markos shrugged. He turned to his crew, cupped his hands to his mouth and shouted,

"Take them!"

The pirate turned in on us.

Men appeared on the pirate deck with grappling hooks in hand. Five of them, standing well apart. The pirates swung the hooks on the ends of long ropes. They meant to tie us to them, then board and storm.

Kordax cursed angrily and grabbed the steering oar; the steersman relinquished control at once. He was a grizzled, sunburned man whose eyes had stared into too many horizons. Yet he was a cheery soul who always had a kind word for Diotima, a ready joke for the crew, and he even handled Herodotus with aplomb. He was deeply competent or Kordax would not have had him. Now this kind man screamed at the deck hands to break out the axes. The steersman grabbed the first to be handed out. I snatched the second, determined to be useful. I stood alongside him with axe in hand, while he shouted and dared the pirates to throw their hooks. He seemed to view being taken by pirates as a professional insult.

Markos reappeared at the fore with his arrow-shooting machine in hand. Kordax saw it too.

"The bows! Break out the bows!"

61

Those deck hands without axes reached once more into the small hold below deck. They hauled out short bows and quivers of arrows. This was the standard armament of any civilian boat: axes to deal with boarding parties, and bows to fight ship to ship.

Diotima needed no encouraging. She was an excellent archer and had brought her own weapon with her. It was a custom-built recurve bow in reinforced horn, especially crafted for her by a master bowyer who had tweaked the pull to exactly her strength. Diotima couldn't shoot as far as a man, but what she aimed at, she hit. If she'd been a man in the army, she would have been a designated marksman.

The only problem was, Diotima's bow was at the bottom of the luggage. The crew ignored her screams to bring out her own weapon. They had the ship's issue weapons and that was good enough for them. One of the crew told her to shut up and keep her head down.

Diotima cursed in a most unladylike way and dived head first into the hold. All I could see were her legs sticking out as she clawed her way past boxes and chests.

The pirates threw the grappling hooks.

Kordax threw the steering oar far to starboard. *Dolphin* swerved left.

The pirates had expected *Dolphin* to run away from the hooks. Instead, Kordax had steered us *into* the attack. That caused the pirates to completely misjudge their throws. The hooks flew over our deck and landed on the far side. Five ropes hung transverse over *Dolphin*'s deck.

Kordax's maneuver had prevented the grapples from taking hold, but we collided with the enemy. Throughout the voyage, Kordax had winced if a sailor so much as scratched *Dolphin.* Now his beautiful boat bounced hard against the pirate ship.

Everyone went down. One of our axemen staggered backwards and went over the starboard side with a scream. There was no stopping to collect him. Two pirates fell, one after the other. They too were left behind.

The steersman was the first back up. He swung his axe onto one of the ropes. He was a powerful man. The rope parted on the first strike. The axe blade embedded itself in the deck.

As the steersman struggled to free the blade, Markos brought the arrow machine to his stomach and fired. The heavy bolt took the steersman in the throat and passed through his neck. I was standing beside him and I heard the bones crack. The bolt disappeared into the water on the other side of *Dolphin*.

The steersman's body fell to the deck, almost decapitated but for shreds of flesh. His blood gushed across the deck onto Diotima, who only now was emerging backwards from the hold with bow in hand. I hoped she took the crewman's advice and kept her head down.

I took the steersman's place and hefted my axe in two hands that were suddenly sweaty. Meanwhile, *Dolphin*'s other axemen cut the remaining four ropes.

The two boats were flying side-by-side at incredible speed. The gunwales ground against each other in an act of mutual destruction.

Kordax pulled the steering oar the other way.

The boats parted company, but not before several pirates made an attempt to cross. They leapt with short swords in their hands.

I'd never fought with an axe before, but it wasn't the most subtle weapon. I swung at the pirate coming my way as if he were a tree. The axe caught him in mid-jump, center of the stomach. We stared at each other in shock, my weapon embedded inside him, before he fell back into the growing gap. The blood-soaked axe handle slipped through my hands and went with him. I never even heard the splash.

Of the other three pirates who'd jumped, two had been dispatched as mine had. The fourth made it onto our deck alive. He stood forward of the mast.

Diotima didn't miss. He went down with an arrow to the stomach. He was quickly surrounded by four furious axe-wielding *Dolphins.* Their axes rose and fell, and that was it.

The two boats had drifted apart during the fight. If the grappling hooks had held it would have been a different story, but we had defended well. The threat of a pirate boarding was over. Kordax shouted, "Oars!"

The men stumbled back to the benches. Men were pulling even before everyone was in place. *Dolphin* accelerated.

Now that there was a distance between us and with speed on, Kordax slammed the steering oar hard to the right. The experienced crew knew what to do without being told. The starboard side lifted oars. The port side sailors dug in hard. Their biceps bulged and the men cursed mightily under the strain. But they held on.

Dolphin spun on the spot with an agility that would have done a real dolphin proud. Incredibly, the pirate ship passed *behind* us.

We were pointing the other way.

"Pull!" Kordax shouted to his crew. "Pull like Lord Hades is on your tail!"

The crew needed no encouragement. *Dolphin* surged.

"This is where you thank me for making sure the men were well rested," Kordax said to me and Herodotus. I hadn't noticed the writer throughout the whole battle. I wondered where he'd been.

The distance between us and our attackers grew. The only problem was, now the pirates were between us and Egypt, our destination.

"So that was your friend from the other night?" Kordax asked me.

"Markos? Yes."

"I'll kill him for what he did to Olas."

The steersman's body had been carried to the side and dropped overboard. I objected, but was told roughly that it's the only thing to do at sea. If I died this day, that would be my fate too. The thought made me queasy. When my time came, I wanted a decent burial, with the coin beneath my tongue, to pay Charon the Ferryman to take me to Hades.

I had to force my mind back to the immediate problem.

"Markos must have followed us from

Thera," I said to Kordax.

Kordax thought about it. "We were in dock for five days. Yes, that would be just enough time for him to travel to Crete, find pirates and bribe them to go after us."

"How could Markos have bribed pirates?" I wondered. "We're carrying nothing valuable."

"What do you think we're worth in ransom?" Kordax shot back.

"Oh. I didn't think of that."

The captain nodded. "The crew will be sold as slaves. They'll take *Dolphin* from me. You, I, and Herodotus will be ransomed, assuming our families will pay to have us back. Your wife will be raped," he finished, matter-of-fact.

"I'll defend her to the death," I said, and meant it.

"Then you'll be dead. And she'll still be raped."

"I'll ransom her the moment they step on board."

"You'd better have a lot of coin then," Kordax said. "Diotima would fetch an absolute fortune as a brothel slave."

That depressing comment was enough to make me think we'd taken on too big a job. It was time to turn around, go back to Athens, tell Pericles I had failed.

"Can we return to Crete?" I asked Kordax.

"Where do you think those bastards came from?" Kordax said.

"Oh. Right," I said, abashed. If we turned tail for Crete, the pirates need only follow us back to their base.

"There's no safe landfall within sailing distance but the African coast," Kordax said. "We'll have to break their cordon."

"How do we do that?"

"By being faster than them."

The two pirates were to our southeast, exactly where we needed to go. Kordax made a minute adjustment to the steering oar. *Dolphin* commenced a wide, long arc to the east. Some time later, the pirates turned the same way, shadowing us.

"If we continue on this heading, we'll come to Phoenicea," Kordax said.

"That's the plan?" Diotima asked. She had joined us after seeing to the injured men. She had learned basic medicine from doctors back in Athens.

"No. But every *stadia* we travel this way takes our enemy further from home."

"You're deliberately tiring out their men," I said.

"Yes."

"It won't work," said the proreus. The offi-

68

cer of the forward deck had come aft to ask for orders and couldn't resist butting in. "They can attack us in relays," he added. He sounded worried.

"What does that mean?" Herodotus asked. Even in this dire situation, he pulled out his brush and papyrus and prepared to write.

The proreus said, "The pirate boats take turns to come at us fast. Their crews rest in between sprints, but *our* men have to sprint all the time. They wear us out. Then they catch us."

Kordax ignored the pessimism and ordered the proreus to have all lines ready and repair anything that could slow us down.

It wasn't yet midday and already everyone was exhausted. I insisted I rest one of the men at the oars. Our lives depended on the oarsmen and I was going to give them every chance to be rested before the next crisis. Herodotus joined me on the bench.

I took the smooth oar in both hands, put my feet on the footrest, and tried to pull in time. My hands were bleeding and my arms and back were aching before the sun hit noon. The men before and behind me maintained the rhythm while I struggled, and they'd been doing this all day. These sailors must be demigods.

Diotima brought fresh water and food to

every man. Throughout this time the pirates had held station, daring us to come south.

The mast cast very little shadow when Kordax eyed the sky, the water, the pirates, and us. "Prepare to head south," he said quietly.

I relinquished my spot on the bench. *Dolphin* turned to the enemy.

"They have three choices," Kordax said, as we watched the pirates maneuver. "They can split and attack us from both sides —"

"That sounds bad," I said.

"On land it would be," Kordax said. "At sea, it means we can slip between and run away."

"Oh."

"Or they could chase us down in a relay of sprints, like the proreus said."

"That must be bad if it worries a good seaman," I said.

"Have you noticed the wind is behind us?" Kordax said. "*Directly* behind us."

"Uh, yes?"

"What do we have that they don't?" Kordax asked.

"Innocent men?"

"Besides that."

I looked from *Dolphin* to the enemy and back again.

"A mast."

"Yes, and with the wind at our backs we can use it. If they try to chase us down in a sprint relay, we hoist sail and relax."

"That's why you took us out here."

"Yes."

"Kordax, you're a genius!"

"Only if the plan works."

"What can go wrong?"

"They can do the third and most clever thing. One of them can block our path, perhaps even by ramming, and then the other can hit us midships. That would be standard trireme tactics, if we were fighting a navy boat. It's what I'd do."

It was what the pirates tried, after they had chased us long enough to learn that we could hold our speed. I looked up, willing the sun to descend so we could escape in the dark, but Apollo was stubbornly high in the sky. I doubted it was even yet mid-afternoon. The light wouldn't save us.

Kordax grunted when he saw one pirate hold station, while the other swung out wide. "This is it," he said.

Axes and bows were handed round once more.

"We hoist sail now?" Herodotus asked.

"No, that would commit us to a line they can predict. I must be free to maneuver."

Kordax told the rowers to slow down.

"Conserve your strength," he shouted to them.

Naval battles aren't at all like land battles. It takes ages to reach your opponent. In the meantime all you can do is stare at the people you're planning to kill and feel socially awkward.

The pirate to our flank had gone far out and was matching our pace. The one in front was headed right for us. I could see their proreus directing from the bow. He pointed left or right as necessary to make sure they stayed on our line.

"If we hit at these speeds, we're both going to sink," I said quietly to Diotima.

"You're such an optimist, Nico."

"No, listen, if it happens, grab onto something that floats."

"Such as?"

I had no answer. But my mind repeated over and over that Diotima couldn't swim.

She held her bow and I held another axe, but neither did us any good. It was all up to Kordax.

Kordax made no effort to avoid the imminent collision. The two captains stared each other down.

We were ten ship lengths apart when our proreus pointed to the right and shouted, "Pirate midships to starboard!"

Everyone turned their head, except for Kordax.

Dolphin was sailing south as fast as she could go. If we continued on this path we would reach Egypt. But that wouldn't happen, because there was a pirate in front of us, heading north, and at any moment we would collide head-on. When we did, both of us would be dead in the water. Meanwhile, the second pirate was charging in from the side. The second pirate could ram us midships.

Markos stood at the bow of the second pirate. I thought about asking Diotima to take a shot at him, but really, what would be the point?

While we were looking right, the first enemy was upon us.

I was horrified when I turned my attention forward. We were practically on top of each other and closing at crash speed.

Kordax jigged *Dolphin* to the right at the last moment. The pirate turned the same way. When he saw the pirate's bow match his move, Kordax pulled the steering oar the other way and shouted. "Starboard oars in. NOW!"

The oarsmen were ready. They had known one side or the other would have to pull in. But Kordax had given no hint of which side he would choose until it was practically too late. The starboard men swore and heaved. The oars began to come in.

The pirate captain saw the change too late. He'd already committed to the other direction, fooled by Kordax's fake. But he tried hard to correct. The pirate started to swing our way.

The two boats struck, but at an angle. The sides crunched against each other with such a force that I thought they must break, but they held, and dragged against each other as they passed.

The rowers on the pirate had not been fast enough. *Dolphin*'s bow broke through every oar on that side. It was one sharp crack after another, amid the screams on the other boat as the rebounding wooden poles broke the rowers' arms.

Kordax smiled at the sound.

We stared at the men on the enemy deck as we passed. We were so close we could practically smell them. The bowmen on both boats took the chance to fire. A stream of arrows went both ways. I ducked. Diotima stood calmly and managed to get off two shots. I heard a couple of shouts from the enemy, but whether any of our shots had struck I couldn't tell. Our proreus took an arrow in the arm but otherwise we had survived.

The cracking of oars finally ended as the boats parted.

"Damage report!" Kordax ordered.

"The bow is not good, Kordax," reported the proreus. "We're taking water." The arrow stuck in his arm hadn't prevented him from doing his duty. He had hung upside down over the front of the boat to see what state we were in. But he had to hold his arm away from his body. The blood dripped on the deck.

"How much water?" Kordax asked. He looked crest-fallen.

"The enemy oars caved in the stem where they struck. Our back's not broken, and the holes are above the water line . . . barely." The proreus shrugged. "The faster we go, the more water we'll take."

"If we were a trireme, we would have cut through those oars like they were paper," Kordax said.

"You're not in the navy any more, Captain."

"I know, my friend. See to your arm."

I held the arm of the proreus still while a crewman cut both protruding ends of the arrow.

"Don't pull it until we reach a doctor," Kordax advised. "Lest he bleed to death."

Diotima tore the hem of her dress and wrapped it around the wound. The proreus said he had never felt better, but his face was pale.

Kordax's ploy had partially worked. The boat we had attacked shipped half his port-side oars to the damaged starboard side and made for Crete, slowly. The boat carrying Markos was still on our tail. If we flagged for an instant, he would have us.

"Make sail," Kordax ordered, to give his men a rest.

The crew had been waiting for that. The sail rose in an instant, a light sail of magnificent blue linen hung square from the yardarm.

"We have a heavier sail of hemp, but with damage at the bow we're better served with light material," Kordax said. "I bought the blue cloth last time I was in Egypt. We're taking it home."

Even with the light sail, the nose dug in too much and *Dolphin* took water. Kordax ordered every man not working to stand at the back of the boat. When that didn't quite work, he ordered luggage hauled up from below and stacked at the rear too. I sat amidst sweaty men atop crates and amphorae. We looked like a floating house sale. *Dolphin*'s nose rose, and we skidded along.

The weird configuration meant that *Dolphin* didn't sail as quickly as Kordax expected. The remaining pirate caught up to us. Kordax ordered a half-crew to resume rowing. That was enough to keep us ahead. The pirate moved directly behind, in an attempt to block our wind. He was too low in the water to succeed, but it was worrying.

It felt like we'd been fighting all day. I said as much to Kordax.

"We almost have. Any normal pirate would have given up long ago," Kordax said.

"Markos is paying them."

Markos stood at the bow of the pirate. He looked annoyed.

Diotima took the opportunity to try to kill him. Her aim was good, but he wasn't dumb enough to stand still. When he saw her rise with bow in hand he hit the deck and her shots passed over his head.

Her action proved a good idea, though. Soon the crewmen with bows were taking aim at our pursuer. We didn't have enough arrows to shower them, but potshots were enough to disrupt their rowing. It's hard to row when you know someone is aiming at your back.

That idea lasted until some bright man aboard the pirate — it was probably Markos — thought to tear up their decking to use as a shield. We watched while the pirates shoved and pushed the barrier into place. We could see nothing but the slope of the wooden wall propped up at the front of their boat. Not only did it protect them, but it seemed to make them go faster. The pirate ran into the back of us.

We had fought for so long that the African coast was in sight and coming up fast, but it was still too far away to reach before the pirate would overhaul us. It was almost dusk, but the two boats were so close, they couldn't lose us now. I cursed our fate.

Kordax said, "Pass out the axes." Now even he sounded worried.

"Warships on the port bow!" called the proreus. "Two of them."

They were headed directly for us and we'd never noticed. All our attention had been on the pirate.

I'd never before appreciated what a mighty beast a trireme is. I'd traveled on them plenty of times, but when you look at them from below they seem terrifying. Their streamlined battering rams were clearly visible just below the surface of the water. Either of those warships could sail right through us and barely notice we were there.

One of the triremes split away and headed for the pirate, who made a sharp turn right.

He headed the only way he could go and live: straight for the African coast. If he made for open water the trireme would easily run him down.

The other trireme came straight on, then turned at the last moment with unnerving accuracy to come alongside. That battering ram must have come within half a ship's length of us.

A man leaned over the side and shouted down to us. "Where do you hale from?"

He had an Athenian accent.

"Athens!" Kordax called back.

The man threw us a line. "Would you like a tow?"

THE NAUARCH

During our running battle with the pirates we had blundered into the Athenian fleet, the one that had been sent to assist the rebels. *Swift* — for that was the name of our rescuer — cast us loose in the middle of two hundred triremes. We were safe at last.

The Admiral of the Fleet — the *Nauarch* — was the well-respected Charitimedes. He was known as a competent man and a brave one. For several years running he had been elected one of our ten military commanders. Pericles was another such, but whereas Pericles's forté was grand strategy, Charitimedes was a natural commander at sea.

Swift had dropped us beside the Nauarch's command ship. Kordax and I were invited to climb up the rope ladder. Herodotus, not being a citizen of Athens, didn't get an invite, much to his disappointment.

"Ah, Kordax, I'm glad to see you," said Admiral Charitimedes. "You're just in time for the battle."

I felt a trifle faint at those words.

"How can I help?" Kordax asked without hesitation.

The Admiral said, "One of my trierarchs is dead. Can you take command of *Vengeance* while we wait for his replacement to arrive?"

"Of course," said Kordax, the retired naval officer.

"Good man," Charitimedes said. "I understand you had a difficult crossing?"

"We had a minor problem," Kordax allowed.

I wondered what he would consider a major problem. Navy men, I'd discovered, would never admit to a situation they couldn't handle.

"We've been expecting a relieving force to arrive from Persia," said the Admiral. "When I heard reports of a fight to the north I sent *Swift* and *Harpy* to scout it. But it was only you. Pity. I'd been looking forward to a decent fight."

"Sorry to disappoint you, sir," I said.

Charitimedes turned to me. "Not your fault. The last lot of Persians we wiped out weren't much chop. But I must say the ones holding out in Memphis seem to know their business."

"That's why I'm here, sir."

"Oh? Who are you?"

We had outrun any possible messenger who might have foretold my mission to the Admiral. I had foreseen this problem. I took from beneath my tunic a letter of introduction written by Pericles.

Charitimedes read it. When he finished he looked me up and down. "So you're Nicolaos. I've heard of you. They say you're Pericles's attack dog."

That wasn't quite the way I would have described it. But there was no point in arguing.

"You're rather young for this, aren't you?" Charitimedes said.

I was twenty-five. Not old enough to hold public office, but old enough to serve Athens. I pointed that out to Charitimedes. He grunted.

"Well, at least your attitude is good. I'm aware of this scheme of Inaros's. I must say, I think his idea is crazy. You'll probably get yourself killed."

I resisted the urge to ask about the next boat back to Athens. Instead I said, "What *is* the plan, sir?"

"The whole thing is so very Egyptian, I think perhaps Inaros better tell you personally."

"This Inaros, what's he like, sir?"

"An extremely able man," the Admiral said. "But you'll see for yourself, soon enough."

"I will?"

Charitimedes called over one of his men.

"Is the messenger boat free?" he asked.

"Yes, Charitimedes," said the junior officer.

"Take this man, his baggage, and anyone he nominates to go with him to Naukratis. Get him there quickly. Apparently he's going to solve our crisis."

The Prince of Libya

The messenger boat dropped us off at Naukratis, a city halfway along the Nile Delta. From the moment we entered the waterways, Herodotus had his scroll out and was writing fast. He didn't stop asking questions of the captain, who answered every query with a complete lack of interest.

"What sort of bird is that?" Herodotus pointed at one of the thousands of birds that flocked all up and down the river.

"That's a bird," said the captain.

"Oh." Herodotus was stalled for a moment. Then he brightened when he saw another plumage. "What about that one over there?"

"That's another bird."

Our captain went on to demonstrate equal lack of knowledge of plants, animals, people, lifestyle of the natives, architecture and local politics. He was, however, able to give me detailed advice on all the best places to drink in Naukratis, which I carefully memorized.

Diotima was as absorbed as Herodotus. The two of them looked like a comedy act as they rushed from one side of the ship to the other, determined to see everything.

I admit I was fascinated myself. Egypt looked nothing like Hellas. For instance I wondered why there were so many logs floating by the shore. Then one of the logs surged in the blink of an eye, and snatched one of Herodotus's birds.

I gasped. It looked like some terrible monster had risen from the depths of Tartarus.

"What in Hades is *that*?"

The captain glanced over to where the hideous creature was shaking the corpse. "Those are crocodiles," he said. "Don't fall in. If you do, there'll be no point stopping to collect your body."

I could see what he meant. The crocodile had swallowed the unfortunate bird in one gulp.

"Dear Gods. Do the locals hunt those things?"

The captain laughed. "No. Those things hunt the locals."

Naukratis is a special city. Half the people

who live there are Egyptian. The other half are Hellene. Both sides only live in Naukratis for one reason: to trade with each other. The port would have done credit to a major capital. The docks were filled with ships from every part of the world. I saw trading vessels from Ephesus, from Tyre and Syracuse, from Samos, Rhodes, Mytilene, Cyprus, Carthage, and a place I'd never heard of that the sailors called Massalia.

Though we had arrived at dusk, it was still hot, and the moment we stepped away from the river, it was dusty. Running parallel with the shore, a wide boardwalk connected the well-maintained wharves with the many warehouses. A small army of men waited beyond the boardwalk. They crouched down, so that for a moment I thought they were large birds. The manner of rest of these men was remarkable. They balanced on the balls of their feet, but otherwise stayed as low as if they kneeled. For some reason they found this comfortable. Diotima observed that the posture kept them out of the dust, for there was nowhere to sit that would not end in a mouthful of dust blown by the hot wind.

These crouching men were dock workers. They waited for a ship to arrive, then clamored to be chosen to unload the cargo, for which they were paid.

One of these dock workers told us that for a hundred years, the traders of Naukratis had been exempt from tax. "That is why all the foreigner ships come here," he said, his teeth bright and white. "They go anywhere else, they get taxed."

Herodotus asked then how did the Pharaoh make a profit from that? Our friend pointed south and said, "That way are the camel caravans, laden with the things that men buy here. When they leave Naukratis, they get taxed."

We tipped him to get recommendations on a good place to stay, and he gave directions to an inn by the central agora. "You go far from docks, you get better place. Not so many sailors, you know?"

We walked into town. I wish I could talk about Naukratis's architectural merit, but it had none. The people lived only to make money. The most utilitarian of whitewashed, mud brick buildings was fine with them.

The same, however, could not be said for the women. They were gorgeous, every one of them.

Herodotus was smitten. His eyes were as large as plates every time a woman passed. Twice Diotima and I had to grab him when he turned around to follow a particularly attractive local with wide, swinging hips.

"You don't want to associate with them, Herodotus," Diotima said.

"I don't?" Herodotus was clearly willing to argue that point.

"They're prostitutes," Diotima explained. "Have you noticed they're all walking towards the docklands, where the sailors stay?"

The moment Diotima said it, it was obvious.

I was pleased to see that Herodotus could behave like a normal man at least some of the time. His devotion to that notebook of his was disconcerting.

We found the inn, and it was everything the man at the docks had said, including the price. Fortunately, Herodotus was paying. We took two rooms.

Herodotus said he was exhausted and would retire. I was one hundred percent sure he planned to go meet the local women, but I don't think Diotima guessed and I didn't tell her.

Yet Herodotus had hired me to protect him, so when Diotima went upstairs to inspect the rooms, to make sure they were clean, I mentioned casually to my employer that a wise man doesn't take all his money with him when he visits a brothel. Nor does he leave it alone in an empty room at an inn.

Herodotus didn't reply. After a moment, he turned to the wall and, out of sight of anyone else, pulled out two heavy bags of coins. He handed them to me without a word. I immediately stuffed the bags beneath my own clothing, and then wondered how Herodotus had managed to walk all this time with that much weight. I was flattered that he trusted me.

The two of us shared a conspiratorial look as Diotima returned. I'd brought my own exquisite lady with me and I intended never to need another, but four years ago I might have been tempted to join him.

Herodotus yawned ostentatiously and walked upstairs. I took Diotima by the hand and led her outside.

"Where are we going?" she asked.

"To find Inaros."

The Athenian Admiral had told me that the rebel leader was to be found at Naukratis. He hadn't told me where, but I had assumed that the city would be crawling with troops, one of whom could take me to him. Instead, there wasn't a soldier to be seen. To look at the agora, you would never have known there was a war on.

Though it was getting dark, the central agora didn't need torches. The stars and the moon shone bright enough. The place was as busy at night as any big city. Suspicious-looking loiterers milled about and eyed the passers-by. Partygoers crossed one way or the other. Beggars sat on the ground with their hands outstretched or calling for alms. Rich people dropped a coin into every hand they passed. They seemed to treat it like a tax.

I decided to ask one of these beggars where I might find Inaros. I chose a man with a thick beard. Unlike most of the beggars in their loincloths, this one was respectably dressed in an ankle-length tunic.

The beggar held out his hand.

I had expected that. I reached for my money pouch — tied securely to my belt and hanging *underneath* my chiton — agents know all about pickpockets — when I suddenly realized there was a problem.

"I'm sorry, I don't have any Egyptian money," I said.

"That's because there's no such thing," the beggar replied in accented but understandable Greek.

"There isn't?"

"Egypt doesn't make its own coins. Whatever coins you foreigners spend, we use ourselves," he said. "If you want to make a donation, I'm currently accepting Persian sarics, Babylonian shekels, drachmae from you Hellenes, silphium from Cyrenaica, and siglos, both the Lydian and the Persian kind."

"There's a difference between the siglos?" asked Diotima.

"Oh Gods, yes," said the beggar with some passion. "Don't ever let someone give you a Persian siglos if he owes you a Lydian. Insist on at least two for one."

"I'll remember that."

I gave the beggar three drachmae. That was half a week's wages and more than enough for one bit of information.

I said, "Can you tell me where we can find Inaros —"

The beggar ignored me. He held each coin up to the light and stared at it intently.

"This is a good one. Thanks." He dropped the first two drachmae into his begging bowl. The third that he had labeled good, he continued to hold as if it were something precious.

I thought perhaps the poor fellow must not understand about coins. He didn't seem to realize they were all the same value: three one-drachma pieces.

"They're all the same, you know," I said gently.

He shook his head. "No they're not. Every coin is like a person. They all got different personalities."

Out of all the beggars in this city, I had to pick the one that was insane.

"Sure," I said. "Now, about Inaros —"

"When you sit around here begging all day, all you got to do for entertainment is look at the coins people drop. I see all kinds," he said, then added, "In low denominations, of course."

"I can imagine."

"That third coin you gave me's got no moon. All the coins you Athenians make have got an owl, but only the really old ones got no moon beside the owl."

"Getting back to Inaros —"

"I got interested in coins, you know? Not just to spend, but coins are like art. I keep the unusual ones for my collection."

"You collect coins instead of spending them. And you're a beggar?" I said.

"Best way to get more coins!"

"I'm sure."

"If you're interested in coins, you should talk to the other collectors. They all know me. I keep an eye out for them. Whenever I find something unusual, I sell them the coins."

"You sell money . . ." I repeated. I had some trouble with that idea.

"Yeah. There are guys who will pay good money for this money."

"Let me get this straight," I said. "That one drachma piece is worth more than one drachma?"

"Right. Because there's no moon beside the owl, that means you guys minted it before the Persians attacked you, which was — what? — thirty years ago? This coin is *old.* I could get maybe five drachmae for this." He tucked the one-drachma coin into a leather bag beneath his clothing, a bag rather like my own.

"That doesn't make sense."

The beggar shrugged. "He's over there." He pointed.

"Who is?"

"Inaros. You kept asking about him. I don't know why you'd bother talking to him though; he's not interested in coins."

The man whom Athens was backing to be the next Pharaoh of Egypt had taken residence in a mansion just off the agora.

Inaros held counsel before a group of fifteen men. He sat upon a large, straight-backed chair, his arms lying perfectly parallel on the unpadded rests, his spine flat against the wooden back. Whether it was subconscious or by design, he already sat like a Pharaoh. So much so that I felt like we had entered a throne room, though we were in a mere merchant's house.

One of the men who stood before Inaros was holding forth.

". . . and I say to you, Inaros, that the news is pleasing, up and down the Nile. Here in the north, in the Land of Papyrus, you are Pharaoh in all but name. It is as if the Persians never existed. To the south, in the Land of Reeds, the governors of the *nomes* await your coming and that of your armies. Soon, Inaros, you will wear the Double Crown of the Two Lands."

"Hardly soon," Inaros said. His voice was mildly ironic, and deep, with a pleasant timbre. "What of Memphis?"

"There is Memphis," the advisor admitted.

Another man spoke up. He was gray-haired and looked a hard man. I guessed he was an officer. "The army cannot march south to liberate the Land of Reeds while Memphis remains under control of the Persians," he said crisply.

"I understand this, General," Inaros said.

"Does the enemy weaken?"

"If anything, the Persian grows stronger in his fort," the General said. "They have been given far too much time to rest and recuperate."

"The people of Memphis feed the enemy garrison," the advisor said glumly. "They prefer Persian rule."

"In the name of all that is holy, why?" asked another man.

"They do not accept Inaros as a true incarnation of Horus," said the political advisor.

"Of course he is," the man said. "The God has chosen Inaros. How else could he have won the astounding victories that he has?"

Heads nodded about the room.

"The city dwellers are less sure of the God's intention," the advisor said.

"Or else they're less pious," the hard-bitten military man added drily. I saw Inaros hide a smile at those words.

"Inaros is a true descendant of the Pharaohs," the third man insisted. "He said so."

There was general silence to this remark.

The silence was finally broken by the military man. "Let me assault the city, Inaros," he said.

"No!" The advisor held up his hands in horror. "Think of the civilian deaths."

"So?" replied the officer. "Have you ever known a war when people didn't die?"

"The Pharaoh cannot kill women and children!"

"The Pharaoh will not be Pharaoh if he doesn't!"

The two men were shouting at each other.

"Gentlemen," Inaros said.

They turned to him.

"You are both right," Inaros said.

"We cannot both be right," said the advisor, and the military man nodded. They had found something they could agree on.

Inaros said, "General, you are right that Memphis must be taken. By assault, if no other way can be found. But if another way can be found, we must try it."

"We need an answer for Memphis," the General insisted.

"There will be an answer," Inaros said.

They ceased speaking when we were noticed. Every head turned our way. Inaros's eyes swept over us, then he said, "Here we have friends from Athens, I take it."

Diotima and I hadn't yet said a word. He must have deduced it from our clothing. I wore my best chiton, which Diotima had made for me using quality linen. It covered me from my arms to my legs; the material

96

was key-patterned in bright blues. Diotima wore a dress of rich red to set off her long, dark hair and silver earrings. All of this was quite different to what the Egyptians wore, which for the powerful men in this room meant voluminous clothing that hung loose and flowed with every movement.

Diotima and I stood out more than I had realized. I made a note that we would have to buy some local clothes.

"Greetings," I said. "I bring a message from Pericles to the esteemed . . . er . . ." I trailed off in confusion. "I'm sorry, do I call you Pharaoh?" I asked. Pericles hadn't bothered to mention that detail.

Men laughed. The political advisor scowled.

The man on the throne said, "I am Inaros, the chosen of Horus to assume the Pharaohship. But for the moment, my highest title is Prince of Libya."

The Prince of Libya held out his hand.

I handed over the letter of introduction that Pericles had written. Inaros read it. When he finished, he said to the assembly, "Gentlemen, our answer may have arrived. I invite you to welcome Nicolaos and Diotima, sent by our ally. They are . . . diplomats."

"These two are diplomats?" the General

said. "They make them young these days."
He looked Diotima up and down. "And a
damn sight better looking than the ambas-
sadors we used to get."

Inaros mentioned that dinner was long
overdue for his advisors. They took it as a
polite dismissal.

When they had left, Inaros asked, "Are
you hungry?"

We hadn't eaten since lunch on the boat.
Diotima and I said yes.

"So am I. Come this way."

Inaros stood. Two guards fell in behind
the Prince of Libya. They were tall and thin,
and stood straight as the spears they held in
their right hands. They wore nothing but
loincloths.

They were also bright red. Not sunburn
red. These men had coated their entire
bodies in a dye so loud that they looked like
they'd been dipped in artists' paint. That
alone would have grabbed my attention, but
there was more. The hair on the right side
of their heads hung all the way to their
waists. The hair on the left had been shorn
to the scalp.

They looked totally lopsided. I almost
expected them to fall over sideways. But
they didn't. Instead they stared at me.

"Don't mind them," Inaros said. "They're

from my homeland."

The Prince of Libya led us into a back room where there was a table and chairs. He invited us to sit. One of the slaves brought beer, another carried food.

This gave the rebel leader plenty of time to inspect us.

"The commander of my armies is right. You appear to be young for this assignment."

"I am twenty-five —"

"As I said, young."

Inaros himself could not have been older than forty-five by my reckoning. I decided not to mention that.

"Hmm, well," Inaros said. "If Pericles sent you, then you must be the best that Athens has."

It wasn't exactly a ringing endorsement of confidence.

"So, what do you think of me?" Inaros asked as he sipped his beer.

I choked on the apple I was eating. How was I supposed to answer that?

"Your approach is refreshingly informal," Diotima said.

Inaros laughed. "I have no delusions about being anything other than a man with the ability, *perhaps,* to take control of a country." Inaros ate dates and cheese from the plate before him as he spoke. "You listened in on the conversation. There has been a great battle, which we won with the excellent help of your Admiral Charitimedes and his fleet. I rule all of Egypt from the capital Memphis, up the Nile, through the Delta and on to the sea."

"You rule with a light touch," I said. "Naukratis seems barely to notice you."

"Nor do I want them to," said Inaros. "It is in my interest that they be undisturbed."

"It is?"

"Every man, woman and child in this city is a trader. Traders don't want to be governed, Nicolaos and Diotima. They want to be left alone to make their profits."

"You don't mind?"

"Mind? Are you insane? Have you ever noticed how cheap it is to rule a law-abiding citizen who just wants to be left alone? I *love* citizens like that."

"So you deliberately moved the army out of Naukratis," Diotima said. "We wondered where they were."

"I had somewhere else to send them," Inaros said. "After I conquered Bubastis and several other cities on the Delta, I discovered the people there have a problem with crime. So I flooded the streets of Bubastis with my troops."

"Did it work?"

"After I impaled the more egregious offenders, the crime level reduced markedly." Inaros sighed. "But there are always the dumb ones, and the overconfident. So it is that my soldiers patrol the streets in those places, and the people are pleased to see them and greet my men with kind words. In Bubastis the citizens are safe and the crocodiles grow fat upon the flesh of miscreants."

"Whereas here you leave the people to make money," Diotima said.

"Which can only be good for Egypt. Precisely. And then among the farmers along the river I take a more paternalistic approach. Men of the soil do not always plan well. There I exact a tax of one tenth of all grain."

"To feed your troops?" I raised an eyebrow.

"No, to store against time of need. Have you ever known a farmer to think more than one season ahead? Nor have I. We would all starve in a poor year if I didn't force them to save."

It all seemed mind-bogglingly complex. I said as much.

He gestured at our plates. "Must every man like the same food? No? Then why should he like the same government?" Inaros shrugged. "I give to every citizen the rule that he wants, or needs."

Charitimedes had told me that Inaros was very able. He was right. This man was a genius.

"Why are you doing this?" Diotima asked. I knew what she was thinking. The way he planned to rule, this talented man was setting himself up to be a virtual slave to his subjects for the rest of his life.

"You ask why, young lady?" Inaros leaned forward and looked into her eyes. His voice became intense. "For power, of course. I lust for power as the traders in this town lust for coin. You see, I am like all the other tyrants, all the other kings you have heard of. But the difference is, I know the price I must pay for power, and that price is good government." Inaros leaned back in his chair and relaxed. "Fortunately, when it comes to that I have the coin to spend," he said immodestly. "I need not offer the people a counterfeit."

"What about Memphis?" Diotima asked.

Inaros frowned. "In Memphis we have a problem. What the people of Memphis want is rule by the Persian overlords. I'm afraid there we must disappoint them. That's the problem."

"Is this why you wrote to Pericles, asking

for our help?" I asked.

"It is. Some months ago, my army and that of the Persian met on the sands at Pampremis. At the same time, Charitimedes took on the Persian fleet anchored in the Nile. We won mighty victories, both on land and at sea. With their fleet destroyed, the enemy had no line of retreat. The remnants of the Persian withdrew into a citadel within Memphis that we call the White Fort. There they await the coming of a relieving force."

"Are they so sure the Great King will send one?" I asked.

"Yes," Inaros said with complete assurance. "Egypt is a rich province. Also, during the battle the enemy was commanded by their Satrap, a man named Achaemenes. He was the brother of the Great King's father."

I didn't like that past tense. "Did you say *was*?"

"Achaemenes died in the battle," said Inaros calmly.

"You *killed* the uncle of the Great King?" I said, aghast.

"I might point out that *he* was trying to kill *us,*" Inaros said.

Beating a Persian army was one thing. Slaughtering a member of their royal family took the insult to a whole new level. Dear Gods, the Persians were going to come down on these rebels with an iron fist.

"This is where we need you," said Inaros. He paused to drink his beer. "With the Athenian fleet controlling the sea, the only route for an attacking army is the very hard journey across the desert."

"Yes, I can see that."

"If by that time the Persians have been cleared out of Memphis, then my army can safely face the new attack on the *East* bank of the Nile, with no fear of an enemy at our rear. These new Persians will have no access to the Nile; their supply line will stretch across the desert and we can wear them out with ease. They'll have no choice but to turn around and go home."

Suddenly an Egyptian victory looked possible. Maybe this crazy rebellion would succeed after all.

"I see your plan," I said. "This will work."

Inaros smiled. "I am pleased you agree, and that's why I need you to capture the White Fort for me."

The plan suddenly went back to being impossible.

"I'm an agent, not an army!"

It was the second time I'd had to say that. The first had been back in Athens, to Herodotus. I wondered how the historian was getting on with his women, while I sat here discussing suicide missions with a Prince of Libya.

"Hear me out." Inaros barely seemed to have noticed my outburst. "The situation is more fluid than my advisors would have you think. I have been in contact with the leaders of Memphis. They have certain . . . concerns about my bid to supplant the Persians. Most of these involve their personal wealth and safety. When I raised the rebellion, you see, there were more tax collectors in Egypt than there were teachers for our children. The tax was intended for the coffers of the King."

"So the Persians were sucking the life out of Egypt," I said.

"Graphic, but accurate. My simple policy of executing every tax collector I came across did much to endear me to the populace."

"I can imagine."

"All that tax money used to pass through the capital, Memphis, on its way to the Great King. A certain amount of it stuck to the Egyptian bureaucrats who collaborated with our overlords."

"Ah ha! No wonder the bureaucrats in Memphis are resisting you."

"Indeed. In the normal course of events I would impale these creatures, but expediency has forced me into negotiation. I have guaranteed them their lives and their fortunes if they submit. They might even retain their government jobs."

"That's immoral!" Diotima blurted.

"I would not be the first politician to buy a victory, don't you think?" Inaros said gently.

Diotima nodded.

"It is not as bad as it sounds," he went on. "A corrupt man is like a drunkard. Once he has sipped from that cup, he cannot stop himself. Sooner or later these bureaucrats will embezzle from the state again, and then I will have them."

"More fat crocodiles?" I suggested.

Inaros smiled. "I may hire you for my justice department, Nicolaos. Your thinking agrees with mine."

"Then you have everything under control, Inaros. I don't see where we can help."

"There is another condition to be met, the most important of all. These men in Memphis will not bow to anyone but a child of their royalty. They require proof that I am a true descendant of the Pharaohs of past times."

I remained studiously silent on that one. For although Inaros was clearly the best man to be leading Egypt, he was also a man

of notably dark skin who resembled the Aethiopeans, while every powerful Egyptian
we had seen notably was not. He didn't look
like any Pharaoh we'd ever heard of. Diotima also held her tongue. Despite which,
Inaros had no trouble divining our thoughts.

"My father was indeed related to the last
family to wear the Double Crown," Inaros
said. "The royal lines of Egypt, Libya and
Aethiopia have sent their daughters to
marry into each other's families since time
immemorial. It is one of the ways we keep
the peace. The farmers, the merchants, the
artisans . . . everyone who was under the
Persian thumb has accepted my claim."

"I'm sure."

"But not the bureaucrats of Memphis.
They demand that I produce the insignia of
the Pharaoh."

"What's that?"

"*They* are the crook and the flail. The
crook and flail are passed down from one
ruler to the next. The crook symbolizes the
Pharaoh's role as a shepherd to his people.
The flail embodies his responsibility to —
how shall I put this? — to *encourage* good
behavior."

"I've got the idea," I said.

Diotima said, "I thought the Double
Crown that people talk about was the

insignia of the Pharaoh?"

"That's different again. The crook and flail symbolize the Pharaoh's relationship with his people. The Double Crown is political. It symbolizes the unity of Upper and Lower Egypt, which we call the Two Lands."

Diotima shook her head. "That's a lot of symbols."

"When you come to know this place, you will realize that Egypt is nothing *but* symbols. The crook and the flail are instantly recognizable by any true Egyptian. When the bureaucrats see that I hold the genuine articles, they will bow before me, the Persians will be bereft of their vital support, and the invader's final stronghold in the land will fall to me. But none of this will happen unless I can prove that the crook and flail were passed down to me from the last Pharaoh."

I asked, "Where do we find this crook and flail?"

"I have no idea," said Inaros. "Because quite obviously the crook and the flail were *not* passed down to me."

"Then we don't even know where to start!"

"Begin in Memphis. The crook and flail were last seen there."

"How long ago was this?" I asked.

"Sixty-eight years, when the last Pharaoh died and this land fell under the Persian yoke."

"Terrific."

Inaros thought about it for a moment. "I think you should see my agent, the one who negotiated this agreement. Her name is Djanet —"

"*Her* name?"

"She is a singer, from Memphis."

"Is that some sort of cover?" I asked.

"No, that's her day job."

I hadn't known much about this rebellion before I took on the assignment, but one thing I was learning fast: it was being run by amateurs.

"I will send with you one of my men, to smooth your path."

Inaros gestured. One of the bright red men stepped forward.

"My future, and the future of all of Egypt, relies on you finding the crook and flail. Good luck."

THE RED MAN

We didn't see Herodotus until late next morning. When we did, he smelled of incense and had an enormous hangover. He sat at one end of the tavern room of the inn, hunched over with his head in his hands.

Diotima was solicitous but didn't recognize the source of the problem — she had never had a hangover in her life, and it never occurred to her that Herodotus might be guilty of riotous living. "Perhaps it was something you ate," she suggested. She offered to bring him an enema.

Herodotus turned green and had to run for a bucket.

"That will do you good," Diotima said cheerily to the sound of retching. She went to fetch him some wine. "Wine will make you feel better," she said as she left.

"Did you have a nice time?" I asked Herodotus once he'd emptied his stomach.

"Enough material for a whole chapter," he said with a weak smile.

"You're not going to put that night in your book!"

"Perhaps I might omit certain details."

Diotima returned with the wine.

"Who's he?" Herodotus asked. He pointed at the escort Inaros had assigned, who stood behind us. He had accompanied us back to the inn, after dinner with the rebel leader. Diotima and I had left our escort downstairs when we went up to bed. He was still there when we came down next morning. I presumed that in between, he had slept somewhere. Up to now he hadn't said a word.

"Who?" I said. "Oh, you mean the big red guy with half his hair missing."

"Yes, that's who I mean." Herodotus looked the man up and down. "I don't recall hiring him."

I suddenly realized we had some explaining to do.

"Uh, well, Herodotus, it's like this . . ."

I told him the truth, except for a few bits that I distorted to avoid making myself look untrustworthy. I explained that since we were going to be in Egypt anyway, that Pericles had asked me to look in on our Athenian ally. And that since we happened to be there, that Inaros had offered us a commission to find the crook and flail. I didn't mention that if Herodotus had proven to be a spy then I was under orders to kill him.

This was a complex subject to be discussing over breakfast (which Herodotus felt he might now manage to hold down). The innkeeper's daughter brought us cheese and bread and light beer.

Herodotus was upset, but not in the way I expected.

"You went to see the rebel leader, and you didn't invite me?" he said, aggrieved.

"You had . . . er . . . other plans for the evening," I said, glancing at Diotima.

"Oh. Yes, so I did," Herodotus said, abashed. Then he rubbed his hands in glee. "This is the perfect opportunity to see more of Egypt and pick up who-knows-what exotic tales for my book, with an entrée from no less than the rebel leader himself. Where do we start?"

"In Memphis," I said. "Apparently this man" — I indicated our red-dyed escort — "can arrange our passage, but he's obviously very primitive. I'm not sure how intelligent he is."

I turned to the barbarian.

"Can — you — understand — me?" I spoke slowly and loudly. I figured the

barbarian would be more likely to understand a civilized man if I spoke up.

"I comprehend you quite adequately," the
barbarian said. He spoke in the most cul-
tured baritone that I'd heard since I'd left
Athens. "Though if I might beg you to
speak more softly, that would be agreeable."

Herodotus, Diotima and I stared in shock.
His Greek was so good that if I'd met him
at a symposium I would not have blinked,
as long as I was totally blind.

"Your Greek is excellent," Diotima said
wonderingly, and Herodotus nodded. I
could imagine Herodotus with his scroll and
ink brush working overtime as he inter-
rogated this man. "Who are you?"

"You may call me Max," the red man said.

"That's your name?"

"My name is Maxyates. But all my friends
call me Max. I choose to call you friends,
despite the terrible war of aggression your
people perpetrated against mine."

"Your people?" I said, perplexed. I
couldn't recall Athens attacking any bright
red people with only half their hair.

"My tribe are the descendants of Troy.
After you Hellenes did your best to wipe
out my ancestors, the few survivors made
their way to Libya, where they started again.

I am proud to call myself a child of Hector."

If this man was a Trojan then I was the King of Persia. But there was no doubting that he was civilized.

"Where did you acquire your education?" Diotima asked.

"My father is chieftain of one of the great tribes of Libya. As the third and youngest son, I had no future as leader, so he sent me to Egypt, to learn at the temple at Saïs, where I acquired the tongue, and to read and write, and studied the thoughts of the wise men. I discovered that I enjoyed this. I traveled on to the great center of learning at Ephesus."

"Why would you do that?" I asked.

"I am a philosopher."

I groaned. There was no escaping them.

"It was there that I learned your Hellene tongue, at which I hope I am not entirely inadequate."

He could have taught elocution to Pericles.

"While I was in Ephesus I took the chance to search for Troy, the land of my forebears. My ancestry is very important to me."

"Did you find it?" Herodotus asked eagerly. "I could put that in my book."

"I learned the works of your Homer in

search of hints. But alas, there was nothing. I traveled to Ilion — it's a minor city up there, inland — from whence I scoured the coast in search of the fabled city. But every day I returned to Ilion empty-handed. In the end there was no choice but to abandon the search. So it was that I returned home, to assume my destiny as the least important man in my family."

"Then how did you end up here?"

"My father owes his allegiance to the Prince. Thus when our Prince went to war, to conquer Egypt, Father sent me to serve him. I am ready to serve you in accordance with his wishes."

"We need to get to Memphis," I said.

"Yes, this is possible."

"To Memphis, by all means," Herodotus said. "I have already . . . ah . . . experienced the most interesting parts of Naukratis."

THE SINGER FROM MEMPHIS

Max arranged our passage for the next morning. From this point on, his language skills would be essential, for everywhere south of Naukratis the common people would speak only their own Egyptian tongue, though Max assured us that the educated would be able to speak Greek.

Max returned from his excursion with an unexpected visitor. It was the Nauarch, Admiral Charitimides, with ten officers in tow.

"How are you?" he asked.

"Fine so far, sir," I said.

"I'm actually here to see Inaros. It looks like there won't be another fleet action any time soon. Scouts report no activity in any ports to the East. It's even quiet up in Phoenicea, the traders tell me."

"That's good news, sir."

"Only if you like being bored," the Nauarch said. "I plan to lead our sailors onto land, to help our Egyptian allies in the next battle. The Persians have to hit us *somewhere,* you know."

"Yes, sir," I said politely.

"Oh, I got a message from your boss, Pericles."

"A message for me?" I said, startled.

"No, for me, but you might like to know. A Spartan army marched against Athens," he said calmly.

"What!"

"Our lads met them at Tanagra. The battle was a draw."

"Dear Gods, why?" I said. "We were at peace when I left."

"That's the interesting part," Charitimides said. "We captured some of their auxiliary troops. From them Pericles learned that a Persian ambassador has been visiting Sparta. A Persian in Sparta — seems rather odd, don't you think? They say this Megabazos fellow turned up with a boat load of gold and bribed the Spartans to hit us."

"That sounds bad."

"No, it's good. It means the enemy is scared of us in Egypt. Pericles thinks it's a strategic diversion."

"What does that mean, sir?"

"Just as we are in Egypt to force the Persians to send their troops here, so the

Persians are paying the Spartans to cause a ruckus back in Hellas, so that we have to return home."

"Are we going home, sir?" I asked.

"Good Gods, boy, of course not!" he exclaimed.

"Oh."

"The enemy wouldn't spend that gold unless they feared my men. So my fleet is staying right here. Anyway, it appears our lads back home have seen off the Spartans. What's your next move?" Charitimides switched from grand strategy to intelligence work in a single breath.

"We depart for Memphis tomorrow, sir," I said.

"The place is crawling with enemy troops."

"Yes, sir."

"You'll probably get killed, but that's the way it goes when you serve your country, eh?" He clapped me on the shoulder.

Charitimides chuckled at my expression and took his leave. The Nauarch acted like everyone's favorite uncle, but I'd never met a man more determined to fight.

Despite the warning, we got a shock two days later, when our boat docked at Memphis, the capital of Egypt.

Persian soldiers. They patrolled the docks and the wharves and no one seemed to take any notice. They wore their standard floor-length uniform of heavy cloth without any accommodation to the incredible heat. Some carried spears and shields upon their backs. The spearmen patrolled in squads. Other men were armed with bows and quivers full of arrows. The bowmen had taken up position on the roofs of the warehouses and the other high points.

It was a stark reminder that we were in a country divided by war. It also drove home the extent to which Inaros had returned Egypt to the Egyptians. He might be Libyan, but the soldiers who fought for him so willingly were Egyptian. In the north, where Inaros had conquered all, you would never have guessed that this was a country occupied by a foreign power. Here in the capital, we were in a Persian province, no doubt about it.

The Persians were obviously on the lookout for any advancing military, but they didn't give us a second glance. I brushed past one as I came down the wharves. He smiled at me with perfect teeth and very sunburned skin.

"What do they think we are?" I whispered after they had passed us by.

"They think we are foreigners," Maxyates replied calmly. "Do any of us look local?"

We didn't.

Funnily enough, Herodotus was the least concerned of us.

"I come from Halicarnassus," he reminded me, when I asked. "I'm used to seeing Persian troops in the street."

I had managed to forget that Herodotus was, technically, a citizen of this empire. Diotima and I had also once lived in a place with Persian occupying troops in the street — in Asia Minor — but that didn't mean I had to like it.

I had expected Memphis to be a big city, but I never thought it would be so crowded. We had to push our way through from the docks to the center of the city. Athens had narrow streets, but in Memphis there were places where you had to walk single file to squeeze between the buildings. In Athens there is a law to ban people from building over the street — everyone ignores it, but at least there's a law. In Memphis they didn't bother with even the pretence to stop builders encroaching.

It seemed half the women in Memphis wanted me to buy their chickens. We could barely take ten steps in any direction without a mass of squawking feathers being thrust in our faces and toothless women demanding we pay them money. Small children would take this opportunity to pickpocket. Herodotus found that out the hard way.

"Hey, bring back my purse!"

Fortunately I'd already taken his money bags from him — for a man who had traveled so much, he was astonishingly naïve. I had the money firmly tied against my chest. Those bags contained our only means of support, and all my wages.

I asked Maxyates if Memphis was always like this. He shrugged. "So many people are willing to live like ants. I don't understand it either."

I understood now the reluctance of Inaros's political advisor to send troops into this labyrinth. Soldiers trying to force their way through these passages . . . the slaughter among the civilians would be fearful. Nervous men who had no idea where they were, surrounded on all sides by buildings from which a knife could emerge at any moment. Not knowing what they'd find around the next blind corner, but knowing the enemy was waiting for them somewhere, such men would be prone to kill anything that moved and then look to see what they'd hit. I could just imagine one of these small girl-pickpockets creeping up on a jumpy soldier with his sword in hand. No, it would never do. If finding the crook and flail would save the people in these streets then it had to be done.

We somehow emerged into a large agora. Though they didn't call it that. They called it something else but I didn't catch the name. There was an inn that Inaros had recommended to us. We found it easily, with Max's help. Then I choked at the inn's prices. I should have realized that someone called Prince of Libya would work to a different budget than normal people.

Herodotus took his money bag from me and paid without demur. The good news was, the rooms were the most comfortable I'd seen at any inn, anywhere. They had real beds made of wood, not merely a sack of hay on the floor. There was a cupboard for our clothes, *two* chairs, a basin, a chamber pot that was actually clean. A window looked over the agora and beyond that, rising in the distance, a fine view of a magnificent building, surely a temple, though it looked nothing like the ones we had in Hellas. That was directly to the south.

The innkeeper was used to tourists. He told us which road out of town would take us to the pyramids, then warned us that to see them properly we would need to leave at first light, and be prepared for a long day.

Herodotus was desperate to see something at once. Our host recommended the Palace of Apries, built by a long-dead Pharaoh. The palace was close by and one of the smaller monuments. You know you're in a place of monumental architecture when one of the *smaller* buildings is a king's palace.

"Allow a whole day for the Temple of Ptah," the innkeeper warned us.

"Is that the magnificent building I saw out our window?" I asked.

He said it was, that the Priests of Ptah would welcome any donation, and that the Temple of the Apis Bull was situated immediately behind.

Herodotus almost swooned at the thought of such tourist attractions.

"Do not donate to one god and not the others," the innkeeper warned us. "Lest the spurned god be offended and cast a curse upon you. Whatever you do, don't return to the inn if you've been cursed by anyone. I don't need this place burning down."

The innkeeper, his wife and his teenage daughter were all loaded down with charms, necklaces and bracelets. All three of them jangled every time they moved. Three or four charm necklaces each, more bracelets than I could count on each wrist — the wife explained that each bracelet had been magicked in a different way to ward against various curses — and rings on every finger to protect against the evil eye. Any evil curse that came through the door to this place wouldn't stand a chance.

I left Herodotus in the care of Diotima and Max. My wife was if anything a better bodyguard than I was — for some reason I'd had bad luck in the past with keeping people alive — and Max was available if muscle was required. Their plan was very simple: to see everything worth seeing in the city.

"We'll start from the north and work our way down," Diotima said. She produced a wax tablet and started a list. "The Palace of Apries, then the Temple of Ptah, the Palace of Merenptah, the Temple of Ramses —"

"You couldn't possibly see all that in a day," I pointed out.

"Who knows how long it will take?" my wife said happily. "Days, probably."

"Many days, certainly," Max added. "As philosophers it is our duty to converse with the wise priests of the temples, to learn what we can."

"Good thinking, Max," Diotima said.

Herodotus rubbed his chin thoughtfully.

"We must not forget the pyramids, and the outlying temples. Perhaps a month?" he suggested.

It occurred to me that I was sending two philosophers and an author out to play in a city full of ancient wisdom. I would have to hope they remembered to come home.

Nevertheless the arrangement suited me very well. I intended to go in search of the mysterious Djanet. Inaros's agent probably didn't want a small committee to turn up and blow her cover. Besides, though I trusted Herodotus, I didn't trust him *completely.*

Inaros had told me that the singer could be found at an inn close by the fort. The moment the others left to explore the city to the north, I departed south.

As I got closer I saw that the White Fort really was white. The walls were made of limestone. The soldiers I passed didn't give me a second glance. They had nothing to fear from a single man, or so they thought. The gates were open but the guards posted there wouldn't let me in. Persian confidence didn't extend that far. They had no qualms though about passing through various local Egyptians who led donkeys loaded with supplies: quality fruit and vegetables and heavy containers of beer.

The Persians had cleared away the houses surrounding the fort. The rubble told me it had been a recent demolition. I didn't need a military man to tell me why they'd done that: the Persians were expecting to be besieged, and they didn't want to give their attackers any easy access to the top of the walls. I was willing to bet that at the tops of those turrets there'd soon be plenty of rocks to drop and oil ready to boil and pour. I for one wouldn't want to be standing at the base when that happened.

The White Fort sat directly beside the river. It meant there was one side from which the fort couldn't be attacked. It also meant the people inside would not go thirsty. Inaros had told us that the White Fort had never been taken. I could believe it.

I still hadn't found the tavern where Djanet the agent sang. I solved that by walking back to the guards at the gate. "Where do you men go to drink?" I asked them in Persian.

The Eye of Horus was one of the better sort of taverns frequented by soldiers. Which is to say, even the officers came there to drink. The board out front had, inevitably, been painted with an Eye — the symbol was a single, stylized eye with a line above it for eyeliner and a funny squiggle below — the name and the sign designed to keep away bad luck. Even in the short time we'd been in the country, I'd come to realize that Egyptians were the most superstitious of people. But I guessed that a horde of off-duty soldiers who didn't want to be bothered while they got quietly drunk would have contributed to the good luck, by keeping away anyone spoiling for a fight. Say what you like about Persians, they knew how to deal with troublemakers.

I stood at the door to survey the scene. Even in late afternoon, there were innumerable Persians sitting at the benches. Some of them were already slumped over the tables. Maybe they'd been on night duty. Among the drinkers were plenty of natives, easily recognizable by their dress, their hair and their accents. There was no segregation. The natives and the soldiers were happy to socialize. They laughed and smiled together. They all chattered in Persian, even the locals. It went to show how much the city had accepted Persia.

Someone at the back of the room was playing a flute. It was dark in that corner, but as my eyes adjusted I could see that the flute-player stood upon a small stage, and that a woman stood beside him. The woman crooned a song. She was tall, and dark, and lissome.

I would have to get her attention, for surely this must be Djanet. I thought about waving, but decided that would be a disaster. I must under no circumstances let the Persians in this room know that she was an agent for Inaros. So instead I took a table as close as I could, wondering how I could get her attention. In the meantime I enjoyed the song.

The music didn't sound like normal Hellene music to me. The notes were different, the tunes like nothing I'd heard before, and the rhythm was strangely engaging. I had tried over the last days to pick up a few words of the local language, with help from Maxyates. Max had told us he was a natural student, but he had also proved a natural teacher who was very patient with my attempts to speak Egyptian. Now I applied my hard-won linguistic expertise to the lyrics.

I bent my ear to understand the words. As far as I could tell, Djanet seemed to be singing that I resembled a small hunting dog. I guessed that probably wasn't right. I made a mental note to ask Max for more lessons.

I tapped my hand on the table in time to

the music. That caused the serving wench to think I was impatient for my drink. She hurried over with a mug of the local beer. It wasn't wine, but it was better than nothing.

The appearance of the serving girl gave me an idea. I would write a note to Djanet and have the girl carry it to the singer. Men wrote notes to tavern singers all the time. The singers almost always ignored the suggestions in the notes. No one would take notice of such an approach. I pulled a piece of broken pottery toward me — like most inns, the tables had a few pieces lying about — and scratched a message, telling the singer that a mutual friend had suggested I look her up while I was in town. As written it was the usual sort of salacious scribble, but I was sure any agent good enough for Inaros would see the true meaning.

I had just finished writing the note, and was about to signal for the serving girl, when I saw a man walk in. I think my heart must have stopped at that moment, if only for an instant. Because I knew that new arrival, and I never, ever thought to meet him at a tavern in Egypt. We had met before, and the last time Diotima and I had been lucky to escape with our lives.

I would know that dark hair anywhere, and the beard, black as night and curled

The Eyes and Ears of the King

Barzanes wore his brightly colored officer's tunic with the careless ease of one who held so much authority that he'd ceased even to think about his rank.

After my last run-in with Barzanes, I had put some effort into discovering the extent of the man's powers. I'd learned that he had no limits. The Eyes and Ears reported directly to the Great King, his job to watch over everything that happened within the empire of the Persians. Wherever Barzanes went, he spoke in the King's name. Barzanes could order even the execution of a satrap, if he thought the situation required it, and he would be answerable only to his sovereign for whether the action was justified. He could certainly execute a humble Hellene agent and no one would blink an eye.

I wondered if I sat quietly in the corner, would Barzanes miss me?

131

He didn't. The Eyes and Ears of the King searched the room as if he expected something to be here. Or someone.

Our eyes locked — I couldn't force myself to look away — and Barzanes walked across the room to stand opposite me at the bench.

"Athenian," he said. That single word made my heart sink. At our last meeting I had pulled a little trick on Barzanes, one that he would probably still be angry about.

Barzanes sat down. As he did, I pushed the pottery shard with the message to the side of the table, in the hope that the Persian agent wouldn't notice it.

To my relief, he didn't. He said, "I would say that I am pleased to see you, Athenian, but I never tell a lie. So instead I will ask, what are you doing in Memphis?"

"I was wondering the same thing about you," I said, in an attempt to show some bravura.

Barzanes was entirely unaffected. "Do not be ridiculous," he said. "You are surrounded by soldiers of the empire. In this place, I have power and you do not. So you will answer my questions."

I decided only the truth would do. "I got a job as a tour guide. I'm escorting a book writer around Egypt."

Barzanes snorted. "This is no good, Athenian. Cannot you at least attempt a lie I could believe?"

"It's true!" I protested. This was what came of being honest. Life is so unfair. "How did you find me, here in a random tavern?" I asked in an attempt to change the subject.

"I could hardly miss, after you blundered into the guards at the gate not a hundred paces away. You even talked to them. Do you think I'm such an idiot that I would not notice?"

"I didn't even know you were in Memphis, Barzanes. Whyever you're here, it's nothing to do with me, and I still don't understand how you knew I was in the city," I said.

"I posted a man at the docks. I gave him descriptions of the ten most dangerous men in civilization, with orders to alert me if any of them arrived by boat."

I preened. "I'm flattered," I told him.

"You shouldn't be. I can barely believe that someone as apparently incompetent as you deserves to be feared, Athenian, yet my own experience tells me that somehow you always seem to succeed where better men would fail."

I said, "I notice that didn't stop you from writing a description of me so good that even a complete stranger could spot me."

"It was admittedly difficult," Barzanes said. "Your looks are non-descript, your face unremarkable, your manner entirely un-noteworthy. You appear to be a complete non-entity —"

"Thank you very much!"

"But the same cannot be said of the dark-haired beauty you married. If you wish to remain anonymous, Athenian, then you must leave your wife at home. Every man between the docks and the agora watched her pass with great interest. I needed only warn the guards at the White Fort, and sure enough, you walked right into them."

"You didn't come to Egypt merely to wait for me to arrive," I said with certainty. "I myself didn't know that I was coming until a few days ago. You had no way of knowing I'd be here."

"This is obvious. You are a mere distraction. My mission is otherwise." His voice was short, he spoke with the slightest hint of anger. For a man of Barzanes's self-control, that spoke volumes.

"Problems?" I asked sympathetically.

Barzanes said nothing.

Why in Hades was Barzanes in Egypt? His presence could only mean that something had attracted the personal interest of the

134

Great King of Persia. What could it be?

Then I had the answer. I smiled.

"Let me think," I said. "Oh yes, the Great King's uncle is dog food, isn't he? Slaughtered by a bunch of amateur rebels. His body is lying out there in the desert, somewhere —"

"The body was recovered," Barzanes interrupted. "The Dowager Queen demanded it."

"Surely the body wasn't shipped home!" I exclaimed. "A corpse carried across the desert, the smell alone —"

"Achaemenes was cremated, you idiot. The ashes were returned to the court at Susa."

"Embarrassing moment when they arrived, I imagine?"

"Very. The King's Mother sobbed in public. Artaxerxes himself was furious. He demanded answers."

How many men could refer to the Great King of the Persians by his familiar name?

I said, "That's why you're here then, isn't it? The King wants answers. He sent you, his most trusted agent, to find them. He wants to know how this disaster happened. How did a professional army of the Persians end up cowering inside a fort?"

"Not cowering," Barzanes said. "Look

about you, Athenian." He gestured at the relaxed soldiers. I couldn't judge their competence, but they certainly looked comfortable.

"Are they Immortals?" I asked. I was genuinely worried about that.

The Immortals were the elite special operations force of Persia. It was the Immortals who had finally beaten the 300 at Thermopylae. It was the Immortals who had climbed the unclimbable face of the Acropolis when a small force of Athenians had held out there to the last man. If the White Fort was garrisoned with Immortals then we could give up now.

"No, these men are mere regular soldiers," Barzanes said. Though he was Persian through and through, he could not keep the disdain from his voice.

At that moment, one of the more relaxed soldiers slipped off his bench onto the floor, where he lay comatose.

Barzanes gave a moue of distaste. "Of course, I will address any discipline issues that I find."

If I was the garrison commander, I would be very nervous with Barzanes looking over my shoulder.

Barzanes shrugged. "But I admit the obvious. I am to report into the administration of this province of our empire. It does appear that there have been some errors."

"Inasmuch as half the country is now in the hands of your enemy, I'd say that was an understatement."

"I have not been here long enough to form a definite opinion, but I suspect my report will not be entirely complimentary to the previous Satrap," Barzanes said.

"That would be the dead uncle of the king. Won't such a report require some tact?"

"The King does not want lies. He wants truth," Barzanes said.

Barzanes was more confident about that than I would be. I would be a trifle wary if I had to tell an absolute monarch that his uncle had not only brought about his own downfall, but had lost a province in the process. I said as much to Barzanes.

He paused for a moment, then said, "It is possible the King might not share this truth with his mother."

If Barzanes was being honest with me — and I had never known him to lie, though he was the most ruthless man I had ever known — then he really did not know why I was in Memphis. By implication he also did not know of the crook and flail, and its importance to Inaros and the rebels. I

137

would have to make sure he never found out.

"I'm sorry about your problems, but I'm telling you the honest truth. There's no need for us to be in conflict."

Barzanes might dislike lying, but personally I had no objections.

"You think so, do you?" Barzanes said. I could here the contempt in his voice. "Then why is it that the rebel army surrounded Memphis the moment you arrived?"

"What!"

"Memphis has been ringed by the enemy. They moved into position just moments after you stepped onto the docks."

That bastard. Inaros had ordered his army to Memphis. He must have known he was going to do it, but he'd never told us. He'd hung me out to dry.

"You're not going to tell me this is a co-incidence, are you?" Barzanes said.

No, I wasn't. I said nothing.

"Then I repeat. Do you want to tell me what you are doing here?"

I was saved from having to answer by a commotion at the door. Two soldiers pushed their way in. Between them was a man whose arms they held trapped. It was Markos.

The soldiers dragged Markos to our table.

One of the soldiers was carrying his arrow-firing machine.

Barzanes didn't show the least surprise at this sudden entrance. I did, though.

"Hello, Nico," Markos said. "So they caught you too."

The soldiers dumped Markos. The one with the machine laid it in front of Barzanes. The two saluted the Eyes and Ears of the King, then moved to stand guard at the front door, the only way out.

Since Barzanes sat opposite me, Markos took the only other seat, at the head of the table, so that the three of us formed a triangle. I was determined not to show any reaction. Barzanes for his part stared at Markos, and Markos at Barzanes.

"I don't believe I know you," Markos said.

"But I know you," Barzanes said. "You are Markos, the son of Glaukippos. Your father died when you were young. You subsequently came first among your cohort in the deadly test known as the *krypteia*. As a result, you were picked by the Spartan elders for assassin duty, a job at which you excelled due to your complete lack of morals." Barzanes said the last part with great distaste. He considered himself to be a highly ethical man. "You were imprisoned when you became over-enthusiastic in the application of your skills, but you were never executed, due to a power struggle among your leaders. At that point I become hazy. I have been in Egypt dealing with affairs, and thus out of touch with my usual sources. Obviously you were released, but why I do not know. However, you will soon tell me this."

Both Markos and I blinked at that remarkable speech. Barzanes had just revealed that he had an information source inside Sparta, one so good that he could reel off the biography of a senior agent of the Spartans. Did Barzanes have a similar source inside Athens? Of course he must. I wondered what the source had told him about me. Probably everything. Barzanes could give strangers directions to find my home.

Barzanes was far too smart not to realize what he had just done. Then why had he done it? To send a message, of course, a very scary message. *I know where you live.*

"I'm impressed," Markos said. "But how did you know I was in Memphis?"

"Don't ask," I told the Spartan. "The answer is embarrassing. We both should have noticed the spotter at the docks."

"Curses," Markos said, good-naturedly. "That *was* sloppy of me, wasn't it? But in my defense — and to answer your question,

140

Barzanes — I'm a mere tourist, come to admire the sights of Memphis. I didn't realize I needed to worry about a hostile reception."

"Me neither," I said, trying to sound innocent.

Barzanes looked from one to the other of us as we spoke. "This defies belief," he said. "The premier agents of Athens and Sparta both descend upon Memphis, a place where I happen to be, a hot spot in the war between the Persians and the Egyptians, and you expect me to believe that this is a coincidence?"

I knew why Markos was here. Markos had come to Memphis to kill Herodotus. The situation was getting more dire with every moment.

"Who's your friend, Nico?" Markos asked.

I said, "Markos, meet Barzanes. He's the Eyes and Ears of the Great King. I wish you joy of each other's company."

If I hurried I could round up Herodotus, Diotima and Max, and get out of town fast. I rose to go. Both Markos and Barzanes put a hand on me and pushed me back into my seat.

"Do you persist in this ridiculous story that you are a tour guide?" Barzanes said.

"Actually, he's telling the truth about

that," Markos said. "A fellow named Herodotus. He's a writer."

"I have never heard of this man," Barzanes
said. "And I have read every book ever written."

"He hasn't finished the book yet. He says
he has to do some research first," I said.

"A likely story," Barzanes said coldly.
"And a fine excuse to go snooping. How do
I know *he* is not a spy?"

That was what I'd been asking myself.

"How come you're still alive?" I asked
Markos for the second time in days.

"Is there a reason why he should not be?"
Barzanes asked.

I said, "The last time I saw Markos, he
was on a pirate ship, being pursued by an
Athenian trireme with orders to sink him."

Barzanes raised an eyebrow at Markos.

Markos shrugged. "The trireme caught
up with us just off the African coastline —
when a trireme's after you, you make for
the nearest land, right? The trireme hit us
hard. The pirate sank. I managed to swim
for shore." Markos looked to me. "I'll point
out that the trireme was trying to kill me on
Nico's orders."

Barzanes turned the raised eyebrow my
way.

"Because you were trying to kill my client!" I protested.

"I seem to recall Diotima took a few shots at me," Markos retorted. "A couple of those arrows came close to gutting me."

"She wouldn't have been shooting if you weren't trying to sink us in the first place."

"Well, back in that tavern you hit me first!"

He had me there.

Barzanes's head had swiveled back and forth as the argument went on. "I could end this now by killing you both," he said. "You're surrounded by Persian soldiers."

"We'd take a lot of them with us," Markos said at once. "And we'll make sure you're the first to die, Barzanes. Do you think you could hold off both me and Nicolaos?"

"There's no need for such talk, Markos," I said smoothly. "We might be surrounded by Persians, but the Persians are surrounded by Egyptians."

"Where?" Markos peered around the room.

"They're ringing the city," I told him. "Barzanes said so himself."

Barzanes scowled at me. "Are you saying the rebels will attack the city merely to avenge you?"

"Do you want to find out?" I challenged him. We both knew the Persians needed to delay a siege for as long as possible, to give reinforcements time to arrive.

"It's an impasse then," Markos chuckled. "This could get messy."

"Gentlemen, I have a proposition," I said.

Barzanes and Markos looked at me expectantly.

"As it stands, there is every chance that only one of us will leave this city alive."

Barzanes and Markos glanced at each other. They nodded.

"Nothing is to be gained by us killing one another," Markos agreed.

That wasn't strictly true, but this wasn't the moment to get picky about details.

I said, "What I propose is this: that we declare a truce."

They both looked dubious.

"What kind of truce?"

"The kind where we don't kill one another. We are all here on missions. None of us is willing to admit what they are, but we all know it's true. The fact is, if we spend all our time trying to kill each other, we'll never get any work done," I said. "I propose we agree not to get in each other's way."

I prayed to whatever gods would listen that they would agree.

"What if our mission requires us to interfere with one of the others?" Markos asked.

"Are you saying *your* mission does?" I asked.

"Er . . . no."

"I give you my word of honor that I am not here to harm either of you. I didn't even know Barzanes was here! As for you, Markos, much as I would enjoy dancing on your grave, I didn't come here to do it. I thought you were drowned, dead for the second time."

"This cannot work," Barzanes said. "I do not know about the Spartan, but *you,* Athenian, I am sure are here to act against Persia. I must act to protect the empire."

"Barzanes, I swear by my gods that I am hired by Herodotus to protect him. You can check that any time you like. You probably already have."

Barzanes said, "Of course I have."

"Then you know it's true. Herodotus will see the sights. We'll pick up a few souvenirs." Such as the crook and flail, but I wasn't going to mention that. "And then we'll depart."

"If I discover you have lied to me, Athenian, your death will make impalement seem like a happy option."

"We *all* reserve the right to defend our interests," I agreed. "I'm merely pointing out that they don't intersect."

145

"You believe the Spartan when he says he's not here to attack you?" Barzanes asked, clearly bemused.

"Well, he *says* he's not. If he breaks his word, I'm free to kill him, am I not?"

"I will not object," Barzanes said.

I appeared to consider his words, though I had already planned out the next part when I made my proposal.

"Why don't we make this more certain?" I said. "If one of us attacks another, then the third man is *obliged* to assist the wronged party. After all, crime and disorder is hateful to the Great King, is it not?"

"This is true." Barzanes nodded.

"Here now!" Markos objected.

I smiled. "You don't have a problem with that, do you Markos? After all, you're just an innocent tourist. You didn't lie about that, did you?"

"Well, when you put it that way . . ."

"Good."

I silently exulted. It would be very much harder for Markos to attack my party if he had to worry about Barzanes joining in the fight.

"An agreement requires that we drink to it," Barzanes said. That was a Persian custom, one that I could well understand.

Markos nodded, very reluctantly.

Fortunately we were in a tavern. Markos went over to the bar, where he had a lengthy conversation with the serving girl. He returned with a mug in hand, along with the girl, who carried a mug each for Barzanes and me.

"It's agreed then. We'll refrain from attacking each other."

Heads nodded all round.

"Let's drink to it," Markos said.

I stared down at my mug of beer, and was assaulted by a sudden fear. I knew I hadn't tampered with the drinks, but I couldn't guarantee one of the other two hadn't. It would be so easy for an agent with a small flask of poison and a deft hand to eliminate his rivals.

Barzanes and Markos were the best around. Both of them had the skill and the knowledge to slip poison into my cup.

"We'll all drink on the count of three," Markos said. "One, two, three!"

Three cups remained sitting on the table.

"There is a difficulty," Barzanes said, as we sat there staring at the beer. He was thinking what I was thinking.

"All right, I've got it," I said. "What say we switch drinks randomly? So that no one knows who has what cup?"

I shoved my cup at Markos. He in turn

pushed his to Barzanes, who pushed his original cup in front of me, and then swapped Markos's and my cups. Markos in turn moved Barzanes's cup to me, then took mine. Not to be outdone, I pushed mine at Barzanes, took Barzanes's cup, gave it to Markos and grabbed Markos's cup just as he was about to make his own move. Barzanes was already grabbing my cup, joined it with his, and shuffled them back and forth at blinding speed until I couldn't tell which was which. Markos snatched one of these and performed his own shuffle, while I randomly took the cup in the middle and snatched one from Markos to swap their positions.

Our hands became blurs of motion as we shoved cups back and forth. After we finished, there was a beer in front of each of us.

I had lost track of which cup was which, but could I be sure Markos and Barzanes had? What if one of them had tracked the cup he knew to be untainted?

"Are we ready now?" Barzanes asked. "One, two, three!"

Three cups remained on the table.

We all looked at each other.

"What say we get the serving girl to

randomly place the cups?" Markos suggested.

I snorted. "That's no good. She could be acting for you. You've probably seduced her already."

"Not yet," Markos said. "But we have a date for tonight. What do you think we were talking about at the bar? International politics?"

"I would suggest one of the soldiers place the cups," Barzanes said. "But of course you could not trust me to be honest."

In the background, Djanet had been changing not only songs, but also languages. When Barzanes entered she had switched to a Persian love song. I spoke some Persian and her accent sounded perfect to me. Now she was singing in Greek — very good Greek — something about suspicious minds.

"Who's your girlfriend, Nico?" Markos asked.

"What do you mean?" I said, confused. "I don't have a girlfriend. I'm married."

"Then explain this," Markos said. He held up the pottery shard on which I had written the message for Djanet. When I had pushed it out of sight of Barzanes, I had put it where Markos later sat. "You ask the singer for a meeting. Tsk, tsk, Nico. What would

Diotima say? But then, you also called yourself an agent. Is this business or pleasure?"

Barzanes's eyes narrowed. He looked at me, then at the singer, and back to me again.

The singing abruptly stopped. All three of us looked over to the stage. Djanet had disappeared, leaving an empty spot where she had been standing, and a confused-looking flute player. Barzanes signaled to the guards at the door. They hurried out back, but soon returned, shaking their heads.

"Who is the woman, Athenian?" Barzanes said.

"A good singer?" I suggested. "I don't know." I made a sudden decision. "I'm going to trust you two. I'm going to drink this beer in front of me. Join me or not, as you will."

I took hold of the mug, closed my eyes, and knocked back the beer, all of it, one big gulp after another, until the mug was empty.

I slammed the mug down on the table, my eyes watering, to see that Barzanes and Markos had drunk too. They both slammed down their mugs at the same time I did.

We stared at each other for an instant, then Markos began to choke.

He coughed and spluttered, but he didn't turn blue.

"Sorry," he wheezed. "Some went down the wrong way."

I was sure it was an act.

THE TJATY

I emerged from the dark tavern and blinked at the bright light outside. There was no point trying to search for Djanet. If she had any sense she was long gone. I couldn't understand how Markos had divined my interest in her. Perhaps I'd looked in her direction once too often.

Diotima's party would soon be back at the inn. I set off to meet them there, thinking that after the deal I'd just made, I was safe at last.

As I turned the corner, a hand with a cudgel emerged from a nearby doorway. I saw it coming out of the corner of my eye, but I couldn't move in time. The anonymous arm brought the cudgel down hard. My last thought as I fell unconscious to the dusty street was that I should have been more careful.

I opened my eyes to stare into the eyes of a

cat. Its fur was pure white. The cat stared back at me with dark eyes that didn't blink.

How long had I been out for? I knew I was somewhere strange. I lay upon a stone floor that was perfectly polished. But it was also very cold.

The cat jumped away to reveal the view behind. I saw a massive chair carved from solid marble. A man sat upon the chair. Behind the man, and towering above him, was the statue of a god. The god held a strange-looking staff in front of him. I couldn't guess what it meant. Beside the god was a goddess. She was well proportioned with wide hips and large breasts. But above her shoulders she had the head of a cat. She stared at me with a stony expression.

Something jumped over me. Another cat. I saw now that the room was filled with cats, a whole clowder of them, more than I could count, all of them sleek and well-fed.

The man who sat before me was fat. So fat that his belly didn't just protrude, it flowed across his lap, almost reaching his knees. The man's jowls were enormous. The wide folds of skin at his neck made his brow look narrow and his scalp had been shaven clean, so that his head resembled nothing so much as a turnip.

Set within all this flesh were dark eyes that stared at me.

"So. You are awake." His voice was deep.

I had the sort of headache that normally only comes from three days of solid drinking. I pushed myself off the cold stone floor, rubbed my head and asked, "Who are you?"

"I am the Tjaty."

He said it as if I should recognize the name. I didn't. I hoped the next question would clear things up.

"Where am I?"

"You are in a secret chamber that lies deep beneath the Temple of Bast."

Well, that explained all the cats. Bast was the cat goddess.

The plump, white cat jumped into the lap of the Tjaty. The Tjaty tenderly stroked the feline as he spoke. I noticed he had rings on every finger, expensive ones if the jewels were any indication. The cat purred loudly over the sound of his bass.

"You are privileged to be here," the Tjaty said. "Access to this chamber is normally reserved only for the most elite of our organization."

"I have no idea what you're talking about," I said. "What organization?"

"We are the senior bureaucrats of the Black Land, the public service of Egypt. I am the Tjaty, the prime minister, what our friends the Persians call a vizier. I am the head of the Public Service."

The Tjaty gestured to something at my rear. I turned, to see a semicircle of men at my back. Every one of them glowered at me.

"I present to you the Heads of Department," the Tjaty said.

These were the men whom Inaros had talked about, the ones who had enriched themselves with the taxes reaped from peasants. I had suggested feeding these men to the crocodiles. Now having met them, I found the idea even more pleasant.

The Tjaty continued speaking.

"In addition to being the goddess of the well-fed feline, Bast is also patroness of public servants. Do you know why?"

"Let me guess."

"Don't bother. I will tell you. The Lady Bast is consort to the Lord Ptah. You see them behind me, standing side-by-side. As Ptah is patron deity of Memphis, so Bast is patroness to the Public Service who serve Memphis and the Black Land. Ptah and Bast abide in perfect union, as do Memphis and the Public Service."

The Heads of Department chanted something in reply to this, in words I did not understand. It felt almost like a religious rite.

"Bast is an exquisite goddess," the Tjaty said. "She is anointed in perfumes, she is served by slaves, she takes as her due only the finest in all things —"

"This is pretty much in line with my guess."

"But within that precious exterior she has the heart of a vicious, sadistic predator," the Tjaty finished. He brought down one massive fist onto the arm of his chair, and the whole room seemed to shake. He thundered, "Yet you, Nicolaos . . . *you* seek to trifle with men such as us!"

"I do no such thing," I protested. "I'm just a tour guide —"

"Don't lie. You are on a mission to recover the crook and flail of the last Pharaoh. You do this for Inaros," the Tjaty said.

This was becoming ridiculous. I was supposed to be a secret agent, but everywhere I went I was recognized by someone. Sworn enemies ran into me at nondescript taverns. Complete strangers hailed me by name after they'd captured me. At least in the case of these men I knew the source of half their knowledge. These were the men to whom Inaros had promised to display the crook and flail, as proof of his royal descent.

"Well you should know," I said. "You have a deal with Inaros."

"That is true."

"Then I don't see why you have a problem with me."

"Because we want him to *fail*," the Tjaty said.

"Why?" I asked.

"Can you imagine men such as us bowing to a man of no pedigree? Do you expect us to work for a mere . . ." He shuddered. ". . . For a mere member of the *general public*?"

There were groans, and exclamations of horror from the men at my back.

I could imagine these men bowing to anyone who maintained their privileges.

"I'm not so sure," I said. "Have you met Inaros? I've rarely met a more competent leader."

"This is the Public Service. We never take competence into consideration."

"Would you rather work for the Persians?" I asked.

I thought I was posing a rhetorical question, but to my surprise the Tjaty considered his words while he stroked the white cat. The cat snarled at me. The Tjaty said, "We prefer rulers who leave us to run things. Such is the case with the Great King. The Persian court is far away. The Great King does not bother us with minor administrative details. As long as Egypt remains stable and the tax money flows, he is happy."

Inspiration struck. "Ah, I understand, you want to continue to misappropriate public funds!"

"A stipend for our excellent service has long been a perquisite of the position," the Tjaty said smoothly. "We think of it as a performance bonus."

"I see," I said, and I did. Inaros would never tolerate these men, and they knew it.

"I was sure you would see things our way," the Tjaty said. "We agreed to Inaros's terms because we never expected him to succeed."

"Well, you're safe with me then. I have no idea where the crook and flail are."

"We wish to be more certain. Therefore we would like to offer you a job."

"I already have more jobs than I can cope with," I said, and I meant it.

"This one is very simple. All you have to do is . . . nothing." The Tjaty smiled.

It only took me a moment to realize what he wanted me to do. "You mean I don't find the crook and flail," I said flatly.

"Make a pretence, if you wish," said the Tjaty with an air of disdain. "But deliver failure. Guide your writer around our lovely country and then return home. When you do, you will find waiting for you a letter from me, asking you to write a Very Important Report."

I could hear from his voice that the Tjaty liked getting reports.

"For this you will be rewarded amply," the Tjaty finished.

"What sort of report?" I asked suspiciously.

"I see you are a detail-oriented sort of person." The Tjaty waved his arm dismissively. "Does it matter? This can be decided later. Probably a strategy report. One can never have enough strategies, you know. We're particularly fond of five-year strategy plans. We like them so much we produce a five-year strategy every year. The important point, my dear Nicolaos, is that you will be *well rewarded.*"

"A bribe then."

"Payment for services rendered. Surely an agent understands that concept."

I shook my head. "I'm sorry, I'm already commissioned to do the exact opposite job."

The Tjaty scowled in anger. Even the cat scowled. "You must understand that in opposing us, you oppose an organization that has existed for three thousand years. We existed when you Hellenes were wearing skins and living in huts. We were filling out forms and writing reports when the Persian Empire was a few villages strung together. We outlasted the Hittites. We outlasted the Assyrians. We will outlast these Persians and we will outlast whatever comes after them." The Tjaty was shouting now in passion. "Men come and go, civilizations rise and fall, but the Public Service of Egypt goes on forever!"

Cheers from the Heads of Department.

"An organization of mere public servants," I said contemptuously.

"You underestimate us. The greatest man who ever lived was a public servant. All reverence to His Name."

"Whose name?"

"Imhotep. Greatest of the Tjaties. I am his direct successor. There he is." The Tjaty pointed to an alcove in the wall, where there was the bust of a bald man who looked very serious. "Imhotep was the greatest architect who ever lived. He *invented* the pyramids. He invented medicine. He made discoveries in mathematics. He was the son of Ptah himself, so great was he. And this man, you must understand, was a public servant."

"Proves nothing."

"Then let me put it this way. Have you ever noticed, Nicolaos, how cats like to play with their victims? And the fatter the cat, the more it likes to see its victim squirm. So too public servants."

"So?"

"So that is the fate you face, if you deny us. Do you understand?"

"Yes."

"Do you have any questions?"

"Only one. Do you know what happened to the crook and flail?"

After all this nonsense over a few pieces of wood, I'd become genuinely interested in what had happened to them.

"Work with us, Nicolaos, and you will prosper." The Tjaty gestured. "Release him."

A blindfold suddenly appeared from behind to cover my eyes. I didn't resist.

I was led through a series of twisty passages. At one point we stopped, and I heard stone scrape before being led forward again. We came to steps that I negotiated with difficulty. They were uneven. The smell was musty and, as we rose, the air became hotter. Despite which, I was surprised when I suddenly felt the fading sun upon my face.

The blindfold came off. I found myself facing the everyday crowd of a busy street. Behind me stood the Temple of Bast.

I turned around. A dark man stood there, holding the blindfold. I thought he was probably the man who had slugged me. He smiled at me with pure white teeth and courteously told me to have a good night.

I made my way back to the inn. As I stumbled along I stopped once or twice in search of some wine to drink, but there was none to be had in common Egypt. I had an enormous headache from the knock to the back of my head. By the time I got to the inn it was dark. Diotima sat in the common room, looking thoroughly over-heated, with her feet in a bucket of cool water.

"You have no idea how much I've suffered while you went gallivanting about Memphis," she groaned.

"You're the one who wanted to see everything in Memphis," I pointed out. I clutched my throbbing head.

She looked at me oddly, then sniffed. "Have you been drinking?"

"Unfortunately not. I'm sorry you didn't enjoy the tour. What about Herodotus?"

"The man never stops," Diotima said with a mixture of despair and wonder. "I think we must have walked up and down every palace, every temple and every street in the north of the city. The next time we split up, *you* go with Herodotus and *I* get to have the fun. Where in Hades have you been?"

"Not so much fun," I said. "Markos is in

162

town, and I'm glad you're sitting down while I tell you this, because so is Barzanes."

Diotima paled. "I was afraid of that."

"You were? How did you know?"

Diotima pointed. "Because *she* turned up."

I turned around to see a woman, sitting in the dark corner of the room. It was Djanet. She stood up.

I put out a hand in greeting. "Djanet, I'm pleased to meet you —"

She punched me out.

Apparently it was my day for being hit in the head. I didn't quite fall unconscious, but the world spun. I staggered back into the table behind me.

I rubbed my jaw and said, "Is that any way to treat a fellow agent?"

"You exposed me to Barzanes," Djanet said. "I thought Inaros would send someone competent."

"He did!"

"Then why am I on the run?" She almost shouted, but managed to keep her voice down.

"Sorry about that," I said.

"I can't go back. *You* might be safe from Persian repercussions —"

"Not likely!"

"But *I'm* certainly not. You do realize,

don't you, that this is technically Persian territory? Barzanes could put me on the pole, or feed me to the crocodiles, and no one would object."

She was right. "I'm sorry, Djanet," I said, feeling guilty. "You listened in on the conversation, back at the tavern?"

"As I was singing? Yes. I tried to warn you when I sang about suspicious minds. I was trying to tell you that Barzanes was already suspicious of me."

"I thought you were singing about our attempts to kill one another."

"Who cares about that?"

"Well, I do have this preference not to be killed."

"What will you do now?" Diotima asked Djanet.

"Do? I haven't thought about it." She sat down at the table. "I wasn't planning to close this gig any time soon. I suppose I'll have to go with you."

Diotima and I exchanged a surprised glance.

"With us? With us where?" I asked.

"Aren't you searching for the crook and flail?" she said.

"That's what we came here for, to ask you," I said. "I was under the impression you know where they are."

She looked at me oddly. "What on earth gave you that idea?"

"Oh dear," Diotima muttered. "But Nico's right, Djanet. We came to Memphis so *you* could tell *us* what to do."

There was a depressed silence. Then Djanet sighed. "It's a stuff-up then."

"We need to start from the beginning," Diotima said decisively. "Who are you, Djanet, really?"

"You mean, what's a girl like me doing in a mess like this?"

"Yes. If you're going to join us, we need to know."

"Is there any beer in this place?"

I went to get some. There was an amphora that the innkeeper kept behind the bar.

"I'm a local," Djanet said, as I poured beer into a cup. "I was raised in Memphis, but my family was poor. My parents died when I was young."

"That sounds tough," I said.

Djanet shrugged. "What can you do? I was raised by my grandmother. But there was no hope of a dowry, and that limited my options. I took to singing." She grimaced. "The arts pay better than begging, though only just, and it's slightly higher status than the . . . er . . . *other* form of entertainment business."

"I know what you mean."

"That's how I got to be an agent," she said. She finished the beer and put down the cup. "You meet a lot of people in my business. The rich and the poor, the powerful and the weak, everyone likes to hear a nice song, you know? Before long I was connecting people with other people."

"What do you mean?" Diotima asked.

"Say I'm singing at a rich man's house, at a party. I hear one guest say to another that his wife wants new-painted walls. Well, maybe I know an out-of-work painter. I met him when I was singing at a low dive the day before. He's drinking his woes away because he has kids to feed and no work. So I recommend the painter! He does a fine job, because he needs the money. Everyone's happy. The rich man pays me a good fee, because I made his life easy. You see?"

"I see."

"Before long, people were coming to me, because I'd acquired this reputation for being able to supply anyone to do anything. My circle of acquaintances is . . . shall we say . . . broad."

I wondered how many dodgy enterprises Djanet was involved in. It didn't seem polite to ask.

"Inaros said you were his agent," Diotima

prodded.

Djanet sighed. "That's only partially true, and it's kind of against my normal rules because I'm not getting paid a single coin for a lot of work. But I'm the only person in this mess who *everyone* talks to. I have access to the White Fort. The Persians like a song as much as the next man, and I don't look threatening. The bureaucrats tolerate me as a conduit of information. I obviously have no ambitions so I don't threaten them, and the rebels like me because I'm a down-trodden Egyptian, just like them."

I had also brought some hard cheese and dates. Djanet munched on these as she spoke. "The net result is, when anyone says anything interesting, I pass it on to the other parties. Suitably spun of course to sound best to my audience. That's something a singer knows how to do. You play to your audience, right?"

Diotima and I nodded.

"Before I knew it, I was an agent acting for everyone. Dear Gods, you wouldn't believe the contortions of negotiation I have to go through." Djanet drank the beer in a few swallows and asked for more.

As we were speaking, Herodotus had come downstairs. He looked at Djanet oddly, then began to listen in.

"The bureaucrats are covering their bets by negotiating with both sides," Djanet said. "They're making sure that whoever wins, they won't lose. They don't really want Inaros —"

"So I discovered," I said.

"What do you mean?" Djanet and Diotima asked simultaneously.

I told them of being waylaid by the Tjaty.

Djanet looked even unhappier after that.

"It doesn't really change things," she muttered. "If Inaros displays the crook and flail to the people, they'll have no choice but to acknowledge him."

"Inaros has guaranteed their positions," Diotima said.

"Yes. That was my idea. I had to persuade him, but it was the deal maker for the Public Service."

"Then it remains only to find these accursed insignia," I said. "What do you know about them?"

"Not as much as I'd like. The crook and flail were last seen in the hands of the Pharaoh Psamtik. He was defeated by Cambyses, who was the Great King back then."

"Inaros said this happened sixty-eight years ago?"

"That's right. Psamtik wasn't killed immediately. He was kept prisoner in a palace, for about a year, I think. The Double Crown was taken by Cambyses. The Great King was seen wearing it in public. The crook and flail, however, were never seen again. Apparently the Persians didn't realize their significance."

"No surprise there. Everyone knows what a crown is. But those insignia are weird. Who'd recognize them for what they are?"

"Perhaps," Djanet said. "When they finally executed the Pharaoh, no one even thought to ask about them."

"This is hopeless, Nico," Diotima said. "The last Pharaoh died ages ago. Our grandfathers were small children back then."

"You're right," I said.

"They don't need an investigator," Diotima said. "They need someone who can work out what happened in ages past."

At those words the realization hit us. Diotima and I turned simultaneously to stare at Herodotus the Historian. We had inadvertently brought with us the one man in the world with any chance of solving this puzzle.

I said, "Umm, Herodotus?"

Herodotus said, "Eh? What is it?"

"You wanted to learn unique things about Egypt, right?"

"Yes, of course."

"Well, here's your perfect chance," I said. "How would you like to lead an expedition to find a lost treasure?"

"What sort of lost treasure?" he asked. He sounded dubious.

"As in, a treasure that's been lost," I explained helpfully. "Something precious that went missing sixty-eight years ago."

"To return the treasure to its rightful owner?" Herodotus asked.

"In a manner of speaking," I said smoothly.

Herodotus rubbed his chin, deep in thought. "My readers would love it," he said, half to himself.

"They certainly would, Herodotus," Diotima said with feeling. "It might even be worth a whole chapter in your book."

Herodotus nodded gravely. "Yes, on this I feel you are right."

"So you'll do it?" I asked.

"I will." He nodded.

"Excellent," I said. "What should we do first?"

"We must consult the written words of someone who was there at the time. Who has written about what happened to the items."

"If we had something like that, we wouldn't need you!"

"There is no written record?" Herodotus said, perplexed.

"None."

Herodotus was clearly annoyed. I thought he was about to stamp his foot, but he resisted. "This sort of thing is exactly why people need histories," he grumbled. "All right then, what about someone who was there? Someone we can interview?"

"From that long ago?" I said incredulous. "They're all dead."

"Not quite," Djanet said. "What about the Blind General?"

That brought us all up short. "Who's he?" Diotima asked.

"He's the King of the Beggars."

THE BEGGARS OF MEMPHIS

The next morning, Herodotus, Diotima, Max and I followed Djanet out onto the street. She accosted the closest beggar — he was a man with both legs off at the knees, calling for food for an old war veteran — and whispered in his ear. The beggar nodded.

"I just requested a meeting," Djanet explained. "This man will take the request to the General."

Diotima exclaimed in horror. "You asked a man without legs to carry a message for you? Are you thoughtless?" She bent to offer the poor man a handful of coins from her money pouch. "Here, take these," my wife said.

"Thank you, miss." The beggar scooped the coins from Diotima's hand and into a hidden pouch. Then he unwound the filthy bindings from his stumps, and stood up on two sound feet, with legs firmly attached in the usual place. He had bent his legs double at the knees and with the rags bound them tight to his thighs. "Aargh!" He jumped about, in obvious pain. "Pins and needles," he said. "Excuse me."

He hopped about a bit more, then scurried up the road.

"Nice trick," Herodotus commented. Diotima kept a frosty silence.

Djanet stepped into the shadows while we waited. "In case the Persians are looking for me," she explained. "No need to make it too easy for them."

"Barzanes has promised to leave me alone," I said.

"Yes, but he didn't say the same for me."

I forbore from pointing out that we were probably the most oddly assorted party in the entire city. If anyone wanted to find us, they wouldn't have much trouble. But Djanet's move was sensible. Though it was early morning, I could already feel the sun burning my skin. We all stepped into the shade.

As it happened, a man did approach us, but he was an Egyptian, not a Persian. It was the fellow who had led me from the underground chamber at the Temple of Bast. He was probably the same man who had coshed me unconscious and carried me there in the first place, but I hadn't wanted to ask. That was business, and there was no point getting upset about such things.

"Good morning," he said politely. He handed me a sheet of papyrus.

"What's this?" I asked.

"I don't know, I'm just the messenger."

"A message? You people send messages written on *paper*?" I said, aghast. "Isn't that expensive?"

"Not in Egypt."

He turned around and walked back the way he'd come.

"What does it say, Nico?" Diotima asked.

I turned the papyrus one way, then the other, trying to make sense of it. "I don't know. It's covered in weird squiggles."

"Allow me," Max took the paper from my hands. He turned it the other way round, and read. As he did, his eyebrows rose higher and higher.

"I congratulate you, Nicolaos," Max said, when he was done. He handed back the papyrus sheet.

"Oh?" I asked.

"This missive is from the Department of Public Health and Safety. You have been officially declared a plague carrier."

"What!"

"You are officially and formally warned off from sleeping in any public hostel, inn, tavern or other place of rest," Max said with a straight face.

"What plague does my husband carry?" Diotima said. "I ask only in case I should fear for my own health."

"Bedbugs," Maxyates said. "I regret to inform you, madam, that your husband is overrun with bedbugs. The document goes on to say that copies of this warning have been sent to every hostel in Memphis. In triplicate, of course."

I recalled the Tjaty's words, that public servants were sadists who liked to toy with their prey before they destroyed them. I should have listened to him.

That brought to mind the landlord's fear of bad luck and curses. There was no way he was going to let me through the door after he saw a message like this.

"Where am I supposed to sleep?" I asked.

"In the street?" Max said.

"I'm sure the beggars could suggest something," Djanet added.

At that moment the beggar with two legs returned. He asked us to follow him.

THE BLIND GENERAL

The beggar led us from sunny streets to a district of dark lanes, somewhere far from the river. At that place our guide turned to a deserted warehouse, where the door hung off its hinges. He pushed his way through — the door squeaked noisily — and we found ourselves in a large, empty space. The roof above had half rotted away. In this derelict building, under a small, poorly rigged awning, sat an old man and a young girl. Scattered around them were the things of a camp: a couple of bedrolls, some stale bread and cheese, a flask of beer and an oil lamp.

The Blind General was a thin man, and old. He was half-shaven. You couldn't call the face hair he wore a beard, more like a three-day growth that was gray enough to be almost invisible against his leathery skin. He seemed as ancient as the Gods, but as hale as you can be when you're dressed in rags and living off scraps.

The girl sat beside the man. I guessed her age for eight. She wore a dress and looked far better fed than he. As we approached, she whispered into his ear.

"Greetings, Djanet," he said. "What do you bring me?"

He looked up at us with eyes that were . . . I almost gasped. Herodotus did gasp. Diotima strangled a sob.

Whatever had destroyed the General's eyes, it had been hot, and it had seared the flesh, so that the sockets were scarred, empty holes. The skin about was scarred and pitted too. If someone had told me that this was not a man but some creature from the depths of Tartarus, well, I would have believed it.

"Greetings, General," Djanet said. Her voice was solemn. "I bring you querents."

The General harrumphed. "Querents? Then you have come to the wrong place. I am no oracle like the one at Siwa, to dispense wisdom."

"You are better than an oracle, General. Every beggar in Memphis has benefited from your wisdom," Djanet said.

"Hmmph," he said, clearly unimpressed. "What wisdom do these querents seek from an old beggar?"

I said, "General, sir, my name is Nicolaos, from Athens. We wish to learn of the last days of your Pharaoh Psamtik."

He turned to look straight at me as I spoke. It was disconcerting.

"I never speak of those days. Why should I?"

"It would help us," was all I could offer lamely.

"Do you give alms to beggars?" he asked abruptly.

"Er . . ." I thought about the coin collector in Naukratis, but I was fairly sure he didn't count.

The beggar who had led us here spoke up. "The Athenian lady gave me a handful of coins, General."

"She did, did she?" His head turned to look at Diotima. "That would be the pretty lady with the dark hair, who stands silent between the two Hellene men?"

The girl-child was still whispering nonstop into his ear. Now I realized why.

The General said in approval, "Since you gave alms to the poor, I will speak with you."

"Thank you, sir," said Diotima. "It is as my husband says. We seek the crook and flail of the last Pharaoh."

"In the name of Ra, why?"

"A deal has been struck," Djanet said. "If

Inaros can prove his descent, then the bureaucrats in Memphis will acknowledge him Pharaoh."

"Inaros? He's a bloody Libyan," the General said.

Maxyates stirred, but showed remarkable restraint.

"Nobody's perfect, General," Djanet said. "At least Inaros wins battles, and he wants to expel the Persians."

"To remove the Persians from Egypt?" he said dubiously.

"To send them across the desert with such a defeat that they never return," Djanet said sincerely.

"Then I am your man." The General sat up straighter. "Though everything I tell you will be to my discredit."

This was excellent news.

I said, "Good, then please tell us — where can we find the crook and flail?"

"I have no idea."

This was bad news.

"But I was there when the crook and flail were lost," he said to us. Then he sighed. "I was there for the entire disaster."

"It must be quite a tale," Herodotus said.

"Only if you enjoy disaster stories."

"But I do, General," Herodotus said smoothly. Extracting stories from people was Herodotus's specialty. He took over. "Tell us what happened, so that we can learn from the past. That's a worthy goal, is it not?"

"Hmmpf," the General grunted again. It seemed to be his favorite response. He thought for a moment, then said, "Pharaoh was new in the job. He'd only just inherited from his father, Ahmose, who had ruled for forty-four years. Psamtik was not the man his father was."

"What sort of man was he?" Herodotus asked.

"Hatred was his daily bread, and he fed well upon it."

"Oh."

The Blind General shrugged. "It was . . . difficult. Pharaoh would strike us when he was displeased, for the slightest reason. Even we military men of the highest rank. I once saw him strike my predecessor across the face with the sacred flail. My predecessor turned against Psamtik because of that."

"Were you really a General?" I said, astonished.

"Of course I was a General, you dolt! If I had been a Lieutenant then I would be the Blind Lieutenant."

"I mean, I had thought it a courtesy title."

"Not at all. King of the Beggars is a

180

courtesy title. They call me so because I have the most experience. I've been begging for sixty-eight years now. But I was a true General." He sighed. "I was a young man in those days, and tall, and straight of limb. I commanded my first division at twenty-two years."

"That's a very young age to be a General," Herodotus said.

The General nodded. "You are right, yet it was a natural appointment. I will say, without false modesty, that I was the finest warrior in Pharaoh's army, and my father was among the highest noblemen in the land. I will not tell you my sire's name, I do not wish to sully his memory by any connection with me. But know that my forefathers had served Pharaoh since the Black Land became one nation. Thus as soon as I was blooded in battle, Pharaoh appointed me commander of the Division of Ra, we of the many-weapons."

"Many weapons?" Herodotus asked. He wrote notes as he spoke.

"My men could fight with anything," he said proudly. "We carried spears, bows, slingshots, daggers, swords of good bronze. You name it, and we could kill you with it. We were . . ." He paused. "I don't know the word in your language."

181

"Like the Immortals of the Persians?" I suggested. "Top line troops?"

He nodded. "Just so. I vowed never to fail Pharaoh, nor did I. I brought him victory in all my assignments." His shoulders slumped. "That is, until the final onslaught."

"The battle against the Persians?"

"Yes. My predecessor was a mercenary, Phanes of Halicarnassus by name. In revenge for the shameful blow Pharaoh had struck across his face, Phanes sought out King Cambyses of Persia. He showed the Persians how Egypt could be attacked."

Herodotus had stopped writing. "The Phanes you speak of led the Persians into Egypt?"

"When our armies met upon the sands, Phanes stood beside Cambyses. Psamtik saw this and shook his flail at Phanes, the very same one with which he had struck Phanes in the first place."

"So we have the flail at the battle," Herodotus muttered. He made a note.

"There is something you must understand, if you wish to find the crook and flail . . ." The Blind General drew a deep breath before continuing. "Psamtik ordered the sons of Phanes brought with us to the battlefield. I didn't understand why until, right before the fighting began, he ordered the two boys brought forward. Psamtik cut their throats before our eyes. Before the eyes of their father, too. Phanes stood on the other side of the field and saw his sons die. Then he watched while Egyptians drank the blood of his boys. Pharaoh was the first. He drank from a cup."

"Are you serious?" I exclaimed. I had never heard of such barbarity. Not even from uncivilized savages.

"I told you that hatred was his bread."

"I can't believe it."

"It shames me to admit it," said the General, "but I didn't object. I think Psamtik had gone mad. If I had tried to stop him, I might have shared the fate of the children."

"How did Phanes react?" I asked. I couldn't imagine what I would do if I had sons.

"During the battle he slaughtered every Egyptian within reach."

"Understandable."

"It gets worse. After we had been routed, Cambyses sent an ambassador, by boat, to Memphis, to ask us to surrender on terms. The Persian ambassador had barely finished speaking before Psamtik had him torn limb from limb. Then he ordered the crew of the boat that had brought the ambassador dealt with the same way."

"I'm beginning to see why the Persians aren't so keen on Egyptians," I said.

"They got their revenge," said the General. "After we had been defeated, they selected two thousand youths from our best families and executed every one of them, starting with Pharaoh's own son. Then they enslaved the maiden daughters of our noblemen, including Pharaoh's daughter. I shudder to think where most of them went."

"Is that when they exacted their revenge upon you too, General?" Herodotus asked quietly.

"They held me down while one of their men pressed hot blacksmith's irons into my face," he said dispassionately. "I thought I would die. But I lived, as they intended. Then they released me onto the street, to be a blind beggar for the rest of my life."

It was an ugly story, with terrible atrocities. There'd been no side in this war worthy of my sympathy. I wondered if we should continue with the assignment. Then I thought of Inaros, the only man who would suffer if we gave up. He seemed a good man, and a better ruler than anyone else on offer.

"They didn't hurt Psamtik," the General said. "Not then, anyway. He was kept alive at the Great King's court here in Memphis, for many months, until he caused more trouble and they killed him. But long before that, Cambyses was wearing the Double Crown."

My heart fell. "What if the Great King also has the crook and flail?"

"I don't think that's likely," said Djanet. "He has the Double Crown for sure. The Persians made a big thing of it. Cambyses wore the crown during a parade through Memphis. When he departed, he took it with him. I doubt the crown will ever return to Egypt. But Cambyses did not carry the crook and flail. I'm sure he would have, if he'd had them."

"Djanet is correct," said the General. "I was invited by the Pharaoh to join him in his prison, when he learned of my plight. It was a sumptuous prison and information got in and out with ease. If Cambyses had found the crook and flail, I would know it."

"Then some time between the battle and the final defeat, the crook and flail disappeared," Herodotus said.

"Yes."

"Maybe Psamtik destroyed them?"

"No," said the General and Djanet simultaneously.

"You don't know how it is for us Egyptians," Djanet explained to our surprised Hellene silence. "The crown is the kingship.

But the crook and flail are Egypt. No true Egyptian could harm them."

"Hidden then," Herodotus said. "Or spirited away."

"Yes."

"I wonder how he managed that?" Herodotus asked.

"Did he have the crook and flail then?" I asked.

The General laughed. "Do you think he would tell me? Besides, I spent that year in fever and agony. Nobody could trust me with anything."

"Oh, of course, excuse me," I said.

"But rest assured, if Psamtik had displayed the insignia while he was a prisoner, they would have been taken from him," the General said.

"Then he hid them while he was there," Herodotus said.

"Or he gave them away," Diotima suggested.

Cheery optimism was lacking across the party.

Into the depressed silence the General said, "That's all I can tell you."

"Thank you, General," Diotima said. "May I ask, who is this girl with you? Is she your granddaughter?"

The General laughed, an oddly harsh

sound. "You are absurd. I may be blind, but I know what I look like. I would never have imposed myself on a woman. No, the girl is an orphan. She has my protection, which is valuable. A small girl on the street is . . . vulnerable."

"I understand," Diotima said.

"With me she has food, a dress to wear, a place to sleep. In return she tells me what she sees. Little Tia here" — he patted her on the head; the girl looked solemn — "she is one of a long line. When she is old enough to make her way in the world she will leave, and I will take in another orphan." He sighed. "There's always another orphan."

"You are kind."

"It's a fair arrangement," he said gruffly. He hesitated, then said, "Your question puts me in mind of someone who might be able to help you. Let me make enquiries. One of the beggars will contact you tomorrow."

As we left, I asked Djanet the obvious question. "How do you come to know the General?"

"I know all sorts," Djanet said, off-hand. "In the case of the General, it's easily explained. The line between an artist and a beggar is finer than most artists would like."

"What's his real name?"

"Nobody remembers," Djanet said. "He's been the Blind General since before any of us were born."

Knowing now that he had been a nobleman and a genuine commander, I was fairly sure that his true name could be discovered if we wanted, but the poor man deserved his anonymity. I said, "I wish we could do something for him."

"Don't be ridiculous," Djanet said. "Don't you think he could rise from poverty if he wanted? He does this deliberately, to punish himself for losing the fight against the Persians."

THE ARROW

I slept in the street. The innkeeper refused to let me through his door, let alone near his beds, not with an official public service notice in his hand that said I was crawling with bedbugs. Diotima had insisted on joining me outside, and I had insisted she sleep in our rented room. I eventually prevailed because, beneath that headstrong exterior, my wife is at core a sensible woman.

So Diotima retired to our comfortable bed, and the beggars showed me a good place outside, under a tree in a secluded courtyard, off a lane from the main road. I'd slept in worse places, but that was when I'd been doing my time as a recruit in the army. It had been some years since I'd slept rough. Married life has that effect on a man. I discovered I'd lost the art of sleeping in the soft dirt.

Not that the dirt was soft. It was more like gritty sand on hard rock. Nor was there even a single blade of grass anywhere within the city to be my cushion. Egypt is that kind of place. (The beggars had gleefully told me that out on the farms, sleeping under the stars was considered very pleasant as long as the crocodiles don't get you.)

I tossed and turned, unable to get comfortable. No matter how I lay, there was some part of my anatomy digging into the sandstone. Eventually I turned onto my stomach, which was good enough to send me into a doze, until in my sleep I ate a mouthful of sand.

I sat up, choking and spitting grit.

I heard thumping. It wasn't my heart. Someone, somewhere, was hitting something.

The back wall of the inn in which Diotima and Herodotus slept bordered the courtyard. I looked up — it was a big building, three stories tall — but all the lights were off. That reassured me. Yet that was the direction of the pounding.

A thin voice called, "Open up! Please open up! The General is dying!"

Lights came on in the inn. I heard voices demanding to know what was happening.

I pushed myself up and ran.

I got there first. As I turned the corner to the front of the inn I saw a girl beating her fists on the door, the girl who had been with the General. She turned, startled by my sudden appearance. She took one look at me and screamed, then fainted on the spot.

The door opened at that instant. Diotima stood there. She saw me standing over the unconscious child.

"Nico, what have you done, you brute!"

"Me?"

Herodotus, Djanet and Max arrived. We carried the girl inside. She came to quickly, aided by some cool water applied to her face by Diotima, while Max fanned air across her.

"The General, he's dying," were her first words.

Djanet gasped.

"What? How?"

"An arrow . . . in the dark . . . someone shot him . . . I don't know . . . he said to bring help . . ."

"Can you run?" I asked.

"Yes."

But she couldn't. The beggar girl had spent all her energy in getting help. When she stumbled the second time I picked her up and carried her under my arm. In that way we ran through the dark streets of Memphis.

"Does this sort of thing happen to you

often?" Herodotus asked as we ran.

"More often than you'd believe," I panted. I was carrying the child and it was hard work. "I'm sorry about this, Herodotus," I said. "You hired us to keep you out of trouble, and here we are getting you into it."

"Don't apologize," Herodotus said. "I'm having fun. I thought I was going to write about history, but here I am making it. This is going to look terrific in my book."

The historian was barely puffed by the exercise. He was in the sort of condition that would have made him a good inquiry agent. If I ever needed a partner, I could do worse.

We got there second.

We burst into the old warehouse to see a group of men clustered about a body. Every one of them was dressed in Persian army kit. They turned at our entrance, and I saw that they were big men. Several of them drew swords. They stood there, ready to attack us.

A smaller man pushed his way between them to stand in front. It was Barzanes.

Djanet swore softly and disappeared back out the door. Max followed her. Herodotus, Diotima and I stood our ground, with the girl child between us.

Barzanes had only two words to say.

"Arrest them."

I stepped across in front of the doorway to stop the troops chasing after Djanet and Max. But that was no help for me.

When Persians decide to arrest you, they do it properly.

Men surrounded me. Someone tripped me and I hit the ground hard, face first. Two feet came down on my back to make sure I stayed down.

Fortunately Diotima had the good sense not to join the fight. She knew we could never win here. She pulled the girl against her to protect the child, grabbed Herodotus by the arm when he moved to help me, and protested loudly at the treatment meted out to her husband. The armed troops ignored her.

I couldn't see what was happening, but I felt hands grapple both my arms and both my legs. I rose into the air.

They carried me in this undignified position to Barzanes, where the soldiers stood while I dangled.

With some effort I looked up to find Barzanes staring down at me.

"What are you doing here, Athenian?" he said coldly.

I could think of several witty replies, but

none seemed a good idea while I was hanging face down.

"We were summoned by the child," I managed to gasp. It was hard to breathe suspended from my arms and legs.

"Why?" Barzanes asked. "How can you possibly be concerned with the death of a beggar?"

That was going to be tough to answer.

"It's this writer with us," I moaned quietly. "I don't understand it. He questions *everyone*. He questioned the beggar just yesterday," I added, because surely Barzanes would have that piece of information soon, if he didn't already. It was important to tell as much truth as possible.

Barzanes looked over to where Herodotus stood.

"Is he some sort of spy?" Barzanes asked, echoing my own original thoughts.

"Have you met him? I can't believe anyone with that much boyish enthusiasm could be up to no good." To change the subject I said quickly, "What are *you* doing here, Barzanes? You're not going to tell me the Eyes and Ears interest themselves in the death of a beggar."

"We do when the beggar once commanded an army against us." Barzanes stared at me. "You are either naïve, Athenian, or you are trying to deceive me."

I had nothing to say to that.

"Crime and disorder is hateful to the King," Barzanes said. "All who live within his domain are protected by his laws, and contrary to what you think, I have investigated death among the lower classes before this. Normally when a beggar dies by violence, the miscreant is another beggar who killed for the few coins the victim carried."

I had seen the same thing myself. I nodded at the Persian agent's words.

Barzanes said, "This was not the sort of death an ordinary beggar meets."

He stepped to the side, to reveal the body of the General. An arrow protruded from his face, exactly where one of the scarred pits replaced an eyeball. The General had been flung onto his back by the force of the blow. It had probably been a quick death, but the sight was ghastly.

"Look at that man's face, Barzanes," I said. "Your people did that."

"It is the fortunes of war," Barzanes said without emotion. "This man's fate is the risk I take every day, to serve my king and country. How do you think I would fare, Athenian, if I fell into the hands of the rebels?"

I thought of Inaros's preference for feeding criminals to crocodiles, and impaling tax collectors, and had nothing to say.

"You see," Barzanes said, correctly interpreting my silence. "It is the risk you, too, have taken, Athenian, to serve your city."

Barzanes's words oddly echoed what Charitimides had said the last time I had seen him.

"What was done to this officer is not what I would have done," Barzanes admitted. "A clean death would have been preferable."

"You Persians wonder why we Hellenes resist your rule," I said. "Take a look at that man and you'll see the reason why we'll fight you to our last breath."

I had become foolishly angry.

Barzanes said, "Release him."

They let go.

I hit the ground chest first. The air rushed from my lungs so quickly that I belched. I rolled onto my side and gasped for breath.

"Your words convince me that you did not kill the old man," Barzanes said, with no sign of either hatred or sympathy. "That is all that matters in this place." He pointed at Herodotus. "Bring him."

The men who had held me dragged Herodotus to stand before Barzanes.

"You are Herodotus of Halicarnassus," Barzanes said.

"I am," Herodotus said. He must have been scared, but he didn't show it.

I wondered how Barzanes came to know Herodotus's home city. Had he investigated the writer?

"I am a citizen of your empire."

"A citizen who talks to beggars," Barzanes said.

"I'm writing a book."

Barzanes said, "I have read every book in the world. Perhaps, when you are finished, I will read yours."

"If you buy a copy, I'll sign it." Herodotus stared back at Barzanes, which isn't easy to do. "I have committed no crime," he added, which was true.

"Then you are free to go." What Barzanes thought of Herodotus, I couldn't tell, but he seemed to have decided the author was no threat.

Barzanes and I knelt beside the body.

"How easy to shoot a blind man," I said contemptuously.

"Yes," said Barzanes. "All the killer needed to do was walk in, aim and shoot. The victim would not see it coming, and there is no risk to the attacker."

"He's a coward," I said.

"He is sensibly efficient," Barzanes countered.

"Maybe the killer dropped a clue at the entrance," I said in hope.

"I have already searched," Barzanes said. "The ground is so littered with rubbish that there is no hope of discerning what is important."

That was depressing.

"Then there is no way to tell who killed him," I said.

"Had he any enemies?" Barzanes asked.

"Only you," I said. "And other Persians."

"This is not a Persian killing," Barzanes replied, too distracted by the problem at hand to be offended. He fingered the arrow. "The arrow is of Egyptian design. There are thousands of standard issue Persian arrows afloat in this city, but the killer has chosen Egyptian ammunition. Why?"

I thought perhaps to throw us off the trail, but I didn't say it.

Barzanes looked closely at the damage. "The arrow has penetrated to a normal depth for such a wound."

"He probably stood a normal distance away."

"And used a normal bow," Barzanes added.

He was obviously thinking what I was thinking: that Markos carried a crossbow.

We looked at each other.

Barzanes seemed to come to some sort of a decision. He stood and held out a hand. A soldier passed him a cloth of fine linen.

Barzanes wiped his hands on the cloth and passed it back to his man. He didn't offer me the cloth. I wiped my hands on my tunic.

Barzanes said, "Walk with me, Athenian."

I walked. We left the soldiers behind. We passed by Diotima and Herodotus, who watched us pass with raised eyebrows. Barzanes and I stepped through the exit, where we ambled down the deserted street. The wind blew street grit into our faces, but at least we couldn't be overheard.

"This country is a mess," Barzanes said. "I cannot understand why the Great King wants it."

"For its enormous wealth?" I suggested.

"Yes, that I understand. But the disorder. Think of the terrible disorder."

Barzanes sounded distraught. If there was anything he hated, it was disorder.

"Nothing here works as it should," Barzanes went on. "Crime and disorder is hateful to the King, yet these Egyptians are all thieves. Even I have been pickpocketed as I walked through the marketplace. Me, the Eyes and Ears! What must it be like for normal men?"

"They seem to get by."

"I cannot arrest the entire population!" Barzanes ignored my reply. "Yet to get the criminals off the street that is what I must do."

"Maybe you could go home instead?" I suggested.

"There is crime, but the worst criminals are the men who run the country."

"I see you've met the Egyptian Public Service," I said.

Barzanes scowled. "In any other satrapy of the Empire I would have them executed. Here, I must tolerate them. The advisors to the Great King have insisted upon it."

"Why?"

"Because they are the only men who support us."

"I feel for you."

"I freely admit, Athenian, that I loathe those creatures."

"You know, Barzanes, you should have a chat with Inaros. You two have more in common than you think."

"So you *have* been in contact with the rebels," Barzanes said.

I cursed my stupidity. My mouth had run far ahead of my brain.

"I could hardly avoid it since we came down from the north," I said lamely. "The fact is that Inaros is an ally of my city."

"Yet here you are, in Persian territory."

"Like Herodotus, I have committed no crime," I said in all honesty.

"Let it remain thus," Barzanes said. "Crime and disorder are —"

"Hateful to the King. Yes, so I've heard."

"Athenian, there is an important matter upon which we must speak," Barzanes said.

"What is it?" I said suspiciously.

At that moment a man and a boy entered the street in which we stood, coming from the desert end. They led a donkey that was overloaded with more farm produce — mostly barley — than I would have thought any beast could carry. Obviously these two were on their way to the city market.

Barzanes took me by the arm and led me away from the travelers. The familiarity shocked me. We were hardly friends. Barzanes was the stiffest, most formal man I knew. We walked slowly as we spoke.

"There is a point on which we might have common interests," Barzanes said.

"I doubt it," I said.

"Hear my words. When Markos joined us at the inn —"

"You mean when your soldiers frog-marched him in," I interrupted.

"It amounts to the same thing," Barzanes said, unperturbed. "At that time the Spartan assassin carried an unusual weapon. You must surely have thought upon it?"

"I certainly have," I said with feeling. "I've been on the receiving end."

Barzanes raised an eyebrow. "Then Ahura Mazda, the Wise Lord of the World, must favor you, for you are lucky to be alive. I tell you now, that weapon is one of the most powerful in the Persian armory."

I said, "I'm not surpris—" But then the implications of Barzanes's words hit me, and I stopped in mid-sentence. "Did you just say that Markos is carrying a *Persian* weapon?"

Barzanes scowled. "In a special palace outside the capital, Susa, lies an armory of unusual weapons belonging to the Great King. I have been to this palace."

I raised an eyebrow. "For special weapons training?" I asked.

"That need not concern you," Barzanes said shortly. "What should, however, is that at this palace I observed the very same weapon that Markos wields. My observations were not so close that I can say for certain that his weapon definitely came from the palace, but I think this must be true."

"Why?" I asked. "If one Persian could invent this thing, another could build it for Markos. He probably got it in one of your provinces."

"No, this is impossible, because we did not invent these crossbows," Barzanes said, surprising me.

If the Persians didn't invent them, then who did?

"We bought them," Barzanes said, answering my question. "To the east of our Empire there is another land, separated by a great desert, which is why we Persians have never conquered them, but we trade. The road across that desert I spoke of is very long and populated by lawless brigands. The traders who cross are always accompanied by guards. It was the guards who carried the crossbows. When the Great King saw them he acquired several at a high price."

"Who are these traders?" I asked.

"We call them the Silk People."

"So *that*'s where it comes from," I said. "I have seen silk. Diotima has some."

"I have seen the people themselves," Barzanes said. "They are very strange. But you understand, Athenian, that it is impossible for the Spartan to have acquired a crossbow from anywhere else."

That explained why I'd never seen anything like it before.

The sun had risen as Barzanes and I talked. Memphis was waking up. More people were passing us by, so that we had to speak softly. But I understood now why Barzanes had insisted we talk in the street: not to prevent Herodotus and Diotima from hearing, but to keep this news from his own troops. If a few common soldiers discovered that their king had lost such a weapon, the news would be all over the empire before the month was out. That raised an interesting question.

"How did Markos come by a secret Persian superweapon?" I said.

"Funnily enough, I myself thought to ask that same question." His voice dripped sarcasm. Barzanes, the Eyes and Ears of the King, was not a happy man. "Crossbows are supposed to be a state secret."

"Then why are you telling me?"

"If a Spartan is not only carrying one, but shooting people with it, then how secret do you think they are?"

"Good point."

Barzanes said, "I sent a King's Messenger to Susa, to inquire. But it will be many days before I can expect a reply."

I gave it some thought, and suddenly I had the answer.

"Obviously your friend Megabazos gave it to him," I said. I was exasperated by the games we were all playing with each other. I yearned for at least one thing to be clear.

Barzanes stopped dead. He turned to me and said, "Repeat your words."

Did Barzanes really not know what had been going on in Hellas? "It seems we can help each other," I said. "I might know something you don't."

"Explain."

"A Persian ambassador turned up in Sparta with a shipload of gold. He bribed the Spartans to attack Athens. And they did! Surely you know this."

"I know no such thing," Barzanes said.

He sounded like he meant it. I remembered that Barzanes prided himself on never having told a lie. I had seen him cut off a man's toes. I knew he had ordered any number of executions. He would commit almost any atrocity in the name of his King. But he never, ever lied.

"How am I to know this is not some Athenian fabrication?" Barzanes said. "Where did you learn of this?"

"From Charitimides. He's the Nauarch, the man who commands our fleet."

"I know of him. An able commander but not a statesman."

"Charitimides had word from Pericles."

"A statesman and a liar."

That was Barzanes's summation of Athens's greatest man, and I couldn't say I disagreed.

"Tell me again the name of this ambassador," Barzanes said.

"I was told his name is Megabazos."

"This man I know all too well," Barzanes said. "You called him a friend. He is not. I once investigated Megabazos for enriching himself at the expense of the state."

"And?"

"He was guilty. His sin is great. When he dies his soul will be cast into a pit of molten iron for all eternity."

"That sounds painful."

"But it won't happen soon enough. The Great King chastised Megabazos but did not punish him."

"Political influence?" I suggested. I knew how that worked.

Barzanes was expressionless. "Artaxerxes the King decided the man was more useful alive than dead."

"Presumably because your king had this Megabazos earmarked for the trip to Sparta. By any chance did this investigation happen recently?" I asked, because another thought had occurred to me.

"Immediately before I left for Egypt," Barzanes said.

"Is Megabazos the sort to hold grudges?"

"He hates me as few other men do," Barzanes said. "Why do you ask?"

"Just curious. I think it obvious, Barzanes, that in addition to gold this Megabazos carried one of your king's crossbows to Sparta."

"This is outrageous, Athenian," Barzanes raged. "The whole security of my nation has been endangered by a foolish nobleman who thought to give a new weapon to the Spartans. The *Spartans* of all people! Ahura Mazda preserve us all. We may as well just turn the weapon around and shoot ourselves in the head."

"Well, I'm glad it's your problem and not mine," I told him.

"You think so, Athenian?" Barzanes said. "Then what happens when an army of Spartans armed with crossbows arrives outside the walls of Athens?"

That brought me up short. Dear Gods, we were all in trouble.

"The crossbow can penetrate armor." Barzanes put the boot in.

I had personally seen a bolt fired from that thing fly through a mud-brick wall. Yes, of course it could penetrate bronze armor.

"We have to get that weapon back," I said.

"What a good idea," Barzanes said.

Barzanes let us go. As he said, it was obvious we hadn't killed the General.

We walked away with the only worthwhile clue: the girl-child. Barzanes seemed unaware of her existence, or that she habitually stayed with her protector.

Gentle questioning from Diotima elicited the unhappy news that the girl hadn't seen a thing.

"It was dark. There were footsteps. Then a twanging sound." The girl burst into tears.

It took the best part of the morning and a very expensive slice of honeycomb to calm her down.

During this period Herodotus had been thinking. He said, "Child, think back to yesterday. After we left, what did the General do?"

"He ate some bread," the girl said solemnly.

"What about after that?" Herodotus pressed. "Did he go anywhere? Did he talk to anyone?"

The girl nodded.

"What did he do?" Herodotus asked.

"He went to the undertaker." The girl hiccupped, either from crying or eating too much honeycomb.

The undertaker? You normally go to the undertaker *after* you've been murdered, not *before*.

"Why?" Herodotus asked the obvious question. "What did he say to them?"

"I don't know. He bade me wait outside."

"Was that usual?"

"No." The girl hiccupped again.

Not knowing what else to do with her, we took the child with us back to the inn, where we found Maxyates and Djanet. The inn-keeper let me stand inside the door, so long as I wore five special amulets to ward against spreading bedbugs. After they slipped away, Max and Djanet had made their way back to our street, where they had waited across from the inn to see if Bar-zanes's soldiers appeared. When they didn't, they went inside.

"What do we do with the girl?" Herodotus asked.

It was a good question.

"We can't take her with us," I said. If nothing else, she would be in too much danger.

"Give her back to the beggars?" Maxyates suggested. "This seems the only option."

"I have an idea," Djanet said. She stood and walked out the back, to where the innkeeper and his family lived.

"Problem solved!" she announced on return.

"How?"

"I did a deal with the landlord," Djanet said. "His daughter's getting married next month." Djanet pointed at the girl-child. "Meet the inn's new serving girl."

This seemed a fine solution, but something bothered me. "You mentioned a deal," I said.

Djanet shrugged. "I told the innkeeper that this child brought particularly good luck to anyone who cared for her."

"I take it you didn't mention that her last protector died horribly."

"Slipped my mind completely. I suggest we load her down with every good luck charm we can find in the marketplace."

"Good idea."

That evening, Herodotus and Maxyates sat at the table in the common room. Maxyates was telling Herodotus all about his homeland.

". . . and in the far south there is forest, vast swathes of forest. Many extraordinary animals and people live there."

"Such as?" Herodotus asked. He was scribbling furiously.

"There are snakes that can eat a man whole. I have seen this with my own eyes."

I wondered if Maxyates was having Herodotus on, but I said nothing. Herodotus took

210

Max's story at face value.

"Any other animals?" he asked, pen poised.

"Elephants, lions, bears. I believe Hellas does not have these animals."

"We have bears!" I put in. "I once had a run-in with a bear —"

"Go on, Max," Herodotus said. They ignored me completely.

"Horned donkeys," Maxyates continued.

I raised an eyebrow.

"Then there are the dog-headed men."

Now I *knew* Maxyates was making fun of Herodotus.

The historian looked up at Maxyates, fascinated. "Do they truly look so?"

"The head of a dog, on the body of a man," Maxyates said solemnly. "The men are dwarves. I have never seen one of these strange men alive, but I once saw the body of one. A hunter had brought him in. Apparently the two had fought."

Herodotus wrote more.

"This forest seems a dangerous place," I said.

"Many die there," Max agreed. "But the rewards are great for a successful hunter."

"What of your own people?" Herodotus asked.

"We lead ordinary lives," said the man

dyed red from head to toe, and with all the hair on one side of his head shaved off. "We live in villages and grow plants for food and we hunt."

"Does anyone live inside the forest?" Herodotus asked.

"There are the wild men and wild women," Maxyates said. "They do not live in villages. Nor do they wear clothes."

"Don't they get cold?" I asked.

"No, for they are covered in thick, black fur all over their bodies."

I had always thought Maxyates was a truthful and humorless man. But after this I resolved to judge his words more carefully.

THE HOUSE OF DEATH

The news that the General had visited an undertaker before he was murdered was suggestive. In particular, it suggested we should talk to the undertaker.

"Perhaps the Gods sent him a vision of his own doom," Herodotus said. "The General might have gone there to arrange his affairs."

"The man was a beggar," Djanet scoffed. "He had no affairs. Besides, the House of Tutu is the most expensive undertaker around, and in the land of the pyramids, that's saying something."

"The General might have been richer than you thought," Herodotus said.

"I happen to know the General gave all his money to the poor," Djanet said.

"But he *was* the poor!"

"Yes, well," Djanet huffed. "That's why he was poor."

"How did you come to know the General

in the first place?" Diotima asked. She sounded suspicious.

"Oh, I know just about everyone," Djanet said grandly.

"Hmm." I could tell from her manner that Diotima was suspicious. I could also tell that she wasn't sure *why* she was suspicious.

I paid close attention to Maxyates during this exchange. For all that he looked odd, he was the closest we had in the party to another Egyptian. Maxyates seemed to take Djanet at face value.

It was unbearably hot walking down the streets of Memphis. I stopped at every drink vendor we passed, in the hope of a decent cup of wine, but all they had was beer.

Meanwhile, Maxyates and Herodotus were arguing about the Gods.

Maxyates, the weird-haired Trojan philosopher, and Herodotus, the inveterate traveler, had both seen much of the world and thought much upon it. Maxyates had taken objection to Herodotus's idea that the Gods might have sent a vision to the Blind General.

"Would the Hellene gods send a vision to an Egyptian?" Maxyates said. "The people of the Black Land worship different gods to yours."

Herodotus scratched his head. "It's a vexing question. I've always wondered about the gods in other lands. I think they must be one and the same."

"Different peoples have different gods," Maxyates said. "This all men know."

"That cannot be true," Herodotus said. "I think rather that the same gods must manifest themselves to different peoples in different ways."

"Why would they do that?"

"I don't know," Herodotus said. "But does it make sense that there could be more than one king of the gods? We Hellenes have Zeus. The Egyptians I've learned have Amun-Ra. Clearly therefore Amun-Ra must be Zeus."

"They are nothing alike," Maxyates said.

"But they *have* to be the same god," Herodotus insisted. "You can't have two lots of gods running the world. What happens if they disagree?"

"Did that not happen when your Hellene gods fought the Titans?" Maxyates said.

"Well, yes," Herodotus said, reluctantly.

"There you are then. Two sets of gods are perfectly possible," Maxyates said.

But it was obvious Herodotus didn't agree. The two of them squabbled every step of the way to the funeral home.

The House of Tutu rested on an elegant

street in the southern part of the city. The street was so wide that there was room for a row of palm trees down the middle, to give shade. I was struck by how different the architecture was in Egypt compared to Athens. In Egypt the buildings were flat, white and square. Flat walls and flat roofs. I suppose they got away with it because it never rained. Athenians would have painted everything in sight in bright colors, but the Egyptians used whitewash and left it at that. In Egypt, a man judged the quality of his home by the cleanliness of his white walls. I asked Djanet about this.

"It's cooler inside if it's white outside," she said.

Herodotus made a note.

The glare made me shield my eyes and made the sun seem ten times worse.

A man stood at the entrance to the funeral home. He blinked at the sight of us — obviously, we didn't look like customers — but he opened the door anyway.

Inside was the coolest, most pleasant building I had yet seen in this country. The layout was much like an Athenian home: rooms surrounding an open central courtyard. Yet here someone had stretched sheets of white linen across the open inner space. The sun's light was a diffuse glow. A fountain bubbled in the center and vines climbed the walls and stone columns to make the place seem more like a garden than a place of funereal business.

A man entered from the other side. He arrived so quickly I thought the doorman must have signaled that there were visitors. His hair was gray and straight and his face immaculately shaved. I had never seen a man with less stubble. Though he was obviously old, perhaps in his sixties or seventies, he was trim rather than thinned by age. The clothes he wore were like something out of the frescoes dotted all over the temples: a loin cloth of the purest white linen. His chest would have been bare had he not wrapped about him a wide stole of some sort, also of white linen. The effect was impressive, set off against the dark olive of his skin. It was then that I realized there was barely a hair on his chest. Had he had his chest hairs plucked out? I thought he must have. If so, he was braver than I was.

He began a greeting in Egyptian, saw the look on our faces, then switched smoothly to Greek. "I am Tutu, of the House of Tutu. I bid you welcome. I see that you are not among our regular customers. How, then, may I serve you?"

Regulars? At an undertaker?

I said, "Thank you, Tutu. My name is Nicolaos. I'm from Athens —"

Tutu held up a hand to stop me. "Rest assured that will be of no difficulty. I am always happy to embalm foreigners."

"Er . . . you misunderstand. We wanted to ask you about a conversation you had yesterday, with the man known as the Blind General. What did he want?"

Tutu was silent for a moment. Then he said, "You will understand, I am sure, that I never discuss other people's business."

My shoulders slumped. The embalmer spoke with such firmness that I knew we would get nothing from him. We had wasted our time.

"Your reply is very right and proper," Herodotus said approvingly.

"Thank you," said the embalmer to the historian.

Herodotus spoke warmly. "I am most pleased to meet an embalmer of Egypt. All men know that the skill of the Egyptians in these matters is the greatest in all the world, and I am given to understand that the House of Tutu is unsurpassed amongst the Egyptians."

Tutu fairly glowed.

"I find funeral customs a fascinating subject," Herodotus went on. "I like to learn

218

of them wherever I go. Did you know that in the land of Scythia, when the king dies, they dig an enormous grave? They lay the body on a mattress, so that in death the king will be in comfort."

"This is a good custom." Tutu nodded.

"Then they strangle to death one of the king's concubines," Herodotus said with happy enthusiasm.

Diotima gasped. "Dear Gods!"

"They do it so that the king will have companionship in the afterlife," Herodotus said. "They lay the woman's body alongside the king. Then they kill the king's servant, his cook, his groom, and his favorite horse. These too attend the king in death. Lastly they fill the grave with dinnerware made of purest gold. Over this they heap a vast mound of dirt."

"A Pharaoh — even a barbarian one — deserves such comfort," Tutu said in approval.

"I wonder if the concubine and servants feel the same way," Diotima said in ill-disguised disgust.

Herodotus ignored my wife. "Then the king's mourners ritually cleanse themselves," he said. "They erect tents made of hide, in which they place stones that have been heated to a red-hot glow upon a fire.

The people lather their heads with soap made of ash and goat fat. Then they enter the tents, where they throw the seed of the hemp plant upon the hot stones."

"Why?" Tutu asked dubiously.

"I don't know," Herodotus admitted. "But when they do this, the Scythians shout for joy."

"A strange custom," Tutu said. "Is that the end of the ceremony?"

"Not quite. A year later, the king's subjects return to his grave with fifty fine horses and fifty fine youths. The youths are strangled with a garrote and placed upon the horses, which are sacrificed and placed so as to ring the grave."

Tutu nodded in approval. "These Scythians of whom you speak obviously know the importance of honoring their king. I see too that you are a man of fine taste to interest yourself in such things. May I ask your name?"

"Herodotus."

"Have you seen the pyramids?"

"I hope to."

"You should. In the days of my forebears it was much the same as you describe. Hundreds of servants willingly took poison to provide the Pharaoh with a proper retinue in death." Tutu sighed. "Alas, those halcyon days are long gone."

"Good," Diotima muttered under her breath.

Tutu didn't hear her. He said, speaking to Herodotus, "I admit, when I saw foreigners in my vestibule I had not thought to meet someone of such refinement and culture. May I return the favor by demonstrating to you our own methods?"

"That would be admirable," Herodotus said.

But I didn't like the sound of that. "Demonstrate on whom?" I asked.

This caused the embalmer to turn his attention from Herodotus to me.

"Tell me, young man, have you given any thought to your own Afterlife?"

"I confess it's something I've been hoping to put off."

Tutu shook his head in dismay. "You can never start planning early enough. After all, your journey to eternity begins from the moment you are born." He took me by the arm and led me through a wide entrance at the back of the courtyard. The others followed behind.

In the room beyond were more coffins than I had ever seen in my life, each placed upon a stone pedestal as if they were wares for sale.

"Lie in this," Tutu said.

"But it's a coffin!" I objected.

"It's a sarcophagus, to be precise. Notice that the outer case matches the shape of a person. I'd like you to try it on for size."

I opened my mouth to say that I would sooner lie on a crocodile, but Herodotus said, "Go ahead, Nicolaos. This is perfect material for my book."

"I'd rather not know," I muttered. But my paying client had urged me, and I saw that our witness had become friendly under Herodotus's relentless interest. I took off my sandals and climbed into the man-shaped box.

It was surprisingly comfortable, except for my arms.

"Fold your arms over your chest," Tutu said. "Like this."

He demonstrated. I copied his pose.

"It's a bit too roomy," I said, getting into the spirit of the thing. "Do you have something in a smaller size?"

The embalmer appraised me in the sarcophagus with a knowing eye. "We will need the extra room after your body has been wrapped," he said. "Now you will object that the chartreuse of the inner case isn't suitable for a man of action such as yourself, and I must say I would agree. For you I

222

might suggest something in crimson. Or perhaps a sky blue. We have an excellent portrait painter who will place your visage on the face of the casket. Rest assured, too, that the inside will be perfectly smooth. No one wants to spend eternity looking at some carpenter's sloppy woodwork."

"I see that you take everything into consideration," I said.

"We are professionals. My family have been embalmers to the highest in the land for countless generations, including Pharaohs, I am proud to say."

"I'm sure you have many happy customers," I said.

"Most of them tend to be dead."

"Oh, good point."

He helped me out of the casket, then led me by the arm. "Now do please come over here and relax while I demonstrate how we'll remove your organs." Tutu held up an iron probe that looked perfectly innocent. "This is what we use to remove your brain. It goes through your nostril into your skull, then I twist like so —"

I stepped back so he wouldn't demonstrate on me. The embalmer rotated the tool rapidly in the air. "The trick is to catch the brain stem," he said knowingly. "Then the whole organ comes out in a long stream. It goes straight into one of these jars, to which we add preservative."

Herodotus was making rapid notes. "Is that normal?" he asked.

"Quite so. The brain, liver, kidneys, intestines . . . all have to be removed, else they rot and the earthly remains become a little . . . er . . . squishy."

I felt this was more information than we or any other sane people needed, but Herodotus was scribbling furiously, Maxyates leant forward in concentration, and even Diotima was following closely.

"Is that important?" Diotima asked.

"Of course it is. The *ka* and *ba* must have their house in good shape for eternity."

"*Ka* and *ba*?" Diotima frowned.

"The life force and the eternal spirit. The patient's heart must remain in place, of course."

"Why?" Herodotus asked.

"I should have thought it was obvious. It's so that on the deceased's journey to the Afterlife, his heart can be weighed against the Feather of Truth. If the heart weighs less than the feather, then he passes on to eternal life in the Field of Reeds. But if his heart weighs more than the feather, then the deceased goes to the Devourer of Souls."

If all it took was a heart heavier than a

feather, then the Devourer must eat well.

Tutu added primly, "Of course, in the case of a Pharaoh there can be no doubt that his heart will be pure."

"Of course," I agreed, while reflecting that the most recent Pharaoh had cut the throats of innocent children.

Tutu put down his hideous brain-remover tool.

"May I offer you refreshment?" Tutu spoke directly to Herodotus.

"We would be pleased."

Tutu led us to comfortable seats. These were not dining couches, but upright chairs. It was an odd custom of the Egyptians that they expected to eat while sitting up. I thought this must be bad for the digestion, for surely when upright the food must fall through you faster. Perhaps that was why Egyptians always seemed so argumentative.

A girl servant appeared with trays of barley bread, dates and a meat that she said was duck. Diotima immediately reached for the dates. She loved anything sweet. I thought the duck excellent, the best meal I'd had in Egypt.

Herodotus and Tutu set to talking about different ways of burying people. It was an odd subject for any meal, but they spoke with enthusiasm and seemed charmed with each other's company.

A man appeared with cups of beer. I asked if they had any wine. They didn't.

The embalmer overheard my quiet request. "I'm a traditionalist, as I'm sure you've noticed," he said. "The ways of my forefathers were good enough for them, and they're good enough for me. This wine you speak of is an import from your own lands. Here in Egypt, real men drink beer."

"You speak knowledgeably about the funeral customs of the Pharaohs," Herodotus prompted. I could tell he was displeased that the subject had changed.

"I have dedicated my life to the proper treatment of the dead. I should hope to have some small expertise."

"Have you really been embalmers to the Pharaohs?" Diotima asked.

"I may say without undue pride that for countless generations we have served Pharaoh in this most delicate of personal needs."

"Then it was you who buried Psamtik, the last native Pharaoh?" Herodotus said.

"My father was the embalmer, in fact." Tutu gave a moue of distaste. "I was only young, but I remember it well. The whole affair was most unsatisfactory in every way."

"Oh?"

"It was a rush job, I'm afraid. The Persians turned up with Pharaoh's body and gave us three months to embalm it. Three months! In the days of our forebears it would have been three years."

"Unfortunate," I commiserated.

"You know Egypt has fallen on hard times when not even a Pharaoh can get a decent funeral."

Diotima, Herodotus and I went *tsk-tsk* in unison.

"In the old days, the nobility of Egypt came to our house for all their embalming needs. I am horrified to say I can't remember the last time a client of good birth crossed our threshold."

"Business is bad?" I asked.

"Business is booming, but the clientele isn't what it used to be. These days we see a lot of newly rich. Members of the public service, mostly."

"Oh dear." I looked about rapidly, for fear some of them might be present.

"You may well say so," Tutu said. "In the old days, gentlefolk of distinction would gather here in our lounge, to relax with fine food and cold beer and share their plans for eternity in an atmosphere of refinement and culture. Try doing that with these new rich. They walk in and expect to be served *quickly.*" Tutu shuddered in horror. "They demand a mausoleum bigger than their neighbor's, then complain about anything that costs more than a coffin of paper mâché. It would never have been allowed back in the days of our forebears. How I yearn for those past times. On my days of rest, I take my personal chariot into the desert, to Saqqara, I look upon the pyramids and I weep at the thought of how we have fallen from glory. Weep, I tell you."

"So am I right in thinking you never spoke with the last Pharaoh?" Herodotus pressed on the point he cared about. "You were young then, as you said, and when he arrived at your house he was dead."

"It would be remarkable if he were not. Psamtik came to us in two parts, the body on a bier, his head in a bag."

"That does seem conclusive. Then Psamtik was decapitated," Herodotus said. "What did the Pharaoh do to deserve such treatment?"

"One doesn't like to enquire," Tutu said. "Not when the people bringing him are the executioners."

"Understandable."

"A most undignified way for a Pharaoh to die," Tutu said. "But I must say it made it so much easier to remove his brain."

Herodotus said, "I imagine the Persians didn't bring any grave goods with them."

I suddenly saw what Herodotus was driving at. My hopes lifted.

"None," Tutu said. "These Persians are barbaric."

My hopes fell again. This was depressing news.

Herodotus shrugged and said, "Oh well, I'm sorry, Nicolaos. I thought perhaps the General knew where the crook and flail were and had come to retrieve them."

"It was a good try, Herodotus," I consoled him. "Even the best detective sometimes ends up in a dead end," I said.

Then it occurred to me that dead end was perhaps not the best description for a funeral home.

"Thank you for your time, sir," I said to Tutu, to cover my mistake. "Rest assured sir, that if I die I could think of no one better to embalm me."

Tutu rose from his seat. "I assume your next visit, since I could not help you, will be to see the General himself."

"Alas, sir, that will be impossible," I said. "The Blind General died last night."

"Dead?" Tutu's face turned a shade of gray. "This is terrible news. He didn't seem ill yesterday." Tutu sighed. "But I suppose that's the way with the elderly."

"Not in this case," Djanet said. "The General was murdered."

Tutu staggered as if he had been struck. "May Amun-Ra preserve us! Who killed him?" Tutu demanded.

"We don't know," I said.

"It will be the Persians," Tutu said, almost to himself. "It has to be. They still hate him, after all these years. A defenseless old man." He brought himself up short. "Where is the body?" he demanded.

As far as I knew it was still at the warehouse. I said as much to Tutu.

Tutu clapped his hands. Two young men came running. They were assistants, dressed like their master in a white loin cloth. Tutu gave them instructions to collect the earthly remains of the General.

"Bring his body to my embalming table," Tutu finished. "You must hurry. He has already been out in the heat of the day far too long. Take the cart and the fast horse. Now go. Quickly!"

The young men went.

"So the General did have an arrangement with you, for his funeral," Herodotus said. He shot a triumphant look at Djanet. "I thought as much."

"Not at all," Tutu said. "The General was

my country's last link to a bygone era. You know he was descended from the nobility, don't you? I don't care if he didn't have a coin to his name. The General will receive my best service. I promise you his ka and his ba will be provided for as befits a man of his noble spirit."

"You are kind."

"No, I am Egyptian. To you I may seem only an embalmer. I know how you foreigners look down upon my honorable profession. But I am also a true Egyptian, the son of a true Egyptian. For countless generations my family has paved the way for good Egyptian souls to reach the Field of Reeds. I will not fail in my duty to the last great Egyptian."

"The *last* great Egyptian? What about Inaros?" I asked.

"Nobody in their right mind thinks Inaros is an Egyptian, let alone descended of the Pharaonic line. It is a lie we accept in order to rid ourselves of the hated Persians. Still I could wish he were of the true blood."

"What if Inaros produced the crook and flail?" I asked.

"That would be a different matter," Tutu said to me. "Though you are a barbarian, you surely know that the true Pharaoh is the living incarnation of Horus."

231

I hadn't known that, but I wasn't going to give Tutu any opportunity to think less of me, so I nodded.

"Pharaoh is also the son of Amun-Ra, as all men know," Tutu continued. "It is inconceivable that Amun-Ra and Horus would allow the crook and flail to fall into the hands of an imposter. Thus, if Inaros were to exhibit the insignia, it could only mean that the Gods had selected Inaros to represent them on earth." The embalmer shrugged. "It would not be the first time that a dynasty has changed."

Well, that was one way of looking at it.

"You would be happy, Tutu, if this were to pass?" Djanet asked.

"Anything would be better than what we have now," he said fervently. "I cannot credit that a Persian king is the living Horus. The insult to Egypt is great."

"Know, then, that we sought the advice of the General to present the crook and flail to Inaros," Djanet said. "He told us there was someone who might be able to help us, that he would make enquiries. That was yesterday. Today, he is dead. In between, the only person he visited was you, Tutu."

"The General agreed to assist you?" Tutu asked.

"He did. I fear that might be why he was killed."

"The General was such a man as to recognize the chosen of Horus," Tutu muttered, half to himself. He added politely, "May I ask you to refresh yourselves while I think upon this matter?" He clapped his hands. More food was brought.

We ate in silence, while Tutu considered whether he would help us.

There was a knock upon the front door. A man entered. He went straight to Tutu and handed him a piece of papyrus, then bowed and exited the way he came. Tutu read the letter with raised eyebrows.

Tutu turned to me. "You said your name is Nicolaos?"

"That's right."

"Are you Nicolaos, son of Sophroniscus?"

"Yes." How did he know my father's name?

"I have just received a message about you."

Uh oh.

Tutu held up the papyrus. "This is an official notice from the Public Service. It warns that you are a dangerous seditionist who works against Egypt. Anyone who gives you aid will never again receive business from the government."

I groaned. The bureaucrats had stopped me at the last moment.

Tutu tore the official notice into little pieces.

"What do you want to know?" he asked.

Into the otherwise stunned silence, Maxyates said, "You're ignoring a government directive?"

"I certainly am. I don't know who you people really are, I'm not sure I believe you work for Inaros, but the Public Service hates you, and that's good enough for me."

"But they're your biggest customers!"

"Did I not already explain what boors they are? How lacking in nobility? Do you not know the bureaucrats work for the Persian against the Egyptian?"

"We want to know what the General said to you," I told the embalmer. "Most of all, we want to know where to find the crook and flail. The General said he didn't know where they are."

The youths returned. They carried the Blind General between them. Tutu watched them pass by and disappear through the doorway to the embalming room. He suppressed a sob. Then he said, "Bide a moment." He spoke in such a commanding voice that we all stood still while Tutu paced back and forth with his head in his hands.

He walked over to a corner where he stood before a statue of the jackal-headed god Horus. Then the embalmer stepped sideways to a statue of Amun-Ra, where he remained for some time with his hands clasped like a supplicant. Herodotus, Diotima, Djanet, Max and I watched this with some astonishment, and sidelong glances at each other.

Tutu returned to us.

"I find that to act honorably to one man, I must break a vow to another."

We waited.

"You wanted to know what my friend the General came here to say."

"Yes."

"He didn't come to say anything. He came here to *ask* me something. The General told you the truth when he said he did not know where the crook and flail were. He wanted to know if I could tell him."

"I suppose you don't know either," Herodotus said.

"On the contrary," Tutu said calmly.

"What!"

"The crook and flail are in Psamtik's sarcophagus."

"How do you know that?"

"Because I put them there."

THE MUMMY'S CURSE

"It was the perfect hiding place," Tutu said. "After the Persians delivered Psamtik's body, my family got to work very quickly. Fortunately, we had been the embalmers for Psamtik's father, the Pharaoh before him, who had died not two years before. There are special rituals that attend only to the burial of a Pharaoh, you see."

"So it was entirely predictable that the Persians would come to you," Herodotus said.

Tutu nodded. "We were the natural choice. Perhaps the *only* choice. What other family could embalm a Pharaoh with the speed the Persians demanded? We were the only House with everything still set up from the previous job."

"Go on."

"A few nights later, there was a knock on the door. My father opened it personally to reveal a blind man, with a rag wrapped about his eyes, led by a child."

"The Blind General."

"He was a young man then, and I was younger still. Yes, we have known each other that long." Tutu wiped away a tear. "He knew we had Psamtik. The General carried a parcel, wrapped in rags. It looked like any rubbish that a beggar might carry, but within were the crook and flail of Egypt. He said that he had been in the palace where Psamtik had been kept prisoner. The General had taken the crook and flail when Psamtik was removed to be executed. He knew that sooner or later the Persians would notice the insignia gone, and then they would search him. He wanted my father to hide the insignia."

"Which your father did," Herodotus said.

"Not quite. The General left before my father could decide what to do with them. The General didn't want to know where the crook and flail went, so he could never be forced to reveal the location."

Djanet nodded. "That was sensible."

"Then my father said these words to me. You must understand that he was a very wise man. He said, 'Tutu, I am old, and you are young. When the day comes that a new Pharaoh arises, I will surely rest in the Field of Reeds, but you, my son, might still be here to advise him where he might find the crook and flail. Take the insignia of the Pharaohs, and hide them where you think best, but never tell me what you have done with them, nor tell any other person, until you think the time is right.' "

"What did you do?"

"I buried them, for the months that my father embalmed Psamtik. I spent the next three months assisting him, and helping the carpenters build the sarcophagus. Eventually my father declared the body ready to go in the sarcophagus. In fact he grumbled that much more time was needed, but the Persians had told him to be ready three days hence. That night I placed the crook and flail within."

"Surely the Persians would look inside," I protested. "They'd see the crook and flail."

Maxyates added, "Your father could not fail to see them when he placed the body."

"You are both wrong. I artificed a cunning hollow in the base of the sarcophagus, covered by a solid-looking board, only accessible from inside."

"Clever!"

"Thank you. My father did not see it when we placed the body, or if he did, he made no comment. As I said, he was a wise man. The Persians would not see a thing.

Once the body was in, you would have to lift it from its coffin to have any chance of seeing the secret compartment, and even then they would have to know what to look for. I thought this unlikely."

"You were right, and this is wonderful news," I said warmly. "Tutu, you have succeeded beyond all expectation. No one but you has had the faintest clue where to find the crook and flail. But now is the time for the Pharaoh's insignia to return to the world."

"I think you may be right." Tutu nodded.

"Then tell us, where do we find Psamtik's coffin?"

"I can't be certain," the embalmer said.

I groaned. "You don't *know*?"

"I'm sorry."

"You must know *something*," Herodotus said.

Tutu said, with obvious reluctance, "I suspect, but I do not like to say what might not be true. You understand this?"

Herodotus nodded. "That is very natural and honorable."

"Then hear my thoughts. A few days after Pharaoh Psamtik was delivered to our House, it was announced that the Persian King was to depart Memphis. He was to visit the Palace at Saïs."

239

"Saïs?" Diotima asked.

"It is a city in the Land of Papyrus, what you people call the Delta. This was significant."

"Why?"

"Because Psamtik's father, the Pharaoh before him, who was called Amasis, was buried there. Of this I am certain. My family had embalmed Amasis a mere two years before."

"Go on."

"An enormous train of men, women and carts full of luggage accompanied the King. The baggage train was so long, they required an entire day merely to drive out of the city. We realized that the Great King did not intend to return. This proved to be true. From Saïs he went back to his own country. We were happy to be rid of him. But from Saïs we heard stories that upset my father a great deal."

"Concerning the Pharaohs?" Herodotus asked.

"I told you that Amasis, the father of Psamtik, was entombed at Saïs. The Persian King had the body of the old Pharaoh removed from his House of Eternity. The body of Amasis was brutalized in ways that I will not mention. His ka and his ba were scattered to the winds. The ka-priest whose

240

job it was to maintain the Pharaoh's final resting place was executed. Finally the mummy was burnt to cinders."

"Dear Gods, why do such things to a dead man?" I said.

Tutu shrugged. "Who can understand the mind of a Persian? You must know that to destroy a body by fire is the worst fate that can befall an Egyptian. The Persian had done everything in his power to offend Egypt."

Tutu was a man in his old age, and this had happened in his youth, but even so he wept at the memory.

"My father was devastated. He it was who had prepared Amasis for the Field of Reeds, and now all was ashes."

"They didn't cremate Psamtik too, did they?" I asked. That would be disaster for us.

Tutu shook his head. "Psamtik lay in our House. He was with us long after the Persian King departed Egypt. In fact, he lay with us long after the sarcophagus was supposed to be collected. We had done the best we could in the allocated time, all was prepared. A month passed, but still nothing happened. My father was reluctant to remind the authorities, after what had happened to Amasis."

241

"Understandable."

"Then, one day, some priests came to the door. They were very polite when they spoke to my father. The priests made an extraordinary request. They said openly that they had no authority, but they asked for the body of Psamtik. They said they would treat him with dignity."

"What did your father do?"

"He gave them the body!"

"Who were these priests?"

"They said they came from the temple at Siwa."

The Blind General had mentioned Siwa. When we first met him, the General had said he was no oracle like the one at Siwa. I asked Tutu about this, but surprisingly it was Maxyates who answered.

"The oracle at Siwa is the most famous in Africa, a very holy place dedicated to the god Amun," he said. "I have been to Siwa many times, as it is a place of learning. The temple was rebuilt in the days of the Pharaoh Amasis. He sent them much gold and resources and workmen to make the temple great."

Tutu nodded. "It was this that persuaded my father. The priests of Amun are well disposed to Amasis. When they heard what had happened to their benefactor, they were determined to save the son."

"That makes sense."

"The priests carried away Psamtik in the dead of night. I never saw that sarcophagus again. Then another strange thing happened."

"What was it?"

"Four months later, three Persian soldiers came to our House, a sergeant and two soldiers. The sergeant said he had been sent to collect the body of Psamtik."

"That must have been awkward."

"This was four months after the priests had taken the body; it was *five* months, mind you, after the time the Persians said they would be back."

Herodotus chuckled. "Administrative error. It happens all the time. What did your father do?"

"He lied to them. He said other soldiers had come at the appointed time, five months before, and that these other soldiers had taken away the sarcophagus. The sergeant looked cross and went away. The soldiers never bothered us again."

On a sudden impulse, Herodotus clasped Tutu's hands and said, "Sir, you may have done Egypt a greater service today than any in your past. I thank you."

Tutu smiled thinly. "Your words are kind.

I must hope. But I am not hopeful. Things were better in the days of our forebears."

"You seem to prefer the past," Diotima said gently. "If you don't like the way things are done these days, should you not plan for a better future?"

Tutu looked at Diotima with something akin to horror. "Young lady, I am an embalmer. An embalmer works only with that which has passed. The future and the people who live in it will be some other embalmer's problem."

"Oh. I see," said Diotima, somewhat nonplussed.

"There is something else you must know," Tutu spoke hesitantly.

"Go on."

"When the work was complete I placed two scrolls inside the sarcophagus. The first was the Book of the Dead."

"Which is?"

"Our sacred religious text. It contains instructions to the deceased on how to pass the various tests that will confront him on his journey to the Afterlife. It's a standard inclusion in every proper burial," Tutu said. "However, the second scroll was specific for Psamtik. It was a long list of curses that will befall whoever opens the Pharaoh's sarcophagus."

"What sort of curses?" Herodotus was making rapid notes.

"In brief, the man who opens that grave will suffer nothing but disaster for the rest of his life, and when he dies, his soul will go straight to the Devourer. Personally I would not want to be the one who opened that sarcophagus. I tell you this because whichever of you volunteers to open it will suffer these things. I hope your loyalty to Inaros is very great."

I gulped. My loyalty to Inaros was close to non-existent. I wasn't sure I believed in the Egyptian gods, but no man willingly takes on a curse.

Tutu's words cast a pall over the group. We all wondered who would be the one to sacrifice himself — or herself — for the good of Egypt. There were no volunteers.

THE SPARTA CONTRACT

We left the House of Tutu with much clasping of hands, kind words from the embalmer and our heads spinning from what he had told us.

"We must assume that Tutu's idea is correct," Herodotus said. "The sarcophagus containing the crook and flail is at Siwa."

"Tutu is almost certainly correct," Djanet said. "If Psamtik had been buried or cremated in Memphis, I would know it."

This dogmatic statement caused us all to look at her askance.

"I made enquiries once, long ago," Djanet explained. "Nobody could tell me a thing, not even the beggars, and they know everything that goes on in this city. Psamtik wasn't buried in Memphis. Even a quiet funeral in the palace grounds would have been impossible to cover up; a soldier or a servant would be bound to talk."

"So if it isn't in Memphis, it must be at

Siwa." I said. "That makes sense."

"Then that's where we're going," Herodotus said. "Max, what else can you tell us about Siwa?"

"It is an oasis," Maxyates said. "In the Egyptian tongue they call it the Field of Trees. Siwa lies *very* far to the west. So far west in fact that one must cross the desert. Siwa is in Libya, not Egypt."

I laughed. "If Inaros finds out the crook and flail have been in his own homeland all this time, he's going to kick himself."

"And the oracle?" Herodotus prompted.

"It is most ancient and of the greatest holiness," said Maxyates solemnly. "The Oracle at Siwa is like . . ." He thought for a moment. "You Hellenes have your Oracle of Delphi. Siwa is like that for the Egyptians and Libyans."

"Then it is very important indeed," said Herodotus.

"Yes."

The matter seemed to be settled. I felt like a weight had been dropped from my back. We had a plan, and it took us out of Memphis. The whole party felt the same way; the mood became lighter.

Being in the southern part of the city meant we were close to temples that Herodotus was desperate to see. One of these was impossible to miss: a colossal statue of an ancient Pharaoh. Some fellow I'd never heard of, named Ramses. Like all Egyptian statues, the figure stood rigidly upright. Why couldn't these Egyptians do a proper statue, like we Hellenes? But I had to give them credit for sheer size. This Ramses stood taller than any building in Athens. Standing at his feet, I had to look straight up to see his face.

"What did he do?" I asked, for surely anyone with a statue this big must be important.

"You've never heard of Ramses?" said Djanet, in shock. "What do they teach you Hellenes?"

"Mostly to quote from Homer," I said.

Djanet sniffed.

"Ramses was the greatest ruler who ever lived," Maxyates said.

"I thought that was King Menelaus, or Priam?" I said. "That's what Homer says."

"Ramses was greater than both," Maxyates explained. "He was the greatest. At his mausoleum there is an inscription that says: *I am Osymandyas* — that was another name for Ramses — *I am Osymandyas, the king of kings. If you would know how great I am, then excel me in my works.*"

"Hmmpf," I said. "That's just saying, if

you think you can do better than me, then let's see it. Typical boasting." Diotima quietly kicked me in the shins. This was her gentle way of reminding me to be polite to our hosts. Seeking to make amends, I added, "Well, I'm sure he was greater than our current crop of leaders. I can't imagine anyone saying that about Pericles."

We walked on to the gates of the Temple of Ptah. Herodotus wanted to go in. I said I wasn't keen. All about the entrance were cats, too many cats to count. Every man and woman who passed through treated the cats with deference, to the point that they would walk around the felines to avoid disturbing them. The cats were a bad sign. The Tjaty had said that Ptah was the husband of Bast. There was too much chance I'd run into a bureaucrat in the temple of Ptah, maybe even a Head of Department.

Herodotus said stubbornly, "I didn't come to Egypt to miss anything."

A direct order from my employer was going to be hard to resist. But I would try. I opened my mouth to argue.

"May I make a suggestion?" Maxyates interrupted. "I will escort Herodotus to the temple. I know it well enough. You and Diotima can make your way back to our lodgings."

"Good thinking, Max."

The Trojan was a fine peacemaker.

Djanet said she had her own arrangements to make. If we were to depart Memphis on our quest for the crook and flail, then first she must see to some business matters she had in progress. Nobody was brave enough to ask what business she meant. The singer from Memphis was also an agent for a rebel prince, and the gods only knew what other dubious enterprises she was involved in.

Djanet went her own way.

Several cats lounged upon the top of the surrounding wall of the temple. They looked down on the visitors below them with an air of superiority. One of these felines was pure white. I had a feeling I'd seen it before. The white cat stared at me with a knowing look. I shuddered. I grabbed Diotima's arm to drag her away.

As I did, she grabbed my arm back. "Nico, over there!"

I looked where she indicated with her eyes. There was a man walking out of the grounds of the Temple of Ptah. At first glance the man was a Persian soldier. He wore the flowing brightly checkered tunic with its enormous sleeves, the hat with gold braid and no brim, and the leather shoes with curled-up toes. Typical Persian infantry kit. Anyone would take him for one of the soldiers stationed here. But on his back, instead of the bow and quiver of a typical soldier, there was hung a crossbow and a packet of shorter bolts.

There couldn't be two such weapons in Memphis, could there? Barzanes had made it clear enough that access to the crossbow was restricted.

No, it had to be Markos.

He hadn't seen us. Markos turned east, in the direction of the White Fort.

"What do we do?" Diotima asked.

"We follow him," I said.

He retreated into the distance. Diotima crossed the road, in case he turned that way, and so that we wouldn't be recognized as a pair.

I kept my eyes firmly locked on the crossbow and walked after Markos.

As I walked, I worried. What had Markos been doing at the temple? Had he been visiting the same bureaucrats who had captured me? Had they captured him, too, and then released him as they had me? Why was he dressed as a Persian?

Markos's route took him to the street on which lay the main gate to the White Fort. My heart constricted. For a moment I thought he would turn in. That would have been a development that made me pack up and run for home. But instead he walked past. The Spartan assassin took no notice of the guards who stood their duty, nor did they pay any attention to him.

It was remarkable how well Markos blended into the background, especially with the crowds of Egyptians all around him. He pushed them out of the way and swore at them in good Persian. I spoke the language myself and admired his accent, which was better than mine.

Markos turned a corner, going left. I hurried to follow. Diotima cut through a back alley. I reached the new street just in time to see him turn right. Diotima was closer than me. She made the turn.

I hurried to catch up. As I rounded the busy corner I ran smack bang into my wife.

"Oof!"

I caught her as she stumbled forward.

"What kept you?" she complained.

"Well, he turned your way. What are you doing here?"

"He stopped. He's in that tavern over there." Diotima nodded in the direction of a seedy-looking building. In fact, everything looked seedy. Markos's path had taken us to the docklands. Not the respectable part where commercial river boats came and went — this street ended in a pile of dingy fishing craft, dirty barges and dodgy-looking Egyptians who called out that their moldy row boats were for hire. I wouldn't have got in one unless I wanted to catch a disease. Other men with shifty eyes lined the street. They were on the lookout for an opportunity, and I was determined not to be it.

This was a strange place for Markos to come. He had better taste than this.

"That tavern had a large window fronting onto the street," I said.

"Most do," Diotima replied.

"I wonder what he's doing in there?" I asked.

"Nico!" Diotima said, urgently and as quietly as she could. But she was too late. I was already edging my way forward.

Though it was bright in the street and dark within the tavern, the sunlight shone through well enough that I could see Markos within. He sat at a table, with his back to a wall. He was drinking.

"Hey, mister! You and the lady friend, you are from Athens, yes?"

I looked down. A boy stood there. He had a runny nose.

"You from Athens?" he repeated. He spoke Greek with an atrocious accent, but I understood him well enough.

"I'm from Athens," I said.

"Got a message for you," the boy said. "The man inside says, wouldn't you be more comfortable if you sat with him?" The boy spoke quickly, as if repeating his lessons. Then he added. "The man paid me to say that!"

I sighed. My wife, who had joined me, scowled. "Well, we may as well go in," she said. "We can't look any more stupid than I already feel."

Markos had already ordered for us. Three cups sat upon the table before him. The chairs were arranged so that Diotima's and my backs would be to the door. I felt nervous, but I sat. Then I immediately looked behind me.

"Well done, Nico," Markos said. Irony had always been one of his strengths.

"When did you spot us trailing you?" I asked.

"Shortly before you spotted me. I had a hard time getting you to notice me. I suppose it was the Persian uniform."

Somehow that news almost made me feel better, even though it was even more embarrassing. It was also very disturbing to hear that Markos had deliberately led us to this place. The thought made me look over my shoulder once again.

Markos saw my reaction and laughed. Angry, I turned my chair sideways so that I could both talk to the Spartan and watch what happened behind us.

"You led us here for a reason," Diotima said.

"My last conversation with Nico was constrained by the presence of Barzanes," Markos said. "I was hoping for something a little more private."

"You could have simply walked up to us," Diotima said coldly. Markos had once made a serious offer to marry Diotima. She had never forgiven him.

"In this city?" Markos arched an eyebrow. "Dear Diotima, you're not using those brains that Nico keeps telling me you've got. This city belongs to the Persians, or hadn't you noticed?"

"So?" Diotima said.

"So if you were Barzanes, what would you do? Scatter informers across the city, maybe? Of course you would. So would I."

Diotima nodded.

That was the annoying thing about Markos. Even when he was your mortal enemy, what he had to say made sense.

"The Persian uniform's very fetching," I said. For Markos did indeed look good in the flowing robes of a Persian infantryman.

"But I fear you're in the wrong army. Is there a reason for that?"

"It's not a fashion statement," Markos said. "I noticed no one ever stops to question a soldier. Not even the other soldiers. It makes it easier too to carry my toy." He patted the crossbow as if it were a favorite pet.

"How did you come by that thing? It's not Spartan, is it?" I asked. After what Barzanes had told me, I was curious to hear the Spartan's side of the story.

"I'm told it's a *gastraphetes.*"

"A tummy shooter?" Diotima said derisively. She smiled.

"Yes, I laughed too, my dear Diotima," Markos said. "Until I saw it in use. Then I had to have one."

"Where did you see it?" I pressed. "Where did it come from?"

Markos smiled. "I'm . . . how shall I put this? I'm not at liberty to say."

I said, "You probably got it from that Persian ambassador. The one who visited Sparta. What was his name? Oh yes, Megabazos."

Markos looked astonished. "How do you know about that?" he demanded.

It was my turn to smile. "I'm . . . how shall I put this? I'm not at liberty to say."

"All right," Markos grumbled. "We both have our sources." He grimaced and took another deep drink. He emptied the cup, wiped his mouth with the back of his hand, and called for another. The waiting girl brought a cup at once. She glanced at the cups in front of Diotima and me, saw that they were full, and retreated back to the bar.

Markos said, "This beer doesn't taste anything like wine, but it grows on you."

"Personally, I prefer wine," I said.

"Me too," he admitted. "But I'll take beer in a pinch. I may as well tell you the story about the gastraphetes. It's relevant to what we need to talk about, and you seem to know most of it anyway."

"Go on."

"You're right. Sparta had a visitor from Persia. He wanted us to attack you. Brought a whole boat load of gold with him. For our expenses, you understand. The elders took the money," Markos admitted.

Admiral Charitimedes had told me the same thing, but until now I hadn't fully believed it. The 300 had died to the last man to hold the pass at Thermopylae. Now, only twenty-three years later, their sons were taking money from the Persians to attack their former ally Athens.

I said what I thought, not normally a good

policy between agents, but I couldn't help it. "This is the worst thing I have ever heard."

"Oh, come now Nico," Markos protested. "It was business."

"I mean it, Markos," I said. "I've seen men impaled, I've seen a child torn apart, I've seen crimes that would sicken anyone. But I never thought I would see Spartans hire themselves out to the enemy for money."

"Well, there's no point blaming *me*. I don't run Sparta," Markos said. "If I ever rise that high, I'll be sure to take your advice. Will that satisfy you?"

I grunted.

"Markos, tell me something," said Diotima. "Surely King Pleistarchus would never have allowed this deal with Persia."

King Pleistarchus was the son of Leonidas, who had led the 300. We had met the Spartan king and Gorgo, the dowager queen, at the last Olympics. Though the Spartan king had technically been our enemy, I had liked him very much. Diotima and Gorgo had become friends.

"Then you haven't heard," Markos said. "Pleistarchus is dead."

In the silence that followed, Markos said, "Don't look at me like that. *I* didn't kill him."

Pleistarchus had been in the prime of life. "How did it happen?" I asked.

"It was a battle." Markos shrugged. "I don't know any more. At the time I was in prison, you might recall, on the king's orders."

I tried to think of a way Markos could have done it, but I had to concede that not even he could exterminate a king while chained in prison.

"What of Queen Gorgo?" Diotima asked.

"She's dead too," Markos said. "Old age or disease. I never asked."

Tears welled in Diotima's eyes. She dabbed at them with the sleeve of her dress.

This news explained a lot. With both Gorgo and Pleistarchus in Hades, the last moderating influences in Sparta were gone. All that was left were the hawks who were ready to fight Athens, and if the Persians paid them to do it, then all the better.

Markos went on. "As I was saying, before you decided to rant, the ambassador from Persia brought this crossbow with him. I think he meant it as a present for our leaders, but as it turned out, there was another use for it. One I think you'll approve of, Nico."

"I'm listening."

"As part of the deal for the gold, the

Spartan leadership offered my services as an agent for Persia in Egypt."

"Aha," I said. Markos had to be the Hellene agent that Pericles had warned me of, so long ago in Athens. "You know, for a while there I thought Herodotus must be the Persian agent. Obviously it was you."

"The man from Halicarnassus?" Markos said. "Well, there is his obvious family connection to Persia. Your assumption wasn't so unreasonable."

"What family connection?" I asked. Then I realized what Markos meant. "Oh, you mean that he comes from a Persian-ruled city. Many men born in Ionia support Athens against Persia, you know. Herodotus supports Athens."

Markos waved his hand dismissively. "It doesn't matter. What *does* matter is that in addition to hiring Sparta to attack Athens, Megabazos also made a semi-private offer to me, with the knowledge and permission of our leaders, of course."

"Of course." There was no such thing as independent action among the Spartans.

"It made sense for everyone," he said. "After all, I was firmly ensconced in prison, as all men knew. From Sparta's point of view they could say I had escaped and was now working as a private agent for Persia.

You see?"

"If you were caught, you were deniable."

"Exactly. For my part, the deal got me out of jail. I was hardly going to say no."

"I understand," I said, and I *did* understand. No matter how morally dubious Markos's position might be, it was only rational of him to prefer this assignment to incarceration in a Spartan prison.

"There was only one problem," Markos continued. "The Persians didn't want another agent in Persia. They already had their own very good man on the spot."

"Barzanes," I said.

"Barzanes," Markos agreed.

"Then the deal fell through," Diotima said.

"Not quite," Markos told her. "Megabazos the Ambassador was intrigued when he heard about me. He asked to see me. I was brought before him. We had a lovely chat."

"I can imagine."

"This Megabazos has a mortal enemy in the Persian court. Would you like to guess who it is?"

I didn't have to guess. I already knew the answer.

"Megabazos hates Barzanes," I said. "Barzanes accused Megabazos of corruption before the Great King. The Great King

261

refused to condemn Megabazos because he's too useful."

Markos raised an eyebrow. "Is that the reason? I asked, but my client wasn't inclined to tell me why he wanted Barzanes dead."

"Your *client*?" Diotima repeated.

"Megabazos decided that although Persia didn't need an assassin in Egypt, he had a personal need."

Diotima said, "Are you telling us that one high ranking Persian has commissioned a Spartan to assassinate another high ranking Persian?"

"That's about the size of it." Markos confirmed.

"Wouldn't their king be upset, if one of his senior men killed another?"

"I asked the same question," Markos said. "You can imagine I had a personal interest in the answer."

"Which was?"

"That this sort of infighting happens all the time, that the Great King tolerates a certain amount — if the nobility are plotting against each other, then they're not plotting against *him,* you see — but that if some act is too public then the Great King will have no choice but to take notice. You can see why the deniability factor is important to Sparta."

"Dear Gods!" I said. "We three only just swore an oath not to attack each other!"

"I think of it as a tactical ruse," Markos replied with apparent sincerity. "When the blow comes, Barzanes won't be expecting it."

"Is that how you excuse being an oath-breaker?" I asked.

"Oh, come now, Nico," Markos chided, as if I were a slow child. "How often do cities swear eternal friendship, then attack each other a year later?"

"That's different," I said.

"How? Aren't we three representing our cities? I'm acting for Sparta, you represent Athens, and Barzanes is the very essence of Persia. Don't tell me Athenians are above such tricks. When was the last time Athens attacked a city merely because it was convenient?"

"Er . . ." That was a question I didn't want to answer. I was well aware that under Pericles, Athens had followed a rather aggressive foreign policy.

"Let me help you," Markos said. "When Aegina made a treaty with Sparta last year, you Athenians attacked them merely because you didn't like the idea of our alliance."

"There was a minor incident," I conceded.

"You almost wiped them out!"

"All right, it was a major incident."

"Aegina will probably never be the same again," Markos said. "So if I trick a Persian, don't go looking for any moral high ground. You won't find it."

"That was Athens, not me," I protested.

"Didn't we just agree that we represent our cities?"

He had me there.

"There's no point arguing about this," I said. "I take it Megabazos gave you the crossbow to kill Barzanes."

"I'm sure you can see why. It's deadly at short range."

I could see where that would appeal to Markos.

"It's a strange weapon," I said.

"It took me a while to get the hang of using it," he said.

"How did you test it?" I asked.

Markos shrugged. "Sparta had a few sick slaves surplus to requirements."

I should have guessed. Diotima looked disgusted. This was typical Spartan thinking. In Athens that would have been called murder, even if the victim was a slave.

"How is it at a distance?" I asked. If I ever again had to run from Markos, I wanted to know how secure my back should feel.

"Wildly inaccurate past twenty paces," Markos admitted. "But that's not the point. In my weakened state, the crossbow was the perfect weapon." He patted it fondly, like a favored dog. "My knife work used to be the best," he said immodestly. "But in the first months after they released me, I couldn't have killed a child."

I was afraid to ask how he knew that.

"So you see, Nico, we're not in conflict here," Markos said.

"Except you tried to kill us every step of the way here," I pointed out.

Markos shrugged. "That was a personal matter. Now that we're all in Egypt, you're beyond my reach. Or rather, to kill you now would interfere with my real mission. We can help each other."

"How?" I asked dubiously. Now that I knew what he was about, I was worried to be seen in Markos's company. Barzanes obviously had no idea that he was a target, else he would have killed Markos on the spot when they first met. When Barzanes learned of this plot and that I had spent time with Markos, he would assume I was part of the conspiracy. That was the last thing I needed.

"That's why I led you here," Markos aid.

"I need you to help me kill Barzanes."

"No." That was an easy decision.

"I thought you might say that." Markos waved. The bar girl returned with another drink for him.

"Should you be drinking that much?" I asked.

"Yes, I should," Markos said seriously. He pulled back the sleeves of his tunic, to reveal the ugly white scars that we'd seen before. "These hurt," he said. "They never really stop bleeding. Just when I think they're healed, there's another break, and more blood."

To my alarmed look he chuckled. "Not enough blood to kill me. You're not going to be that lucky, my friend."

Markos seemed a changed man from when I had met him last. I supposed three years in a Spartan prison could do that to you.

Markos shrugged. "It could have been worse. They might have put me back in boarding school."

"Very funny."

"Funny indeed, but I mean it. Seriously." Markos spoke earnestly. Then he drained half the next mug of beer.

All of a sudden I realized he was somewhat drunk — he had been hiding it well.

"You want to know what it's like to grow up in Sparta?" Markos said.

"I know," I said. "The men starve the boys, to teach you field craft and how to deal with adversity. If you want to eat enough to live, then you have to steal the food."

"Then they beat us if we were caught," Markos said. "The weak boys die. The fathers don't care. They treat it like battlefield casualties. A Spartan boy's at war from the moment they take him from his mother."

"So that when you face a real battle, it will seem easy," I said. "The other cities admire Spartan discipline. I thought you were happy with this, Markos. They used to call you the best of the best."

"I was the best. I still am." He shrugged. "I can't complain. I was one of the survivors. But I saw my fair share of dead children being carried from the boys' barracks. It was like culling animals on a farm."

"Tough childhood," I said.

"If you can call it that. The funny thing was, the boys were even harder on themselves. They beat each other up. The elders expect a certain amount of 'rough play,' as they call it. What I called it was a constant struggle to not be the guy on the receiving end. It was all about having friends, you see. Allies. It never much worked for me though. I never was any good at making friends. I was always the loner. I was the target more times than I want to remember. I can't tell you how often I went broken and bruised. Then my father or our mess leader would beat me again, as punishment for losing."

"You found an answer," I said.

"Yeah. I told jokes. Nobody ever hits the funny man. I got *really* good at making people laugh."

I'd always admired Markos's sense of humor, even when he was trying to kill me.

Markos paused. "That worked until we were adolescents. Then it got serious. You know we Spartans are allocated to a mess — like a platoon, a fighting unit — very early in our lives?"

"Yes."

"Once you're allocated, that's it, you can never change. There's a lot of social status in your mess. Some are better than others. Everyone's desperate to be in the best. The competition is like nothing you Athenians ever experience. Then the hazing gets worse, deliberately worse, because the worse you can make your fellows look, the less likely they are to beat you for votes to a good mess. You understand?"

"Yes." I could imagine.

"Being the funny guy didn't matter any-more. This was serious stuff and, well, as I grew it turned out I was pretty handy with a blade. Just natural aptitude, I guess. My reflexes were way beyond the other boys. The first day they taught us knife fighting, I disarmed our teacher."

"That would be good then?"

"Not if you want to live long enough to see twenty!"

"Oh."

"While I lived, I was a competitor for the very best messes. Men who weren't as quick as me but whose fathers had more influence saw me as a threat. But it's funny, you know. Telling jokes and killing people has become my life. If I wasn't an assassin, I wouldn't mind being a comic."

"You must be joking," I said.

Markos grinned. "Yes, precisely. I *must* be joking. I could be one of those actor fellows you Athenians have, traveling from place to place, making people laugh."

I tried to imagine Markos as a stand-up comic, and surprisingly, it wasn't too dif-ficult to do. Somehow in my mind's eye I could see Markos performing prat-falls and making people laugh with pig's bladders and farting sounds.

"It's not too late, you know," I said earnestly. Because I would like nothing better than to have Markos out of my life. Or at least, not trying to kill me.

"It is too late," he said quietly. "Sparta doesn't have comics."

"You could leave?"

"When was the last time you heard of a Spartan leaving Sparta?" Markos said. "Besides, do you seriously think Athens would have me?"

It was a fair question, and deserved a fair answer.

"Never," I told him.

"There you are then. I couldn't go to a lesser city, could I?"

"No, certainly not," I agreed. Markos was like me, we both wanted to serve the very best. In Hellas, that meant Sparta or Athens. Every other city was an also-ran.

"How about you look the other way while I kill him?" Markos said.

"What?"

"Barzanes."

I remained silent.

"Nico, think for a moment. Athens would like nothing better than Barzanes removed, right?"

Markos was right, but there was a problem.

"It would start a war," I said.

"You mean, like the war we're not having now?" he pointed out.

"It would start a *worse* war."

"Not if I kill him," Markos said. "Then it's not your fault. All you have to do is look the other way."

This was the Markos of old. The one who could make any plan that helped him seem reasonable.

The problem was, the plan *was* reasonable. How could removing Barzanes not help Athens? The man was worth half an army to the Persians.

"All I ask is that you look the other way, if it comes to a fight."

Markos was making sense. What he proposed in essence was an alliance between Sparta and Athens against Persia. There was plenty of precedent for that. What's more, I knew that Barzanes was the man most likely to stop me in my quest for the crook and flail. But what Markos proposed was also dead against the oath that the three of us had sworn. How could I go against my word?

I knew what Pericles would say. Pericles never let ethics get in the way of a good

271

decision. He would make his choice based purely on one single criterion. It was a phrase he used so often I thought he must mutter it in his sleep. *For the good of Athens.* Pericles would do whatever he did for the good of Athens.

On the other hand, killing the Eyes and Ears of the King might possibly annoy the King. Ever since the Persian invasion in my father's time, Athens and Persia had been locked in a low-level conflict. We fought each other in proxy wars, like this one in Egypt. Neither side dared attack the other directly. If Barzanes died at the hand of a Hellene, it might trigger Artaxerxes to assemble his armies once again. I didn't like that thought at all.

Here was I, a humble agent, forced to make a decision that might mean war or peace across the civilized world. I didn't know which decision meant war, and which meant peace.

"What do you say, Nico?" Markos asked. He looked me square in the face with his most sincere expression.

I didn't dare open my mouth. I knew my voice would squeak if I tried to speak. Instead, I looked away.

Markos got the message.

"Then it's a deal?" he persisted.

I took a deep breath. "It's a deal."

He put a hand on my shoulder. "Thanks, Nico. It's good to know Sparta and Athens can still work together against Persia."

Markos stood to leave.

"Wait, Markos," I said. "There's one more thing."

He leaned over to hear me. I could smell the beer on his breath. "What?"

"This."

I slugged him. Hard. But from a sitting position. I didn't know if I could knock out the Spartan assassin with a single blow, but I gave it my best. Perhaps his recent weakness and the beer made it easier. His eyes rolled up and he fell back like a rag doll.

The other patrons of the tavern swiftly looked our way. But when they saw that it was a simple punch up they went back to their own business. It was that kind of place.

I eased Markos back into his seat, made sure he could breathe, then pulled the crossbow from his warm and unresisting hands.

"Thanks, Markos," I said to his unconscious form. As an afterthought I relieved him of his crossbow bolts.

Diotima sprinkled our cups of beer liberally down his front, and pushed an empty cup into his right hand. Anyone who came across him would think he was sleeping off a drunk.

There was a reason for my perfidy. I now had the upper hand on every important mission that I had undertaken. In accordance with my agreement with Barzanes, I had relieved Markos of the crossbow. I had never promised that I would give it back to Barzanes. Instead I would take it back to Athens. If Spartans armed with crossbows could only be bad for Athens, then Athenians armed with crossbows could only be good. We Athenians would never again need to fear a Spartan army.

In accordance with my agreement with Markos — the one I had concluded with him just before I knocked him out — I had left him alive and free to assassinate Barzanes, whose elimination could only benefit Athens. Markos would have to do it without his favorite weapon, but I had never promised I'd make it easy for him.

I could even argue that by taking the crossbow but leaving Markos alive, I had fulfilled the non-aggression oath that the three of us had sworn together in the inn beside the White Fort.

Best of all, my party had discovered the location of the crook and flail. Soon we'd be on our way to retrieve the items, thus making both Inaros and Pericles happy.

All in all, I felt very pleased with myself.

This feeling lasted as long as it took us to return to the inn.

FIRE IN THE NIGHT

Djanet was standing at the door of our inn, despite the very late time of night. I had thought everyone would be asleep.

"What is it?" Diotima asked. She sounded worried.

Djanet pointed. A fire blazed above Memphis.

"Those flames are to the south of us," she said.

It could have been any building in the south that burned. There were hundreds of them. But that was the direction of the House of Tutu. I had a bad feeling.

Word spread quickly. Fire is the most dangerous threat to any city, anywhere. In Egypt where the sun turned the wood to dry kindle it would be even greater. Men streamed past us, all heading to the source of the flames.

Herodotus and Max came downstairs. They'd been woken by the noise of the crowd. We joined the throng heading south.

It was as we all feared. The House of Tutu blazed. We stood in the street and watched helplessly. Locals who knew the area better were quickly forming a chain to pass buckets of water. I wondered where they were getting it from, until I realized that this was not Athens without a river. This was Memphis, where the enormous Nile flowed by.

The men at the head of the chain began to throw water on the fire. I had never seen anything so futile. They could no more put out that blaze with buckets than I could drink dry the Nile.

The Egyptians thought so too. They began to tear down the adjoining houses, to the wails and imploring screams of the owners. The firebreak would save the rest of the city.

"How can it burn so hot?" Djanet said. She had to speak loudly over the noise of the burning house.

"Do you recall all the amphorae in the embalming room?" Herodotus said.

"Yes. There were many rows of them."

"Those amphorae contain spirits and oils to preserve the dead."

"Dear Gods."

We didn't need Herodotus to tell us what that meant.

Diotima said, "Tutu must be in there."

"We're not going in to find him," I said firmly. It would be suicide.

As I spoke, the roof caved in. The door blew out, and from within staggered a man. He was on fire, but he barely seemed to notice. It was Tutu.

I ran forward. So did Herodotus and Maxyates. Together we picked him up and carried him away from immediate danger.

We only had to lay him gently on the ground to see that there was no hope. His skin was charred and peeling away. The blood oozed from his body in more places than we could hope to staunch. His hair was gone.

He whispered in a voice that sounded somehow wrong, through lips that had been almost burned away, "My House . . ."

"Your House is gone," Herodotus said, as gently as he could.

Tutu closed his eyes. "I do not fear death, but I fear failure," he said in that strange voice. I realized his lungs had been burned beyond repair. "I have lived alongside death all my life. How could I fear it now?"

"You have smoothed the path for so many who have gone before," Herodotus said. "Your heart is pure and there will be many friends who await you in the Field of Reeds."

Tutu nodded, then coughed. Much blood came up. Diotima wiped it away with the hem of her dress.

"There is something I must say before I die," Tutu whispered.

We all leaned closer to hear.

"When the General came to my house the other night, he spoke of something I did not tell you about before."

"What?"

"He talked of a child."

"A child? You mean the child who sees for him."

"No." Tutu coughed again. Flecks of blood struck our faces. Tutu was whispering now, so quietly that we struggled to hear. "The General spoke of a child of the Pharaoh. He said he must speak to the child. That the child must decide, before he would tell you what he learned from me."

"Where do we find this child?" I said urgently.

But it was no good. Tutu belched an enormous amount of blood. He died before our eyes.

As we walked away Herodotus asked, "Who will embalm the world's best embalmer?"

"The second best?" Diotima suggested.

"It hardly seems fair, does it?" Herodotus said. "For such a man to receive second-best treatment seems almost . . . sacrilegious. Of all men his ka and his ba deserve the best."

There was nothing we could do about it. We left Tutu's body in the care of his neighbors and servants, and went in search of the next step in our quest.

"A child," Maxyates said in wonder.

"Is this why he was killed?" Diotima asked. "To stop him from telling us more?"

"Probably," I said, considerably annoyed. I'd had a vision of finishing this job, now that we'd learned that the crook and flail were in a sarcophagus that had probably gone to Siwa. Instead we had yet another mystery to solve.

"Do you recall the General's last words to us?" Herodotus said. " 'I will have to ask permission.' "

"Yes."

"He said the same to poor Tutu. The Blind General didn't strike me as the sort of man who asked permission of anyone."

"I agree."

"Then why did he need to in this case? After so many years?"

"Could it be that Psamtik is still alive?" I

asked, in a moment of inspiration.

"After the embalmer sewed his head back on?" Diotima scoffed. "It's not likely, is it?"

"This news does make a certain amount of sense," Herodotus said. "The Blind General might not have been friends with the Pharaoh, but with the Pharaoh a prisoner in his own former palace, the Blind General was perhaps the only man with access whom the Pharaoh could be sure wasn't in the pay of the Persians."

"Who is this child Tutu spoke of?" I wondered. "Could it be Psamtik's son? Or his daughter?"

"We know the answer to that," Diotima said. "The son was killed. The daughter was enslaved and sent to Persia. She must be a very old woman now. She's probably dead. No one would call her a child."

"The General was an old man," I said. "Even a middle-aged adult might count as a child to him."

"True enough," Diotima said. "But this daughter, even if she's still alive, would have to be almost as old as the General. I can't believe he meant her."

Herodotus said, "Could there be a third child?"

"No one's mentioned one."

"What about his time as a prisoner? Psamtik wasn't too old to sire a child in the months before he died."

There was a brief, stunned silence while we all realized that Herodotus was right.

"Dear Gods, a true child of the last Pharaoh," I said. "If the Persians found out, they would be wild to kill him." Then I did a double-take. "Wait a moment. That child's not Inaros, is it? Could it be that he's telling the truth about his ancestry?"

Diotima did some mental arithmetic. "No, it's impossible. Any child of the last Pharaoh would have to be at least sixty-seven years old. Inaros can't be older than forty-five."

"The father of Inaros is not in doubt," Herodotus said. "Everyone knows his father was the previous Prince of Libya. The question is, could *Inaros's father* be the true child of the Pharaoh?"

We all looked at Max. He was the only one among us who might know the history of his country.

Max shrugged. "Certainly Inaros claims it is true, but if I am honest then I must say this is unknowable. You ask me about a time that was three generations ago. Not even my father was born then."

"That's why we need history books," Herodotus said. "So we know what happened in the past."

"Alas, there is no such thing," Maxyates said.

"I'm working on it," Herodotus said. "Are you noticing a pattern here? Every time we talk to someone, they get killed."

"It does seem beyond coincidence," I admitted, rubbing my chin in thought.

"Do you often have this effect on people?" Djanet asked.

"No! Never before," I protested. But then honesty compelled me to add, "Well, there have been one or two incidents . . . but those were on previous jobs . . ."

"That makes me feel so much safer," Djanet said in her most sarcastic voice.

"I'm beginning to wonder if I did the right thing in hiring you, Nicolaos," Herodotus added.

For some reason I was to blame for all our witnesses dying. It was hardly fair.

"But Herodotus, think of all the book research," Diotima countered. "Can you honestly say you would have learned all these things if you were a mere tourist?"

"No, that's true," Herodotus said. "I just wish fewer people were dying for my education."

"Whoever is doing this is not very philosophical," Maxyates said.

"Few murderers are," I replied, and then,

because Max rarely spoke until he had something important to say, I added, "What do you mean?"

"Someone is following us, and killing the witnesses *after* we have spoken to them," Max said. "It hardly seems logical. Should they not kill those we are *about* to speak to? To kill them afterwards does nothing useful."

Max was right. It made no sense.

"Perhaps whoever it is doesn't know the answer to the mystery either," Diotima said. "They don't know the path to follow, so all they can do is follow us and hope to get to the next witness before we do."

"Then why kill the ones we have spoken to?" Max asked.

"Maybe he finds it cathartic," Diotima said. But it was obvious she didn't have an answer for Max.

"Then there is the question of why murder witnesses, when this person could go straight to the source of his anger and kill us?"

"Maybe they're not following us," Herodotus suggested. "Maybe they're on the same trail for their own reasons, and they don't know we're a few paces ahead."

"In that case, when they discover our existence, we are going to be in enormous danger," Max said.

That night as we ate dinner I told the party about Markos, and how I had acquired his crossbow.

"That makes it all the more important that we get out of town," Djanet said gloomily. She had listened to my tale with close attention. "This Markos, you say he is a good man in a fight?"

"The best there is," I said sincerely. "I wouldn't want to face him."

"Hmm."

"Did you discover anything interesting at the temple of Ptah?" I asked Herodotus.

"Did you know the first race of people were the Phrygians?" he said.

I didn't. Nor did I care. Diotima, however, had to know everything.

"Oh? How did you work that out?" she asked.

"The priests told me!" Herodotus said. "In the time of Psamtik I — he was the great-great-great-grandfather of our Psamtik, if the priests are to be believed — the Pharaoh ordered two children to be raised without anyone ever speaking to them. These two children never heard a single human voice utter a single word."

"Why?" Diotima said. "That was cruel."

"But ingenious. He wanted to find out what language the children would speak if left to themselves. You see, the Pharaoh reasoned that without any adult to teach them, whatever words the children spoke must belong to the very first language ever spoken by people."

"You're right, that is clever," Diotima marveled. "What were the children's first words?" she asked eagerly.

"They said 'bread' in the tongue of the Phrygians. So Phrygians must have been the first people, older even than the Egyptians."

"We don't have time for this," I interrupted. I had been thinking about Djanet's words. She was right about the need to leave. Whoever was killing witnesses would surely come after us, sooner or later, and now Markos would be in the queue to kill us too. The only sensible option was to leave at once. "Max, I'll need your help."

"Where are we going?" he asked.

"To find a boat."

DEATH ON THE NILE

Getting out of Memphis was harder than getting in. I went with Maxyates to the docks, where by luck we ran into the captain of the river ferry that had brought us here, the ferry that traveled between Naukratis and Memphis.

The ferry captain backed away warily.

"Oh no! Don't come near me. You people are poison."

"What do you mean?" I said, confused, because we had departed from the captain on friendly terms.

"The word is you have bedbugs."

"That's a calumny. Don't believe it."

"Then how come the Public Service sent everyone this message?" He held aloft the unfortunate notice. "You're not saying my government would lie to me, are you?"

"It's funny you should mention that —"

"And then there's this other notice."

"What other notice?" I asked.

287

He rummaged in his bag. "This one. Here," he handed it over, from a distance. "It says anyone who deals with you won't get no government work."

I read it quickly. It was the same as the one Tutu had received. Not only did the ban name me, it also described me in detail. "Oh."

"I got a family to feed. I'm sorry, but I can't afford that sort of trouble. Do you know how much money I make shipping tax collectors up and down the river?"

It was a fair point from an honest man. I didn't want to damage his business.

"Thanks anyway," I said, loudly, to make sure anyone listening heard that the captain had rejected us.

"I'm glad you understand," said the ferry captain. He made his way off.

There was no point asking anyone else for passage. Probably some agent working for the Public Service was watching us. I knew I'd never spot him. Any local could fade into the background to fool a foreigner like me; I wouldn't know what to look for. It made me realize how much I relied on local knowledge when I took on work back in Athens.

"But Nico, how shall we travel to Siwa?" Maxyates asked when I told him we were trapped.

"Psst!" a voice hissed.

I looked around, but I couldn't see the source.

"Psst!" It was a man lurking in the shadows of a dark side alley. "Psst!" he repeated.

"Do you want my attention, or have you sprung a leak?" I said.

"Hey, I heard you want to get out of Memphis." He spoke quietly.

"That's right," I said suspiciously.

"The Public Service got it in for you?" he asked.

"Maybe."

"Word on the street is, some guy named Nicolaos is a troublemaker. Would that be you?"

"Maybe. What's it to you?"

"Nothing, except I got a way out of Memphis, one that doesn't involve walking across trackless desert."

He had my attention.

"I'm in the import/export business," he explained. "Except my business doesn't pay taxes, you know what I mean?"

A smuggler. Yes, of course. Smugglers were the one people who need not fear the labyrinthine regulations of the Public Service. Smugglers would have fast and efficient transport in and out of Memphis.

Maxyates spoke up. "Nicolaos, are you sure this is a good idea? These people are criminals!"

I shushed him. "I deal with criminals all the time, Max. Leave this to me."

Max looked dubious, but he said nothing.

"How much are you charging?" I asked the smuggler.

He named a sum that was five times the going rate.

I staggered back in shock. "You must be joking!" I choked.

He laughed. "Take it or leave it, mate. This isn't a charity."

He knew he had me cornered, the bastard. There was no faster route out of Memphis.

"We'll take it," I said through gritted teeth.

"Meet me tonight at the old shack north of the docks." He gave us instructions by rote in a rapid speech. He had obviously done this many times before. I paid him half the money — I knew better than to demand a receipt, or to ask his name — and left at once with Max in tow. We had to prepare our party to depart.

"Are you sure this is a good idea?" Diotima whispered.

"Of course I'm sure," I told her. "We're spies and they're crooks. What could possibly go wrong?"

Our party waited by the boatshed. It was a dark night, and surprisingly cold. I wrapped my arms around myself to get warm, then realized that was silly and wrapped my arms around Diotima instead.

A boat glided out of the night. It was so quiet that I didn't see it until it was almost beside us. They carried no torch. To have navigated blind like that their pilot must have memorized every tiny bit of the river. As they touched the bank I saw how they could be so silent. Men stood on each side and propelled the boat by pushing against the bottom with poles. There was not a single splash to their movement.

"You are all here?" a voice whispered from the boat. It was the man from the docks.

I nodded in the pitch black, realized that was useless, then said, "Yes." My voice in the night sounded loud as a shout.

"Speak quietly!" he hissed. "There are soldiers patrolling this area."

We clambered on board.

"Do not try to stand," the smuggler said. "The boat is built for speed, not stability."

Indeed it was. More like a long, thin rowboat than a ship. I asked about this.

"On a river there is no room to maneuver," the smuggler said quietly. "Our only way to evade the tax collectors and their soldiers is to be faster than them." He held out his hand. "You pay me the second half now."

"I pay you when we get there."

"Then the boat will not move," he said. "We will have half our money, and you will have nothing."

I paid him the second half.

The smuggler grinned and went aft. The boat made way.

I knew a great deal about how to move unseen within a big, crowded city. Athens was my usual hunting ground; dark alleys, rooftops, crowds and disguise were second nature to me. I had always thought this was a difficult skill — after all, when you're surrounded by people, someone could notice you at any moment — but now I realized that out here in the country the problem was infinitely worse. When you're the only person in plain view, then you're *very* noticeable.

"You must lie down," the smuggler said.

"Why?" I asked.

"Soldiers patrol the banks," he said. "Even in the dark, they will see your silhouette and know that you are not one of us. We bribe the soldiers to look the other way when we carry goods, but criminals such as yourselves are another matter."

"We're not criminals," I said.

"Of course not. That is why you are sneaking out of Memphis in the dead of night in fear of our government."

"It's more complex than that," I assured him.

"We have transported many men who assured us that it was all a misunderstanding," said the smuggler. "You do not need to justify yourself to me, Hellene stranger. Your gold is good, and that is all that matters."

I gave up trying to convince the smuggler that we were a party of innocents. We all lay down on the very uncomfortable floor of the boat and hauled over ourselves a tarpaulin that smelled of mildew and dead fish. Because the boat was narrow we had to lie head to toe. It wasn't the best arrangement. I shifted about in a desperate search for a more comfortable position.

"Hey!" A voice at my feet complained.

I had kicked Herodotus in the face.

"Sorry."

"Tell me again why we're doing this?" Herodotus asked from somewhere close to my feet. I remembered then that it had been some time since I washed them.

I said, "Because whoever's killing our

informants probably doesn't like us very much either."

"Sounds like a good reason," he said grudgingly.

It was a good thing we had departed in the middle of the night. If we'd had to hide like this from dusk to dawn I might have died of cramp. We stayed in that position until the sailors said to us that we were clear of towns, at which point we were very happy to shed the tarpaulin and ease our sore muscles upright. If nothing else the fresh air was a relief.

As dawn broke we found ourselves in the middle of nowhere. Wherever we were, the Nile looked the same as it did everywhere else. To the right and left were farms growing barley, rich, tall, strong plants like nothing I had ever seen in Hellas. The soil was black as Hades — I could see why they called Egypt the Black Land — nor were there any rocks, and the fields were not stony hard, like every farm in my homeland.

Truly, Egypt was a land rich in food. With all this bountiful wealth, I wondered that no one could make a decent cup of wine.

The boat pulled over to the side, where there was a stone wharf and nothing else.

"You get out here," the smuggler said.

"Here?" I said. I could barely credit his words.

The smuggler shrugged.

"You paid us to get you out of Memphis. We got you out of Memphis." He pointed at a low sand dune. "Over that dune you will come to a village. There you can hire a guide for your next leg."

The Oracle at Siwa lay far inland, across the desert. It didn't make sense to follow the river any further, so I agreed.

The boat docked precisely at the wharf.

"Mind the crocodiles," the smuggler said, as he handed us across the dry land. "The children of Sobek are particularly fierce on this stretch."

With those words the men with the long poles shoved, and the smuggler dwindled into the distance, returning the way they'd come.

Apollo chose that moment to appear over the horizon, driving his chariot with the sun in tow. Or if the Egyptians were to be believed, then the god Ra came into view, casting golden light. I supposed it was all a matter of perspective.

In either case we watched this spectacle, all of us exhausted because we had not slept and our wits were slightly addled. That is the only excuse I can give for what happened next.

Herodotus remarked idly, "You know, it's a funny thing, but in all my travels, this is the first place I've come to where the sun rises in the west. I must remember to mention that in my book."

"What?" I said, confused.

Herodotus said, "Siwa is to the west of Memphis, right?"

"This is true," Maxyates said.

"And our plan is to depart from the territory to the north controlled by Inaros, from there traveling west along a road that is under his protection, to approach Siwa from the northern road, which you say is the safest route."

"That is correct."

"So we've traveled north all night," Herodotus insisted.

"Of course," I said.

Herodotus pointed. "Then how come the sun is rising on the *left* bank?"

We all stared at him, open-mouthed. But I already knew what had happened.

Those bastard smugglers, in the dead of night, had carried us south instead of north. No wonder they had told us to lie down and cover ourselves. We hadn't noticed.

Diotima realized the same thing as quickly as I did. She asked the obvious question.

"But why?"

No one had an answer.

Maxyates spoke up. "I think our first step must be to ask someone where we are," he said.

I nodded. "Good thinking, Max."

An arrow came from nowhere and took Maxyates in the chest.

He was thrown backward and writhed on the ground.

Diotima shouted, "Don't pull it out!" She had studied some medicine and knew, as any doctor did, that while the arrow was inside him it would plug the wound and stop the blood from rushing out. She ran for our baggage.

Max ceased his struggles at once. For the rest of us, however, the struggle had only just begun.

More arrows came our way. Three at the same time. We ducked and they flew over our heads.

Djanet threw herself into the narrow ditch behind the low wall. Then cursed when she realized it was a latrine.

If I'd had any doubt that Herodotus was an experienced traveler, his reaction would have dispelled it. He hit the ground in the blink of an eye and dragged himself behind a low rock, barely larger than a stone. It was the most useless cover I'd ever seen, but he had instinctively made maximum use of what little there was.

Meanwhile I stood there. The biggest target of all.

But someone had to find the enemy. I desperately scanned for whoever was shooting, hoping it wouldn't hurt too much if I was hit.

There they were, their heads poking over a low rise. I counted seven men and a leader. Bad odds.

They looked at me; I looked at them. They surely saw that Maxyates was hit. They certainly saw that we were immobilized. They let loose the arrows they held, and I fell back onto my behind. Two of them missed me by a whisker. Another went wild. I was suddenly aware that Diotima was somewhere behind me.

"Diotima! Duck!"

I didn't have time to turn, but I heard noises like she was dumping the contents of our bags. I didn't stop to wonder why, because the soldiers — for that was what they were — dropped their bows and advanced with swords drawn.

It was then that I saw something astonishing. They weren't Persian soldiers. They weren't Egyptian either. These men were

Hellenes. They were dressed in hoplite armor.

They must be Charitimides's men, from the fleet. I shouted in relief. "Hey, we're on your side!"

They didn't break their stride.

"We're Athenians!" I shouted. Which wasn't entirely true in the case of Djanet, Max and Herodotus, but it was close enough for the purposes of saving our lives.

"We're *not* Athenians," their leader shouted back.

Uh oh.

Many Hellene men hired themselves out as mercenaries. They would fight for whoever offered the most pay.

"Surrender or die," their leader added.

Herodotus rose during this exchange. "Do we surrender?" he asked.

I shook my head. "That would be certain death. The way they shot at us without warning, surrender will end in execution, don't you think?"

Herodotus nodded grimly. "All I have is a knife."

"Me too."

I pulled my dagger. The enemy had swords and shields.

The mercenaries lined up in two rows, exactly as per standard drill. These men knew their business.

I said to my client, as we faced overwhelming odds, "Herodotus, I owe you an apology. You hired me to keep you safe, and here we are about to die horribly at the hands of trained killers. Is there anything I can do in compensation?"

"It's a little late to ask for my money back," he said.

I laughed, perhaps a little hysterically.

I said, in a comradely way, "You know, it's funny, but when we first met, I thought you must be a Persian agent. Now I know better."

Herodotus looked at me oddly. "But I *am* a Persian agent. Didn't you know?"

"You're *what*?"

"Attack!" The mercenary leader shouted at his men.

There was nowhere we could run on this riverbank that they couldn't follow, and they were hardened soldiers, and there were twice as many of them as us. Really there was no option. We would have to fight them, probably to the death. That was assuming of course that Herodotus, who I had just learned was a Persian agent, was willing to fight alongside me.

I shouted to the rear. "Diotima, Djanet! Run!"

300

I could buy them some time. It was the best I could hope for.

"Nico! Catch!"

I turned my back on the enemy. Not normally a good idea, but Diotima's yell was urgent.

She threw the crossbow at me.

I had stored it in our baggage, which was emptied and scattered about my wife's feet.

Thanks be to the Gods. This was what we needed to save our lives.

There was only one problem. I had no idea how to fire a crossbow. The string was already pulled, but something prevented it from releasing. I could see bits of metal holding the string. I pushed on them, tentatively, but nothing happened. What should I do now?

"Well, what are you waiting for?" Diotima demanded. "Fire the accursed thing!"

I looked down at the weapon in my hands in confusion. "How?" I asked. I couldn't see anything that might make the crossbow work.

"Don't you *know*?" Diotima fairly shrieked. The men were getting close.

"No," I said. "Do you know, Herodotus?"

Herodotus shook his head.

"Dear Gods, what is it with you men?" Diotima snatched the crossbow from me.

She nestled the stock against her stomach, as Markos had done. "It's like a bow," Diotima lectured me as she aimed. "If I can shoot a bow then I can fire this thing."

Diotima looked down at the weapon, then up at the rapidly approaching mercenaries. She made an adjustment in her aim. She stared at the mechanism.

"There has to be a release," she half-mumbled to herself.

The soldiers were twenty paces away.

"Er, Diotima, could you fire that thing please?"

"The catch . . . Oh, yes. Here it is!"

She flicked a lever at the side.

The heavy bolt flew into our attackers.

The soldiers paid for their perfect discipline. The bolt pierced the first man in line. It went straight through him into the man behind, who screamed and fell, revealing the bolt embedded in their leader, who whirled about as the bolt struck and then fell heavily.

The mercenaries suddenly found themselves leaderless, and two of their men dead, from a strange weapon they had never seen before.

But there wasn't time to reload. And it was still five trained soldier against two men with daggers.

The crossbow had fallen to the ground. I picked it up, held it to my stomach, and shouted, "Stand back, Herodotus, I'm firing again!"

The weapon was unloaded, but they didn't know that.

The remaining five soldiers took one look at me, then looked down at their fallen comrades.

They ran.

"Good shooting, Diotima!" I said.

When there was no answer I looked to my left.

She wasn't there.

"Diotima?"

I heard a splash behind us.

Diotima was a slight woman. The force of the crossbow had flung her backwards, over the parapet, into the Nile.

I thought to myself it was a good thing she fell into the water and hadn't landed on hard ground.

Then I remembered that the Nile is full of crocodiles.

"Diotima!"

I rushed to the parapet. There was Diotima, floundering in the water. The natural buoyancy of her breasts kept her head above water, as they had on the beach at Thera.

"I'm all right, Nico!" she shouted up to me.

No, she wasn't. She couldn't see what I could see from above. A crocodile in the muddy water, right behind her.

I jumped.

I landed straddling the beast. Crocodiles have an incredibly tough skin. I discovered this the hard way when a particularly important item between my legs crashed onto the crocodile's hide. The pain almost made me black out. Dark circles filled my sight. But I didn't dare lose consciousness here. If I did, I was a dead man. And so was Diotima. Or a dead woman, rather.

So instead I gasped and breathed heavily and felt my balls crawl up inside my body to get away from the crocodile. My sight cleared and I felt as ready for action as I was ever going to be.

That was when I realized I didn't know how to kill a crocodile. I remembered the captain's words on the courier boat. *If you fall in, there'll be no point stopping to collect your body.*

I had to do something. I drew my dagger and held the weapon in an overhand grip, raised my hand high and struck down into the animal's neck with all my force.

The blade bounced off the skin. The shock

of the blow jarred my hand and sent the blade flying into the air. I watched it fall into the muddy Nile and disappear from sight.

This wasn't going to end well.

The crocodile had barely noticed that I'd tried to kill it. It advanced on Diotima, who had swum to the shallows. She turned to see the ravenous mouth about to consume her.

She screamed. "Nico!"

The crocodile snapped at her leg and barely missed. Diotima fell over into the mud and crawled backwards as fast as she could through the stickiness. The crocodile lurched forward while I rode upon it. Diotima scrambled in the mud for something to hold onto, but there was nothing. At any moment the crocodile would have her. I beat my fists against the monster, but it had no effect.

Yet the futile action gave me an idea. I leaned forward and pulled myself along its back, ignoring the pain of the rough skin, until my hands could touch the top of its awful snout. I felt around there until I found two depressions. They were only small, but they were what I wanted. With a hand over each I stuck in my fingers, felt something soft, and then I pushed hard.

The monster retreated back into the water, away from Diotima. She scrambled on hand and knees out of the water.

The crocodile had finally noticed I was on its back. It rolled.

"Whoa!" I wrapped my arms about it. I didn't dare let the creature dislodge me, or it would eat me.

I went under.

My back jammed against the silty bottom of the river. Then I felt the weight of a crocodile on top of me.

I would have died then and there, except the brute rolled again. My head breached the water and I gasped for air.

Diotima stood on the riverbank, covered in mud and looking concerned. "Nico! Are you all right?"

"I'm just fine!" I shouted back.

The crocodile rolled again.

At least this time I remembered to hold my breath.

I surfaced once more, but I was weakening. I could feel pain everywhere that I was pressed against the crocodile. I had to get clear of this monster.

How do you get off a rotating crocodile?

"Lean back!" It was Herodotus, shouting.

"You must be joking!" I shouted back.

"Trust me, Nicolaos!"

Trust a man who had just told me he spied for the enemy?

But you get to know a man when you travel with him for long days in tough circumstances. I had seen him drunk. I had joked with him. I knew he was a good man.

I could feel the crocodile's legs move. It was about to roll again.

I had to make a decision.

I leaned back.

A crossbow bolt whizzed over my shoulder. It actually clipped my ear as it flew past. I felt blood spatter my face.

Was Herodotus trying to shoot me? I was the only one to whom he'd admitted his Persian connection. It would be so easy to have an aiming accident in this situation.

Then I realized the crossbow bolt that had almost killed me had thudded into the crocodile's head. The bolt end stuck out like some weird, wooden appendage.

The great beast lay still for a long moment. Then it gave a long juddering, roaring sigh.

The crocodile died.

THE MERCENARY

While I'd been fighting for my life — and Diotima's — Herodotus had loaded the crossbow and worked out how to fire it. He had pointed it downwards and pulled the trigger.

I remembered Markos's words, that the tummy-shooter was wildly inaccurate beyond twenty paces. Herodotus could have as easily hit me as the crocodile.

In fact, he *did* hit me. My ear bled copiously, but otherwise, it wasn't as serious as Diotima's wound. There were gouges in her leg, from when the crocodile had tried to bite her. The mere scrape of the creature's hide had been enough to tear skin. I worried that she would catch the flesh-eating sickness and die, but Herodotus claimed knowledge of medicines. He explained, inevitably, that he had heard useful things from foreign doctors. He cleaned the wounds with the beer in our flasks and made a batch of lotion that he said would stop infection. I had to hope he was right.

Max was in a very bad way, but typically he was more concerned about the rest of us. I didn't dare move him, but I made him comfortable while we sorted ourselves out.

We recovered Djanet from the latrine. She was a mess. Diotima covered for her, standing by the side of the Nile with the crossbow armed and ready to shoot, while Djanet washed her clothes and bathed off a considerable amount of muck.

"The good news is, there must be civilization near here, wherever we are," Djanet said when she returned.

"What makes you think that?" I asked.

"Where do you think all the poo I just fell in came from?"

It was a good point.

Max was dying.

Diotima and Herodotus both inspected our Trojan friend, and came away shaking their heads. The arrow had embedded itself in his chest, close to his heart. Any attempt to pull it would certainly kill him.

Max already knew the diagnosis. He asked in the most astonishingly calm voice to compose a final letter to his father, which Herodotus took down. Herodotus wept as he wrote.

"I would like to be properly dressed for my descent to the underworld," Max said.

"Of course, anything we can do," I said. Herodotus, Diotima and Djanet all nodded their heads.

"I am dirty, and my dye has worn thin. I wish to die a proper red color. There is dye in my bag. And my hair . . ."

Max needed say no more. Diotima was already going through Max's bag. She returned with a flask, which she held up for Maxyates to see.

"Yes, that is my dye."

We washed him, being careful not to touch the arrow, for fear that it pierce his heart. Then all four of us knelt around Maxyates and rubbed the dye into his skin. It wasn't the moment to ask how the dye was made, but I wanted to because it was a very strong solution that seeped into the skin. Djanet, Herodotus, Diotima and I would have bloodred hands for days to come.

When we were done we dressed Maxyates in his best clothes. He suffered these indignities with amazing grace. He even went so far as to thank us for our attentions.

But now the preparations were over. It was time for Max to die.

"Hey, what about me?" A voice yelled from the distance.

It was the mercenary leader.

Diotima had shot three with a single bolt. After the bolt had passed through two men, it had wounded a third. The crossbow might be inaccurate, as Markos had said, but when it hit it did astonishing damage.

I walked over to where the three bodies lay. The first two were indeed dead. They had the hard mercenary look about them: sunburned skin and calluses, and their equipment was old and worn — a mercenary has to supply his own gear — but well serviced too, which meant they were veterans. Seeing our opposition, I counted us lucky that they had run when they had.

The third man was their commander. He lay face down on the ground. He'd turned his head to get enough air to breathe. I had thought from a distance that Diotima's shot had taken him in the stomach. It hadn't. He had turned at the last moment and the crossbow bolt had ripped his back.

He heard me approach, but couldn't turn enough to look me in the eye. Facing the dirt, he said, "Help me. Please."

This man had tried to kill us, would certainly have done so if we hadn't fought back. I wasn't feeling particularly merciful, but he had something I wanted, and I was willing to go a little distance to get it.

I said, "If I do what I can for you, then you tell me everything you know."

He said, "Yes."

I said, "Can you get up?"

He said that he couldn't. One of his arms was splayed out and the other by his side, his legs akimbo. It was an awkward position. I wondered that he hadn't shifted, wounded though he was. But he said, "I can't feel a thing. Can't move my arms or legs either."

"Oh."

I knelt beside him, pushed his side up with my left hand. He was a dead weight — he gave me no assistance at all. I felt with the fingers of my right hand along the length of his spine. He didn't complain; he knew what I was doing, and why.

Everything felt normal, starting from the small of his back, until, close to the base of his neck, something moved beneath my fingers, a knot of some sort. I stopped, pressed a bit more firmly, felt around.

He said, "I know you're touching me, but I can't feel it."

There was no doubt about it, my fingers felt a jagged lump beneath the skin where there should have smooth vertebrae.

I said, "Your back is broken."

We both knew what that meant. Though

he still breathed, he was as good as dead. A man with a broken back never healed. He could linger for days — if his family cared for him, sometimes for months; the result was always the same: a disgusting, undignified, inevitable death.

He said, "I guessed you'd say that."

It seemed odd, talking to a man who didn't move at all. I hadn't realized before how much attention I paid to the way men fidgeted when they spoke, their body language. A man without body language was half-mute.

I said, "What's your name?"

"Alekto. Alekto from Rhodos."

Rhodos was an island in the Aegean. Many men from the islands took to mercenary work.

"Nicolaos!" It was Maxyates calling, weakly, but audible.

"Yes?"

"Does the soldier live?"

"He lives." For now, I said under my breath.

"Will you bring him to me?"

It was an odd request, but I would deny nothing to a doomed man.

I unstrapped Alekto's armor. There was no point carrying that too. He was a big man but I was strong. I hefted him in my arms and carried him back to our group. I expected the mercenary to cry out in pain, but he didn't.

I deposited him beside Maxyates. The two dying men lay side by side, both unable to move. They stared at each other. I wondered what they were thinking, but it seemed impossible to comprehend what must go through the minds of men in such straits. I hoped never to find out.

Maxyates reached out to hold the mercenary's hand.

"You must not fear death," Max said to the man who had killed him. "Death is a chance to gain knowledge. It's a . . . er . . . once-in-a-lifetime experience."

"Is this supposed to make me feel better?"

"And then to experience the afterworld," Max finished. "There can be no greater opportunity for a philosopher."

"You're not Egyptian," the mercenary said.

"I am Libyan," Maxyates said. "I followed Inaros to free this country. You are Hellene. Tell me, why did you come here?"

Alekto sighed. "For money. I fight for money. I got a wife, and a son. Can't farm, can't fish, so I fight to support my wife and boy."

Max nodded. "It is a worthy motive."

He was being far more generous than I would have been.

"I'm sorry I killed you," Alekto the mercenary said to Maxyates. "You seem like a good man."

Max looked to me. "Nico."

I knelt beside him. "My friend, when we first met, you called yourself a child of Hector."

"It is my greatest pride."

"Know then that we will give you the same ceremony that Hector received."

Max smiled weakly. "Does that include dragging my body through the dirt behind a chariot?"

"We might skip that part," I said. "We'll move on to a mighty bonfire for the fallen hero."

"This is good. Thank you, Nicolaos. Now, may I ask you for your final gift."

I had known it would come down to me.

I didn't give myself any time to think about it. I grabbed the arrow shaft and pulled.

It wouldn't budge. Suction. They'd taught us in army drills how to deal with this. I didn't want to do it to poor Max, but there was no choice. I twisted the arrow as I pulled. Max's body jerked in pain, but he uttered not a word.

The arrow came free.

For a moment, nothing happened.

"So this is what it feels like to die," Max said as he lay there. "It's very philosophical."

He gasped. His body shuddered for a moment. Then he was gone.

I reached out to close his eyes. He had died staring into the sky.

The mercenary had killed my friend Maxyates, who for some unexplainable reason chose to forgive him. For that reason alone I would be gentle with Max's slayer. Yet now he was my captive. I would make him talk.

"Why did you attack us, Alekto?"

"We were hired," he said.

"By whom?"

"Look, I don't want to get into any trouble—"

"Trouble? Your back is broken. How much more trouble do you think you can get into?"

I had said something he could understand.

"It was the Public Service," he said. "They hired us."

Dear Gods.

"Look, they're the government, right?" he said defensively. "It can't be wrong to do what the government says."

"What did they tell you?"

"They said you would be delivered to this spot. All me and my mates had to do was come here, wait for you to land, kill you all, then go back to Memphis for our pay. They didn't say nothing about some super weapon. How did you hit three of us with one shot?"

"It's called a gastraphetes."

"Well, it should be banned. That thing's not fair."

I was beginning to understand. The Public Service must have paid the smugglers to bring us here. The Public Service had issued the decree for legitimate businesses not to deal with me, to *force* us to take passage with the smugglers, who in fact had approached me first. I had followed their plan, every step of the way.

Max had asked me, back in Memphis, whether it was a good idea to deal with the smugglers. I had ignored him, and now he was dead.

I had failed my people.

Why hadn't the Public Service used Persian troops? The bureaucrats and the occupying army were tight enough that the Persians would have lent the Egyptian bureaucrats enough troops to finish off a

317

few troublemakers.

Then the reason hit me. Barzanes had sworn an oath that we would not attack each other. Barzanes *never* lied. He would not countenance the use of his troops. That was also why the Public Service had waited for us to leave Memphis before they attacked. Only the sheer luck that I had taken the crossbow from Markos had saved us.

"Couldn't you find a better job?"

He shrugged. "Times are hard. I got a family to support. Who's gonna look after them when I'm gone?" That led him to another problem. "Here now, you gotta take my final pay to my wife. Will you do that?"

"Yes," said Herodotus. I would have said no.

"Camels," Alekto suddenly said.

"Camels?"

"Over the hills here, south up the river, far enough away that you wouldn't see or hear them, we tied up our camels. They got us here quickly. You've been good to me, taking money to my wife and all. So I'm telling you in return. There're camels that way. Take them."

"Won't your other men have them?"

"Those idiots ran the other way. They're probably in the nearest town by now. It's a run-down village to the north. They won't be coming back."

I had to agree. Mercenaries who've failed their job don't hang around.

"Thanks, Alekto. Listen, we'll tell your son that you died a hero in battle."

"I wanted to see my son grow up." I thought he was about to sob, but he managed to hold it in. "I guess this means that's it. For me I mean. There's no way I can recover from a broken back."

"I'm afraid so," I said gently. "How would you like me to do this?"

"I dunno."

"I thought you hardened mercenaries always thought about how you wanted to go, if it came to that."

"Standard campfire talk. Tough guys talk about it all the time, but I never could make up my mind."

Terrific.

"I used to think maybe being decapitated would be best," he offered. "Real fast, you know?"

I rubbed my chin while I thought about it. "I can probably find an axe around here somewhere," I said.

"But then I decided it'd be terrible," he finished.

"Oh."

"Think of the mess."

"I know what you mean. How about I stab you in the heart? That'd be quick."

"But then I'd see the knife go in. Besides, what if you missed? I've seen guys writhe around for ages with a dagger stuck in them."

"All right. How about I choke you to death."

"Gods no. Imagine struggling to breathe."

"Then I could hit you on the head with a club?"

"And have all my brains squelch out? No thanks."

"Drowning? I could carry you to the river."

"I couldn't bear to feel the water flooding my lungs. Besides, I can't swim."

I decided not to argue the logic of that.

"Poison?" I suggested in desperation.

"I'd have to swallow it, knowing it was going to kill me. No thanks."

"Dear Gods," I said in exasperation. "There must be some way of dying that you're happy with."

"Look, mate, I seen a lot of men die in a lot of ways, and you know what? Not a single one of 'em looked happy." He paused, then added, looking at Maxyates's body, "Except for your friend here. He took it real well."

"Then be like Maxyates," I said.

"Yeah, well, I'm not coated bright red, either. And I'm no philosopher."

"Then I don't know what to do, Alekto," I said, now very irritated. "Unless you want us to let you lie here while you waste away. It'll probably take a couple of days and you'll hate every moment, but that's your choice. I'm doing you a favor here."

"I'm sorry. I'm having trouble getting used to this. In a moment I'll be dead. I never expected to die."

"Most people do, you know. Die, I mean."

"But do they ever think about it? Do you?"

"Sure I have. In my business, you've got to think about what could go wrong."

"You don't believe it though, do you? If you did, you wouldn't be cracking jokes. No one ever thinks they might actually die. I know I didn't, until this moment." A tear trickled down his cheek. "I'm scared."

"There's no need to be scared." It was Diotima. She'd walked up behind me and I'd never noticed. "You'll pass from this life to the next." She knelt beside Alekto and held his hand to comfort him, then realized he couldn't feel a thing and put it down again. "Do you know what they drink in Hades?"

"Yeah. Dust."

Diotima shook her head. "They drink good wine in a beautiful meadow called the Elysian Fields. It's a peaceful place of fine, warm weather. Believe me, I know. I'm a priestess."

Her words calmed him.

Alekto said, in a quiet but clear voice, "All right, I've decided. I think a sword might be best." He thought about it some more. "Yes, definitely a sword. That's the best way to go. Straight in the heart."

I said, "I don't have a sword." But I knew someone who did. "Hold on, I've got it! Wait here," I said, and then realized what a stupid thing that was to say to a man with a broken back.

I ran to the other dead soldiers. I snatched a sword from a hand and ran back. I stood above Alekto with sword in hand and said, "This ought to do the trick!"

I gripped the handle in both hands and raised it, point down, ready to plunge into him.

"Not with that!" Alekto shouted in horror.

I lowered the sword. "What's wrong now?"

"We got that gear from the White Fort. It's a Persian sword. I don't want to be killed with a Persian sword," Alekto said. "I want to be killed with a proper Hellene weapon." He paused. "Well, to be honest, I don't want to die." Now he began to cry. "My son . . . I have a son. I want to see my son."

Beyond his head, where he couldn't see it, Diotima had quietly drawn her priestess knife, which she always kept in a pouch about her. It was the knife she used to make sacrifices. The blade was short but very, very sharp.

She looked me in the eye and I looked back and gave the smallest nod.

Djanet saw our plan. She said, "Close your eyes, Alekto, and tell me about your son."

Alekto closed his eyes and managed to stop his sobbing, but he said nothing. He was silent for so long that I thought he might have gone unconscious, but then he said, "We got a place near the beach. I take him on the sand to play. He likes to run on the sand. Runs into the water and out again and I chase him around." He smiled. "Best times of my life, on that beach, with my son."

His eyes still shut, the tears gone, he smiled at the memory.

With one swift motion Diotima leant over and cut his throat.

The blood spurted into my face.

Alekto opened his eyes and gave me an aggrieved look for the briefest moment. Then his eyes dimmed and rolled up into his face and he was gone.

We all three stood up and silently walked away from the corpse. None of us could bear to be near it.

"Was it true what you said?" I asked Diotima. "About the Elysian Fields?"

"Yes, it's in Homer, but the Elysian Fields are only for the favored of Zeus. I have a feeling that doesn't include Alekto. I lied to him."

To call us exhausted would have been a wild understatement. It was barely mid-morning, and already we had fought off mercenaries, survived a crocodile attack, and given our friend Maxyates the gift of death. We lay in the shade of a date tree and ate the dates.

Too many good men had been lost in this struggle for Egypt. I was becoming almost afraid to talk to anyone, for fear it marked them for an early demise. I was furious with Pericles for putting me in this situation.

There was one subject however that had to be addressed as soon as possible.

"Herodotus, you told me you're a Persian agent."

"It's true," he said. "Well, sort of. It's a

324

family tradition. We've always been happy to find out things and let people know, including the Persians. My father says that's why I'm so obsessed by history. It's really very similar to spy work!" Herodotus prattled on, blithely unaware of our shock. "It all began with my Great Uncle Phanes —"

That name was familiar. I struggled to recall where I had heard it before. Then I remembered that the man who had betrayed Egypt to the Persians all those years ago had been called Phanes. Phanes of Halicarnassus. That was what the Blind General had called him when he told us the tale. Phanes had gone over to Persia, and in revenge the Pharaoh had murdered the sons of Phanes.

Phanes *of Halicarnassus.*

I was lying next to Herodotus *of Halicarnassus.*

Diotima made the connection at the same time I did.

"Do you mean to say that the man who betrayed the last Pharaoh of Egypt to the Persians was *your uncle*?" Diotima said, aghast.

"Er . . . yes," said Herodotus. "That is to say, he was my great uncle." Herodotus was a stickler for getting his facts right, even when it made him look bad.

"The Persians have been friends of my family ever since," he said. Into our cold silence he added, defensively, "My family is as Hellene as you are! It's only that we can also see the Persian side of things. I try to be balanced about loyalties —"

"Are you reporting to them now?" I asked.

"No."

"Is that the truth?"

"If I had access to the Great King's court, do you think I'd be lying under this tree surrounded by corpses?"

It was a fair point.

"Why didn't you tell us this before?" I demanded.

"It was irrelevant until you told me we were looking for the crook and flail. I came here as a tourist, remember? Then, when the Blind General told his story, it didn't seem the best moment to mention that Phanes was my grandfather's brother."

Diotima ignored this argument and instead said, "Until now, there were only two men with a connection back to those days: the Blind General and Tutu. They both died for their knowledge. Now there's a third man. You, Herodotus."

Herodotus said, "You think that I am —"

"Marked for death," Diotima said. "Yes. I

326

wonder if the Public Service knows about you?"

"They must," I said.

"The Public Service keeps records about *everything,*" Djanet said. "It's what they do."

"That, and arrange assassinations," I added.

"No, they're terrible at that," Djanet said seriously. "Look how many attempts they've made, and you're still alive. Typical Public Service inefficiency. They should have hired a private individual."

"But I know nothing that anyone would want to kill me for," Herodotus said.

"Hmm. What can you tell us about your Great Uncle?"

"He returned from Egypt a bitter and disappointed man. Of course I knew his sons, my second cousins, had died here. He never spoke of the manner of their death. I must say I was horrified when I heard what the Blind General had to say."

"Did he talk of anything else? Such as for example the crook and flail?"

"If he had, I would have mentioned it before now! It's a terrible thing, what age does. Here was a man who was a mover and shaker in the world. His acts decided the fate of nations. Yet his own sons died and he was reduced to bitterness."

He had also betrayed Egypt. I glanced over at Djanet to see what effect these words had upon her, but she seemed to take the story with equanimity.

Herodotus spoke on. "As an old man, Phanes would sit on his own in the agora at Halicarnassus — there was an inn that kept a table out front, just for him — and he would watch the people go by. He would talk about things, but I'm ashamed to say that as a young boy I didn't listen."

As the day wore on, Herodotus and Djanet slept. Diotima and I stepped away to prepare the bier for Maxyates. Living wood is no good for fuel, especially not for a funeral pyre. But the Nile was lined with many palms, and the dead ones had quickly dried out in the intense heat. Not far away was a grove that must have been standing for many years, because half the trees were leafless and lifeless, but still standing. I had pointed them out to Djanet. "Will those burn?"

She looked and said, "Yes. They're called Doom Palms."

The name wasn't encouraging, but they would do for what we needed. Diotima and I went to collect some. The dead palms proved to have only shallow roots. By pushing on one side I was able to get each trunk onto a tilt, after which I could bring it down by climbing the other side and letting my weight do the work.

"This news clears up a lot of questions," I said as another palm hit the ground. "We think the Public Service knows about Herodotus. What about Barzanes?"

"He *must,*" Diotima said, as she stooped to collect branches that had fallen from a nearby sycamore. They would make fine tinder. "It was his own side that employed Great Uncle Phanes."

"Barzanes never gave anything away," I said glumly. "But Barzanes being the Eyes and the Ears, he was the one man who knew for sure that his own side hadn't hired Herodotus. When you and I turned up with the nephew of Phanes, Barzanes automatically assumed that we knew what we were doing."

"Do you realize that the moment we turned up in this country with Herodotus, we advertised our intentions?" Diotima pointed out.

"I keep feeling that all through this mission, everyone but me has known what was going on."

"Everyone but us," Diotima corrected. "I missed it too."

Diotima was strong enough to carry the

thin ends of the trees. We raised a platform by placing pairs of palm trunks crossways until they were just high enough to let a fire burn below. Then we placed a row of palms sideways to make a bed on which Maxyates could lie, then covered this with dried palm leaves. It was the best we could do.

"Do we have a chance here?" I asked my wife. "Should we declare failure and return home?"

"If we do, then Max died for nothing," Diotima said.

"There is that." After a pause, I said, "We have to assume Barzanes knows we're here for the crook and flail, or if not that, then certainly something connected with Inaros."

"He guessed that all along anyway, I'm sure of it," Diotima said.

"Yes. I wonder why he let us loose for so long?"

"On the strength of our results so far, I'd say it's because he had nothing to fear."

"I'm here to find the crook and flail for Inaros. Barzanes is here to find it for the Great King. Markos is here to make sure Barzanes doesn't leave Egypt alive. Maybe also Herodotus."

"I thought we'd decided that Barzanes came to Egypt to investigate his own people: the commanders who were losing the war for Persia."

"He was," I agreed. "But as soon as he saw us and Herodotus, he must have changed his mind. Remember he's the Eyes and Ears. He can make decisions for the Great King."

"This is guessing, Nico," my wife said dubiously.

"You're right," I said. "But it makes sense, doesn't it? I feel like I know the inside of Barzanes's head. When he learned that *we* were after the crook and flail, he realized that the same logic applied to his Great King. If Artaxerxes arrives in Egypt with the crook and flail in hand, he can claim that Psamtik bequeathed them to the Persians. Enough Egyptians will believe it that Inaros won't be able to unite the people. Barzanes could win a bloodless victory for Persia."

"What about Markos?" Diotima said.

"I can't see inside his head," I said. "I don't think anyone could."

"All right then."

"This changes things again," I said. "If we can't have the crook and flail, then we have to make absolutely sure that Barzanes *doesn't* get it. That would be the worst of all possible worlds."

We cremated Max in the evening, after

331

Apollo had left the sky. To my shame I didn't know anything about Max's religion. I had never thought to ask him. Nor had Djanet. Nor had Herodotus, despite their long conversations about the nature of religion. But Diotima was an accredited priestess who had once served at the Artemision, the same place where Max had chosen to study, and we decided a Hellene rite would be best.

Herodotus and I carried the body to the pyre, while Diotima sung hymns to Artemis. I placed a coin under Max's tongue. He would use it to pay Charon the Ferryman to cross the River of Woe, on his journey to Hades. Djanet lit the pyre. It took a little while to catch, but when it did, the fire roared high.

The one thing we did know about him was that Max had been proud of his Trojan heritage. As the flames consumed his body, Herodotus recited from Homer's *Iliad*. He spoke of the Death of Hector, that valiant hero who had died defending the walls of Troy.

CAMEL DELIGHT

We discovered the camels next morning, tied up exactly where the mercenary had told us to look.

Djanet was the only one who knew how to ride them.

"It's not that hard," she said. "You just have to hate the camel more than he hates you."

"Sounds easy," I said.

"Camels can do a lot of hating."

We also found spare supplies. Lots of them, enough for eight soldiers and more than enough for two men and two women.

The mercenaries had brought flasks of bath oil with them, and a *strigil* for scraping off the dirt. The two women crowed with delight and made off to give themselves a proper clean.

Best of all, there was wine. Two flasks of real Hellene wine.

"If you drink that all at once we'll have to

sling you over the camel," Diotima warned.

"No fear of that," I said, as I liberally watered a cup. "I have to make this last."

The only thing they didn't have was paper. Herodotus grumbled about this. He had used up his entire supply in taking notes. I'd never known a man to fill so much paper. But this was Egypt, the home of paper. I was sure we'd find some soon.

That was assuming we ever got the camels moving.

"Do you know what to do once you're on?" Djanet asked.

"Of course."

I was an expert horse rider. I figured that a camel was merely a lumpy horse.

Djanet whacked my camel with a stick.

"You'll hurt it!"

"You can't hurt a camel. You can only irritate it."

The camel knelt on its front legs.

"It's a bit uneven," I pointed out.

"It'll even out once you're on."

I clambered on.

The camel instantly rose.

"Aaargh!"

I still wore my *exomis,* standard wear for a working Hellene man, but it didn't include underwear. That was how I discovered that camel hair is tougher than horse hair.

"Are you all right, Nico?" Diotima asked. She had changed into local Egyptian dress when we were in Memphis, discovered she liked it, and had worn nothing else ever since. She was already on her camel and looking comfortable.

"Never been better," I said, rubbing the damaged parts. They were still bruised from landing on the crocodile. Before we left I would have to tuck some material between me and the camel, or that part of me might wear away.

Herodotus, needless to say, wouldn't get on until he'd taken endless notes. He too had changed to Egyptian clothing and didn't seem to have my problem as he rose into the air.

"Do you think we can make good time?" I asked.

Djanet looked at me oddly. "These are camels," she said. "They come in two speeds: very slow, and way too fast. You don't want way too fast unless you want to eat sand."

"Right. Got it."

Djanet handed out sticks.

We were on our way, to the Oracle at Siwa.

THE PYRAMID PLAN

If there is anything slower than long-distance travel by camel, I don't know what it is. We could have walked faster, except that we would have died of exhaustion before a day was out. What the camel lacked in speed, comfort, agility and manners, it made up for in its ability to walk on, and on, and on.

As we rode, Djanet told Herodotus a story of a man who died on camel back while crossing the desert. Nobody knows how long the camel carried him, but when it finally halted on the other side his corpse was mummified. Herodotus listened politely, but he didn't write down her tale. It was the only time I ever saw Herodotus not credit a story.

The ambush against us had taken place south of Memphis. It had to be plotted that way, because Inaros's army was to the north, and apparently not far away. Barzanes had hinted as much when we first met.

That meant Memphis was between us and our destination. It was impossible that we should go through the city. I couldn't begin to imagine the chaos that would ensue if Barzanes, Markos and the Public Service all suddenly saw us ride into the marketplace. Barzanes surely must know by now that we had skipped town. The Public Service would want to know why we were still alive, and would probably try to correct that error. Perhaps scariest of all, Markos would want his crossbow back.

All in all, there was a fair chance that if they knew where we were, there would be at least three collections of annoyed people chasing us.

Accordingly we detoured far inland. It meant an extra two days in the terrible heat, but we simply had to endure it.

Our path therefore took us to the great tombs of the ancient pharaohs. We arrived in the morning, when the sun shone off them in all their glory.

"Dear Gods. They're *enormous.*" I couldn't keep the awe from my voice. "Did people build those things?"

"Of course people built them," Djanet said derisively. "When was the last time you saw gods do manual labor? No, Nicolaos, these are the product of tens of thousands of hard men, laboring for years and years of their lives."

It was mind-boggling.

Djanet tapped her camel on the backside with her stick. The camel walked on, and ours followed behind. We entered the most astonishing graveyard.

"There can't be too many kings buried here," Herodotus commented.

"Only one per pyramid," Djanet said. "Plus attendant slaves of course."

"Never have so few been buried in so much, by so many," Herodotus said.

I didn't even try to think my way through that. Instead I thought of Tutu the embalmer. He had spoken of this place with reverence. I said, "I can understand why Tutu came here to admire the works of his forebears, and then wept. It makes perfect sense to me now."

"Why?" Djanet asked.

"If I knew that my ancestors had been capable of such magnificence, if I had this daily reminder that they were so much greater than me, if I lived in an age where my country was a puppet in world affairs, like you Egyptians are — sorry, Djanet, but it's true — then I think I'd . . . I don't know . . . maybe I'd stop trying."

"I'm not offended," Djanet said mildly. "Perhaps someone in that position wouldn't try to achieve glory. Maybe they'd simply work to their own advantage."

"*You* don't do that," Diotima said. "You're working for Egypt."

Djanet shrugged. "I'm unusual in many respects. But I admit I know many people like Nico describes. They think only of their own comfortable lives."

"This pyramid is different from the others," Herodotus said. He pointed to one of them.

He was right. All the other pyramids were . . . well . . . pyramids. In fact, they were the same shape as the wheat cakes we ate back in Athens. They had smooth sides, or as smooth as you can get from worn stone. But the pyramid that Herodotus pointed to seemed to be made of giant steps, not smooth at all.

"It is the tomb of the Pharaoh Djoser," Djanet said. "Legend says Imhotep himself designed it, that when he built that tomb Imhotep *invented* the pyramids."

I'd heard that name before. Then I remembered, the Tjaty had talked about Imhotep in worshipful tones.

"Yes, he was a real person," Djanet said in answer to my question. "Prime Minister of

339

Egypt, architect, doctor, mathematician, philosopher. His own tomb is probably close by, but no one knows where."

"How come I hadn't heard of him before I came to Egypt?" I asked. "In Hellas, all the great men of past times are famous."

Djanet gestured to the pyramids. "Right in front of you are the largest buildings ever built by the hand of man. He didn't need any more fame."

"We have to camp here tonight," Herodotus said.

"Is that a good idea?" I asked.

"This could be my only chance to see the pyramids," Herodotus said. "If you think I'm passing through here without doing a thorough survey, then think again."

In all fairness I had to grant him the point.

Herodotus spent the rest of the day scouring the burial ground. He questioned Djanet mercilessly.

Diotima and I used the opportunity to spend some time together. Though there's not much you can do when the only places to sit or lie down are either hot sand or hot rock. At least we could be alone for the first time in days.

We camped against the base of one of the big pyramids. I thought it would block the light of the campfire from at least half the ground.

As we sat about our campfire, Herodotus said, "I suppose you realize that tonight we'll be sleeping in the world's largest graveyard."

"You have the nicest way of putting things," I said.

"It's a knack," he said modestly. "But you must admit the idea is rather macabre."

Herodotus's observation stayed in the back of our minds. Our conversation was muted, lest we disturb the spirits of the dead.

Thus it was that when dark shapes appeared out of the night, the women screamed. I almost screamed too.

Silhouettes stood beyond the edge of the light of the flames. They looked like men, but could equally be evil spirits, for they watched us in silence.

I stood up to confront them. "Who are you?" I demanded loudly.

I tried to count them, but they were too many. If these men — or spirits — meant us harm, then we were doomed.

A form pushed his way past the silhouettes to step into the light. It was the man who had coshed me in the streets of Memphis, and then carried me to the secret chamber beneath the Temple of Bast. The same man who distributed the orders of the Public Service.

"The Tjaty wishes to speak with you," he said. "Come."

We were in the greatest danger.

"Stay here," I said to the others. Not that they had any choice.

In the distance set upon the sand was a palanquin, a large one, which I could see by virtue of the men with torches standing about it. Other men sat on the ground. They were the bearers. They wore nothing but loincloths. They rubbed their muscles and looked tired.

We stopped alongside the palanquin, which was richly painted. The door slid open to reveal the Tjaty, the Prime Minister of Egypt and head of the Public Service.

"We meet again, Nicolaos," he said smoothly. "You have proven remarkably difficult to kill."

"Sorry about that."

On his lap lay the white cat that I had seen in the chamber beneath the Temple of Bast, and then later at the gates to the temple's grounds. The Tjaty stroked the cat as he talked. The cat purred contentedly and stared at me with complete disdain.

"There is no need to apologize. I admire

a man who excels at his profession. I myself am the best Public Servant in Egypt. Since Egypt has the best bureaucrats in the world, it follows that I am the world's best bureaucrat."

"I'm sure you are. May I ask a question?"

"Please."

"How did you find us?"

He smiled. His fat fingers didn't stop stroking the feline. "When I heard that my men had failed their assignment, it was clear that you would make for the north. You could not travel through Memphis. The other side of the Nile is filled with troops loyal to the government. Thus it was inevitable that you would pass this way, and with that historian you have in your party, that you would stop here for the night. It was only a question of setting observers and awaiting their report. I was very happy to come here to meet you. The trip to the pyramids is pleasant at this time of night."

His bearers might have felt differently about that.

"May I ask another question?" I swallowed my fear to ask, "Do you intend to kill us?"

"I am sorry about your friend. You were the intended target, not him."

"That is my point," I said. "If someone must die here, let it be me. Let the women and Herodotus go."

"No one will die tonight, unless you make it necessary."

"What?" That wasn't the answer I'd expected. As soon as those men had surrounded the campfire, I had seen my own death. My only concern had been for Diotima to escape.

"There have been developments since we last spoke," said the Tjaty calmly. I couldn't tell if he was genuinely indifferent to my distress, or quietly enjoying it. "I'm afraid your death is no longer required. Quite the reverse in fact."

My jaw dropped. "Do you mean Maxyates died for nothing?"

"There lies an interesting philosophical question. We must discuss it some time. But in the here and now, let us consider more pressing matters. The last time we spoke, I asked you not to find the insignia. Alas, too many people are now aware of the crook and flail. Word has spread, largely I must say due to all the questions you've been asking. I personally know of two private expeditions that are being organized. Neither is anywhere near as advanced as your party."

"Private expeditions?"

"Treasure hunters. They do not care for political symbolism. They care only for the treasure that invariably accompanies a Pharaoh's sarcophagus."

"Ah." That made more sense.

"As a result it is now impossible that the crook and flail *not* be found. Failure to produce them when their existence is generally known would be a sign of impotence on the part of the Public Service. People might even question our credentials. That would never do, for if there is any rule to which Egypt must cleave, it is that what is good for the Public Service is good for Egypt."

"I'm sure no one would question that."

"And yet, somehow I have a feeling that you do," said the Tjaty drily. "I see that I must explain myself, for it is important you understand the vital nature of our work. We of the Public Service have been the government of Egypt since the Two Lands were united. Do you know how long ago that was?"

"No."

"Nor does anyone else. It was that long ago. Egypt was already ancient when my predecessor Imhotep built that first pyramid you see beside us. Today it looks like weathered stone. Have you wondered how long it takes for blocks of stone that big to wear away?"

"Er . . ."

"Pharaohs have come and gone, good Pharaohs and bad ones, great men and shocking fools — I may say, without fear of contradiction, that Psamtik was just about the worst of the lot."

"So I gathered."

"And yet, Egypt endured even that disaster, because for thousands of years the Public Service has given our people continuous, consistent government."

"I thought the Pharaohs did that?"

"Pharaoh graces us with his godlike presence. From time to time he issues commands. We of the Public Service interpret Pharaoh's words and execute the plan. In those rare circumstances where Pharaoh's wisdom is less than godlike, the Public Service has been known to be flexible in its interpretation."

"Sensible of you."

"We take the long view, and I am a very flexible person," he said from beneath rolls of fat. "I am therefore revising my approach to you, Nicolaos. You are no longer a source of anxiety, but rather the solution to another, perhaps larger problem. I previously offered you a substantial sum to fail to find the crook and flail."

"I turned you down."

"I now offer an even more substantial sum

346

to find these implements and bring them to me."

"You're not going to claim to be descended from the last Pharaohs, are you?" I said.

"I confess we did have a strategy team look into that option. There have been countless long meetings."

"I can imagine."

"It was decided in the end that it would be better if Pharaoh Psamtik bequeathed the crook and flail to his brother and conqueror, the Great King of the Persians. Unfortunately, during the confusion of the times, the items were mislaid. That is how the story will be represented to the public. But now, thanks to careful research and an expedition funded by the Public Service, the crook and flail have been discovered."

"I'm beginning to see your plan," I said.

"I was sure you would. We are already composing the invitations for the handover ceremony. Pure white best-quality papyrus with nice bordered edges sounds about right, don't you think? Great King Artaxerxes will be invited to visit this loyal satrapy to receive in person the crook and flail of the Two Lands. I will make a long speech. It will be a fine event with many opportunities to ingratiate ourselves to our normally distant ruler. A most satisfactory situation all around."

"Aren't you forgetting Inaros's army?"

"When news spreads that the crook and flail are in the possession of the government — indeed will soon be in the hands of our rightful ruler the Great King — opposition will crumble, and this bunch of deluded rebels who support the Libyan will drift away."

"Hmm." I wanted to be non-committal, but I was afraid the bloated bureaucrat was right.

He continued. "In addition, I've become aware of yet another foreigner in my country. This is starting to become annoying. Don't you Hellenes have anything better to do than invade Egypt?"

"You mean Markos?"

"He indeed. The Spartan assassin threatens to upset the balance."

"What do you mean? What balance?" I asked. Then I realized the implication of the Tjaty's words. "You've had a run-in with Markos, haven't you?"

"I don't have run-ins with anyone. We had a civilized discussion, to the extent that such is possible with a Spartan. Incidentally, I thought the Spartans called themselves laconic."

"Markos talks more than most of them."

"So I discovered. His plan to kill the Persian Barzanes would not be beneficial to the Public Service. Our relations with Persia are of the utmost importance."

"Did you do something about it?"

"I warned Barzanes of his imminent danger. But the Eyes and Ears has proven strangely reluctant to adopt certain actions that would be in his own interest and that of his king."

"That can happen when you're dealing with an honest man," I pointed out.

"Yes, it's unfortunate," said the Tjaty.

"Don't worry," I said. "What Barzanes lacks in corruption he makes up in ruthlessness. The moment Markos breaks his oath, Barzanes will destroy him. Come to think of it, why aren't you talking to Barzanes about the crook and flail, and not me?"

"Ruthlessness is an admirable quality, to be sure. Yet for the two missions I have in mind, I require a man of more, shall we say, flexible temperament. Athenians are renowned for their flexibility when it comes to matters of their own advantage. In your own way, you Athenians would make good public servants."

"You're too kind."

"Also, the manner in which you retrieved

the weapon from the Spartan speaks of a certain originality."

"How do you know about —" But I didn't bother finishing the question. Of course he knew about the crossbow.

The Tjaty wiped his brow, where a slight trace of sweat had appeared. "This Spartan is beyond the skill of my own people. In any case it would not be propitious if Egyptians were to eliminate the Spartan. It might prompt Sparta to invade. The last thing this country needs is more Hellene invaders. No offense intended."

"None taken."

"Thus we have a limited number of people with the skill to take care of this Markos. The Eyes and Ears refuses to move. The army of Inaros might achieve success, but they are singularly unlikely to stop a Spartan from killing a Persian."

"No. Barzanes's death would be a present from the Gods for Inaros," I said.

"Your Admiral Charitimides probably feels the same."

"I imagine so."

"That leaves you. The only person who can deal with the Spartan for me is you."

"You want *me* to kill Markos?" I said, aghast. "He's a trained assassin. How in Hades am I supposed to do that?"

The Tjaty stroked the white cat. The feline purred loudly. "I have offered a large fee for this service."

"I refuse."

The Tjaty sighed sadly. "Then we must revert to the night's other option. The one in which you die impaled upon a stake set by the riverside, where the crocodiles will feast upon your rotting carcass."

"Let me revise that last answer," I said quickly. "How about I accept your proposal?"

"I applaud your decision. I leave you then to your tasks. Bring me the crook and flail, and kill your Spartan opponent. May the Lord Ptah and his Lady Bast watch over you."

The cat snarled.

THE PHARAOH'S CHILD

I saw no point in hiding what had happened from the others. I could hardly tell them that the Tjaty and I had enjoyed a pleasant evening of idle chit-chat.

Herodotus merely nodded.

Djanet said, "No." She fingered the dagger at her belt. "If you deliver the crook and flail to the Tjaty, Nicolaos, it's over between us."

"What's to stop us from delivering the crook and flail to Inaros?" Diotima asked.

"Nothing," I said. "But keep in mind that the last time I refused the Tjaty, Maxyates ended up dead."

We argued into the night about what to do, came to no conclusion and went to bed exhausted.

Next morning, Herodotus went about his survey with determined, deliberate coldness. Up until now he'd been in good spirits about what we'd put him through. No longer. I had a feeling the novelty of being an agent was starting to wear off.

Djanet went with him to explain which pyramid was which, and also I suspected to distance herself from me. The singer from Memphis was enraged that I would even contemplate giving the crook and flail to the enemy.

That left Diotima and me to pack camp and talk disconsolately about the whole mess.

"I've never known a job where I had more conflicting missions," I groaned. "Pericles wants me to help Inaros. Inaros wants the crook and flail. The Public Service wants it too. I've agreed to give it to both of them. Pericles wants me to eliminate Herodotus if he proves to be an agent for Persia, which it turns out he isn't, but his family is. Herodotus is a good man, and we need him to find the crook and flail that everyone wants, not to mention that Herodotus hired me to keep him safe. If Pericles knew that Markos was the Hellene agent working for Persia, he would certainly want me to kill the Spartan instead. Which the Tjaty also wants me to do, but so that he can keep good relations with Persia, which is not to Athens's advantage. Thus I should both kill and not kill Markos. Meanwhile I've agreed an oath of non-aggression with the other agents. Markos will break his oath at any moment, and I've agreed not to interfere, because Barzanes's death can only be good for Athens. Yet we swore that oath, and if Markos is an oath-breaker, I am not. Thus I should both abandon and save Barzanes. Barzanes wants back the crossbow that Markos got from a corrupt Persian official. I stole it from Markos, but am not inclined to return it to Barzanes. We are now about to cross a trackless desert to reach a famous oracle where we hope to ransack a Pharaoh's grave. Which incidentally has been cursed so that whoever opens it will have their life destroyed. Have I missed anything?"

"Only the detail that it would be nice if we got out of this alive."

"What should I do, Diotima?"

"If we give up and return to Athens, men will call you a coward."

I recalled something that Admiral Charitimides had said to me before we left Naukratis for Memphis. *You'll probably get killed, but that's the way it goes when you serve your country.*

I repeated the Admiral's words to Diotima.

"What do you think of Charitimides?" Diotima asked.

"He's a fine man. I admire him very much," I said.

"There's your answer then. We go on."

"If I die out in that desert, you probably will too," I warned her.

"I'm your wife, Nico. We do things together."

"That's not exactly the sort of togetherness activity I had in mind when I asked you to marry me."

Diotima hesitated, then said, "Nico, have you wondered what Djanet is doing involved in all this?"

"I did wonder," I admitted.

"Djanet's a special case," Diotima said. "Max's family owes Inaros allegiance. You and I are professional agents. Inaros's army is made of soldiers and patriots for Egypt. What is Djanet? A singer? How does that fit in?"

"She's a patriot then."

"Did you notice when she said that she once, years ago, tried to determine Psamtik's final resting place?"

"Yes, it struck me as strange at the time."

"Not strange if she was searching for her grandfather's grave."

"That's about the most tenuous link I've ever heard!"

"Yes, I know," she said glumly. "But Nico,

if the last child of the Pharaohs is involved in this, then it can only be Djanet. Nobody else fits all the requirements."

"And if the last child is not involved, then he's probably a cobbler in some run-down street and has no idea any of this excitement is going on."

"Then how would the Blind General have known about him, or her?" Diotima challenged.

"Then why didn't he acknowledge Djanet when we spoke to him? She was standing there beside us!"

"Because the General didn't want us to know."

Diotima had an answer for everything. But there wasn't enough proof to convince a court in Athens. Still, I had to agree that if Inaros wasn't the true heir, then Djanet was the next best choice.

Herodotus and Djanet returned from their tour of the pyramids late in the day. They were both tired. Herodotus had insisted on climbing the tallest one, and Djanet had been foolish enough to go with him. They both complained.

"I feel like my legs are about to fall off," Herodotus moaned.

"If they fell off, they'd hurt less," Djanet replied while she massaged her calf muscles.

The two were friendly with each other, and polite to Diotima, but they remained cold and distant with me. My enforced deal with the Tjaty had destroyed their trust.

Nevertheless, Diotima had deputized me to be the one who broached the subject.

I said, nervously, "Djanet, I have a question for you."

"What is it?" She sounded distracted. "If you want me to cook, you can forget about it."

"We were wondering . . . umm . . . you're going to laugh yourself silly when you hear this . . . but Diotima and I were wondering if you might be the last true descendant of the Pharaohs?"

Djanet did laugh, loudly.

"What makes you think that?" she asked.

Diotima covered the same ground as she had with me. She concluded by saying, "What it comes down to, Djanet, is that your presence makes no sense. Everyone involved in this mess has a reason for being here. Inaros, Barzanes, Markos, Nico and me, even Herodotus, we all have good reasons for being here. But not you. Tavern entertainers don't mix themselves up in deadly politics unless they have a very good reason."

"I have my own reasons," Djanet said.

"It was you, wasn't it," Diotima went on, "who suggested to Inaros that the crook and flail would persuade the Public Service. I'll bet it was. It was you who negotiated the deal at both ends. You orchestrated this whole thing."

There was a brief silence after Diotima finished. We all waited for Djanet to speak.

"I need to cover my tracks more carefully," she said, half to herself.

"You mean you are?" I said, astounded. I hadn't thought it could be true until that moment.

"You're not very good detectives, are you? It took you all this time to realize. It's all true. My father was the son of Psamtik. My father's mother was the daughter of a nobleman. She escaped enslavement by pretending to be a palace servant. Not a much better fate, I'm afraid. Psamtik never knew he sired another son. He died before my grandmother even knew she was pregnant."

"Unfortunate."

"Not as unfortunate as what happened next. Grandmother knew she was doomed if the Persians found out she carried an heir to Egypt. She escaped into the streets, where she was forced to beg. There she met —"

"Not the Blind General!"

358

"The very same. It was after he had recovered from his own downfall, and established himself as the premier beggar in the city. Grandmother didn't stay a beggar for long. The General saw to that. By the time my father was a small child she had a business sewing and a stall in the market-place. Father lived long enough to marry and have me. When I was very young, my parents were taken by disease. One of those plagues that sweep through this country in the winter and kill the poor people — it happens all too often."

"I'm sorry."

"Grandmother raised me. She died last year."

"Oh." Diotima had tears in her eyes.

"Why didn't you reveal yourself earlier?" I asked.

"In this environment? Do I look suicidal?" Djanet shrugged. "I'm not a complete cipher. My grandmother and my father stayed in touch with the royal families in Aethiopia and Libya. I did too, when I came of age. Secret messages, that sort of thing. The kings of our three lands have intermar-ried their daughters since time immemorial. It helps keep the peace. I was able to keep the Aethiopeans and Libyans up to date on what's happening in Memphis. It's how I

359

got into agent work."

"Libya? Then Inaros knows who you really are!"

"He knows."

"This is outrageous," Diotima fumed. She was genuinely angry. "Inaros should be fighting to restore your throne, not to put himself on it."

"I accepted long ago that a singer from Memphis could never be the king. Inaros has an army. I don't. If he can free Egypt, then good luck to him."

"This changes things," Herodotus said.

"Does it?" Djanet replied. "I don't see why."

"What do we do then?" I asked.

"We go on, Nicolaos," Djanet said. "We go on to find the crook and flail."

THE LAST CAMEL DIED AT NOON

Sand. Sand and dust and rock and salt and heat.

The wind did nothing to cool us. Its only effect was to blow grit and salt into our mouths and eyes. We tied cloths about our heads in the Egyptian manner. It helped a little, but not much.

"Where are we?" I asked Djanet as our camels plodded along.

"We're in a depression."

"Can you blame us?" I said, spitting salt and grit from my mouth. For the first two days we had trekked over dunes that had rolled on like a sandy sea, but then had given way to the rock, stony grit and salty dust that surrounded us now. On the whole, I had preferred the sand.

"Not that sort of depression, you idiot. This is the Qattara Depression. The land here is lower than it is at the sea coast. The soil is as salty as the sea. That's why nothing grows."

Nothing did grow. This barren disaster area was how I imagined Tartarus to be, far below Hades, where those who had been evil in life were punished.

"I thought deserts were supposed to be always sandy," I complained.

"Some bits are. Be glad you're no longer in one of them. The going would be even slower. If it's any compensation, we're almost there. Only another day or two."

"A *day*? Or *two*?" We'd already been traveling for seven days. Or was it eight? I'd lost count. I guessed we'd crossed the Egyptian border long ago, but there'd been nothing to mark it.

"So this depression full of salt, rock, heat and no water is Libya?" I asked.

"Part of it."

"Then I understand why Inaros wants to conquer Egypt. I'd be desperate to get out of here too."

"Just shut up and ride," Djanet suggested. "The more you keep your mouth shut, the less sand gets in."

I followed her subtle hint.

The revelation that Djanet was the true Pharaoh had done little to ease the tension in the group. Herodotus and Djanet still blamed me for having done a deal with the

Tjaty. The only other choice had been death, but apparently that was no excuse.

I rubbed my eyes, which were red, raw and sore. That was a mistake; it served only to put in more salt and grit. I'd made the same mistake at least ten times now, but each time I forgot.

My appreciation for camels had increased with every day. These creatures were remorseless machines when it came to crossing deserts. Djanet had insisted we stop, rest and feed our beasts for two days at a small town on the border of the desert before we commenced the crossing. For a high charge she had even had a camel handler check them over for disease, sores or wounds.

The camel handler had spat on the ground as often as the beasts he tended. He smelled like them too, but the man knew his business. The camels had held up. I understood now why Djanet had insisted on such care. The equation was simple: if the camels died, then we died.

My camel — which, incidentally, I had named Pericles — was more than capable of plodding along without my steering. I nevertheless steered him a little sideways, to join Diotima, who rode to our right flank.

"How are you doing?" I asked her.

"I'm thirsty."

"I know. So am I. But there's not much water left. Wait till tonight, when it's cooler."

She peered at me closely, through the folds of her own head wrap.

"Your eyes are blood red, Nico. You look like one of those *daevas* out of that religion Barzanes belongs to."

Barzanes was a devout Zoroastrian. His people believed in evil spirits called *daevas*.

I said, "Speaking of Barzanes and evil spirits, what's happening with that other caravan?"

"Still following us."

We both looked over our right shoulders.

This was why Diotima held the right flank.

Three days before, another caravan had appeared at our rear, far off into the distance. On each subsequent day it had become larger in our sight, turning from a small dot on the horizon to a size where we could discern individual camels, and a clear camel train of supplies. Whoever they were, they had clearly been traveling faster than us. But when they reached us, they had slowed down. For the last day they had kept station, just distant enough that we couldn't discern the individual riders. Distant enough that we didn't know who was following us.

364

Opinion was divided on the identity of this train.

Djanet had looked at them and shrugged. "Caravans come this way all the time," she'd said.

That might well be true, but the co-incidence was nevertheless worrying. Di-otima thought it must be Markos. He was coming after us for the crossbow. My own theory was that it was one of the treasure hunting expeditions that the Tjaty had referred to.

I had suggested that someone should ride over to them, to see who they were. "I'll do it," I said.

"That's a good idea," Djanet said in her most sarcastic voice. "You can learn Egyptian on the way so you can speak to them."

"Oh, I didn't think of that."

"But I do speak the language. So I'll go," Djanet said.

"No you won't," I replied quickly. "It would be beyond embarrassing if I allowed the last descendant of the Pharaohs to be killed."

"Then we'll both go," Djanet said.

"Splitting the party in half would not be a good idea," Herodotus warned.

"We'll all go," Diotima said.

"Then we may as well wait for them to

approach us!" Djanet said angrily.

So in the end, nobody went, and the other caravan continued to trail us.

Djanet had been short on patience the entire journey across the desert. I didn't know if it was because of the terrible conditions, or because she was becoming more tense as we approached the end of the quest. At least, we hoped it was the end. I myself had become increasingly on edge, but hadn't realized it until Diotima asked me why I was snapping at her. I apologized and told her that the desert was getting on my nerves.

"I know what you mean," Diotima said. "If we arrive at Siwa, only to find out that the body had been shipped on to somewhere else even more remote, I'm going to scream."

"What could be more remote than this Gods-accursed place?" I asked.

"How about Carthage? I was talking to Herodotus. He thinks we're heading in the right direction. After we've found the crook and flail he wants to go north to the coast and then take a boat to Carthage. He asked if we'd take him."

"You told him no, didn't you?" I said anxiously.

"Of course I did. I'm not crazy, Nico."

I edged Pericles over to Herodotus to make sure that he was all right. Oddly, of the party he was the only one in decent condition. I asked him about this.

"Experienced traveler," he said in brief. "One has to keep a cheery outlook when everything goes wrong."

"Have you traveled far?" I asked.

He shrugged. "Across Persia. It's easy with their roads. I've been up north to the cold barbarian lands, but I didn't cross the border, I'm too interested in keeping my skin on. Down south of the Empire there's a place called India. I've met men from there. Traders. You meet all sorts on the road."

"Did you go to Susa?" I asked. It was the capital of the Persians.

Herodotus shook his head. "Nor Athens until the day I met you. It's a funny thing; I've seen more of foreign countries than of my own. But isn't that always the way?"

It wasn't the way with me, but that was Herodotus for you. After meeting him I knew I'd have trouble with Diotima, who would want to visit those places too.

"But I must say that out of all of them, this is easily the worst place I've ever been."

"Sorry about that."

"Have you noticed the second caravan?"

Herodotus asked.

"We've been talking about it all day!" I said.

"Not that one. The small caravan *behind* the one that's trailing us."

Herodotus pointed.

There, far behind but closing, was a single camel and, as far as I could tell, a single rider. It was very hard to be sure. Something about the desert made everything blurry in the distance.

"He seems to be struggling," Herodotus commented.

Indeed he was. Camels don't have the most regular of gaits, but even from a distance it looked to me more like a stagger than a run.

The camel fell.

It didn't get up.

The man did though. I saw him pick himself up off the ground. He walked for a few steps. And then he ran.

"He'll die out there," Herodotus said dispassionately.

The wind chose that moment to pick up. Djanet had warned us that could happen. It meant there was about to be a sandstorm.

"Hey! Nico! Where are you going?" Herodotus shouted at my back.

I'd decided not to wait for Djanet to tell

me not to go.

I whacked Pericles on the backside. The camel surged into what passed for a gallop. I could barely hang on. The gait was throwing me backwards and forwards like a child's doll.

I continued like this for a long time, aiming for where I had last seen that poor man, but mostly keeping my eyes shut, for the grit was swirling everywhere.

I opened them again just in time to see that I was about to run over the man I'd come to rescue. I swerved to the side. He stumbled, exhausted.

I reached down to help him. His hat was blown backwards by the wind and I saw his face.

It was Markos.

"What in Hades are you doing out here?" I shouted over the noise of the wind.

"Why didn't you tell me there was a treasure out here?" he shouted back, aggrieved.

"How do you know that?" I asked.

"Half of Egypt knows it! You should hear the marketplace rumors."

Wonderful. Inaros had specifically said to keep our mission quiet. But then, I thought to myself in consolation, after the General died, and then Tutu, it had been impossible to avoid word spreading.

"Can I climb up?" he said hopefully.

"There's no room," I told him. "Grab the camel's tail." Then I realized pulling on a camel's short tail might have negative consequences for both of us. "No, grab the cloth," I said. I had placed a blanket between myself and the camel. Markos grabbed one corner of it.

I tapped Pericles into motion. The beast pulled Markos along when he needed the help, and gave him support when he stumbled, which he did constantly on the uneven stony ground.

We talked as we moved.

"What did you think you were doing, riding your camel to death?" I said.

"Trying to reach you before it died!" he said. He stumbled and cursed. "Would you believe I started with three of those horrible animals? They died, one by one."

A camel is like a moving rock. I couldn't imagine how anyone could dispose of three of them.

"I bought them from a camel dealer outside Memphis," Markos explained. "The bastard sold me three sick ones. How was I supposed to tell the difference? I don't know the front end of a camel from the back."

He stumbled again. This part of the desert

was mostly hard ground, littered with loose rocks well designed to break your ankle if you trod on one. Pericles pulled Markos along for a moment before he found his feet.

"Though come to that, I do now," the Spartan said. "The front end is the part that spits on you, and the back end is the part that farts on you."

"If you hurt Pericles's feelings, he might refuse to save you!"

"If I get back there alive, I'll kill that dealer," Markos said.

For once I found myself sympathizing with the assassin. Having experienced the desert, I knew that selling a man a sick camel to cross this place was the next best thing to murder.

"Thanks, Nico," Markos said. "You saved my life."

"I haven't yet."

Nor had I. The wind was now so strong, and the dust in the air so great, that I could barely see past Pericles's head. He had to turn from time to time to get around an obstruction, and every time he did, I couldn't be sure that he set himself back on the right path afterwards. I had lost track of which direction to go. In this wall of sand, I could walk right by my own caravan and not know it.

"This way," Markos urged. He tugged us slightly to the left.

"Are you sure?"

"I've had Spartan field training. I'm good with directions. Trust me, Nico. Your caravan is this way."

I had no choice but to trust him. To stand still and wait for the storm to end wasn't an option. Markos and I stumbled through the blasting dust that was the next best thing to Tartarus.

Somewhere in the distance, someone was blowing a horn. At first I didn't recognize it, thought it was part of the wind, but as we pushed forward the sound became clearer.

By common consent, Markos and I made for the horn as best we could.

Eventually we sensed something ahead.

"Hawnk!" Pericles grunted.

Pericles had run into something.

There were similar noises in reply. We had run into a herd of camels, tethered to the ground.

The horn was now loud above the sound of the storm. I shouted, "Who's making that racket!"

The horn stopped.

"Nico!"

It was Diotima's voice.

"Diotima!"

Hands reached out, dragged Markos and me into a gray thing that turned out to be a tent. The inside of the tent would have been unpleasant at any other time. Now, it was like the Elysian Fields. Inside, hunched together, were Djanet, Herodotus, Diotima . . . and Barzanes and four of his men.

We had come to the other caravan, the one that had been trailing us.

"When the storm rose, and we saw that the other caravan had erected a tent, we made for it," Djanet said. "We would have died, otherwise."

"And there was Barzanes," Diotima added. "He let us in."

"Thank you," I said to Barzanes.

He inclined his head. "To fill my pocket with good deeds is an obligation to Ahura Mazda."

Barzanes's strange religion had come through for us again. The Persian agent could be ruthless one moment, and a perfect gentleman the next.

Markos looked like some weird creature arisen from the sand.

"You look like one of the *Spartoi*," I said, and laughed at my own joke.

Markos stared at me oddly, then he got it. "Very funny," he said. For in the legend of

Jason and the Argonauts, the Spartoi were the men who sprang fully formed from the ground, wherever were sown the teeth of a dragon.

I wasn't any cleaner than him. We wiped ourselves down. Until that moment, the others hadn't recognized the Spartan assassin.

Barzanes pointed at Markos. "He goes back into the storm," he said.

Well, I couldn't blame Barzanes for that call. But I hadn't risked my life for a man only to see him killed moments later. I had to intervene.

"We need him, Barzanes," I said. "I know exactly how you feel, believe me, but we need Markos."

"Why?" Barzanes asked.

"He's an experienced scout. All Spartans trained for independent action are. I became lost in the storm, and Markos pointed the way. Could *you* do that? If the storm doesn't let up, we're going to have to march through that muck. How long do these storms last, by the way?"

"Sometimes for days," said Djanet glumly.

"We must unite against the common enemy," Markos broke in.

"What enemy?" Herodotus asked.

"This accursed desert," Markos said.

I couldn't imagine all three parties managing to make it to Siwa without a knife ending up in someone's back. I said as much.

"Then tie me up at night," Markos said. "I'll be at your mercy."

"There is something I must warn you of," said Barzanes. He spoke reluctantly, I could tell from his voice.

"Yes? What is it?" I said.

"I must speak of past times. Sixty years ago, Cambyses, the Great King of the Persians, the grandfather of our current king —"

"The same Cambyses who defeated Psamtik?" I interrupted.

"The same," Barzanes said. "King Cambyses ordered a small army to travel to Siwa, there to destroy the temple, raze the oracle to the ground, and enslave the priests."

"That seems a little extreme."

"I do not know what caused the King to issue this command. I speculate that Cambyses sought to punish the priests for interfering in his affairs, now that I have learned they stole the body of Psamtik."

I asked, "When you say small army, just how small are we talking here?"

"Fifty thousand men," Barzanes said.

We all gasped.

"Fifty thousand," I spluttered. "To slaughter

a handful of priests? What was he thinking?"

"The Great King was perhaps vexed with the priests."

"Yet the temple still stands," Herodotus pointed out. "If anything, its fame has grown with every year. From which I deduce the Persians did *not* ransack the temple. What happened?"

"That army never got to Siwa," Barzanes said. "They died to the last man." He paused, then added, "In this desert." He paused again, then said, "In a dust storm."

There was a long and unhappy silence, while we listened to the sound of the storm outside.

Eventually someone spoke.

"We work together," Djanet said firmly.

THE SAND MARCH

For three long, tortuous days we marched in that storm. We ate dust and we drank dust. It was like Hades. I had been through some terrible experiences in my time, but those three days were possibly the worst of my life.

Markos led every step of the way, and I mean step. He said he found it easier to keep his direction if he walked. So Markos walked and we rode behind, with a rope running the length of the train, so we would not separate in even the worst visibility.

Despite the elaborate precautions we did lose a man. At the end of the march on the second day, one of Barzanes's men was no longer with us. No one had seen him disappear. We didn't even know at what part of the day he had gone; the dust had been too thick. Nor could we go back to search for him. There was nothing we could do but wish his shade peace in Hades.

At night, we bound Markos hand and foot, at his insistence. "I don't want any of you thinking you'd be safer without me," he said. "I want to get there alive as much as you do."

The storm eased on the third day. As it did, we could see the oasis not far in the distance, and I was overcome with the knowledge that we would live. I kicked Pericles forward to stop alongside Diotima, and we hugged on camelback.

Markos wearily hauled himself up onto the camel he'd been leading. He slumped over and instantly fell asleep.

I had wondered what an oasis looked like. Now I knew. It looked like a place where the Gods would choose to live. In the midst of this terrible desert were two beautiful, large blue water lakes, surrounded by many trees. People lived here. Among the trees were the typical white, squared-off buildings of the Egyptians. Between the lakes was a very large hill. It was a natural formation, yet from a distance it was shaped and looked very much like a pyramid. At the top was a surprisingly large complex.

"The temple of Amun," Djanet said.

We rode into town. We did not stop until we reached the water's edge. The camels immediately bent to drink the water. We slid off our mounts, walked into the water, and sat down. The town folk watched this with no apparent surprise. We weren't the first party to arrive from Egypt.

Diotima and I sat side by side in the lake and poured handfuls of water over each other. It was bliss. Djanet ducked herself completely under, then swam. Barzanes uttered a prayer. Even Herodotus put away his writing tools long enough to enjoy the pleasure of being alive.

We continued like this until we'd had our fill of life-giving water — never again would I turn my nose up at a cup of water — before we led away the camels.

It was easy to choose an inn. There was only one in the entire town. We paid for the best rooms the place had to offer — the prices amounted to extortion, but we weren't complaining — then paid even more for a small army of boys to wash down and care for the camels. The beasts had saved our lives; they deserved the very best.

We slept for a day. Maybe more. I honestly don't know how long we lay resting. When Diotima and I woke, we were confused. Was it morning? Afternoon? All we knew was that it was bright sunlight out the window.

We went downstairs to find everyone else enjoying a leisurely breakfast of food that wasn't dried meat mixed with sand.

There we learned that everyone had slept not overnight, but for a day and a half. The others had awoken about the same time we had.

I had lost weight during the journey. Quite a lot, in fact — my exomis hung off me and flopped as if I were a pole beneath a rag. Despite which, I still had little appetite. I supposed it would come back in time. The inn served no wine, which wasn't a surprise. They did have date beer. I drank it without complaint and picked at the flat bread and fruits on the table.

No one wanted to talk about what came next. The euphoria of arrival was gone, replaced by the knowledge that for three days we had worked together to save our lives, but now must return to opposition in our missions. It was a strange feeling. No one wanted to be first to open hostilities. Diotima, Herodotus and I had to be careful for another reason. We knew that Djanet was the true heir of Egypt, but Barzanes and Markos didn't. We didn't dare let it slip.

We finished breakfast by washing our sticky hands in bowls of water. Then by wordless agreement we all began the journey up the hill to the temple. We walked in silence.

At the foot of the steep hill was a stairway made of stone — there was plenty of raw material about — and beside the stairway, a shrine. A large sign was written in the strange language of the Egyptians. Djanet translated.

"It says these buildings were the work of the Pharaoh Amasis," she said.

That was Djanet's great-grandfather.

We continued up the path. My leg muscles ached with every step. I'm sure they did for the others too. At the top was an ornate gate in the Egyptian style, and beside the gate, a priest.

He said, "Welcome to the Temple of Amun. I hope you had a pleasant journey."

The High Priest of Amun received us. He had a private office at the top of the complex, with a view through the window that seemed to go all the way back to Egypt. Acolytes brought dates and beer and, to my joy, a decent wine.

Herodotus thanked the High Priest for his personal attention to mere travelers.

"Every visitor to our temple is someone of importance," the High Priest said.

Herodotus raised an eyebrow. "Is that a religious position? Do you hold that all men are important in the eyes of the God?" he asked.

"No, it's because only important people can get here."

The High Priest was a man of a practical views.

Herodotus looked around at our party, but no one else seemed inclined to speak. Herodotus had somehow become our spokesman.

"The fact is, sir, that for differing reasons, each of us before you is on a quest to find the sarcophagus of the last native Pharaoh, Psamtik, the son of Amasis."

The High Priest of Amun looked from one to another of our expectant faces. Besides Herodotus, who always had a certain air of innocent enthusiasm, the priest saw an Egyptian, two Athenians, a Spartan and a Persian. It was almost like the start of some bad joke.

"I see." The reaction of the High Priest was carefully neutral.

Herodotus was undeterred. "Er . . . I don't suppose you know where it is?" he said hopefully.

"What do you plan to do with the sarcophagus if you find it?" the High Priest asked in return.

Ransack the treasure, tear out the body,

and retrieve sacred insignia from a secret compartment within, in order to prosecute a war. Somehow that didn't seem quite like the right answer to say to a priest. Of all the problems I had anticipated when we arrived, it had not occurred to me that someone might find what we were doing a trifle unethical.

Our combined silence told the High Priest everything he needed to know.

"If I may contribute a point," Barzanes said. "I speak for the Great King of the Persians."

"Yes?" The High Priest said.

"If the contents of that sarcophagus are recovered in the name of Persia, then the Great King will be friend to this temple. There can be no better friend in all the world, nor more powerful. The Great King's friendship is beyond price."

The High Priest arched an eyebrow at these words. "Would that be the same Great King who sent an army of fifty thousand against us?" he asked.

"Er . . . his grandson, actually." Barzanes turned red in embarrassment. Or perhaps it was anger at the mistakes of his predecessors. If so, he would never admit it.

The High Priest said drily, "Forgive me if I find fraternal feelings for Persia difficult to come by."

"Then I shall speak for Sparta," Markos said.

"Do go on," said the High Priest.

"I will not pretend that there is any advantage if you aid me. Sparta is too far away to be of assistance to the temple. But I will say that there is no more fearsome people in the world," Markos said. "It is always good to be a friend of Sparta, because to be the opposite just isn't fun. Ask any Athenian. It is in your interests, my dear High Priest, to be a friend of Sparta."

The High Priest said, with remarkable calm, "You have heard of the Persian army that died. Our god protected us then, and he will protect us again. Nor can any threat against me personally affect my decision. The worst that can happen is that I go to my house of eternity, where I shall have surcease from care. In which case you will have gained nothing."

Markos fell silent.

I said, "Siwa is a lovely place, High Priest."

"Thank you. It is."

"We are in Libya, I believe."

"We are."

"Inaros is your Prince?"

"He is."

"Know then, that it will greatly aid Prince

Inaros if we can have access to that sarcophagus."

The High Priest thought about my words for a long time.

"The prince is known to me. He is a fine man."

"Yes, I know," I said.

"Tell me, does Inaros know what you intend?"

The High Priest had already demonstrated his ability to eviscerate anyone who told less than the entire truth.

"Inaros knows for what we seek," I said. "He does not know where we seek it."

The High Priest spoke slowly. "I cannot help but feel that if Inaros knew you intended to open a grave — *particularly* the grave of one with whom he claims common ancestry — that he would not approve your venture, no matter the advantage to the prince."

I couldn't agree with the priest. Inaros might be a good man, but he was a politician, he was royalty, and he wasn't insane. The prince of Libya would rip open any number of graves if it would make him king of Egypt. But there was no point saying that to a man of the High Priest's ethics.

"Pharaoh Psamtik was not a good man." Djanet spoke quietly.

The High Priest turned to her, in evident surprise. So did the rest of us.

"He was a poor Pharaoh," Djanet went on. "He struck out at inferiors who could not strike back. What sort of man does that? Some said it was because he was insecure in his position. His father Amasis had reigned successfully for forty-four years; no one thought Psamtik could do the same. But by his actions Psamtik drove a man to turn traitor. A man named Phanes."

"I have heard this," the High Priest said.

"Do you know what Psamtik did, in the first battle against the Persians? He took the sons of the traitor Phanes, and right before their father's eyes, and before the eyes of the Persians, and of his own men, he slit the throats of those small boys and bade his men drink the blood of children. Did you know that?"

"I did." The High Priest winced.

"The Great King sent an ambassador to Psamtik, to give him a chance to surrender on terms. It was a better chance than I would have given him. Psamtik ordered the ambassador and his retinue dismembered. Did you know that?"

"Unfortunately, I did," said the High Priest.

"This is the man whose sanctity you are

preserving, and frankly, it isn't worth it."

The High Priest remained silent.

"This request is not about anyone's advantage," Djanet said. "It is about correcting the stupidity, the crimes, and yes, the atrocities perpetrated by the last Pharaoh of Egypt."

Djanet paused. Only Diotima, Herodotus and I knew that Djanet was talking about her grandfather.

"Because of his failings, the people of Egypt have been left slaves to a foreign king," Djanet said. "Now those people are caught up in a war to free themselves. They need help."

"I agree with you completely," said the High Priest.

"Then you will help us?" Herodotus said.

"I would, but unfortunately the sarcophagus isn't here, and I don't know where it is." The High Priest spread his hands in an apologetic gesture.

Four days before, out in the desert, Diotima had said she'd scream if the priests told us that. I had to admire her self-restraint, because she constrained herself to a slight whimper.

Herodotus clenched his hands tight. "That news is . . . somewhat distressing."

"But the sarcophagus was once here. I

hope that we can help you," said the High Priest.

"It was here, but now you don't know?" I said, incredulous. "How do you lose a sarcophagus?"

"You must understand we are talking about a time when the ruling priest was the predecessor of my predecessor. What knowledge I have comes via two generations, who passed on these words in conversation. The final resting place of Psamtik was never central to the work of the temple, and events were somewhat chaotic." The priest shot an aggrieved glance at Barzanes. "The priests back then expected to die at any moment at the hands of the Persians, and that our beautiful temple would be destroyed. When the God intervened to save them, they rejoiced. The fate of one corpse was not uppermost in their minds."

"Understandable."

"Thus at some point during this time, the sarcophagus of Psamtik, the last Pharaoh, disappeared, and no one knows what became of it."

At the sight of our glum faces the priest said, "Do not despair. There is someone we can ask who knows the answer."

"Who?" Herodotus asked eagerly.

"The god of this temple, Amun the Wise."

388

"Oh."

This wasn't the answer we were hoping for. "Forgive me for asking, sir," I said. "But would the God even speak to us?"

"This *is* an oracle, you know," the priest of Amun said gently.

The idea that the oracle could save us didn't fill me with hope.

"What must we do?" Diotima asked.

"If you would each prepare a question for the God, we will arrange for the divination."

"You mean, right now?"

"Why not? The God is always with us," the priest said, reasonably enough.

"Then I shall go first," Djanet said. "My question is very simple. Where shall we find the sarcophagus of Pharaoh Psamtik?"

"I will go second," I said quickly, because I saw a flaw in Djanet's question. I said, "My question is a bit more complex. I ask Amun this: where shall we find the place which is his answer to Djanet's question?"

I felt very pleased with myself. Oracles are known for giving tricky answers. The God might have answered, "In the desert" or "In a tomb" or "At the ends of the earth" and we would be none the wiser. Our entire mission had been spent thinking we'd come to the end, only to find another step. With my question I hoped to circumvent everything and get straight to the final answer.

Herodotus clapped his hands in appreciation. "Very good, Nico!"

Even the High Priest smiled. He said, "I think you will find Amun is not quite as mischievous as your Hellene gods."

"I'm sure you're right," I said politely. But I didn't change my question.

"My turn," Markos said. "I ask the God, who should retrieve the crook and flail?"

Uh oh. Upon the answer to that question would hinge the fate of Egypt. I wasn't the only one disconcerted. Herodotus, Djanet and Diotima glanced at each other with worried faces. Barzanes kept his usual inscrutable expression.

"Next?" the High Priest prompted.

"I will ask," Barzanes said, "who shall rule Egypt?"

This was getting worse.

The High Priest raised an eyebrow. "It's a good thing we have a god on hand. Nothing short of divine wisdom could answer these queries."

The High Priest turned to Herodotus. "Is there anything you wish to ask?"

Herodotus rubbed his chin as he thought. "All the important questions seem to have been asked," he said. "I can think of nothing that will add to the matter at hand.

Would you indulge me in a personal question?"

"Of course."

"Then I ask the God, will anyone read my book?" Then, before any of us could react, he added defensively, "Well, you know, I wouldn't want to spend years writing this thing and then have nobody read it. If the God says it won't work, then I'll stop now."

"You shouldn't do that, Herodotus," I said. "If there's one thing I've learned on this journey, it's that you love this book you're writing. Every time you write one of those interminable notes on your papyrus, you smile, completely lose track of the time, and end up staying awake all night scribbling. Of course you have to finish it."

"No, no, Nicolaos. A book needs readers."

"I promise I'll read it!"

"Er . . . other readers."

"Gentlemen, if you could reserve your discussion for another time?" the High Priest suggested. "The question stands, and the lady wishes to speak."

Diotima glanced at Barzanes with an odd expression.

"I do have a question for Amun," she said. Diotima drew a breath and asked, "Who is the rightful Pharaoh of Egypt?"

Oh dear Gods. What was my wife thinking?

But Diotima had obviously decided that Barzanes's question had to be countered. She sent a sly glance Djanet's way. Djanet, on the other hand, kept an admirably neutral expression.

"Then we are complete," said the High Priest of Amun. "I must go to prepare the sacred vessel for the divination. You will be served refreshments."

We ate and drank in silence. Except for Herodotus, who hummed a quiet, inoffensive tune that got on everyone's nerves.

An acolyte entered to tell us that the priests were ready. I wondered what he meant when he said priests, plural. We followed him downstairs, to the large, wide courtyard, the same courtyard we had crossed when we arrived at the temple. But instead of entering, the acolyte led us to a terrace above, where seats had been arranged to face the courtyard. In the middle of the courtyard was a boat, one large enough to cross the sea. It was almost the size of *Dolphin,* Captain Kordax's craft that had carried us from Athens. That thought made me wonder how Kordax and his men were getting on. Was he still stuck in Africa, like Diotima and me?

The boat in the temple of Siwa was a proper boat, with a hull and a keel, but no mast. It was upright because of triangular supports, of the kind used by shipwrights when a boat had been beached for repairs. About the boat stood a large number of men, perhaps fifty of them, though I didn't count, all of them dressed as priests, all in bare feet, and with no hood or hat to keep off the sun. Going hatless in Siwa risked sunstroke, but I presumed they knew that.

The High Priest joined us on the terrace, arriving through a side entrance. I asked the question that was uppermost in all our minds.

"Why do you have a boat in the middle of the desert?" I said.

"Watch, and you will see," he replied.

From seemingly nowhere a drumming began. It was almost as if the walls themselves made the sound. Then started a rhythmic metallic rattle in tempo with the drums, the sound of many small cymbals being shaken.

This went on for some time. The beat was seductive, hypnotic, the sound reverberated so much that it was all around us. The effect must have been even greater down below, for I realized the courtyard was acting like an amphitheater, reflecting the music up.

So gradually that at first I barely noticed, a flute began to play over the drums. It played at a very high pitch, in an unusual mode with a melody that was deeply foreign and yet strangely attractive.

"The music calls the God," the High Priest explained.

A man with a deep voice shouted an abrupt command. I didn't catch the word, but the priests down below obviously knew what to do.

They swarmed about the boat. Each man rolled up his sleeves and put his shoulder to the hull.

"Are they about to do what I think they're about to do?" Markos said.

The priests hefted the boat. They instantly staggered, as well they might. Those men had to be incredibly strong merely to have got it off the ground.

"Dear Gods," Markos muttered.

"Is that thing as heavy as it looks?" I asked.

"It is, believe me," the High Priest said with feeling.

To our inquiring glances he added, "I used to be one of the carriers, back in my junior days."

Now that he mentioned it, the High Priest's arms did seem to be unusually well muscled.

Meanwhile the priests continued wobbling back and forth under the immense load.

"Do you see those men over there, the three upon the balcony?" The High Priest pointed to a ledge to the side. Three men stood there with stern expressions, their attention locked entirely on the action below. I had seen sergeants in the army with the same look when they drilled their troops. The sharp-eyed look of men who saw everything.

"They are the temple diviners," said the High Priest. "Good men, all three of them. The diviners will provide you your answers. They read the God's answer to each question by the movements of the boat. It is the God's will, you see, that causes the sacred vessel to veer from side to side, and back and forth. Thus Amun communicates with his people."

"So the crew holding it are pushed back and forth by the weight of the vessel, which is in turn pushed around by Amun?" Herodotus said.

"You understand. Precisely."

Herodotus made the inevitable notes on his papyrus.

I said, "Can't the crew sort of . . . ah . . . assist the God with his answer, by pushing the sacred vessel where they want?"

"You obviously have never tried to hold up that boat," said the High Priest. "It's all they can do to keep it off the ground."

Another priest, of middle age and balding, read rapidly from a scroll.

"And the fourth man, beside the diviners?" Diotima asked.

"He is our official querent. The scroll from which he reads contains the questions you gave me."

"I don't understand a word he says," Diotima said.

"He speaks a temple language, the language of Amun. It is a secret taught only to us priests. Question time lasts only as long as the carrier-priests can keep the sacred vessel off the ground," the High Priest said. "Therefore the querent cycles through the list of questions with some speed, to get through everything before they drop the boat."

The High Priest judged the state of the crew with a practiced eye. "Which will be right about now."

A moment later, the carrier-priests dropped the boat with an enormous thud. Now I knew why the courtyard was covered deep in sand. The very solid sacred vessel was unharmed. The men dived out of the way. Other priests rushed in with the supports and jammed these under the hull, while the carriers lay in the sand panting in exhaustion.

Two gates opened along the far side of the court, to reveal a huge empty space. Men placed skids under the vessel. They dragged the oracle back home, its job done for the day. The gates closed behind it. I made a mental note never to become a priest of Amun. It was far too much hard work.

"Excuse me for a moment, I must speak to the diviners to collect your answers," said the High Priest.

He returned quickly.

"Ladies and gentlemen, your answers. Amun has spoken." He shifted through scraps of papyrus. Even from ten paces away, I could see that the papyrus he held had been scraped back for reuse many times. Paper was at a premium this far from the Nile.

The priest looked to Barzanes. "The God answered your question first. Who shall rule Egypt? Amun answered with one word: Persia."

Barzanes rarely smiled, and he didn't now, but the corners of his mouth curved up just the tiniest fraction. The rest of us scowled.

The priest turned to Markos. "Then to

the Spartan gentleman. You asked who should retrieve the crook and flail. The God says this: Not only should Markos the Spartan retrieve the insignia, but he must."

Markos laughed.

The rest of us didn't.

"I like this god," he said. "I will be sure to tell the elders of Sparta of your service."

"Of course, this supposes we find the sarcophagus," I pointed out, in an effort to dampen his happiness.

"The God answered your question next, sir," the High Priest said to Herodotus. "Will anyone read your book?"

"And the answer?" Herodotus leaned forward and looked tense.

"Not millions, but tens of millions will read your history."

That was more people than existed in the whole world. The answer was obviously wrong, but Herodotus was pleased. His normally critical mind had been dazzled by an answer that was better than he'd hoped to hear.

I was disappointed. I couldn't help but feel that the High Priest was telling each of us what we wanted to hear. I had thought the oracle genuine. But these oracular pronouncements were little different from the words a mere charlatan would utter to extract coins from the credulous. Had we wasted our time?

"I come now to the Egyptian lady's question. She asked, where would she find the sarcophagus of Pharaoh Psamtik?"

"Yes?" Djanet said.

We all waited with bated breathe.

"Amun says this: he lies with the Great Tjaty."

"What, back in Memphis?" Djanet fairly shrieked.

"I cannot add words to what a god says," the High Priest answered. "The sarcophagus you seek lies with the great Tjaty. That is what Amun saw fit to tell you."

"That's not exactly helpful," Djanet said.

"Never fear," I said. "This is exactly why I asked my question. Where shall we find the place which is the answer to Djanet's question. What did the God say?" I asked eagerly.

The High Priest rummaged through his slips of paper.

"See question one," he said.

Diotima laughed.

"That's it?" I said.

"I'm afraid so." The High Priest rummaged again. "Oh, a moment. Amun repeated his response, but this time instead of great Tjaty, he said Tjaty of Tjaties. Of course, in the Egyptian tongue, it comes to the same thing."

"Thank you," I said politely, trying hard to hide my annoyance.

"The final question, for the Athenian lady. Who is the rightful Pharaoh of Egypt."

This was the moment all our work would come undone. Barzanes and Markos would learn Djanet's true identity.

The High Priest peered at the response.

"Amun the Wise says this: Siwa awaits the Macedonian."

"Who?" Diotima said. It wasn't the reply she expected. "Is anyone here Macedonian, by any chance?" She glanced at Djanet.

We all shook our heads, including Djanet, which was no surprise since I had never seen anyone who looked less Macedonian.

"It's obvious nonsense," I said. "Macedonians can barely rule themselves. They're far too busy killing each other."

Markos nodded.

"Nicolaos is correct," Barzanes said. "If Persia rules Egypt, as the God predicts, then the Great King is Pharaoh, and the Great King is certainly not Macedonian."

"I'm afraid Amun got that one wrong," Herodotus agreed.

Luckily, the High Priest was not offended by our words. "The God says these things.

We generally find that they turn out to be true."

We thanked him for his courtesy. Herodotus offered a substantial donation to the temple, "For the backs of those poor carriers." Barzanes, too, in the pleasure of knowing that Persia would rule Egypt, promised great reward to the oracle. "A camel train will bring riches," he said.

Barzanes and Markos were both quite happy with the outcome. From their viewpoint, failing to find the crook and flail was as good as winning it for themselves. I noticed that it had been some time since Markos had attacked anyone. I pulled him aside and asked about this.

"Barzanes and I have come to an accommodation," Markos admitted candidly.

I didn't like the sound of that.

"Honestly, there's no point fighting until there's something worth fighting over," Markos added.

"How about that contract?"

"As it happens, I've been offered another contract, a quite different one."

"Oh?" Things had been happening while I wasn't watching. That made me nervous.

"I'm not at liberty to talk about it," Markos said.

"I see."

We rejoined the group, who were making the long walk down the steps of the temple.

Djanet said, "Well that didn't work, did it? I'm in a depression."

"The Qattara Depression?" I said helpfully.

"No, you idiot, a real depression. Could the crook and flail truly lie with the Tjaty, as the God says?"

"If so, the Tjaty's fooled everyone," I said. "I could have sworn he wanted it as much as everyone else."

I mulled over this question as we walked. It made absolutely no sense that the Tjaty had the crook and flail. He had killed Max because of it! The Public Service might be a bunch of sadistic bureaucrats, but not even they would kill a man for something they already had.

I thought through every word that the Tjaty had ever said to me. Was there some clue in there?

Suddenly I said, "Wait!"

Everyone stopped in mid-step and looked at me. We were halfway down the hill, or halfway up, depending on how you looked at it. I said, "Herodotus, you told me you wanted to inspect the boat. For your book."

"Did I?" He sounded confused.

"You did," I said firmly. "Come along

402

now, so we don't have to climb these steps twice."

I grabbed him by the arm and practically dragged him back uphill. None of the others offered to join us. They were all tired of Herodotus's interminable questions.

"Nico, do you mind if we head back down?" Diotima called up to us.

"Go ahead, we'll join you at the inn later," I called back. The party went on without us.

"Where are we really going?" Herodotus asked as we walked.

"To see the High Priest," I told him. "There's one last question we should have asked, and I don't want Markos or Barzanes to hear it. I think you're going to enjoy this."

The High Priest sat at the desk in his office. He looked up as we entered, showed no surprise, and said, "Yes?"

I got straight to the point. "Sir, is the tomb of Imhotep around here, by any chance?"

"I thought you would never ask," said the High Priest.

I told Herodotus he wasn't allowed to make notes. We didn't dare risk Barzanes or Markos reading them.

"We all thought Great Tjaty must mean the current man," I said by way of explanation to Herodotus. "It's normal to place 'Great' in front of the title of an important man, as the High Priest mentioned."

The High Priest acknowledged that with a nod.

"Then on the steps down I remembered that the current Tjaty had called Imhotep *Greatest of the Tjaties.* He said it when I first met him, in the secret chamber under the temple of Bast. The Public Service venerate Imhotep as if he were a god. They even keep a statue of him in their chamber. Suggestive, don't you think?"

"Yes," said Herodotus. "That's all very well, Nico, but what made you think the tomb would be here?"

"Because we know the body of Psamtik was shipped to Siwa! If he lies with the Greatest of the Tjaties, then Imhotep must be here too. Though I don't understand why."

The High Priest looked pleased with me. "Imhotep created the first pyramid, as you probably know," he said.

"Yes, we know that," Herodotus said. "It was the largest stone structure ever built by man in its day. A marvelous achievement."

"Well, you don't think he got it perfect on the first try, do you?"

"You mean —"

"Imhotep came here to practice, out of sight of the Egyptian public, where if the first few attempts at a House of Eternity fell into rubble, it wouldn't be quite so embarrassing."

Herodotus laughed. "And when he finally got one that stood up, he decided to use it for himself."

"Correct."

"I understand quite a few men have searched for Imhotep's tomb at Saqqara," said Herodotus.

"They're grave robbers, all of them, one way or another. There's no need to tell them. The great man deserves his peace."

"I agree with you entirely."

"As to that, I must have your word that nothing in the tomb that is Imhotep's will be touched."

"Definitely not. We will swear it," said Herodotus.

"Sir, what of Psamtik and his grave goods?" I asked. "I must warn you we intend to —"

"Take it. Yes, I know. You are welcome to all of it." He shrugged. "There are some jewels, some gold. Baubles that enrich a man in life but do nothing for his soul. Certainly nothing that anyone alive has any right to."

He was wrong about that, but I wasn't about to enlighten him.

"In fact, I'd be pleased if he was removed. The man did himself no credit in life and his presence in the same tomb as Imhotep is an insult."

Herodotus and I swore by Zeus, by Athena and by Amun that Imhotep would not be disturbed in his rest.

Herodotus hesitated, then said, "High Priest, may I ask a question?"

"Please."

"It seems to me that you may have told a slight fib this morning, when you said that you didn't know where to find the sarcophagus."

The priest smiled, ever so slightly. "Your Persian and Spartan friends were with you."

"So you *did* lie."

The High Priest said crossly, "Every word from the oracle was truth. It came from the god Amun, via our diviners. It is against our religion to alter the God's words, and I would be upset if anyone suggested otherwise."

"Oh. My apologies." Herodotus was contrite.

"As to what was said before that . . . I am a Libyan. The Egyptians are our brothers. Sometimes a priest's words will be phrased for a greater good," the priest said with a straight face.

"Ah." Herodotus smiled.

"It so happens that I have a map of the Siwa locale, showing places of interest for the casual tourist, including the location of any tombs of note." The High Priest pulled out a sheet of papyrus. "Would you like a copy?"

The Imhotep Incident

"We will need bearers," Djanet said.

"Why?" Herodotus asked.

"Well we can't come back here after we've collected the crook and flail, can we? Not if you want to avoid Barzanes and Markos. We'll have to visit the tomb, then *keep on going.* All the way across the desert. So this is it. We collect the crook and flail, take the treasure we find, and we leave. We'll need men to carry the treasure. We'll need supplies, we'll need water."

I was impressed. "You've thought this through ahead of time," I said.

"Very carefully, believe me," Djanet said. "I've thought about nothing else for a long time now."

"When do we do it?" Herodotus asked.

"It can't be at night," Diotima said. "We'd never find anything in the desert, even with torches and a map."

"Nor can we leave in daylight," I said. "It

408

would be obvious."

"Therefore we must leave before dawn, timed so that it is first light as we arrive at the tomb," Djanet said.

This was such perfect planning that we all nodded in agreement.

"I go now to arrange men and supplies," Djanet said.

Not for the first time I mourned the passing of Max. Not only because he was a fine man, but because he too could have talked with the locals in their own language. As it was, Djanet would have to make all the arrangements.

The remainder of the day was spent in rest. Barzanes interpreted our inaction as depression, due to what he thought was the failure of our mission.

"I cannot say I am sorry," Barzanes said to me, as we sat in the cool shade of the inn, drinking the local beer. "Had you found the crook and flail, I would have been forced to intervene. We would both have regretted that."

"I'm sure."

Barzanes ordered more beer for us both and sat back in what passed for him as a state of relaxation, which meant that his back was a little less straight than usual.

"You serve your country and I serve mine, Athenian. It means we are often at odds, but when we are not there is no reason why we cannot converse."

That took me aback. It was the closest thing to a friendly overture that I had ever heard from the Persian.

"Listen, let me give you some advice," I said. "When you're back in Egypt, look out for Markos."

Barzanes nodded. "Megabazos hired the Spartan to kill me. Of this I am aware. Know that one of my men has watched him continuously since we joined forces."

"Why don't you simply kill him outright?"

"Unfortunately the Great King wishes to make a friend of the Spartans. They would not take it well if one of their agents was killed by one of ours. Not without proof of ill-doing, at any rate."

He was more sanguine than I would have been.

Barzanes drank more beer. Then he said quietly, "There is another reason I keep the Spartan alive. When he finally makes his move — and I am sure that he will — I intend to capture him alive. I will then cart him to Susa, where he will stand before the Great King and confess, under torture if necessary, that it was Megabazos who hired a Spartan to murder me. This the King will not be able to ignore, and I will finally have eliminated a corrupt official of my people."

"Dear Gods, Barzanes, you're using yourself as your own stalking horse!"

"Yes."

Barzanes was the coldest man I had ever met, but I admired him as a most competent enemy.

I wanted to see Markos before we left. I found him by the edge of the lake, the beautiful lake that gave life in the middle of this desert. He sat in the shallows with a couple of the local men. They all held cups.

"I'm learning the language," he said, when I joined them. He held up an amphora. "Would you like some beer?"

"I've had enough," I said. "I was drinking back at the inn."

"Nothing else to do, now that your mission's failed," he said. "I'm glad the treasure wasn't here, Nico. If it had been, we would have had to fight over it."

"Would we?"

"You don't think I could go back to Sparta and admit I let an Athenian get away with such a big advantage, do you?"

"Well, it's not a problem now," I replied, and tried to sound sad. "Diotima and I will have to return to Athens and admit failure."

"Will you get into trouble?"

I thought about it. "I don't think so," I said. "Egypt is far away. Siwa is even further away. Everyone knows these things are chancy. Pericles will shout at me. It's not like I haven't heard that before."

"Give my fondest regards to your boss."

"I'll be sure to do that. It'll make him shout even louder."

I sat in the water beside them while Markos continued his conversation with the local men. The Siwans were much amused. At first I thought they were laughing at Markos's attempts. After a while I realized they were laughing *with* him. Markos had picked up the tongue very quickly and, inevitably for Markos, he was using it to tell jokes.

I complimented him on his fitting in so well.

"I rather like it here."

"Why don't you stay?" I said abruptly.

He looked at me with an odd expression. "What makes you say that?"

"In your heart, you're no more a Spartan than I am. You can do better elsewhere. You'd certainly be happier elsewhere. You said to me, back in Memphis, that you could have been a comic. Well, disappear on this continent and no one will ever know.

Be a comic!"

"Now you're giving me career advice?" he said. "What's got into you?"

"Nothing, except I wish you well, strange as that may seem. I admired you from the day we first met, back at the Olympics."

"We talked about this before. I can't do it. I need to be at the center of things."

"All right then, at least do me this favor: when you go back to Egypt, don't continue the contract on Barzanes. Go back to Megabazos and say you failed."

"Why are you saying this?"

"I don't want to see friends fight each other."

"Friends?"

"Colleagues then," I said impatiently. "You're making this difficult."

Markos drank his beer and watched the water for a long time. Then he said, "I'll think about it."

"Thanks, Markos."

As I left, I passed by one of the Persians, who lounged against a whitewashed wall on the opposite side of the street. I realized he was the man that Barzanes had set to watching Markos. He was good at his job, because Markos obviously hadn't noticed. I gave the man a nod as I passed by, and he nodded back

■ ■ ■ ■

We crept out of Siwa in the early morning — so early that the stars were bright in the sky. The logistics had been a major exercise, worked out by Djanet, Diotima and Herodotus while I'd kept Barzanes and Markos busy. The bearers waited outside the city, along with some horses that Djanet had acquired for heavy lifting.

To leave the inn without waking the Persians or the Spartan had been a tense exercise. In the cold morning we had crept downstairs on tiptoe, like lodgers skipping out on the rent. To avoid that being a real issue, Djanet had paid the landlord the entire rent the night before, plus a substantial bonus not to say anything to Barzanes or Markos.

Despite tripping over each other, the scheme had worked. We made it out onto the street with no one inside the wiser. We stood there, shivering for a moment, before we made our way silently to the back of the inn, where were kept the camels. These we loaded with everything we owned, including the pack camels. Once we had what we'd come for, we intended to carry on home. We untethered the beasts and led them up the street.

We arrived at the prearranged place out-side the town. The men were already there, waiting for us.

So was Barzanes.

We stood there, slack-jawed.

Barzanes said, "Good morning. Unfortunately I don't know where we are going. I presume you have that planned?"

I stammered, "How did you —"

"I told you I set a man to watch the Spartan. Did it not occur to you that I might also have set a man to watch *you*?"

It hadn't. I kicked myself.

"Do you mean we didn't have to get up so early?" Herodotus said, aggrieved. He seemed to be more upset about that than that we might be about to lose the Pharaoh's treasure.

"At least we don't have to contend with Markos," I said.

"That's not entirely true," called a voice from beyond the hill. Markos appeared. "Didn't it occur to you that since I was learning the language, I could overhear the local men talking about being hired to dig out a tomb?"

Djanet cursed, loudly. Barzanes looked distinctly unhappy.

"The only party who knows where we're

going is yours, Nico," Markos said. "You'd better lead the way."

THE TOMB

The pyramid tomb of Imhotep had been covered in dirt, dust, and sand. It took us half the morning to find it. In fact, we discovered we'd walked over it twice before we noticed. The tomb looked like every other hill in this accursed desert.

"How long has he been dead?" I asked Djanet.

"About two thousand years."

That explained why it was covered. The dust storms out here were ferocious, and a step pyramid must have acted like a barrier. It would only take a few years before the whole thing was buried.

We sat on the sand — there wasn't the slightest piece of shade — and watched while the workmen cleared the way to the entrance. Herodotus had cleverly loaded shovels and pickaxes onto the horses' backs. I praised his foresight.

As we sat and watched other people work,

we all avoided an ugly subject. What was going to happen when we had the crook and flail? Eventually, unable to stand the unspoken tension any longer, I asked the question.

"*If* we find them," was Barzanes's answer. "We borrow trouble, do we not, to discuss this before we know what lies within?"

"I think we should decide now," Herodotus said. "To avoid any unpleasant . . . er . . ."

"Wars?" Markos suggested helpfully.

"I was going to say consequences," Herodotus said primly.

"I'm sure," Markos said.

"The treasure will be returned to Persian territory," Barzanes said. "Even the oracle agrees that Egypt belongs to Persia. Therefore the crook and flail belongs to the Great King."

"Inaros's armies control the north," I pointed out.

"And Persia's men control Memphis," Barzanes replied. "If we travel due east from here — the shortest route across the desert, I remind you — then we will arrive at Memphis."

"Inaros could move his army," Diotima said.

"So could the commander in the capital,"

Barzanes replied.

Were we really about to restart a war? "Barzanes is right," I said. "We're borrowing trouble."

At that moment one of the sweating men shouted, "We're almost in."

I tried to imagine a room that hadn't been swept for two thousand years. This wasn't going to be good.

They broke through to the door.

The Libyans had worked with astonishing speed. What had saved us was that the entrance had been opened only sixty years before. I couldn't imagine what agony the men must have gone through to open the pyramid when they hid Psamtik in here. Back then, they had had two thousand years of dirt to shift.

The entrance was low but wide. The surrounding stone was in remarkably good condition, I supposed because it had been covered. The doorway had originally been blocked with close-fitting stones. These had been shattered when they put Psamtik in, and the resultant loose rubble merely piled into the doorway. It was sloppy work on the part of the men sixty years before us, but good news for our fellows. They formed a chain and passed out the stones.

When the way was clear, we crowded in.

Workmen passed in torches.

Imhotep's practice pyramid was perhaps half the size of the one he had later built at Saqqara, perhaps even smaller. But within he had left a large space. The smell was beyond musty. The air felt as dead as the occupants. I didn't know if it was my imagination, but I thought it was hard to breathe. I found myself panting.

In the center of the space was an enormous sarcophagus. I walked over, fascinated. It was covered in dust. I wiped some away.

"Dear Gods, is that gold?" I stared at the surface.

"Probably," said Djanet.

"Careful, Nico," Herodotus said. "We swore an oath not to disturb this man." He glared at the others. "Nor let anyone else disturb him."

Markos shrugged. Everyone else nodded and looked solemn.

Herodotus and I wiped it down, then we stared at the beautiful sarcophagus. Herodotus said, "I wish Tutu was here to see this."

So did I. The enthusiastic embalmer would have loved this.

"Tutu was right," I said. "They did do things better in the days of his forebears."

I wanted to look through all the stuff

placed on the floor, but mindful of our promise, I backed away, careful not to kick the jars by my feet. I knew from Tutu's lecture that those jars contained the liver and brain of the man before us, plus other parts of his innards that I didn't want to think about.

Along the side of the wall closest to the entrance, there was a chariot.

"What's that doing here?" I asked.

"Grave goods," Herodotus said.

"Somehow I doubt the occupants will want to go for a drive."

"No, you fools. It's the ceremonial chariot they used to bring Psamtik's sarcophagus," Djanet said. "It's certainly nothing to do with Imhotep. It's in too good condition."

Indeed it was. The chariot was a two-wheeler with a large platform — definitely not built for racing — and in great condition.

"I suppose the heat preserved it."

The men hauled the chariot out onto the desert floor. It was the only way to get at whatever was behind. They had to drip fat from the torches and olive oil from our supplies onto the axles to get the wheels moving, but after that it proved easy enough. The wheels were wide-rimmed.

"I think this might have been built for

desert work," I said.

"Of course it was," Djanet said. "It's an Egyptian chariot, built to travel around Egypt."

"Oh. Good point."

Djanet seemed on edge. That was natural enough. This was her grandfather we were excavating.

With the way clear we came at last to a second sarcophagus. There was no doubting what we had found. The outside matched the description Tutu had given us.

Scattered about the large sarcophagus were boxes, quite large ones, and furniture. A ceremonial shield stood propped against the wall. Diotima opened one of the smaller boxes to reveal jewelry, gold, and stones that glowed in the torchlight. It wasn't a Pharaoh's ransom, but it was a fortune to any normal person. Whoever had put Psamtik here had done right by a defeated Pharaoh. The larger boxes contained precious materials and grave goods, the sort of things that anyone needs to accompany them into the Afterworld: plates and cups, a fine bed and containers of what seemed to be scents and spices.

"This treasure comes with us," Djanet said, and no one argued. We had promised not to rob Imhotep. Psamtik was fair game.

That left the sarcophagus, and whatever might be within.

We looked at one another.

"Who wants to do the honors?" I asked.

"Me," Markos said. "The High Priest said I must open the box. Remember?"

So he had. I also remembered Tutu's words, that whoever opened Psamtik's sarcophagus would be cursed in this life and the next.

I wondered whether to say anything. But if Markos didn't open the coffin, then who? I looked around at the other faces, cast in strange colors in the flickering light. Could I let my wife be cursed? Of course not. Nor Herodotus, nor Djanet. It would have been immoral to ask one of the workmen. It left only Barzanes or Markos, or me. Barzanes was too canny. I was too cautious.

"I insist," Markos said.

Diotima's eyes caught mine. She made no movement, but I knew she was signaling a yes to me.

"Go ahead."

Markos knelt at the side. The catches undid easily, as well they might. They had only been closed sixty years before. He raised the lid to reveal the mummy within. I wondered how Djanet felt.

"What now?" Markos said impatiently.

I inspected Markos for any sign of a curse upon him.

"What is it?" he demanded when he caught me staring at him.

"Nothing." I knelt beside him. "We have to lift out the body."

"What?"

"I mean it."

With Markos at the foot end and me at the head, we lifted the mummy. The body was stiff, probably because of all the wrappings.

We laid Psamtik aside.

"Bring a torch."

Diotima leant over with a torch in her hand. Neither of us could see the hidden compartment that Tutu had told us of. I ran my fingers around the bottom of the casket, felt a slight gap.

"Here it is."

I got my fingernails in and pulled upwards. Part of the base rose to reveal a space beneath, and lying within it a flail, of the type used to keep slaves in line, and a short crook just like the kind shepherds use.

Except that shepherds don't wield crooks made of ebony and gold, and slave masters don't strike with flails embedded with precious stones. The crook and flail shone in the dark. There was no doubt about it:

these items were unique. Anyone would recognize them instantly as the insignia of a Pharaoh.

"We did it!" Diotima shouted in triumph. I laughed. Herodotus wrote a note.

Djanet said, "I'm sorry about this."

"Sorry about what?" I asked.

Djanet hit Herodotus. It was a sharp blow to the temple, that sent the author's head into the wall close by. He fell to the ground unconscious.

"What are you *doing*?" I shouted at Djanet.

But there was no time for a reply, because Markos smashed his fist into my head. It was a blow of Olympic proportions. He was in the perfect position, standing over me. The last words I heard were, "Sorry, Nico."

When I came to, things had changed.

It took me a moment to remember what had happened. When I did, I opened my eyes. My sight went in and out of focus. I shook my head groggily and sat up.

I heard thumps, and the shouts of women. In the center of the chamber, Djanet and Diotima were fighting. Diotima had picked up the ceremonial shield. She was using this to block Djanet, who was wielding one of the workmen's mallets. Djanet's blows against the shield were strong, but so were Diotima's deflections. Neither of them was getting anywhere.

"Go to Barzanes," Diotima shouted. "He needs help!"

Djanet had betrayed us. I didn't know why and this wasn't the time to ask. I didn't want to leave my wife in a dangerous fight, but Diotima knew the situation and I didn't. If she said Barzanes needed help, then his position must have been dire indeed. I couldn't see him inside, nor Markos. I stumbled out into the bright light, and instantly regretted the decision. My eyes hurt and my head felt about ready to burst. I took a step forward, rubbing my eyes to ease the pain.

And instantly tripped over one of the treasure boxes. Sprawled on the ground, I looked to my feet to see what I'd hit. The bodies of Barzanes's two Persian soldiers lay there, one with his throat slit — he stared in open-mouthed surprise — and the other with a dagger embedded in his chest. I wondered if Barzanes was still alive. I hauled myself up and carried on, all too well aware that if Barzanes was gone then I wouldn't last a heartbeat. The workmen were clustered about the low dune beside the tomb. I went that way.

Barzanes was still alive and fighting Markos. Their hands were blurs as they rained down blows upon each other. The workmen were keeping out of it, and I couldn't blame them. They stood back in a semicircle and watched. There was blood flowing from Barzanes's mouth, where I could see Markos had punched him hard. Barzanes was giving as good as he got; as I watched he landed a sly blow against Markos's right knee, which caused the Spartan to stifle a cry of pain. If the situation hadn't been so desperate, it would have been educational to watch Persia's top agent slug it out with a Spartan. As it was, I hoped I could stay conscious long enough to influence the battle, because my sight had blurred again and the desert was spinning. I felt like I might faint at any moment.

I put my hands to my head, in an attempt to hold everything together. I felt warm stickiness. My hands came away drenched in my own blood. The blow Markos had landed had obviously been enormous. Markos might even think I was dead. For that matter, if the damage was great enough, I might soon be. Everyone knew of men who had died suddenly the day after taking a blow to the head.

Meanwhile I had a decision to make. Who

did I want to win this fight?

Did I want Markos to eliminate Barzanes? Or Barzanes to kill Markos? I hated to admit it, but of the three of us Barzanes was the best agent. He was the greater threat to Athens. Markos on the other hand was the most dangerous man I had ever met. There was every chance that one day he would kill me, if he hadn't already. Both were men I deeply admired, one way or another. Both were men I needed to fear.

Neither had seen me, in the midst of their battle. It meant I could intervene on behalf of one or the other. I was in the luxurious but odd position of being able to choose who would be my enemy in the years to come. The assassin or the ruthless agent? The Spartan or the Persian? The friend or the . . . rival?

Though the question was hypothetical, because I was in no condition to fight anyone. At that moment, an angry flute girl with a soft pillow could have beaten me to death, and I wouldn't have been able to stop her.

I needed a weapon. Then I remembered that I had one. I half-ran, half-staggered to where we had left the camels. They had come with us loaded with all our supplies, because we had expected to travel onward after we ransacked the tomb. That plan was dead, but our possessions were still here.

Pericles the Camel stared down at me imperiously. I'd always thought he had much in common with his namesake. I ignored his obvious disgust and tore out everything in the large pack at his rear. The crossbow was hidden at the bottom. I'd told both Barzanes and Markos that the crossbow was left behind in Memphis. I'd lied.

My eyesight went black as I rummaged. I had to lean against Pericles until sight returned. After that I moved more slowly.

I yanked out the crossbow with both hands, then reached for the bolts. They spilled onto the ground. I cursed and picked one up, slotted it into the crossbow, and then with all my strength pulled back the taut wire. That was enough to make my vision go dark again, but I struggled through.

I thought back to the fight on the banks of the Nile, against the mercenaries, and realized there was no point taking a second bolt with me now; in a crisis like this there'd be no time to load another. I ran back to the fight as fast as I could.

The workmen had disappeared. The fight had turned to a close wrestle. Markos and Barzanes were locked together as they each sought a chokehold on the other. That

Death of an Agent

Markos was dead. The crossbow bolt had taken him in the left side, exactly where I had aimed. The bolt had passed through his heart, killing him instantly, and then emerged out the other side of his chest. Barzanes was untouched. That was more by luck than good management, but I wasn't about to admit such to Barzanes.

In a straight choice, I had chosen Barzanes. Barzanes was the smartest of us all, and ruthless, but he was also an honorable man, and I would take that over Markos any day.

For the rest of his life, he would remember that I had saved him from an assassin.

"Thank you, Athenian . . . Nicolaos," Barzanes said. He lay on the ground, panting from the effort. I offered a hand to help him up, then almost toppled when he took it. We found ourselves upright, and almost leaning against each other.

"Who is inside the pyramid?" Barzanes asked.

"Diotima and Djanet."

At that moment we heard a commotion. Barzanes and I both turned to see a chariot race out from behind the pyramid. It was driven by Djanet. She had hitched the hired horses to Pharaoh Psamtik's ceremonial chariot. Trailing along behind her were the bearers, the ones she had hired the night before. They had to run to keep up with her, and each carried one of the treasures that had surrounded Psamtik.

Djanet stood upon the wide platform and drove the chariot herself. At her feet was a long, wrapped bundle. It looked like the body of her grandfather.

Djanet whipped the horses. As she thundered past, Djanet kicked the bundle that lay her feet. The bundle rolled off the chariot floor and hit the ground with a thump and a loud, "Oomph!" from within. It was Herodotus, hastily wrapped up like a sausage in mummy cloth.

As I bent to unwrap him I said, "Are you all right?"

Herodotus spat dust and said, "I'm fine. She tied me up."

"That didn't go quite the way I expected," I said, as we watched Djanet disappear over the horizon, a Pharaoh's treasure trailing in her wake.

"Nor I," Barzanes admitted.

A sudden, horrible thought gripped me. If Djanet was free, what had happened to Diotima? I asked Herodotus.

"Djanet left her tied up, inside the pyramid," Herodotus said.

We found her there, bound hand and foot. She couldn't speak because of the gag in her mouth, but her eyes spoke murder. She spat out the gag as soon as I loosened it and she said, "I presume you let her get away?"

I forbore from pointing out that Diotima hadn't exactly excelled at stopping Djanet either.

"There's a letter over there." Diotima pointed to a rock crevice. "Djanet made sure I saw her put it in."

We opened the letter.

I write this on the night before we depart Siwa, so that you will understand.

What I have taken is no more than my birthright. My parents were killed by poverty in a nation of which by rights they should have been king and queen. I vowed long ago that would not happen to me. When Inaros raised the rebellion, I realized my chance had come.

I confess that you, Nicolaos, and Diotima and Barzanes and Markos, were a complication I didn't need. Never have I seen so few people cause so much confusion among one another. Luckily for me you all proved useful, one way or another.

My final trick was to persuade Markos to help me wrest the treasure from you at the instant we uncovered it, in return for a share. I believe he will use his part to retire from Sparta, to some place where no one can find him. I wish him good fortune and I hope the curse Tutu mentioned doesn't come to pass.

You are probably wondering about my plans. I will not spend my inheritance in the battle against the Persians. That fight was lost when my grandfather fell. I will not give the crook and flail to be carried by Inaros, who is no brother of mine. Nor will I carry the crook and flail myself. A singer from Memphis could never be king.

Instead I go now to the south, where I shall be a Princess of Aethiopia. I told you once before that the royal families had kept in touch. The king there is old. The prince is in need of a wife of royal credentials. Credentials such as, for example, the crook and flail of the pharaohs. So it is that a singer from Memphis might never be king in her own land, but she shall be queen in a distant one.

I thank you for finding my dowry. I could not have done it without you.

In a scribbled note at the bottom she had added:

Sorry I had to hit you, Diotima.

"She would have made a fine Pharaoh," Herodotus said. I could only agree.

Friends and Enemies

We buried Markos in the desert, beside the pyramid of Imhotep. I had wanted to place him within, but lacking an embalmer to prepare the body, that would have been impossible.

Spartan law requires that no man can have his grave marked, unless he dies fighting for his country. I took the view that Markos had more than fulfilled that obligation. Over his grave I placed a sign that read: MARKOS. A FINE MAN.

That job done, we closed the pyramid and resealed the entrance. It took us most of the day. We had to do it ourselves because the frightened workmen never returned. Fortunately we had brought plenty of drinking water, some of which we poured down our backs for relief from the heat.

Then we rode back to the inn, exhausted, wounded and deflated. We had to beg for our rooms back. Word of the disaster at the tomb of Imhotep had already been spread by the men who fled the scene. The inn-keeper told us we could stay, but only if we departed next morning. There was some question whether either Barzanes or I would be fit to travel by then, but there was no choice. Diotima took to doctoring us, by the end of which Barzanes and I were covered in bandages. Markos had done a thorough job on both of us. You had to admire a man who could take on two top agents and come so close to beating them both.

As we sat in the inn's common room that night, drinking beer and nursing our pains, Barzanes said, "Athenian, I wish to ask you a question."

"Yes?"

"When you fired the crossbow, why did you not kill us both?"

"I had only a single shot," I said.

"Do not attempt to fool me," Barzanes said softly. "The crossbow is powerful enough to kill two men with a single shot. You have seen this for yourself. So I ask again. It was in your power to eliminate us both, but you did not. Why?"

I toyed with my beer, wondering how to answer. I chose my words carefully. "Back in Memphis at that inn, we swore an oath of non-aggression."

"I remember it," he said.

"The thing is, Barzanes, you kept that oath. The Tjaty told me that he warned you about Markos. He couldn't understand why you didn't attack Markos first. But I understood. I don't break my oaths either."

Barzanes thought about my words. He said, "Your integrity is great. You would have made a fine Persian."

"Thanks, I think."

"By the way, Athenian, I believe you owe me a crossbow." Barzanes looked me in the eyes as he spoke, to let me know he meant it.

I shook my head slowly. "I'm sorry, Barzanes, but I can't let you send the crossbow back to Persia. It's too powerful."

"I certainly cannot let it go to Athens!" he said. I had to concede that in his position I would have said the same thing.

I'd known this was coming, and I already had an answer. "Barzanes, we've both had a bad day. Do you really feel like fighting about this?"

"Not I," he said.

"Then here's a simple answer. Let's destroy the accursed thing."

Barzanes didn't need to think about it. "Your suggestion is good," he said.

We borrowed an axe, but neither of us had the strength to wield it. Herodotus did the honors. He threw the broken wood onto a pile for the inn's fire, and the metal pieces into the lake.

"Job's done," he said.

The job was indeed done. We could all go home.

THE AEGYPTOS SOLUTION

Inaros was not nearly so angry as I expected.

Diotima and I had insisted upon a private audience when we returned to Naukratis. Inaros had instantly noticed two missing from our party: Maxyates and Djanet. He had nodded and led us into a private chamber. This time however there was to be no intimate discussion around a dining table. We stood while he sat and listened to our tale. We didn't make a very good job of it.

"There have been certain miscalculations," Inaros said, when we finished. "Both on my part and yours. I grieve for Maxyates."

"I'm sorry we failed." It was all I could say.

Inaros held up a hand. "Failure is a relative thing. You might have brought me something more valuable than the crook and flail."

I blinked. "We might? What?"

"The location of the lost tomb of Imho-tep."

"I fail to see the value, Inaros," Diotima said.

"The Public Service will be *desperate* to know where to find Imhotep's House of Eternity. You yourself, Nicolaos, noted how the bureaucrats revere Imhotep. As a bargaining chip, it is most powerful, even more so than the insignia which they would have acknowledged only reluctantly. I can trade the tomb for the White Fort."

"Barzanes has the same information," I warned him.

"But the tomb is in Libya, where I am strong. If I had known that the tomb of Imhotep was on offer, I would have asked for that instead of the crook and flail. You have done well, in the face of difficulties I had not anticipated. I shall certainly say so to Pericles."

A few days later I was walking down a street in Naukratis when I was suddenly confronted by the man who had coshed me, and carried me to the Temple of Bast. The same man who acted for the Tjaty of Egypt.

I backed away quickly and brought up my hands in self-defense, expecting an assassination attempt at any moment.

"You must relax," he said calmly. "I am here to extend an invitation."

He led me to a fine house in one of the better streets, on the opposite side of the city to where Inaros had his residence.

The courtyard within was very beautiful, and filled with cats of all colors and descriptions. I instantly had a feeling of foreboding, which was confirmed when I spied a large cushioned chair, and sitting in it the Tjaty of Egypt. There was, inevitably, a white cat in his lap. It was asleep.

"Greetings, Nicolaos," said the Tjaty.

"Isn't Inaros likely to imprison you?" I said by way of greeting. "You have come to your enemy's headquarters!"

The Tjaty smiled. "There is no difficulty. I am in Naukratis by invitation of the one you mention. Inaros still requires the cooperation of the Public Service if he hopes to capture Egypt, let alone rule it. Though we are enemies, we are also friends."

"I find that difficult to understand."

"It is an Egyptian way of thinking. Let me put it more simply. If Inaros shuts me up in prison, my fellow Public Servants will *never* surrender the White Fort to him. Thus I am safe here as long as I pose no direct threat. I invited you to this house to thank you. You have delivered beyond my expectations,

442

Nicolaos."

"I have?"

Then it occurred to me that everything had fallen together the way the Public Service wanted. The crook and flail were gone. So too was the only descendant of the last Pharaohs. Inaros would never be able to prove his royal blood. Markos was dead, by my hand.

I was astonished to realize I had done *everything* the Tjaty had demanded of me.

He chuckled. It was an evil sound.

"You have done well. We are in your debt. Who is your banker?"

"Banker?"

I didn't have a banker. The only bankers I knew were embezzlers.

"We need to pay you of course. I couldn't possibly ask you to carry home all the gold we intend to give you, your boat might sink. In any case, I find these matters are best arranged through intermediaries, don't you? It makes the source of the money so much harder to trace."

It occurred to me that the Tjaty didn't yet know about the tomb. No doubt Inaros had invited the bloated bureaucrat to bargain. But even that news would please the Tjaty.

"If I ever again require a Hellene agent, I will be sure to call you."

The Tjaty laughed, which woke the cat. The cat looked at me and smiled.

The Nauarch, Admiral Charitimides, released Kordax from naval duty to take us home.

Charitimides clapped me on the back and said, "Glad to see you made it back alive. You had no problems, I suppose?"

"None to speak of, sir." There was no other acceptable answer to a man like the Nauarch. He was a man who commanded two hundred ships of the line. A problem had to be of epic proportions to equal what he dealt with every day.

"Ah well, it's been quiet for us, too, but I'm hearing reports of a Persian army on the move. I suppose you need to report to Pericles?"

"Yes, sir."

"Come back when you're done. I think I can promise you some good fighting."

"Thank you, sir. I'll keep that in mind."

Herodotus saw us off at the docks. He insisted upon staying in Egypt.

"There's still more I want to see," he said.

Diotima and I had to leave Egypt as soon as possible. Inaros had made that clear at our final meeting. We knew too much. I was worried about Herodotus for the same reason.

"Are you sure?" I asked him. "It might be dangerous."

"More dangerous than being with you?" he scoffed.

"You may have a point."

Herodotus patted the pouch hanging by his side. "Anyway, I have safe passes handwritten by both Inaros and Barzanes. With them I can go anywhere in perfect safety, and I still have to finish my book. Inaros has promised me a lifetime supply of papyrus."

That was going to cost Inaros more than he realized.

I said, hesitantly, "Herodotus, about your book . . ."

"Yes?"

"It would be a good idea if you didn't mention . . . that is, if you didn't say anything about —"

"What happened?" he finished for me.

"Yes," I said. "I want to preserve Markos's memory, I don't want Barzanes getting into trouble for the deal he did with us, Djanet wouldn't thank you for it, and I don't need the whole world knowing I'm an agent."

"But I was hoping to put you in my book," Herodotus said.

"Sorry."

Herodotus sighed. "Perhaps it's just as well. Frankly, if I wrote about this, no one would believe it."

"Prepare to depart," Kordax called.

Herodotus waved. Sailors pulled in the gangplank. Oarsmen pushed off, and *Dolphin* began the long journey back to Athens.

AUTHOR'S NOTE

Welcome to the end of the book! Since it *is* the end, I'm going to talk about what's real and what's not in the story that you've just read. If you haven't finished the book, this would be a good moment to turn to the front, because everything from this point on is spoilers.

The war of independence fought by Egyptian rebels against the Persian Empire is completely real. The rebels were brilliantly led by a charismatic Prince of Libya named Inaros. The Athenians did send an enormous fleet to help them. Together they won a massive victory on both land and sea, and the beaten Persian army then garrisoned themselves in the White Fort at Memphis, to await reinforcements from home. So far, so real.

The quest for the crook and flail however is entirely the product of my demented imagination, as are the four agents who hunt for it.

Two of the quest party were real people. The first of these, you might be surprised to learn, is Diotima. She was one of the outstanding philosophers of her time, possibly the world's first great female philosopher, since we know of none before her. We know for sure she was the teacher of Socrates. How she came to that position in my story world is related in *The Pericles Commission.*

The other real member of the quest party is, of course, Herodotus.

Herodotus invented history. That is, he came up with the idea to write down what had happened in the past, so that people in the future could know about it. The very word *history* is classical Greek and means *inquiry.* Herodotus also recorded the habits and cultures of the ancient world, for which he is credited with inventing anthropology. These days we call his book *The Histories.* It is overwhelmingly the most famous book of history ever written.

Herodotus came from a city called Halicarnassus. The same place is called Bodrum today, and it's a lovely tourist town on the Turkish coast. In Nico's time the city was very much Greek, but was ruled by the Persians. Thus when Nico is told that an agent who is Greek but working for the Persians has been sent to Egypt, Herodotus seems a natural candidate.

Herodotus took great delight in recording all the strange and wonderful customs of the people of the ancient world — at least all of those of which he heard tale, and it's obvious he collected everything he could from every traveler he met. In the days before the internet and global villages, the variety in human life was far wider and richer. If you want an example, try this description he gives of Libya (which, in my world, he learned from Maxyates). The Penguin edition says:

. . . Libya is inhabited by tribes who live in ordinary houses and practice agriculture. First comes the Maxyes, a people who grow their hair on the right side of their heads and shave it off on the left. They stain their bodies red and claim to be descended from the men of Troy. The country round here, and the rest of Libya to the westward, has more forest and a greater number of wild animals . . . It is here that the huge snakes are found — and lions, elephants, bears, asps and horned asses, not to mention dog-headed men, headless men with eyes in their breasts (I merely repeat what the Libyans say), wild men and wild women, and a great many other creatures . . .

You can see from this passage where I found one of my more unusual characters. Herodotus is sometimes mocked for the bit about dog-headed men. Yet he makes it clear that he's merely passing on what he's heard, which shows how he went about his inquiries, or book research as we would call it. For what it's worth, there's a modern theory that the dog-headed men were baboons, and the wild men and wild women could have been gorillas.

Clearly at some point Herodotus had been talking to Libyans, and I was very happy to supply him the opportunity.

In this book, every time Herodotus begins a sentence with "Did you know . . ." he repeats something that you can find in *The Histories.*

Nico wonders about the source of Herodotus's wealth. So do modern scholars. To have made all the tours that he appears to have done would have required an enormous amount of money. For that reason, many doubt he visited all the places he writes about. It's highly likely he did rely on the tales others brought back with them from exotic locales, such as India. The one place that we know for sure that Herodotus visited in person is Egypt.

In the book, Herodotus is much taken by the women of Naukratis. It looks like a random, made-up detail, but is absolutely true. In *The Histories* he devotes a surprisingly large section to how lovely the ladies were. One gets the impression a certain amount of personal research was involved.

Nor was Herodotus the only one to fall under the spell of the courtesans of Naukratis. In the century before him, a man named Charaxus — who just happened to be the brother of Sappho, the famous poet — regularly traveled to Naukratis as a trader. There he met a charming and very beautiful slave-courtesan by the name of Rhodopis. Charaxus was completely smitten. Much to his sister's disgust, he spent a small fortune to buy the lady her freedom. Rhodopis instantly dumped Charaxus (he was obviously expecting to marry her), and instead set up her own house of ill repute, from which she became rich. This caused the world's greatest poet to dedicate an entire poem to describing what an idiot her brother was.

The crook and the flail really were the insignia of the pharaohs. Needless to say, there were many versions of the crook and flail over the millennia, with hundreds of pharaohs to hold them. The only examples that survive in reasonable condition are the ones found in Tutankhamen's tomb.

In the author note of my second book, *The Ionia Sanction,* I mentioned how the Greeks mangled the names of Persians. What they did to Egyptian names was even worse. I've called the last Pharaoh of Egypt Psamtik, because that's the simplest of the many variants you'll find in print. He's also referred to as Psammetichus and Psammenitus.

The very name of the country, Egypt, is Greek. Or more correctly, not Egypt, but Aigyptos. The Egyptians in their own language called their country the Black Land, which is a reference to the color of the rich silt supplied by the Nile. Every year the Nile would flood, which spread that black silt across the farms and thus made Egypt the breadbasket of the ancient world.

The ancients also thought of Egypt as two quite different nations. On a map, Lower

Egypt is at the top, and Upper Egypt is at the bottom. The weird naming is because the Nile runs from the south (Upper) to the north (Lower). Upper Egypt was the Land of Reeds. Lower Egypt (the Delta end) was the Land of Papyrus. Each had its own crown, and the Pharaoh wore the Double Crown.

A few other place names are worth mentioning. Libya is the Roman (Latin) name for that country. The Greeks called it Cyrenaica, based on the city of Cyrene, which was originally a colony of Thera, which was in turn a colony of Sparta! Eastern Libya is still called Cyrenaica to this day. I was a bit stuck on which of those names to use in this book. If Nico said Cyrenaica, which is what he would have said in real life, then modern readers would have conceived only half the country he really means, so I went with Libya, which name won't be in use for a few more hundred years.

Likewise, Nico refers to the continent as Africa, because that's how the modern reader knows it. But the name Africa for the continent was unknown in Nico's day. *Africa* is believed to be the one and only surviving word from the language spoken in ancient Carthage. We call them Carthaginians, but they called themselves Africans.

The name stuck for the entire land mass.

As far as the Greeks were concerned, everything south of Egypt and Libya was Aethiopia. Yes, our Ethiopia is a Greek name too. To the Greeks Aethiopia meant all of Central and South Africa, though they had no clue just how vast that area is.

Ethiopia and the people who came from there had been known to the Greeks since time immemorial. Memnon, the King of Aethiopia, was one of the mighty warriors who defended Troy.

The sailors say to Nico that nothing ever happens on Thera, the island at which they stop on their way to Crete. Little do they know that fifteen hundred years before their time, Thera was a volcano that exploded violently. That's why Thera is the shape it is. There's a theory that Thera's explosion caused the end of the Minoan Age. There's also a theory that the Thera explosion is the origin of the Atlantis myth. Nico doesn't mention Atlantis, because he's never heard of it. That nonsense was written by Plato a hundred years after the time of this story.

Thera is officially known these days as Santorini. It's one of Greece's most popular holiday destinations. A lot of the tourist pictures you see of pristine whitewashed homes against a perfect blue sea were taken on Thera.

The statesman Themistocles is the subject of the second book in this series, *The Ionia Sanction*. Herodotus in *The Histories* gives two different versions of the great man's death. In one story, Themistocles died of natural causes. In the second, it was suicide by drinking bull's blood. Obviously they can't both be right, as Herodotus points out in this book.

We now know the source of the paradox: Nico and Diotima lied to him, and in *The Ionia Sanction,* I give a third way for Themistocles to die!

Nico and Diotima have a severe problem with pirates.

The Greeks get credit for inventing a lot of things, but did you know one of them is piracy?

Even the word "pirate" comes from Ancient Greek. When he wrote about pirates, Plutarch uses the word peiratiko.

There have been pirates in the Aegean Sea for at least three thousand years. The Aegean is ideal for this sort of thing. There are hundreds of islands, the coastlines are rocky, and the only way for trade to move about is by sea.

The world's first known pirate was a Greek. His name was Piyamaradus. He's mentioned in a tablet written by the King of the Hittites to the King of Mycenae. That tablet has to be older than 1,200 BC.

By classical times there were highly organized pirates with for-real pirate bases. Many of the bases were on Crete, which was famous as a land of pirates. I'm afraid you'll have to do away with ideas of eye patches, peg legs and parrots screeching for pieces of eight. Your average pirate looked like any other sailor. Successful pirate chiefs became wealthy and could marry well.

Nico and Diotima are saved by the appearance of a trireme. No pirate in his right mind would have taken on a trireme. Triremes were the fighting ships of the ancient world. Before the invention of the trireme, warriors treated ships like a particularly unsteady form of land. Men fought over the water using the same techniques that they used in the army. Then some naval genius (who was probably a Phoenician) realized that the ship itself could be a weapon, and thus was born the trireme, a floating battery ram.

Ships in the classical world did not fly national flags, not even in battle. Hence

Nico can't tell whether a distant ship is friend or foe. We know about the lack of identifying flags because of a famous incident that occurred during the Battle of Salamis. One Persian boat sank another Persian. Three nearby Greek ships thought the attacker must be Greek, when it wasn't, and the Persian King, watching from the shore, thought the destroyed boat must be Greek, when it was actually Persian!

The Blind General is my creation, but the story he relates about the fall of Psamtik and the destruction of the last native royal family is all documented history. You can find it in *The Histories*, Book 3, section 14. In my world, Herodotus wrote this down after hearing it from the Blind General.

In the Herodotus original, Psamtik and the Egyptian noblemen see their daughters being led away as slaves. Then they see two thousand of their sons with horses' bits in their mouths and nooses about their necks. The young men are led off to be executed.

I inserted the Blind General because I needed someone who could live long enough to speak with Nico and Diotima. Psamtik's daughter was enslaved and his son executed after the fall of Egypt. Psamtik had no other child in captivity. I made up that bit.

It must be pointed out that the atrocities were not all on the Persian side. When the war began, Psamtik was none too pleased that his former trusted advisor, Phanes, had gone over to the Persians.

Phanes had unwisely left his sons behind in Egypt when he departed to betray the Pharaoh. Before the battle, Psamtik had the sons of Phanes dragged to the front of the battle line where, before the eyes of their father, the throats of the boys were slit and the Egyptians drank their blood. After this terrible event, the chance of Psamtik receiving any sort of leniency was approximately zero.

Later, when the Egyptians were defeated in battle, Cambyses sent by ship an ambassador to Psamtik to request he surrender. The Egyptians tore apart the ambassador on the spot. They also murdered the entire crew of the ship on which he came. Whence the death of the two thousand sons of Egyptian noblemen, which was judged a fair reprisal.

The ship on which the ambassador arrived was from Mytilene, which is a Greek city. Obviously they were mercenaries working for the Persians. There's nothing odd about this. Greeks were quite famous for their mercenary work. Indeed even Xenophon, one of the great friends and biographers of Socrates, made his name as a mercenary captain in Persia. That there are Greeks in Egypt fighting on both sides is par for the course.

Phanes really did come from Halicarnassus, as did Herodotus. The coincidence was too good to pass by. I made up the bit about Uncle Phanes's being related to Herodotus.

Nico refers to Charitimides as *nauarch,* meaning Admiral. The *nau* part lends itself to the English nautical. The *arch* part means leader, as per *archon* being a leader of Athens. Thus nauarch means leader-at-sea.

The title nauarch for an Athenian commander is problematic because, although Sparta nominated an admiral with that title, the Athenians elected ten men with title *strategos* (meaning strategist, or General) who then commanded on both land and at sea. Some commanders, however, were naturals at fighting on the wet stuff. They always got that job, and I imagine their admirers would have referred to them as Admiral.

Charitimides was a for-real naval commander of the time. He was highly rated by his fellow citizens and is praised by Herodotus, but history has largely forgotten him. With the two hundred triremes of his command, Charitimides crushed the Persians in the last great sea battle between those two peoples. For sheer size, that fight upon the Nile was second only to the Battle of Salamis.

Indeed, Charitimides was almost certainly a junior officer at Salamis, which had been fought twenty-three years before. Which means he and a handful of his veterans are the only men in history who could put their hands on their hearts and declare that they had fought in both of the two largest naval actions up to their day.

After the close of this book, when the Persian relieving force arrived, Charitimides led his sailors onto land to assist their Egyptian comrades. He fell in battle, leading his troops from the front.

Inaros, the Prince of Libya, was a for-real person. He gets enormous praise from Herodotus, who says that no man ever did greater harm to the Persians (when you're a Greek in 455BC, that's praise).

Inaros conquered Lower Egypt, killing in battle a member of the Persian royalty.

However he was stuck trying to capture the White Fort. Ancient sources say outright that the leading Egyptians in Memphis supported Persian rule. Since Memphis was the capital, it seems obvious that means those who administered the government.

The dating on the rebellion is somewhat variable, depending on how you want to interpret the ancient texts. The latest possible date suited Nico and Diotima's very busy schedule for this period. As I noted in *The Pericles Commission,* the years following the birth of democracy in Athens are among the most important in all of history. There was a lot happening all over the place, and Nico and Diotima can't be everywhere at once!

You're probably wondering what happened to the rebellion after the book ends.

The Persians held out in the White Fort for two years. It took that long for a relieving force to arrive. When it did, there was a great battle, during which Admiral Charitimides fell. Inaros surrendered on terms. Part of the agreement was that Inaros's son would continue to rule Libya, which he did. Inaros was guaranteed his personal safety as a permanent prisoner at the Persian court.

Alas, the Dowager Queen of Persia remained angry about the death of her husband's brother. She badgered her elder son, the King, for five years, until he gave in and allowed Inaros to be executed, completely against the terms of surrender. Inaros was impaled on a pole, a particularly gruesome and painful death.

The status of the White Fort in Memphis is something of a mystery. Not a trace of it remains. Some people have suggested that "White Fort" was simply an alternative name for the entire city. The problem with that idea is that Herodotus specifically refers to "the White Fort at Memphis" (in Book 3, section 91, if you're interested), and by context elsewhere there is a stronghold inside a larger city. Diodorus Siculus, writing four hundred years later, refers to the White Fort as close to Memphis. However you choose to interpret it, it is clear that whoever held the White Fort controlled Memphis, and that the place was pretty much impregnable.

In fact, trying to understand the layout of any part of ancient Memphis is tricky. Nearby Saqqara, the site of the pyramids, is probably one of the best surveyed and mapped sites in the world, but once you get to the ancient capital not far down the road, it's a whole lot harder.

Memphis was founded by Menes, the first Pharaoh of Egypt. Menes had to fight a war to unite Upper and Lower Egypt. To save arguments over which of the two former independent nations would host the capital, he founded a new purpose-built city. Thus ancient Memphis was founded for much the same reason as modern Washington DC and Canberra.

The patron god of the city was Ptah. We know for sure where the grand temple to Ptah was. A temple to the Apis Bull was next to it. Both were located at the southern end. Also at this location was found an enormous statue of Ramses II. The statue was moved far away in modern times because pollution was destroying it. We also know the location of the Palace of Apries (a former Pharaoh) to the north. There is known to have been a Temple of Bastet, who was the cat goddess and consort of Ptah. I made up the bit about a secret chamber beneath Bastet's temple.

The famous modern poem Ozymandias is based on an inscription recorded on a statue of Ramses.

Tjaty is ancient Egyptian for Vizier, or Prime Minister, depending how you want to translate it. After the Pharaoh, the Tjaty was the most powerful man in the country. The names of the Tjaties are recorded in much the same way as the Pharaohs.

Contrary to any Egyptian mummy movies you may have seen, Imhotep was not an evil wizard bent on world domination. He was in fact the Ancient Egyptian version of Leonardo da Vinci. Imhotep is credited as the architect of the Step Pyramid. He *invented* the pyramids.

Imhotep was also the world's greatest doctor in his day. He wrote books on ethics and philosophy, and he was a top-class mathematician. But being the world's best in three different fields were just his hobbies. His day job was being Tjaty to the Pharaoh Djoser. One gets the impression from the surviving stories that Imhotep was the one running the show and that Djoser, who knew a good thing when he saw it, was happy for Imhotep to get on with the job.

Imhotep was so awesome that some time after his death, people decided that a god had been living among them and he was raised to divine status.

The location of Imhotep's tomb is one of the great unsolved mysteries of Egypt. There *must* be a tomb. Most people assume Imhotep's tomb will be found close to the final resting place of his boss, the Pharaoh Djoser. If so, Imhotep lies within a few hundred meters of the Step Pyramid at Saqqara. I took great delight in relocating him far, far away.

Imhotep wasn't the first Tjaty, though. Nobody knows who that was. The incredibly ancient Narmer Palette, which is at least 5,000 years old and which commemorates the unification of Egypt, *appears* to show a man who is serving as Tjaty to the first Pharaoh. Either way, the first Pharaoh founded Memphis to be the capital of Egypt, and it's certain that he created a Public Service to administer his new nation.

The Egyptian Public Service is thus the world's oldest running organization, far older than the Roman Catholic Church by several millennia, older even than the Chinese equivalent, since China had several catastrophic social breakdowns which caused them to have to start all over again. The public servants of modern Egypt belong to an organization that has been in operation for *seven thousand years.*

Barzanes says at one point that he has read every book in the world. He would have to exclude books written in China, and a few books written in ancient Mesopotamia, Egypt and India that were already lost, but with those exceptions, this was in fact possible for a good linguist at the date our heroes lived.

The total number of books written before and during the fourth century BC would not fill your local library. The reason for this is very simple. Writing had been invented, and reinvented, several times, but always to do accounting, record proclamations and send messages. The idea of writing either fiction or non-fiction had only just been thought of. The two oldest books in Europe are from Homer (bestselling fiction author of *The Iliad* and *The Odyssey*) and Hesiod (non-fiction: he wrote *Works and Days* which is *The Dummy's Guide to Being a Bronze-Age Gentleman*). Both men had lived a couple of centuries before, but their work had only been written down for the first time a few decades before this story. Likewise on the shelves, you would find poetry collections from Sappho, Archilochos and a few others, plus the Greek plays written in the last fifty years. In the Egyptian section you would find *The Book of the Dead* that Tutu the embalmer mentions, and other religious texts, and instructional texts from Imhotep and a few others.

The two biggest books of the ancient world are about to be written: *The Histories,* by our hero Herodotus, followed by *The History of the Peloponnesian War,* by Thucydides.

The crossbow was invented in China, centuries before the time of this story.

We don't normally associate crossbows with classical Greece, but it's certain that they had them. Their first documented use is at the siege of Motya in 397BC. By the time of Alexander the Great the army had catapults and ballistas (both Greek words) for siege work and infantry support.

The Greek version of the crossbow was invented by Zopyrus of Tarentum. He lived in the last quarter of the 5th century BC, at least forty years after the time of this story.

Thus it's impossible that Markos could have a Greek crossbow. They haven't been invented yet! The weapon that Markos carries is an import from China.

The Persians never used crossbows. I find that puzzling. The Silk Road isn't officially open, and won't be for another two hundred years, but the Persians and Chinese have definitely been trading at this date. The Persians *must* have seen crossbows, if only in the arms of the guards who protected the

Chinese traders. The Persians, being a deeply militaristic people, would have adopted anything that would help them win wars. I can only assume that the Persian powers decided ancient crossbows were too ungainly for standard issue.

The Spartans never adopted crossbows either, despite Markos's having one in this book, and despite seeing them in action in real life forty years later. But that's easy to explain. There has never been a more conservative people.

The Nile is absolutely full of crocodiles at the time Nico and Diotima visit.

The incident where Nico saves his wife from a crocodile actually happened to another couple. Not the crossbow, but everything before that. In 2008 in the Northern Territory in Australia, a woman was caught unawares and was being dragged back into the river by her leg, when her husband jumped on top of the creature. He couldn't even scratch the croc, let alone hurt it. He eventually found its eyes and pushed. The croc let go and swam off. Husband, wife and crocodile all survived.

Ancient Egyptian place names are a real challenge for a modern author.

The Egyptians in Nico's day spoke and

wrote an early form of Demotic. Demotic was descended from the incredibly ancient Egyptian tongue, and thus belonged to the rich and extensive family of languages known as Afro-Asiatic. The bad news is that Demotic is a thoroughly dead language. What's more, written Demotic used only consonants. The words would be wildly unreadable if I used any location names as Nico and Diotima heard them.

Memphis is the *Greek* name for the city. In 455BC the locals wrote the city's name as *mn nfr* (converting the characters into their English equivalent, of course). This gets expanded with a few choice vowels into Men-nefer. I've stuck with what's familiar.

There was an Egyptian writer named Manetho, who lived a couple of hundred years after the time of this story, who referred to Memphis by a completely different name: Hut-ka-Ptah, meaning Place of the Ka of Ptah, in reference to the major temple of Ptah. The Greeks in their typical fashion mangled Hut-ka-Ptah into Ai-gy-Ptos. Which became Aigyptos. Which then became . . . you guessed it: Egypt.

It's important to note that not a single word of Arabic yet existed in Egypt. Despite which, I've used names such as Saqqara for the place where the pyramids are to be found. It gives you the best chance to follow the action.

The good news for both me and Nico is that Greek is already spreading across Egypt. As the power of Athens grew, the Greek language became the *lingua franca* of the Mediterranean. This continued for centuries! A lot of people don't realize that even at the height of the Roman Empire, the language of culture and refinement was Greek. Latin was what the plebs spoke.

Thus in northern cities of Egypt, such as Naukratis, Nico can get by on Greek. In other parts, he can expect the intellectual elite to speak his language, though not normal people. It helps that Nico and Diotima learned Persian in their previous adventure *The Ionia Sanction.* When you're an agent for Athens, speaking Persian is a job skill. In Persian-dominated Memphis they have no problems. In the countryside they have Maxyates and then Djanet to translate where necessary.

It's no coincidence that Djanet is not only the last heir of the Pharaohs, but also an agent. She owes her existence, or at least her name, to my literary agent Janet Reid. Janet is a most awesome agent. If someone made her Pharaoh, I'm sure she'd be just as good at that job.

[Note from Janet: Pharaoh! As long as I don't have to ride a camel, I'm in!]

The Oasis of Siwa is very real. Nico is accurate in his description of the distance and the difficulty of getting there. If anything, he underrates the extreme danger.

Cambyses the King of Persia really did send an army of 50,000 men to reduce the temple. The army died to the last man attempting to cross the desert. Their remains are still out there, waiting for some archaeologist to find them.

The Qattara Depression through which our heroes travel is all too real. It was the location of many battles between Rommel's Afrika Korp and the British during World War II. Indeed, both the British and the Germans used the Siwa Oasis for a headquarters as their fight famously swung one way then the other.

The oracle was dedicated to the Libyan god Ammon. This god is normally associated with the extremely important Egyptian god Amun. Note the very similar spelling. Like most people, Nico makes that connection and never differentiates. In Nico's day, Siwa was actually called Ammonium. I wasn't keen to use that name in the book, but I find it interesting how almost every

Egyptian place name has changed greatly over time, whereas even the most ancient of Greek names have been stable for millennia.

The oracle at Siwa was known to the Greeks from a very early age. Even King Croesus is known to have sent emissaries there. The Greeks considered the Siwa oracle to be on a par with the oracle at Delphi, which by their standard is very high praise indeed.

The oracle really did work by judging the random movements of priests as they staggered under the weight of a huge boat. While this may look mildly crazy, keep in mind that Delphi — the most famous oracle in the world — worked by having a woman utter incoherent words that were interpreted by a priest. In Rome, they predicted the future based on the movements of eagles in the sky, and almost everywhere there were diviners who supplied all your prophecy needs by inspecting the livers of dead animals.

Siwa was visited by Alexander the Great. That visit figures prominently in every biography of Alexander's life, and for good reason.

Egypt fell to Alexander without a single battle. That goes to show how weak was

Persia's control over the province, for which Alexander could have thanked the work of Inaros in the previous century. The Egyptians were happy to be rid of Persian rule.

Alexander then took it into his head to make the same arduous journey that Nico and Diotima do, across the Qattara Depression. Quite why he wanted to do so is unclear. Alexander's best biographer — Arrian — suggests it was because the Greek heroes Perseus and Herakles in their own times visited Siwa. Anything a demigod could do, Alexander had to do too. Whatever the reason, the visit changed Alexander's life.

It was at Siwa that Alexander was hailed as the son of Amon-Zeus, thus making him a demigod and worthy of divine honors. Indeed, in the last years of his short life, Alexander insisted that the Persians and Greeks address him as a demigod.

Other accounts say that Alexander never disclosed what the oracle said to him, but that he reserved what he had learned to tell his mother. That's probably more realistic. But then, if a famous oracle told you that your real father was the king of the gods, you too might want to have a quiet chat with your mother, to find out what she'd been up to.

■ ■ ■ ■

So Nico and Diotima have survived this adventure and are on their way back home. Alas, their good work has served only to stave off defeat for a few more years, when a new Persian attack will arrive to crush the rebellion.

The return of Persian power in Egypt will mean a new threat to Athens from the south. That will trigger Pericles to take a fateful step, one that will change the world forever. It will be the birth of the Athenian Empire, and Nico and Diotima will be there to see it happen, in *Death on Delos.*

GLOSSARY

Agora The marketplace. Every city and town in Greece has an agora. To this day, the Greek word for marketplace is agora. Nico says agora to mean an Egyptian marketplace because he doesn't know any better.

Ammonium What the Greeks and Romans called Siwa.

Amphora/Amphorae The standard container of the ancient world. They can't stand upright because they have a pointy bottom. But the shape is actually very practical. They stack well, and when lying on their side it's easy to reach for the contents.

Bast The cat goddess, also known as Bastet. In Memphis she was considered the consort of Ptah. I couldn't resist also making her the patron goddess of fat cats.

Egypt The official name for the country in Nico's day was The Black Land. The name

Egypt won't exist for another two hundred years.

Also sometimes called The Two Lands, in reference to Upper and Lower Egypt. Upper Egypt is in the *south.* Lower Egypt is the *north.* This is a trap for new players!

Eyes and Ears of the King The FBI of the Persian Empire. They uncovered corrupt officials, saw to internal security, and gathered intelligence. The Eyes and Ears reported directly to the Great King. In a crisis, they could speak in the name of the king.

Field of Reeds The Egyptian afterlife. Not to be confused with the Land of Reeds, which was southern Egypt.

Field of Trees What the ancient Egyptians called Siwa.

Gastraphetes A crossbow. Literally gastraphetes means "stomach bow." The first crossbows had a concave rest at the stock, that was placed against the stomach. That was to control the kickback, which apparently was considerable.

The gastraphetes was the first crossbow in the western world. A similar weapon was invented independently and certainly earlier in China.

Great King The king of Persia is always called the Great King. That's because Persia has turned many of its neighbors into client states, and those states are ruled by 'mere' kings and queens.

Imhotep A genius of mind-boggling ability. Inventor and chief architect of the first pyramid, and prime minister (Tjaty) of Egypt under the Pharaoh Djoser.

Imhotep's final resting place is a genuine Lost Tomb. I have to hope it stays lost, at least until this book is published.

Lower Egypt The Land of Papyrus. It's the *northern* end of Egypt.

Memphis Men-Nefer in the ancient Egyptian tongue. Memphis is what the Greeks called it. Memphis began life as a custom-built city, like Washington DC and Canberra, designed by the first Pharaoh to be his capital.

Nauarch Admiral. I'm mildly amazed this word didn't make it into English, because so many of our nautical terms come from Greek. Such as, for example, *nautical.*

Naukratis A city on the Nile Delta, founded in the 7th century BC. The city was created specifically to allow free trade between the Greeks and the Egyptians. The modern technical term for such a place is *entrepôt.*

The buried remains of Naukratis were discovered by the great Egyptologist

Flinders Petrie.

Ptah God of artisans and builders. He is the patron god of Memphis.

Pyramid It's Greek, and means *wheat cake.* Which tells us exactly what a classical Greek wheat cake looked like.

The ancient Egyptian for tomb was *mer.* Though they were as likely to say House of Eternity, which is *per nheh.*

Saqqara The name is Arabic. Nobody in Nico's time called the location of the pyramids Saqqara, they probably called them part of Memphis, which would be confusing to a modern reader.

Satrap Governor of a province in the Persian Empire. Satraps are powerful men.

Siwa An oasis in the desert and the most famous oracle in all of Africa. The ancient name was Ammonium, meaning the place of Amun.

Trierarch Kordax is the trierarch — the commander — of *Dolphin.* The more modern term, taken from the British Navy, would be master and commander.

Trireme The standard navy ship of the Greek world. Triremes are long, low, sleek, incredibly fast machines with a battering ram at the front. Triremes are the first ships in the world designed to sink other ships. In modern terms they would be classed as destroyers. Athens had overwhelmingly the largest fleet around, with three hundred triremes. Two hundred of these were sent to aid Egypt during the rebellion, under the excellent command of an admiral named Charitimides.

Upper Egypt The Land of Reeds. It's the *southern* end of Egypt.

ACKNOWLEDGMENTS

In every book I begin by thanking my wife Helen and my daughters Catriona and Megan. That's because without their support, there would be no books. I fear that having a mystery author for a father may have given my children a slightly twisted view of life.

An enormous thank you goes to my agent ~~Djanet~~ Janet Reid. I hope she will forgive me for what I've done to her character. It might be some consolation that she ended up a princess.

Juliet Grames is my Patient Editor, whose advice is beyond value. Let me tell you how wise she is. When I wrote *The Marathon Conspiracy,* it was Juliet who insisted I write the scene in which Aeschylus describes the famous battle. Almost every reader who's talked to me about that book has said it's their favorite scene, and I never planned it!

Soho Press is the ideal of all that a publisher should be, and the staff who inhabit its slightly crowded spaces are a wonderful bunch.

Lastly I want to thank the guy who thought it might be a good idea to record his inquiries, that the great deeds of men would be remembered forever. So thank you, Herodotus, for putting stylus to papyrus. I couldn't have done it without you.

The employees of Thorndike Press hope you have enjoyed this Large Print book. All our Thorndike, Wheeler, and Kennebec Large Print titles are designed for easy reading, and all our books are made to last. Other Thorndike Press Large Print books are available at your library, through selected bookstores, or directly from us.

For information about titles, please call:
(800) 223-1244

or visit our Web site at:
http://gale.cengage.com/thorndike

To share your comments, please write:
Publisher
Thorndike Press
10 Water St., Suite 310
Waterville, ME 04901